# Melting

# Melting

Martin Guinness

SPEAKING VOLUMES, LLC

NAPLES, FLORIDA

2012

Melting

ISBN 978-1-61232-933-8

# Chapter One

It was the last thing I expected. I mean, we'd talked about death of course. But it was always *me*. We'd both expected that it would be me. And after I died she'd have to figure out what to do. After all, I was that much older than her. And women are always meant to live longer than men anyway. Aren't they?

We'd been standing in the kitchen, late spring sunshine spilling through the windows. Marie had just finished preparing our lunch. She'd bought a beautiful piece of salmon and grilled it with snow peas and tiny, steamed potatoes. I couldn't resist popping one of the potatoes into my mouth. It was delicious. She'd pulled the cork from a bottle of our favorite Pouilly Fumé, poured the wine into two chilled glasses, and smiled at me as she held out my glass.

But I never managed to take hold of the glass. Instead the smile disappeared from her face, and her eyes widened, as though she'd just recognized some awful truth. Which, in a way, I guess she had. The glass slipped from her fingers and smashed on the floor. She followed it down moments later. Just like that, lying prone amongst the sodden glass shards.

My reactions in quick succession were: firstly, plain surprise. Then raw shock. And, finally, sheer terror. I had no idea what had happened. I just knelt down beside her, ignoring a needle-sharp glass splinter that drove into my kneecap.

"Maddy. What …? What is it? . . . What's happening?"

But she didn't move. And her eyes stared straight back at me….sightless, because there was nobody there to see anything.

"Please! . . . Come on!!"

Strangely, it was a while before I realized that she was dead. When I did, the life went out of me too. My eyes closed and I slowly collapsed on top of her. I wanted to scream and scream. But the words strangled in my throat. And a strange sort of paralysis came over me as I lay there, clinging onto my dead wife's body.

I have no idea how long we lay there together. It could have been hours and it could have been only seconds. Eventually I pulled away from Marie and looked into her lifeless eyes. But it was too much for me. I shut my eyes again, and slowly managed to wrench myself away from her rigid torso. Still in a daze, I sat up and looked around me.

All I could think was: "What am I going to do?"

I reached down to lever myself up, but my wrist found glass and I winced. The blood started slowly, then began to drip. But I didn't notice it. Not then. I managed to drag myself to my feet, and just stood there looking at her. I still couldn't believe that she was actually dead. Eventually I noticed the blood, and reached for a table napkin to cover my bleeding hand.

I stood there for quite some time, unsure what to do. In a daze I looked around and saw the phone. But, even then, it was a few moments before I picked up the receiver and dialed 911.

\*\*\*

Marie Alexandre d'Angelo was born in Casablanca to a French mother and Italian father. Both of them were journalists, often reporting from international locations. They separated when she was three, and for the first few years of Marie's life she went with her mother wherever a story took her. Sometimes this meant traveling around Europe, and sometimes even to North Africa and Asia.

As a small child, she was different to other children. While they were drawing pretty pictures of animals and houses and mommies and daddies, all lit by golden suns, Marie was drawing pictures of people she saw in the street, including beggars and prostitutes. Her teachers had wanted Marie to see a child psychologist, but neither of her parents was worried. In fact they encouraged her.

And then, back in Paris one glorious birthday when she turned eleven, her father bought her a camera of her own. She was delighted. Here was a real opportunity for her to tell more stories with her pictures. And the last thing she wanted to film was family snaps.

When she graduated from the Sorbonne she wanted to follow her parents into journalism, and applied to be a newspaper cadet. After a year, a combination of less-than-exciting stories and, let's face it, not such brilliant writing, almost saw her tossed out of the newspaper.

But, one day, she showed some of pictures to a friend in the newspaper office. The friend insisted that Marie show the pictures to the picture editor. He was impressed and suggested she come and work for him.

It wasn't long before she found herself in Angola and Sierra Leone covering a story about conflict diamonds. Many of her pictures were extremely confronting shots of amputations, rape victims and other atrocities. After that she never looked back, gaining recognition for an individual style and powerful imagery.

And then she seemed to travel from one war zone to another, each new commission bloodier than the last.

Naturally she ended up in Iraq.

Which was where I met her.

***

We were both in Baghdad in 2003 to record the invasion. Or, if you insist, 'liberation', depending upon which way you look at it. The atmosphere was both terrifying and exhilarating. A group of western journalists remained in their hotels waiting for the promised waves of Shock and Awe.

I remember gingerly standing on my tiny bedroom balcony in front of the camera held by my trusty cameraman Ed Wellings. Behind me the sky split open with myriad explosions, more electrifying than a hundred cracker nights. As parts of the city were illuminated by the orange explosions and the resulting fires I attempted to give a running commentary. But the explosions and the sirens were drowning out much of what I was saying. And, in any case, I ran out of things to say. How many times can you say "Oh look, there's another explosion."? I tried to identify parts of the city that were being hit or were on fire. But, in the end, Ed turned off the camera.

"I think we've got it for now."

Frankly I was enormously relieved. I'd been feeling exposed, and was actually starting to fear for my own life.

"Yeah, sure. If anything different happens before the next scheduled upload we can start again. You want to send that up the line and we'll do some more later?"

"Yep."

"I'll be down the hall if anything different happens."

Ed disappeared to another part of the building where the dish for his sat-phone was pointed towards the satellite which would transmit our pictures back to the network.

Ed and I shared a whole suite at the Palestine hotel, Conditions were cramped there, but I'd handed over a wad of cash and, compared to some, we lived in relative luxury. Other journalists were sharing tiny rooms.

After Ed left I lifted the mattress back in place in front of the windows in case the glass shattered. I made some notes about what we'd just shot while it was in my memory, then left the suite and walked along the corridor to a room three doors down. The door was opened on the second knock by an Australian journalist called Paul, who over the years had become a good friend. Paul could always be relied upon to come up with some good, smuggled Irish whisky. And, right now, that was exactly what I needed.

Most of the lights were off in Paul's room, and it was a moment before I realized that there was someone else there. When I saw that it was a woman I thought maybe I should make myself scarce, and I started to make apologies and leave.

"Don't be silly." Paul said. "Come and meet Marie. She's an independent photographer. Just moved over from the al-Safir Hotel. Apparently the Information Ministry told the manager there to get rid of all journalists. Max Wheeler meet Marie d'Angelo."

Maybe it was the intensity of the situation, Maybe it was the three of us huddled against possible death. Maybe it was just the whisky. But, it seemed like strands of electricity threaded around and around Marie and myself. I could barely take my eyes off her. I thought about no-one and nothing else. I was totally in that moment. Only once did I look away when Paul started taping up the windows. Otherwise the three of us shared our personal war stories, and talked about life and death and this and that. The room began to shrink and, though Paul continued to play a part in the conversation, he was obviously aware that we were becoming less and less aware of his presence in the room.

Eventually I dragged my eyes from Marie and checked my watch.

"I have to go. I need to do another piece on the war"

"War? What war?"

She smiled and looked me in the eyes knowingly.

"Now what have I started?" said Paul.

"I'd better go".

I reluctantly dragged myself to my feet.

"I'll see you tomorrow."

"Yes".

It was such a small word. But when she said it somehow it filled me with elation. When I began to give my second piece of the evening the network had to ask me to stop smiling. You could say that I hadn't been shocked, but I was certainly awed.

***

The next day Paul told me that Marie had managed to slip out of the hotel wearing hijab. Against all Information Ministry instructions she'd somehow persuaded her driver to take her. If she got caught the Ministry would probably throw her in the dreaded Abu Ghraib prison. And, if she survived that, they'd throw her out of the country. It was a huge risk.

"She went to take pictures of the damage."

"She's mad!" I said. "Totally fucking insane".

"Yes, probably. I rather admire her though, don't you? And she does take the most amazing pictures."

Marie came back, later in the day, tired, but flushed and exhilarated with tales of a city where certain of Saddam's palaces and other buildings had received direct hits. But buildings on either side were completely intact. "You should see…..you should see."

She disappeared to her room to rest and to load her pictures onto her laptop. I felt a wave of relief, seeing her in one piece, and now I waited for her to come back downstairs from her room.

I was in the middle of a conversation with a Dutch journalist, my mind only half listening, when she strolled into the sand-bagged hotel lobby, looking refreshed and animated. She saw me and came right over.

"There you are." For all the world as though we were old friends. I couldn't stop smiling.

"What are you smiling at?"

"Just happy to see you, that's all."

"Oh good! And I am happy to see you."

She said it simply, without artfulness, her soft French accent making the sentence not a mindless response, but a simple truth.

And that was how the evening continued. We were glued to each other, enchanted by one another. I tried to be discreet as I took in the long, silky brown hair, the sexy body, and the beautiful....Yes, beautiful... face. Not perfect, but certainly she was beautiful. And, while there was faint etching around her laughing eyes, I still thought of her as young. Maybe in her late thirties. But when she smiled at me, which she did often, she looked deep into my eyes and aroused in me a profound yearning and anticipation. I couldn't remember feeling this way. Certainly not for a very long time.

Eventually, reluctantly, I had to drag myself away to file my update on the war. But this time it was different.

"Can I come with you? I'd like to see you in action." She smiled suggestively at me.

I wasn't sure. Was she just teasing me?

"Sure. Why not."

***

Again the bombardment behind me lit up parts of the city. Again I stood gingerly on the balcony, half expecting a stray bomb to end it all for me. But this time Marie lounged on my bed. Her head was tilted to one side, studying me as I tried to give my best performance. I was aware of her the whole time, and I had to concentrate hard on my notes to keep me on track. When we finished Ed discreetly disappeared.

Marie finally spoke, "You're very good."

"Thank you."

"No, I mean it. You're terrific."

I modestly tried to change the subject,

"Would you like a drink?"

She gave a little, Indian-style jiggle to her head.

"Okay. But you don't need to get me drunk."

I was already pouring.

"Sorry?"

"I mean that I don't need to drink alcohol to sleep with you," she smiled sweetly at me.

I choked slightly and my heart literally stopped beating for a moment. The bottle was still poised, mid-pour.

"Oh, don't worry. Paul told me you were married. But, you know, what happens in Vegas….."

I moved towards her, holding the two glasses. She sat up and took them both from me and placed them on the bedside table.

"Marie," I began. "We've only just met. We don't even know each…."

"….Oh, I know *you* Mister Max Wheeler. And I know how you feel. And how I feel. Believe me Max I don't do this all the time. But we could be dead tomorrow."

As if to illustrate her point, there was a violent explosion close to the hotel. We both jumped.

"Shit!' I said "We could be dead tonight."


This alien skin. The curve of this buttock. The weight of this breast with its unfamiliar hardening nipple between my lips. The brush of this belly against my own. These were some of the things I felt as I lost myself in Marie. The way our bodies moved together in perfect rhythm, though we had never known each other before. Strangers, yet eternal intimates.

That night I rediscovered something I hadn't felt for a very long time. There was a freedom to my love-making with Marie. And, within that freedom, there was the young Max. Max the adventurer, Max the lover. And we both felt the connection. And the bombing outside only served to heighten our fervor.


It was only later that I thought about my wife. I thought about Lisa, and how our sex life was these days. Things hadn't been great in that area for some years now, and we both knew it. But what could you expect after, what was it, thirty-three years together? "My God! Thirty-three years." To say that the magic had gone was a cliché, but a sad reality nevertheless. I guess you could say we'd developed a pattern – certain habits. She goes down on me. I go down on her. After a bit of fiddling and kissing and tweaking I kind of climb on top. And then we would both try and come together. Very sad really. It had become simply a way for both of us to get some relief. And maybe to prove that we still loved each other. But that was all. The excitement was long gone. And I knew in my heart that she wasn't satisfied. We'd tried other stuff, including swinging with another couple....What a disaster that had been!....None of it was really what either of us was looking for.

Once.....Once it had been different. When we were young we couldn't get enough of each other. There was a real hunger...a real passion. But that was so long ago.

I guess slowly we'd just fallen into a rut. It was nobody's fault. It just happened. And then, of course, there was the cello teacher. Oh, yeah, the cello teacher. When Lisa was in her mid-forties, and the kids were kind of off her hands, one day she told me that she wanted to do something with her life. Try something new. Well, not 'new' exactly, because she'd taken up the cello when she was at school and had "always liked it". This was actually new information to me. Because, in all the years I'd known Lisa, I'd never once heard her mention playing the cello. Isn't that odd!

Anyway, she'd liked it then and she thought she might like to try again, "You know, something to do. And the best part of it is," she'd said, "I won't have to buy a cello, because I can hire it. So it won't cost very much. And I've found this teacher from South America somewhere." And she'd heard that he plays beautifully and he was a good teacher. "

Hmm.

Well, maybe it was having something vibrating between her legs. Or the teacher, 'Paco', wasn't it, casually brushing her breasts as he sat closely, hard-pressed, behind her and taught her bow strokes. Or maybe she was just worried about never being sexually attractive to men ever again.

Whatever the reason, and it was probably none of the above, Lisa had an affair. And, while I didn't know about it then, looking back I realized how much she'd blossomed during that time. She'd seemed to have a special something about her, a radiance. And I'd actually thought how beautiful she was looking. Yes, indeed: Hmm.

But then Paco had dropped her for someone younger, and Lisa had become unhappy and depressed. And, thinking it was something I'd done, I'd confronted her and she'd confessed it all. After that she seemed to be a bit happier. Relieved to get it off her chest I suppose.

But I wasn't.

Ah, well. That was water under the bridge now, wasn't it. Wasn't it? Well, maybe. But it was a bit like breaking the handle off a precious cup. Because you don't want to lose it you can glue it back on, but somehow you never quite trust the cup – and the glue – again. Especially if it gets a little too hot sometimes.

*\*\**

Marie and I spent nearly two weeks together. During this time the Ministry of Information arranged for journalists to visit various sites around Baghdad. And, even while I was filming with Ed, I was always aware of Marie photographing – distraught children or shattered bodies in the al-Kindi hospital. Its doctors and nursing staff desperately trying to deal with the wounded and dying with practically nothing. In many cases with no anesthetic whatsoever.

Then one day, quite suddenly, Marie disappeared. I'd gone with my government minder to visit the latest bombsite. When I got back to the Palestine Hotel I asked about her, but no-one had seen her. I waited around the hotel all day, but she never returned. That night I couldn't sleep and, by mid-morning, I felt gray and haggard. I tried to find out, through some of my Iraqi sources, whether anybody knew anything, but I had no luck.

The next day I slipped some money to an assistant hotel manager and got her room key. I knew that she wasn't inside but, even so, as I stood outside her door I felt some trepidation. But, of course, she wasn't inside. I closed the door and for a while just stood there in the half-dark, inhaling her perfume. Then I looked about. Her clothes seemed to be in place, but all of her equipment was missing, even her laptop. I searched through her dresser, found some letters, which I studiously avoided looking at. But there was no sign of her passport. I knew that the majority of journalists carry their passports on them at all times, but I couldn't remember whether Marie did.

Three dreadful days later I learned that she was in Amman, Jordan. A French journalist who had just arrived from there had seen her. I found the man and asked him how she was. Apparently she'd been picked up because her visa was out of date and the Ministry had sent her on the awful twelve-hour road journey. She was safe and sound, but still very angry. Then he handed me an envelope,

"She asked me to give this to you if I could."

"Thanks."

I took the envelope to my room to open it. Inside was a photograph that she'd taken of the two of us together. There was no message, just a lipstick impression of her lips.

"So *very* Marie," I thought.

For more than two years we were worlds apart. I went back to my wife, but I thought often of Marie and our weeks together in Baghdad. I also thought many times about trying to get in touch with her. Sometimes I told myself that I didn't know how to make contact. But I knew that was a flimsy excuse. Of course I knew.

The real truth was that I wasn't certain that she wanted to see me.

"What happens in Vegas," she'd said.

Did that mean it was just a fling for her?

And if I did make contact, what then?

Plus there was still the small matter of my wife and four children. Not small children, to be sure. They were all adults now. But I was still affected by what they would think about me.

And so I did nothing about it. Although I often wondered what would happen if I'd run into Marie in some war theater somewhere.

And then I was sent to Paris to cover the riots. Another city was in flames. Disconsolate, unemployed Moslem youths in various neighborhoods of Paris were setting fire to cars and hurling rocks at the fire brigades when they came to try and put them out. The action was getting closer to the better-off neighborhoods and the city center. And then it started to spread to other French cities like, well, like wildfire. And, for a while, it looked as though the whole country might explode.

I was on the plane and halfway to France before I even connected the country to Marie. I wondered whether there was half a chance that she might actually be there. "Probably not,' I thought. "She's most likely somewhere in Africa or Asia."

But I mused to myself, and wondered what it might be like if, by chance, I was able to find her.

"More than two years too. She obviously hasn't tried to find me in all this time."

For the first two days I was busy reporting all the action. For some reason it happened mostly after dark, as though it was all just some outlandish entertainment for the rioters. Like a massive firework show. In the daytime Paris calmed to a mere simmer. As each day progressed the anticipation of that night's events took a hold on the city.

On my third morning I'd had breakfast and had returned to my room. Almost idly I picked up a telephone directory and thumbed through it looking for the surname d'Angelo.

And suddenly I knew why I had never tried to contact Marie in all this time. It wasn't because I wasn't sure whether she wanted to see me. I was afraid. I'd had my adventure in Baghdad and could rationalize that to myself. Any more than that, and I might have to do something about it. Something that might cause, not just *tremors* in my life, but absolute tectonic, volcanic activity. And that possibility terrified me. With all of the imperfections of my life with Lisa, I wasn't sure whether I was ready for those changes.

My mind drifted again to how things had been with Lisa, especially in the last few years. We'd drifted apart, and I knew that it was my fault. I'd spent so much time away from home over the years that she'd forged a life without me. The last of our children had moved out years ago. Now she had her own friends that I didn't even know. Or, dare I say it, care about. When I came home in between trips we met as semi-strangers. All we really had to talk about was the children.

"Have I been so selfish?' I asked myself. "Have I just been thinking about myself all these years? But I wasn't thinking about myself, I was doing my job. And I've provided all them with security. I put all the kids through college. Well, except for Tommy. And he never really wanted to go. Lisa's always had everything she ever needed. And she has her own life. She really had nothing to complain about."

The phonebook nearly slipped from my hands, and I grabbed at it. With the reverie broken I half-heartedly started searching through the 'd's.

And there it was: "d'Angelo, M". Although there were a few d'Angelos, I knew this was her. I read the address, and was stunned to see that it was in the same arrondissement as the hotel I was staying in. Just a short taxi-ride away. Or perhaps, I thought, I could even walk there.

I checked my watch. I had a few hours before my next report. I was supposed to be doing research but, well....

"This is research, isn't it? Mmm..." And I laughed to myself. It would be fun to see the building she calls home. "She won't be there, of course. Probably photographing in some godforsaken part of the planet."

I copied down the address and showed it to the hotel concierge. "Oui, monsieur. Just a short ride. Maybe ten minutes."

So I grabbed a cab and gazed through the window as the taxi driver worked his way through the Paris traffic.

I thought about the time in Baghdad with Marie, and wondered what it would be like if I *was* to see her again. A different place. A different time. I almost asked the driver to go back to my hotel. But I was curious to see where she lived. "Then I'll go back to the hotel." I told myself.

"Ici, monsieur?" asked the driver, as the cab rolled to a stop.

I looked around. I had no idea whether this was the place or not.

"Yeah. I guess."

I paid the man and climbed out.

As the cab pulled away I found the piece of paper in my pocket and read the address, "Number thirty-three. Yep, this is the building. Not bad. Definitely a touch of class. *Very* Marie."

The building had obviously been restored lately. I peered through the thick glass of the door and thought I could see a sort of art deco design.

"Hmm, really not bad."

I started off down the street, and then looked back at the building. I read the address again, "Apartment seven..... Why not!"

I found the buzzer and pushed it, Nothing. Of course. I waited for a few more seconds, then pushed again. Just what I'd expected. Slowly, I started to walk away. Then I heard it, "Oui, qui e la?"

It was unmistakably Marie's voice.

Now what?

I returned to the entrance and leaned in to the entryphone,

"Er, Marie, this is Max Wheeler."

Nothing. Just silence. Had she completely forgotten who I was?

Then, without further ado, the buzzer rang out and the door clicked. I pushed it open gingerly, and barely heard the "Ça va?"

The old three-person elevator had been revamped, but still traveled at snail pace, then clanked to a stop when it reached the third floor. As I opened the gate an apartment door a little way down the corridor opened and I saw her. At first she just stood outlined in the doorway. Then she came rushing into my arms.

"Oh my God Max. Is it really you?"

I held her in my arms and looked into her smiling face. Then pulled her to me tightly. A power surged through my body and I felt totally at peace. "This fit," I thought. "This fit. I remember this perfect fit."

She grabbed my hand and pulled me inside.

As soon as she shut the door behind us she stood back in the little entrance hall and studied me. All I could do was stand there smiling foolishly at her. She shook her head.

"You just turn up? Just like that? No word for, what, two, three years, then just turn up at my door?"

She stood there looking at me with her arms folded across her breasts, her head quizzically to one side

"At least why didn't you phone?'

"I didn't think you'd be here," I said, then laughed as realized how stupid that must sound.

But she laughed with me, turned on her heel and led me into the living room. I was stunned. It seemed like every inch of every wall was covered with photographs.

"Are these all yours?"

"Er, yes." She paused. "Apart from that wall. Those are all by my friends."

Again she studied me without speaking. Eventually, "Are you well?"

"Oh yes. And you?

Later we made love. And now for me the feeling came from my heart as much as my groin. It really felt like an act of loving one another, rather than just having sex. And I felt such a strong union with her, it was like I disappeared altogether.

I wasn't sure when it happened - when I knew that it was all over with Lisa. I just knew that I'd found Marie again. Something had stirred in me. Something I hadn't felt for a very long time. And, as we walked the streets of Paris, and she showed me all her favorite places, I knew that I wanted to spend the rest of my life with her.

# Chapter Two

I looked down at Marie's body. A part of my brain knew that she was dead. Like you know it's cold in Alaska in the winter even if you've never been there. Or even seen a show about Alaska on Discovery. You just know these things. But, somehow, the rest of me wouldn't take it in. Wouldn't, couldn't 'understand'.

I blinked my eyes, not because there were tears there. But because maybe the blinking might cause the synapse that was needed for me to 'get it'.

What I needed was a drink. Mechanically I reached out for the full glass of wine that still sat on the bench. It was Marie's glass. She'd poured it but never picked it up.

"Better not to Sir."

The uniformed cop beside me actually reached out ready to grab my hand.

"The crime scene guys will want to check it."

"Crime scene!"

The explosion came from the short, plump man sitting in my kitchen chair. He'd been cleaning his spectacles with a cloth, and he paused mid-rub. His name is Myron Moscowicz, but nobody ever calls him Myron. It's always 'Mos'. Always has been, ever since he was a child. Even his wife, the fabulous Libby, calls him Mos.

I'd phoned Mos right after the 911 call.

"There's no fucking crime scene here! This poor man's wife has just dropped dead that's all. The only crime is that he's being treated like a criminal. How about some compassion for Chrissakes........"

"....Mos. It's okay. I'll grab a whisky."

I looked at the cop, waiting to see whether he was going to protest. But the cop said nothing. He just looked blankly at us.

"Good idea. I need one too."

Mos slid his glasses back on his nose and followed me into the living room.

When we got there a detective was standing with his back to the door, talking on his cell phone, "Yeah, the DOA's a female, late thirties...."

Mos bridled, but I reached out a hand to him.

"She's not a DOA, Max. That's Marie lying there."

All I could say was, "Yes, I know. It's okay. They're just doing their jobs. It's the only way they know how to do it."

I found the whisky bottle, poured us each a double, handed Mos a glass and took a sip of my own. Then I just fell into a sofa and rubbed my forehead. I was exhausted and drained now.

Neither of us spoke for quite a while. I guess Mos was being respectful, and I couldn't focus. When I finally managed to get something out it was barely audible: "What am I going to do Mos? She was my life. She was my reason to get up in the morning, she was what kept me going through the day…....My soul."

Mos let me talk. He knew better than to say anything at all.

"I loved her so much."

My voice cracked slightly, and I slumped forwards, both hands now holding my head.

Finally Mos whispered, "Yes, Max. I know" A long pause. "Is there anything I can do?"

I shook my head slowly.

"How about a sedative?"

Mos was a pharmacist. His parents had wanted him to be a doctor. And, indeed, he'd originally studied medicine. But he just couldn't stand the sight of blood. It had been a bad sign when they were dissecting frogs and he'd passed out. That was when he knew he just couldn't do it. So he gave up that dream and went for the closest thing he could think of.

"Maybe some Prozac?"

He'd been prescribing things for me ever since we met at an anti-war rally. The Vietnam war that was. In 1967.

"Wow, Mos looked different then," I occasionally thought to myself. "Long, curly hair, even a little beard. Beads around his neck, flowers on his shirt and jeans. Oh my God, was that this lifetime?"

I took a another sip of my whisky and shook my head again.

"Would you like me to call the kids."

And then, very hesitantly, "Or maybe Lisa?"

The detective finished his phone conversation and turned to me, "Mr Wheeler, I'm going to need you to answer some questions."

But I was still reacting to Mos' suggestion, "No. Don't call Lisa. I'll do that. Sometime."

Yeah, telling Lisa was going to be a trip. Would she laugh right in my face?

\*\*\*

Telling Lisa about Marie in the first place had been a real trip. But then what do you expect with someone that you've been joined at the hip with for a lifetime. Someone who's borne you four children, and who knows you inside and out.

It was always going to be tough. But Lisa alternated between screaming rages and passive/aggressive silences. When I wanted to talk she wouldn't. And when I wanted some respite from 'the situation' she continued to give me what for.

In the end I just moved out. At first I crashed with Mos and Libby, but then Libby decided she was being disloyal to Lisa. So I rented a small, apartment in Beverly Hills and waited for Marie to join me in the States.

Each of our children took it differently. Jack is my eldest. I don't know what happened to him, but he turned out to be a rather stiff neo-con merchant banker. He was living in Long Island with Maggie, his Waspy wife and three-year-old son – my beautiful grandson Toby. Well, Jack felt that his mother had been betrayed. Great! I had thought that, being a man, he might have seen my side. But, no. At first he refused to meet Marie. Or even mention her name. Somewhat hilariously, if he talked about her at all, she was 'that woman'. Even now he was still coming around to the way things were. God, wait until he found out about Marie!

Jenny, the older of the two girls, took a strange position. She was very critical of both me and her mother.

"But she's so much younger than you. It's disgusting! It's like marrying your daughter."

"Not quite honey. When you get older the years between people seem to shrink. It doesn't matter so much. It's not like when you're younger. She's…"

"…Dad, she's nearly twenty years younger than you. That *definitely* makes her young enough to be your daughter. Of course I blame mom."

I was aghast, "Why? No, honey this is no reflection whatsoever on your mom…"

"…If she'd kept your interest you wouldn't go chasing after some young…"

"…I never went chasing anybody. It just happened. These things do. It's life. You walk down a path together for as long as it's right. And then you come to, er, a fork in the road…"

I knew I was beginning to sound weird. But I felt I should try and explain. God knows why. But my daughter was obviously hurt and, although she can be highly sanctimonious sometimes, I love her very much, and I felt I owed her an explanation.

"Look, sometimes you just meet someone and fall in love with them, and want to be with them. I hope it happens to you someday."

There, I'd said it.

Jenny was an executive working in business affairs at a large studio. Her 'very busy life' meant that Jenny didn't really have a social life. She certainly didn't have a partner. I thought about that often, and pondered its significance.

Katie, who's only eighteen months younger than Jenny, couldn't have been more different. Katie's a free spirit, an enjoyer of life. A social butterfly. Everybody loves Katie. And Katie loves me. Whatever I do is okay with her. She was the first to greet Marie. She held out her arms and hugged her like a friend. "Welcome to the family," she'd said. And she meant it.

And young Tommy? Well, Tommy is Tommy. There's no-one like him. A dreamer, Tommy lives for one thing: to play his guitar. He was playing in a band that had caught some good press when they played gigs around town – which wasn't often. But they'd had a hit track, which had been downloaded a record number of times over a particular week. So Tommy didn't care as long as he could play. And he was totally down with Marie.

The medical examiner snapped off his rubber gloves as he strolled into the living room. He wasn't sure which was the husband.

"Mr. Wheeler?" He looked from one of us to the other casually.

"That's me."

"Yes, of course," vaguely recognizing me, I suppose. Maybe he tuned into the channel I was on. "Well, Mr. Wheeler, I'm pretty sure your wife died from a ruptured cerebral aneurism. Of course I'll have to do further …"

"But she wasn't sick. Actually she was one of the healthiest people I know. And she was still pretty young.…"

"…Yes. Well, it is pretty rare," he said thoughtfully. "Not aneurisms, of course…."

He saw the expression of puzzlement on my face. "Look, you do understand that an aneurism is a dilation…a swelling if you like…of a blood vessel, part of a vein or artery for example. Kind of like when you inflate a balloon.

Mos, of course, knew what an aneurism was, but he felt that it was important for me to try and understand why my young wife had just died. He quietly poured a little whisky into a glass and handed it to the medical examiner.

"Thanks," he said, taking a sip. "So, when this aneurism…this swelling…gets bigger, the wall stretches and gets thinner and weaker. And that's when it can rupture or burst. It's always going to cause problems, of course. But when it's a cerebral aneurism it bleeds into the area around the brain."

Mos couldn't help himself, "…A subarachnoid hemorrhage…"

"….Precisely. And when this is severe enough it can lead to a coma or even death. As I say, it happens quite rarely. But, in this case…."

He let the last words linger in the air. After all, they explained everything. "And no symptoms?" I asked. I still couldn't believe it.

"Yes, often. Headaches, maybe a stiffness around the neck…."

Almost in sympathy, Mos started rubbing his own neck.

"…But not always. Sometimes, like your wife, it just comes like a bolt from the blue, as it were.

I guess it was the journalist part of me that had taken over now. I'd become interested in the subject. As though Marie was on a trip somewhere, and I was doing a medical story.

"So what causes all this to happen?"

The examiner took another sip, "A number of things. Could be hypertension, say. Or the artery could have a weakness in the wall….Also certain blood infections can be a trigger. With people traveling to some fairly exotic locations these days we're seeing all kinds of peculiar infections."

"And Marie has certainly been to a great many 'exotic' locations," I thought. She'd traveled to every continent. She'd seen things with her own eyes – and her camera lens – that most people only dream about. From the merely colorful, unusual or strange, to the alien, mysterious and glamorous through to outlandishly bizarre.

"I'm interested in people," she'd told me. "Not just interested, but fascinated."

And her photographs reflected that. Whether it was headhunters in New Guinea or NASA flight controllers, she seemed to capture the essence of each subject. Somehow getting inside them, showing them to us, so that we could in turn be equally fascinated.

*\*\*\**

We'd married in Los Angeles. As soon as my divorce came through. It was a very simple wedding. Marie's parents were now dead, and she had very little family in France. Her best friend, Carole, came over to be her Maid of Honor. And a few other friends made it.

Of my kids, Jack informed me that he was too busy, "Well, you know, it's quite a trip from New York. And this is a really busy time for us right now. I'm not sure I can just take the time off like that."

"Fuck him! How did I ever get such a pissy kid? What was it that I did to him? Or didn't do to him?" I thought, even though he's my first-born and I actually love him and have a lot of respect for him.

Jenny was gracious enough to join us for the ceremony, but then slipped out before the small reception without saying anything to anybody.

Katie was there of course, the life and soul of the party. "God bless Katie."

Tommy was playing a gig somewhere. "Well, you can't argue with that.....I guess"

But the guys were there: Mos and Harry and Al. And although the fabulous Libby was there with Mos, she came very much under protest. She wanted to make it known that she was not deserting Lisa, but was coming as my friend's wife.

Several of my work colleagues were also there. And, best of all, my Aussie journalist friend Paul flew in specially. In between covering stories in Afghanistan and Iraq. He brought with him a fine bottle of Irish whisky as a wedding present. And he gave a speech telling the small crowd how he'd introduced the now happy couple during the 'shock and awe' bombing.

In some child-like moment I'd ordered thousands of M&Ms spread everywhere. When I explained to Marie that M&M really stood for Max and Marie, instead of groaning she laughed loudly. I loved her even more for that.

There was no doubt that I was hopelessly, ecstatically, in love. I couldn't actually remember feeling like this. Even as a teenager I'd never been this much in love with anyone. This was the most blissful time of my life.

Then, when I looked down at the marriage certificate and saw Marie Alexandre d'Angelo, I couldn't help myself, "Mad." I said out loud.

Marie looked at me curiously, an unsure smile on her lips, "Who? You or me?"

"No, Marie Alexandre d'Angelo. M A D, Mad." I laughed.

"Oh, yes. I'd forgotten that," And she laughed too.

And so, sometimes when I was feeling capricious, I called her 'Mad'. And then it became 'Maddie'. And that came to be my term of affection for her.

What I remember most was her laughter. She'd laughed at everything. She would stand in Rodeo Drive and have to cover her mouth so as not to upset people. She thought *everything* was hilarious.

Whether it was a trip to Magic Mountain or walking barefoot on the beach, it was like there was a golden halo around us both. A halo of joyfulness and happiness

And, for the first time in my life, I found myself begging off stories. I was reluctant to travel away from Marie. She came with me once to Nepal, and that trip had been amazing for us both. But I'd managed to wriggle out of many jobs. Now I was glad that we'd been together so much of the time.

But six months was all we'd had. Six months of marriage. And then she was gone. Dead. Just like that. I'd been given this wonderful gift. And then it was snatched away from me.

To say that I felt numb wouldn't have been correct. Because that implied that I actually felt something. No, I *was Numbness*. There was no feeling. There was a complete absence of feeling. It would have been no good sticking a pin into me. Or a whole pincushion's worth of pins. There was nothing there. I was the very essence of nothingness.

Mos insisted that I came back to their house. Actually he didn't need to insist. He suggested it, and I followed, zombie-like. Libby gave me some hot sweet tea, which I sipped. Then, later, a bowl of soup, which I spooned into my mouth, neither tasting nor smelling it. And afterwards Mos handed me some Prozac, which I swallowed without protest.

That night, lying in bed bewildered and disorientated, my thoughts turned back to when my father died. It was actually very hard to remember, because I had only been four years old. And my father had come and gone a lot before then. My mother told me that "daddy's a traveling salesman". But I had no concept of what that meant. I just knew that sometimes he was there and sometimes he wasn't. And, one time, he just never came home. It wasn't until I was much older that I found out that it had been a traffic accident somewhere in Virginia.

Maybe it was the Prozac, maybe it was my emotional state, but the harder I tried to remember my father, the harder it was to form a picture. Nothing would come. Just a vague shadow of a thing. Once I'd asked my mother when daddy was coming home. In fact my mom didn't even tell me then that my father was dead. She'd just said that he wasn't coming back to us. I didn't understand. But she'd taken one look at my scrunched up face and all she'd said was, "Please don't cry!" To this day I have no idea why she said that. She didn't say it in a cruel way. She was just firm. Maybe it was too much for her to bear at that time. Maybe it just reminded her of her own sadness.

And I hadn't cried either. I had wanted to cry, but I also wanted to please her, and I managed to swallow my tears. So it became a kind of game between us. Whenever she saw my face crumple she would say that: "Please don't cry!" I don't know if she was afraid of my tears, but she certainly managed to stop me. In fact I couldn't remember *ever* crying. But, when I became an adult, the more I thought about it the stranger I thought her reaction was.

In the darkness I remembered when she *had* told me the truth. I was seven by now, I'd been thinking about my father for a long time, but I came home from school one day to find a strange man sitting in the living room with my mother.

"This is Hank," my mom had said. "He wants to meet you."

I was busy on my way to do something, and I wasn't really listening,

"Why?"

"Because he's heard so much about you."

I blinked. I couldn't understand how this man could have heard of me. Then, when I looked at mom for an explanation, I noticed that she seemed to be all dressed up. Suddenly I began to feel a mixture of half-uneasy and half-excited. Something was in the wind!

It was Hank who broke the short silence, "Your mother's told me a lot about you, and I guess I wanted to meet you."

"Why?"

I still didn't understand.

Hank's already perspiring face turned a deeper shade of pink. "Because I....er....we...."

Finally my mother couldn't stand it any longer, "Because Hank and I are going to get married, that's why."

"Oh."

I computed this new fact. Then I had a thought,

"Does that mean you'll be my dad?"

"Er, yes....I guess so...." Hank sputtered.

I remember thinking about it for a moment. Then, "Good".

And I ran off to play.


I *would* have cried the day I fell out of a tree. Except that I was unconscious. They took me off to hospital, and my mom watched over me there.

"Concussion is all. No bones broken," said the doctor.

I slept for thirty hours straight. When I woke up I was sore, but that was all. No tears. I guess it was too late by then anyway.

Two years later Hank waved goodbye to me and my mom one night and went to the bar for a quiet drink. He'd been there for about half an hour when a fight broke out. Hank kept out of it. But then one of those freakish things happened. A guy got punched and was sent reeling. As he did, he fell against Hank and knocked him clean off his stool. And when he fell he caught his head against the edge of the bar. Bang! That's all it took. One accidental blow. Killed him stone dead. The cops arrived about one in the morning. I heard my mother let out a cry and went to see what was happening. I found her sitting with a dazed expression on her face. A cop brought her a glass of water, but she just took hold of it without drinking, just stared into space. But there were no tears from her. And I shed none *that* time either.

My mom didn't stay a widow for long. Billy-Bob had been lurking, waiting in the wings, and now he seized his chance. They were married within the year and, not long after I turned twelve, baby Elliott was born. *He* sure knew how to cry. But, by then, I felt I was too old to cry and, if anything bad ever happened, I just forced myself not to. And then a funny thing happened. It was as though my tear ducts had dried up completely. There was just plumb nothing there.

Sometimes, watching a movie or something, a lump would form in my throat. But that was all. My eyes might blink once or twice too. But there was nothing there. Zip. Nada!

I'd occasionally wonder what it might feel like to shed a tear. But, strangely, I couldn't imagine it. I even experimented. Once or twice, when I'd stood on the prow of a boat say, and the wind had whipped around my head, my eyes would moisten. I'd turn my face into the wind to see if I could persuade a drop to trickle down my nose. But it never happened.

"You're going to go into work?" asked the delightful Libby.

"Lib, the man's wife just died! What a question."

Mos was horrified. He'd just been about to take a bite out of his breakfast toast. And now he held it poised inches from his mouth.

"I'm just asking…."

"…Well don't. I'm sure that's the last thing Max feels like right now."

"So…what *are* you going to do? If you don't mind me asking, that is."

"What's the matter with you? Why are you badgering the poor man. Let him be. Max, don't pay any attention."

He finally chewed his toast and chased the bite with a swallow of coffee.

Actually I wasn't paying attention to either of them really. I was lost in contemplation. I'd had a night to think about it, but I still couldn't actually believe that Marie was dead.

"Do you need help with anything? You know you can stay here as long as…well as long as you need."

"Thanks Libby. That's very kind. I'm sure I'll manage. Although…" I turned to Mos, "I could probably do with some help with the arrangements."

"The arrange….Oh! Sure, Max, leave it all to me. When..?"

"They said they're going to do an autopsy, so I'm not sure. Maybe in a week's time."

Libby was brushing crumbs off the table. "I'll help you draw up a list of people if you want. To call, that is."

I blinked, "Thanks Lib."

You never knew with Libby. What she'd do or say next.

She lowered her eyes as she searched for any more crumbs,

"Er, what about….Lisa? Are you going to let her know? I could…"

"Yes, why don't you do that. It's not a call I really want to make."

"Sure."

# Chapter Three

Devastate \Dev''as*tate\ transitive verb. [imperative past participle Devastated; present participle verb or noun Devastating.] Deal destruction, desolate, lay waste, ravage, devour, sap, mine, blast, bomb, blow to smithereens, drop the big one, confound, exterminate, . . .

Over the years I'd covered many stories of mud slides and earthquakes and hurricanes and other, awful disasters. I'd talked to people in wars and shootings and the many ways human beings find to bring hell into each others lives. And so often, when I'd interviewed people, one word was used more than any other: 'devastated'. "I feel devastated", they'd say. And they did. And they were.

It was so common now that it had almost become a laughable cliché. Almost.

But if anyone had asked me now how *I was*, I would have to say, "Devastated. I'm devastated." It was almost as though my brain had stopped sending out signals altogether, stopped telling the rest of my body what to do.

Trancelike, I stood in the kitchen of my home and slowly looked around. The broken glass and spilt wine had been cleaned up. And the police had taken away the wine bottle and Marie's glass. But everything else was just as I'd left it. The two plates, with the now-dried up salmon, snow peas and potatoes, still sat on the bench.

I felt paralyzed, my arms and legs lead-heavy. No thought came into my head, I felt no physical feelings. So I just stood there. In the kitchen. In my cotton-wool land.

It was only because the telephone rang. Otherwise I might have stood there all day. Perhaps for the rest of my life. It was Katie, "Dad, I am so sorry. What can I do?" Sweet Katie.

"How did you know? I mean who told you?"

"Libby called mom, and she called Jenny."

"And she called you…?"

"Are you kidding! No, Jenny called Jack. And he called me. Look, I'm coming round…"

"…It's okay Katie….I'm okay…"

"…You don't sound okay. I'll be there in, like, thirty minutes. No, better make it an hour."

"Okay."

\*\*\*

"Dad, I think you should shave." Katie said. "You'll probably feel better, and you'll definitely look better."

I rubbed a hand over my stubble and realized I hadn't shaved since the day….the day before….

I stared at my face in the bathroom mirror. I looked old. Not surprising really. Christ, I felt old. Old like never before. I'd always been told that I never looked my age. I'd loved to tell people, "I'm fifty-eight." Or now, "I'm fifty-nine."

"Really!" They'd say. "Really! Wow! I'd have made you for ten years younger. Or maybe less."

And I knew a secret, little smile would play across my lips.

Well, now I definitely didn't look younger. I peered into the mirror. If anything, I looked ten years *older*. With the gray stubble and my hair all mussed up. "My god." I thought, "So old!"

Had I slept last night? I couldn't remember. I figured I must have, otherwise I would've remembered being awake. But I sure felt like I hadn't slept. Cloudiness surrounded my head and I felt drained. Exhausted. I walked unsteadily into the bedroom and sat on the edge of the bed.

"Just a few minutes." I thought, "I'll lie down for just a few minutes."

And that was where Katie found me when she came to look for me. She saw me curled up on the bed. Not quite in a fetal position, but with my legs drawn up like a child.

"Oh dad," she whispered to herself. And she told me later she'd decided to let me sleep.

A few hours later I found Katie sitting in the living room reading a fashion magazine.

"Hi," I yawned, scratching my head.

"Hi." She uncurled from the sofa and stood up, wrapping protective arms around me. For a moment I felt as though she was the parent and I the child.

"Can I get you anything dad? Are you hungry?"

I checked my watch, "Wow, I didn't realize I'd been asleep that long. I might make some coffee."

I saw her about to protest, and motioned her to sit down.

"I'm fine. Want some?"

We moved together into the kitchen and I saw that she'd cleared away the plates of dried-up salmon.

"Is this...?" she started to ask.

"Yeah, right here. Just dropped right in front of me. No warning, nothing."

I shook my head slowly. "I never saw it coming."

I paused with one hand on the coffee jar,

"Totally alive one minute, and..." I snapped my fingers, "...dead the next. Just like that. I never saw it coming."

"Dad, you mustn't blame yourself...."

"...Oh, I don't. But I sure wish I could have done something."

There was a little pause, while I played with the coffee jar and thought about Marie. Then, when it came out, I was saying it to myself as much as her, "I loved her so much Katie".

"I know dad...I know." she whispered. And her cheeks were wet with tears.

I found the next few days challenging. Going out proved difficult. With my mind a blur, it was impossible to work. I'd get into my car to drive somewhere, and forget where I was going. Even simple tasks became major challenges. And staying at home was worse. As much as possible I avoided the kitchen where 'it' had happened. Sleeping in the bed which I'd shared with Marie was also impossible. So I lounged in front of the television day and night flicking from one channel to another, barely absorbing anything. The whisky bottle constantly stood open in front of me. I just couldn't be bothered to put the cap on. Although I forced myself not to drink before it got dark. Sometimes I dozed. But, always, there was the terrible numbness.

***

"You want some more?" Al asked.

I gazed up at my friend from the depths of the armchair. Al towered above me holding out a whisky bottle. It took me a moment, then I shook my head, "No thanks. I'm good." Al just nodded his head.

Al Geery was not a chatterbox. In fact the only time he talked really was when he had something special to say. And, even then, it was always sparingly, in a deep sonorous voice. He was a gentle, bear-like man, nearly six foot six and broad, with a full beard. There was a solid, placid feeling about him that I liked. It calmed most people and made them feel easy around him. They also liked to hug him. Women especially, but some men also. It gave them a strong sense of reassurance.

I'd never actually hugged Al. Although in the twenty-some years that I'd known him, I had allowed Al to drape an arm around my shoulders. And that always felt good.

Al's wife Rita, on the other hand was a chatterbox. Although that wasn't entirely fair. She was in PR, and she talked for a living. But Boy! had she mastered that art. She was a perky woman who never seemed to stop moving. Like Al, she was in her fifties. But she wore her blonde-dyed gray hair in a short bob, and her constant animation brought a youthfulness to her personality.

She and Al were chalk and cheese. But maybe that was their secret. Because it was obvious that he still adored her and she adored him.

Al worked from home – he ran a small IT company that specialized in anti-hacker software. But he also liked to cook and experiment with recipes. It was his passion. And he loved nothing better than trying a new recipe on his friends or his family and Rita. And she, in turn, loved his cooking, giving the lie to her still slim frame.

I turned my head and looked at the box beside me. Inside it was an urn. And, inside that…were Marie's ashes. I wondered what I would do with them. We hadn't talked about things like that. We hadn't really had time. In fact I'd only guessed about having her cremated. Talking about death and what came after had seemed like the last thing to do.

"Well," I thought ruefully, "I guess it was".

Besides, where should I have buried her anyway? In the USA? In France? I had no idea. I felt a frown crease my forehead. I couldn't believe that she was in there. That this life – this precious life – was now dust sitting in an urn in a box.

The funeral had been a small affair because I'd thought too many people might have made it harder for me. But, in the end, I had the support of my friends, some work colleagues, and family. Katie was there, of course. And Jenny had come. And stayed! Which I really appreciated. Jack, of course, sent his apologies. But surprise, surprise, Tommy had turned up with an acoustic guitar and a song that he'd written specially for Marie. He sang it during the ceremony and it was very sweet, and I was touched, and I could hear sniffles around me.

Tommy also turned up with a raven-haired girl with an exquisite face. Tommy introduced her to me as Anastasia. She was dressed all in black – including her lips and thick kohl around her eyes. She never spoke at all, not even to Tommy, and at first I even wondered whether she might be mute. That was until she'd lent her angelic voice to harmonize with Tommy's. Later she brushed her black lips against my cheek and murmured condolences, and I inhaled a heady aroma of patchouli and cinnamon. Now she squatted cross-legged on the carpet and ran a hand languidly through her long, pre-Raphaelite tresses as she studied the people around her.

Katie left a small group and came over to me, "Hi."

"Hi."

She knelt beside me, "You okay?

I nodded.

"Mom said to send her condolences".

This wasn't strictly true I knew. What Lisa had probably said was, "I'm not surprised. This is God's punishment. It's what he deserves."

"Thank you," I said.

She stroked my hand. The one that wasn't holding the whisky glass. I looked down at our two hands together and back up at her face, and smiled at her, "You're very considerate."

Later I was standing with Barbara Graden and George Colorossi from the network. Their faces were glum. And I knew it wasn't just the funeral. I asked George what was up.

"You heard about the takeover?" asked George.

"What takeover?

"The story is we're about to be 'integrated' into the MRG Network. You know what that means?"

"Not really," I said. But I could guess.

"It means," said Barbara, "that there are going to be some 'rationalizations in human resources'. In other words 'collateral damage'." She gave emphasis to the words the way only a TV presenter can.

"Not good," said George, "Not good at all."

I suppose I wasn't really listening. I was looking at Anastasia. There was something magnetic about the girl. I found my eyes drawn to her and the pool of quiet presence around her. And then, out of the blue, I thought again about Marie. And I suddenly felt an enormous wave of sadness. It overwhelmed me and enervated me and took me over. And I closed my eyes and surrendered.

But the truth was that there was also something deep inside me that was relieved that I could feel the sadness. Because that feeling at least was better than the terrible numbness that I had been experiencing before.

\*\*\*

When Katie drove me home that night I was more than a little smashed. In the car she talked about who'd been there and how each person had reacted. However, she'd realized, after a while, that she'd been doing all the talking, and I suppose that I'd become increasingly quiet. She kept flicking looks at me to see if I was alright.

When she pulled up at my place she looked intently into my eyes, "Are you going to be alright?"

"Sure honey." But I couldn't help letting out a deep sigh and I closed my eyes. I paused for a moment, then looked back at her, "I'll be okay…But thanks."

I kissed her on the cheek and climbed out of the car, then stuck my head back in again,

"Thanks for everything."

I could see her watching me until I was safely inside, then she drove off slowly.

Inside the house I studiously avoided the kitchen.

"Can't handle that tonight," I said out loud.

And I stumbled to the bedroom, and fell into bed.

When I woke the next day my neck was stiff and my sinuses hurt like hell. As I showered, shaved and dressed I tried to figure out how much I'd had to drink, but I couldn't remember.

"Obviously a fair bit," I muttered, as I poured strong coffee.

"I can't keep doing that, or I'll just become a drunk."

I looked around the kitchen.

"And I can't keep avoiding this place. I've either got to move, completely re-do the place or just get used to it."

And, having given myself a severe talking-to, I set out for the network.

***

I steeled myself. I hadn't been into work since Marie died. As I passed through reception and made my way up to my office I knew that everyone was looking at me. Some people even offered me brief commiserations. I knew that it was important for them to acknowledge what had happened. And I accepted their condolences, even though, after a while, I began to feel like I never wanted to hear another word spoken about Marie.

Mike Kenny, my executive producer, was another old trooper. He'd been at the network for twenty years – since the early days – and in the television business his whole life. Mike and I had been through a lot together, and there was genuine fondness between us. Mike, of course, had been at the funeral and, seeing my face now, he felt no need to say anything more.

"Are you sure you're ready for this?" was all he asked.

"Ready? If I don't do something I'm going to go fucking mad. Mike I *need* to do this. I need to get out of the house."

"Okay then," Mike consulted his diary. "We could do with having someone in Baghdad for a week. I don't suppose…"

"…Anywhere but Iraq, Mike. You know…"

"Yes, I'm sorry." How about Israel? A short piece on Arab/Israeli relations now that Sharon and Arafat are out of the picture? Maybe something on the new generation? Or…" he studied the page, "How about Pakistan. Jeff has an interview set up with Musharraf, but wants to finish something here. And, you're there, you could do a piece on the return of the Afghan refugees to Afghanistan?"

I didn't have to think for a single moment. Immediately I said, "Sure. When do I leave?"

# Chapter Four

The plane touched down at Islamabad airport. I was relieved. It had been a long journey. And, even in business class, a journey that had taken me across the States, most of Europe, Dubai, Karachi and finally Islamabad had drained me. And, although I guess I'm a veteran traveler, and know most of the tricks, I still felt rumpled and weary. I'd left Ed in Karachi to find a stringer to work with him on the Musharraf interview later.

Once upon a time, in the Good Old Days, I had traveled with a producer who had organized everything. And a full crew of cameraman and sound man. Now it was just me and Ed. And now, as an experiment, for this part of the trip it was just going to be me. I *was* the crew. The network had sent me with my own camera to try and operate. I missed Ed already, and I wasn't sure how it was going to work. I was now presenter, producer, director, camera, sound, and runner.

After spending an hour clearing Pakistani customs and collecting my luggage I exhaustedly trudged outside and was met by a blast of heat. I looked around the crowd for a sign with my name on it. Nothing. Nothing but the usual bedlam. Taxi drivers called out to me, uniformed 'porters' wanted to carry my bags and boys grabbed at my sleeve, trying to sell me something: accommodation; transport; drugs; their sisters maybe.

Already the familiar dust was starting to catch in my throat and perspiration was forming in my armpits. I walked up and down, peering at the signs held by the patient drivers. I wondered idly whether the hotel might have misspelled my name. That had happened many times. Once there had been a sign that looked an awful lot like 'Mr. Wanker'. "Yeah," I'd thought, "that's definitely me."

I sighed and allowed myself to be led away by one of the taxi drivers.

I showed the driver a piece of paper with the name of the hotel and settled back into the threadbare seat. After a few minutes it started:

"You want nice place? I know good place for you to stay. Very cheap. You will like it very much."

"No thanks, just take me to that place."

I looked out the window at the endless row of tiny shops that graced the streets of so many countries I had reported from, all seemingly selling the same stuff.

"How do they survive?" I wondered for the millionth time. "And did they all have some unique selling proposition, making each particularly appealing to a certain group of dedicated customers?"

"Very clean. You like. I will show you."

"Gotta give the guy credit for persistence," I thought.

In a weary, but firm, voice I said, "No, just take me to that hotel please."

The taxi driver changed tack, "You want nice woman? I get very nice woman for you."

"Yes," thought Max, "I want a nice woman. But she's dead."

Of course the hotel had no record of my reservation. But, after much to-ing and fro-ing – and a small amount of money – a room was found for me. The taxi driver, who had been loitering in the corner, slunk off in disappointment.

As I peered into the bathroom mirror at a face etched with fatigue, I wondered yet again why I was still doing this.

"I should have retired years ago," I thought, "I ought to head for the golf course."

The trouble was I didn't play golf, and didn't like it. Or anything else. This was all I did. And all I liked. And now I wasn't sure I liked this any more either.

I heard a noise at the door and turned around. An envelope had been slipped under the door. I bent, picked it up and opened it. The name and address was longer than the message. It was from the United Nations High Commission for Refugees, and it simply read 'Pick you up at 8.30am tomorrow. B. White'.

\*\*\*

The white Toyota Prado with UNHCR printed on the side pulled up outside the hotel just as I stepped outside. A tall dark-haired young man climbed out and stuck his hand out, "Max Wheeler?"

I picked the British accent right away. "Hello, I'm Barry White." I couldn't help the double take. Barry smiled,      "Yes, I get that all the time. Don't worry. Welcome to Islamabad. Pleased to meet you. Have you been here before?"

I shook the hand, and we both climbed into the Toyota. "Yeah, a couple of times."

The Toyota growled into life and we took off.

"Thanks for this." I said.

"Oh, no problem. Happy to show you what we're doing."

He twisted his head to watch for a gap in the traffic, then pulled out into the great jumble of vehicles large and small, and focused for a while on the traffic. I was happy to just be a passenger. Eventually we turned onto the Islamabad-Peshawar road and then we both relaxed.

Barry turned to me, "How was your trip?"

"Long and tedious."

"I would have thought you must be used to it by now."

"Kinda. Doesn't really get any easier though."

"Any particular focus to this story?"

"The closing of the camps after such a long time mainly. I gather some of these people have been here thirty years or more."

"Oh, absolutely. Many of them were born and raised here, and have never even been to Afghanistan before. Quite an experience for them. They still think of themselves as Afghans though. Still talk about 'going home'."

Barry swerved to avoid a small car that, in turn, was avoiding a bicycle that had swung into the road. Unfazed, he continued, "Actually, we've already helped over two and a half million Afghan refugees return from Pakistan. But there are still hundreds of thousands left."

"Will they go?"

"Hmm. Well, if it was up to the Pakistani government, they would already have gone. But they can't force them, of course."

"Are they worried about the resurgence of the Taliban?"

"Some of them. Security's obviously an issue...."

A truck thundered by us and somehow managed to squeeze in front of us before an even bigger monster coming the other way took us all out.

"...No, the real issue is simply money. That and accommodation. There are simply no jobs and nowhere for them to live. So, often what you'll find is the men will sometimes go back for a visit and leave the women and children behind.

Eventually they find something, and come back for their families….By the way, there's bottled water beside you when you want it."

I looked down at the bottle, but didn't reach for it, "Thanks."

"We're just starting a new program to register those that are left. You might see it. And, um, we actually pay them to go back to Afghanistan."

"How much?"

"Oh, each family will get a 'travel grant'. Somewhere between four and thirty dollars. Depending how far they have to go…"

"…Not much..."

"…And then, when they get there, each individual will get twelve dollars to help them reintegrate."

I mulled this over. For about the millionth time in my life I thought again about inequality in the world.

"I could practically have that much money fall out of my pocket and not notice it."

"Yes, I know what you mean. But we're doing the best we can"

"Oh, I wasn't blaming you. It's just…I don't know," and I sighed, "There's so much poverty and privation in the world. You feel so impotent, knowing there's practically nothing you can do about it."

The Englishman just nodded his head in sympathy. Understanding.

For a very long time we drove in silence, each of us lost in his own thoughts. And then, still jetlagged and tired from the previous day's journey, I nodded off. And even though the Toyota Prado pitched and lurched over several potholes in the road, and Barry had to swerve to avoid various hazards – moving and other-wise – I slept.

When I came to Barry was pulling up at a small café set amongst rows of small, one-man shops. Through bleary eyes I looked at him questioningly.

"Thought we'd stop for a drink. And maybe a bite. Okay?"

"Sure."

We rolled out of the Toyota. The men sitting outside the café eyed us suspi-ciously as we entered. An old fan whirred rhythmically, doing little to displace the stale air. Barry waved at a man sitting behind the counter who was watching a television with the sound turned down. The man nodded, recognizing Barry.

Obviously this was a regular stopping place. But maybe Barry didn't tip him well, because the man didn't smile. Instead he lethargically made his way to our table.

"Would you like something to eat?" Barry asked.

"No thanks. Just some tea." The place reminded me of several places around the world where I'd managed, without effort on my part, to become ill. And, besides, I'd been sitting on my backside in an airplane for the best part of a day – doing nothing. And I'd actually eaten the airline's food. So I wasn't hungry.

Barry spoke to the man in Urdu, ordering tea for us both. I think the man asked Barry if he wanted any food. And, when he declined, the man grumped off to get the tea.

There was no road sign that I could see. Nothing to indicate there was a refugee camp. We were driving along the road, and the next thing I knew we'd turned off. Then the road became even rougher, and the Toyota bucked and jerked and threw both of us around.

"Little bit rough on this road. But it's not too far now," said Barry,

We rounded a bend, and I saw the tent city in a huge, completely flat plain. Of course I'd seen refugee camps before. In Somalia, in Gaza, in Darfur, in Yugoslavia. So many countries. There were differences of course. But, in some ways, there were often many similarities. The air of torpor, a kind of dream-like quality. Human life existing, living one day to the next. One meal to the next. When there was food. Here, at Jalozai, it was all exacerbated by an unbelievable heat.

This camp had been established a long time. At first look it all seemed quite orderly. There appeared to be brightly colored rows of tents which actually protected their inhabitants from the elements. But, looking closer, I saw that most of the 'tents' were tarpaulins or pieces of plastic sheeting strung over sticks, forming merely a kind of separation from the family next door.

The Toyota pulled up at a large prefabricated tent, which was open on three sides. There was an UNHCR sign pinned to the wall of the tent and there were two long lines of people separated by a piece of material. One line was for men and one line for women. They lined up to talk with a man and a woman sitting at desks. Many of the women wore burqas and most carried small children, with other children beside them. And many of the men wore the traditional shalwa kameez, the pajama-like traditional dress. .

"This is it," said Barry, as he climbed out.

I was immediately assailed by the stench from the camp's open drains. A group of small children followed us, giggling. But they were the only animated beings that I could see. All the older children and adults seemed to stand stock still, eyeing us suspiciously.

"These people want to return to Afghanistan." said Barry, "And the Pakistan government and UNHCR want to help them do it voluntarily, with dignity. So, what we're doing is registering everybody and providing documents."

"Why can't they just open the borders and let them go back? Presumably the same way that they arrived?"

Barry White gave me a look of patient sufferance, "Because we need to know who they are and what their aspirations are. Then we can find comprehensive solutions for them all. Each individual will be issued with a 'Proof of Registration' card using fingerprint biometrics and photo IDs."

"And then they'll be able to just go back?"

"Absolutely. Then, once they cross the border into Afghanistan, their registration with us will end and the 'Proof of Registration' card will be invalidated."

I was mystified by the seemingly bureaucratic nonsense.

"Why?" I asked.

"Why what?"

"Why go to all that trouble to register them, then invalidate it?"

"Because the data that we collect in the registration will help the Afghan government to plan their regional governments better. And they can make the best use of the skills. You know, people like teachers and doctors."

It still seemed a strange way to do things and I wanted to ask more, but Barry had already gone to talk with his colleagues. One of the kids was tugging at my pants and holding out his hand. The other kids, seeing this, mimicked their friend. Some touched their grubby fingertips to their lips. "Food." I understood. I shook my head and joined Barry, who introduced me to his colleagues.

"This is Najeeb and this is Rivia," he said, "And this is Max Wheeler. He's a TV journalist come to do a story on the repatriation."

Najeeb pretty much ignored me. But Rivia smiled sweetly and then carried on processing the women in the line, who were still standing patiently.

"Would you like to meet some of the refugees?" asked Barry.

"Definitely," I said. "Just let me get my camera sorted out.

We made our way between the rows of tents.

"They've actually arranged themselves according to the villages that they come from in Afghanistan." Barry explained, "So at least they have that kind of security. But most of them have little else. Just the few things that they could carry with them. Many were ordered to leave by the Taliban, and others simply fled with just the clothes they were wearing."

I stopped to film a man roasting corn cobs on a small open brazier. A small crowd was gathered around him. A few of them looked at him disinterested, but nobody smiled.

"We plan to close this camp very soon." said Barry.

"What'll happen to the people who are left?"

"Weeell…we hope there's nobody left. We would like them all to be repatriat-ed…."

"Hello meester." Would you like to take my photograph?"

A man unexpectedly stood in front of the camera, so that now I was focused on the man's chest. Of course I knew what was coming next. A request for money. But I also knew that if I gave this man any money I'd have to pay everybody. So I tried to ignore the man.

"Everyone loves his country," continued the man, still positioning himself in front of my camera. "but there is no peace. And our land is…has many foreigners who occupy it. It is very difficult to decide. Would you like to take my photograph? It will be very little money"

I pointed the camera into a tent. There were few possessions inside. A woman squatted on the ground. Three small children sat beside her, playing in the earth. In her arms she held an unmoving baby, its arms and legs were stick-thin and its face was gray. The woman turned her face away from the camera. The children just stared at me. I thought about the comparison with a family in middle America, sitting in their luxuriously furnished living room watching television. And I turned off the camera and closed my eyes.

"What am I doing this for?" I asked myself, "So that a family like that sitting watching television can change channels in disgust?"

I looked around again at the dire poverty. How many times in my life had I seen this? How many more times did I need to show it? Christ, if the viewing public hadn't got the message by now, would they ever get it? Probably not. I rubbed a hand over my forehead and eyes.

"Are you okay?" asked Barry.

I thought about the hopelessness of it all.

"Sure." I said. But I wasn't. I really wasn't.

"It's probably just the heat."

"Yes," said Barry. "It's pretty stinking today."

"That it is my friend," I thought.

"Would you like to walk on?"

"Sure. Why not."

I pointed the camera at the end of the row of little tents. A man had built an earth oven and he was busy baking bread. A youth was beside him selling the bread to a few customers. The youth was wearing a T-shirt and a baseball cap.

"Hi," he said. "Welcome to Paradise."

But he didn't smile.

We walked on past a few children who splashed each other at a water tank. Many of the tents that we passed also held women, often with their children, just sitting sheltering from the intense heat.

Inside a lean-to a young tailor squatted, busily sewing. As we drew level with him the young man looked up at us and smiled.

"Hello".

"Hi." I said, automatically smiling back.

"You want I make you some cloths?"

"Do you make many clothes for the people here?"

"Oh yes. Maybe two or three cloths a day. But only for mens."

"How long have you been here?"

The young man laughed, "All my life. I was born here. And I am married here. Now I am twenty years. And this is all I know."

"Are you going back…well…to Afghanistan?"

The tailor was silent for a moment. When he spoke it was pensively, "It is difficult. That is my home. But this too is my home. It is all I know. I will see."

A crowd had gathered around us now. Many children, but also many men – young and old. And also a few curious women in the background. Suddenly there was a commotion between two of the men. I had no idea why it had started. Or what they were saying. But, within seconds, they were pushing and shoving each other. And screaming what sounded like curses at each other. Although I didn't speak a word of Tajik or Uzbek or Hazara, or whatever the language was, I knew that it was getting bad. Without warning a man wielding a large stick began swinging it at both men, striking them on their heads and shoulders.

"Er, I think we'd better move on." said Barry. And moved himself quick smart.

I looked back as we left, still followed by a few intrepid members of the crowd. It now appeared as though an all-in fight was developing.

An old woman sat just inside an open tent. She was keening, rocking backwards and forwards. Beside her on the ground lay the body of woman, the headdress of her burqa still covering her face. Two tiny children sat cross-legged resting their hands on the body. They looked up at us, completely without expression.

"There's a certain level of sickness exists in the camp. MSF do the best they can. But, as you see…."

And, of course, there was no real explanation.


The journey back to Islamabad was a quiet one. At first Barry talked about the camp conditions and repeated that the plan was to close it completely very soon and repatriate its inhabitants. But, after a while, he realized that he was talking to himself and focused instead on his driving.

I told myself that I was thinking about my piece. And, indeed, from time to time I jotted down a few notes. Actually I was trying to process all that I'd just seen. The rock-bottom poverty. The bleakness and general air of despondency. Nothing new to me really. But it had stirred something in me. Something new, yet familiar. I mused again about the hopelessness of it all. It seemed to me then that, no matter how much energy was expended, nor how much money was thrown at it, there would always be millions of people in the world suffering in this way.

As a child, when I was asked what I wanted most of all, I had often said 'World Peace'. Just like that, with a capital 'W' and a capital 'P'. It was something I'd heard adults and other children say. I didn't really understand the concept. Because, where we lived in Pennsylvania, there was *always* peace. Except, perhaps the occasional brawl on a Saturday night.

Later, of course, there was the Vietnam war. And although my mother was never big on "the religion thing", for the first time in my life I started to pray. I prayed for peace in Vietnam. Mostly because, pretty soon, I was going to be absolutely the right age for the draft. All through my school years I could see it coming as the war developed. Then it started to get heavy 'over there'. I received my number, and to my great relief, it was fairly high. But I just knew that, sooner or later, I was going to get drafted. I was safe for a while at Berkeley, although I constantly half expected to get the dreaded letter to go for my physical checkup. Then I left college and it was the late sixties and boys were going to Vietnam after a brief training and, one week later, they were dead.

My pal Danny had lived two doors away. We'd been friends forever. We shared everything, and had been as close as anybody could be. Then Danny got drafted. At first he was excited. He wrote me frequently with tales of horror and glee. 'You should see this fuckin' Sergeant, man.' Or 'We all went out on the town together. Man what a blast.' Later on, when they were in country, Danny started to get scared. And his letters got more and more weird. Then, one day, my mom broke the news to me. The sadness overwhelmed me and I hung my head and couldn't look anyone in the eye. But, of course, no tears came. And I found solace in a succession of co-eds.

When I thought that I might get drafted I prayed hard and I prayed often. And, somehow my number just never came up. I slipped through the net. Or slipped through the cracks. Or slipped through whatever it was the system had laid out for me. And this was almost never heard of, unless your father could buy you a free passage. Or unless you skipped off to Canada. Was it the prayer? I'll never know. What I did know was that I'd lived for years waiting for a missive that never arrived.

And then it was all over, and the US was forced to retreat in those highly televisual helicopter take-offs from the roof of the US embassy. And I realized that I was safe. And that I wasn't going to be a Vietnam statistic. And that maybe, just maybe, my prayers had worked.

You might think that the answering of those prayers might turn a person to religion. But, in my case, I just thanked God and moved on.

But a funny thing *did* happen: Somehow I felt that I'd missed out. Unbelievable. Un-fuckin-believable! Here I had escaped with my life, and now I felt that I'd missed out. So, what it did accomplish was to give me a taste for travel. And, most of all I wanted to go overseas.

As an English major I'd already turned my attention to journalism, and managed to get a job as a cadet on a small newspaper. Now I decided that I would travel overseas and report from wherever.

***

Back in my hotel room, I sat on the edge of the bed. I'd just taken off my shoes and had been about to go into the bathroom to wash. But, somehow, I had got stuck. Stuck on the edge of the bed. I let out a long soft, sigh through my nose. I hadn't meant to sigh, and maybe I was just exhaling. But it came out as a sigh.

And there was nothing interesting on the patch of wall that I was now staring at. But, somehow, I couldn't tear my eyes away from it.

I became aware of the nasal sound of the call to prayer coming from the mosque down the road. But still my eyes were riveted to that patch of wall. I knew that there was a thought percolating in my mind, but I couldn't yet tell what it was. It seemed to me at the time that it was an important thought. And somehow linked to strong emotions. But the thought wouldn't come.

I sat like that for nearly ten minutes. And it was only the strident, insistent sound of the telephone that finally stirred me. I reached out and picked up the receiver, "Yes?"

"Hi Max, it's Mike."

Mike Kenny, my executive producer, sounding surprisingly clear in my ear. "How'd it go today?"

"Oh, you know. Usual stuff."

"Can you get something from it?"

"Yeah." Pause. "I think so."

"Good. Because the interview's off."

My interview with President Musharraf. Off? The interview that I'd traveled all this way for?

"Oh, you're kidding!"

44

"Nope. His office called here about three hours ago. Something more pressing came up apparently."

"So when...?"

"...Not this trip Max. He can't reschedule in the short term."

"But this was the main reason for me coming. The other..."

"I know, Max. But, you know, that's the way it goes sometimes."

"Yeah".

Long pause.

"So, You want me to do something else while I'm here?"

"No, don't worry about it. Just come back. We've already changed your flight to tomorrow morning"

"Oh....Okay."

# Chapter Five

"That's a terrible thing to say…"

"…No, I'm only saying…"

"…It's not the right time. The man's just lost his wife for Chrisakes…"

"…I'm just saying it makes you think, that's all…"

"…It might make you think…"

"…It does. It really does. I could have cancer eating away at me now without me even knowing about it! So why is it so terrible? Any of us could go at any time. Especially at our age…"

"We're not so old. Well, maybe you are…"

I was sitting with Mos and Al in a little Thai restaurant off Fairfax called The Bow Thai. Another great Thai restaurant name pun. Actually, none of us were huge fans of Thai food, and this was always a compromise. When we couldn't agree on what kind of food we wanted to eat we could always agree to come to Bow Thai. We could always get a table without booking and it was quiet enough to talk. Besides, it was located sort of equidistant between our homes. And, besides that again, the Thai waitresses were pretty and attentive. And all of us appreciated those qualities. And once in a while, if the restaurant wasn't too busy, the chef would show Al how to make some of the dishes.

"Look, all I was saying was that it's something that's begun to get to me. That I was just thinking how quickly the years seem to go by. You celebrate the Fourth, and Labor Day. Then it's Thanksgiving. Then it's Christmas and New Years. And, before you know it it's the Fourth of July again. A month feels like just a few days. A year seems like a coupla months. And what's happened in that year? What have you achieved? And then I start to think 'how many of these twelve-months do I have left?'. Five? Ten? Twenty? Or maybe none. Maybe I could go tomorrow like…"

And Mos stopped and realized what he was about to say, and looked at me. So did Al. But I guess I hadn't been part of this conversation at all. Truth be told I wasn't really listening. Although, when they both stopped and turned to me, I felt obliged to say something. I looked from one to the other.

"Sorry?"

Mos was red in the face. It could have been from embarrassment or just his green chicken curry. But, fortunately, he was saved by the appearance of the waitress at our table,

"Everything okay here? All the food is good?"

Mos jumped in, "Everything's fine honey, thank you."

"You want more wine?"

Mos looked at me and Al. We each shook our heads

"Not right now, honey."

"Okay. Enjoy your meal."

And we all watched her swing her ass as she walked away.

It was Al who recovered first, "So how was your trip?"

I toyed with my food. "Kinda disappointing actually. I was meant to do this interview with Pervez Musharraf. But it got called off at the last minute. What a let-down."

"So you flew all the way there for nothing?"

"Well, I visited a UNHCR refugee camp for Afghans."

"And how was that?"

"I dunno," I said, and dropped my fork. "How long have I been doing this? Thirty, forty years? The people in that camp could have been the same people I saw in camps when I first started. Nothing seems to have changed."

Mos wiped his mouth, "But there are new disasters all the time. Doesn't mean nothing's changed."

"Sure, I know. There are earthquakes, mudslides. That sort of thing. I guess we're always going to have that. Although there definitely seem to be more of them these days. But the other thing, mans' inhumanity to man, that hasn't changed. In fact it seems to have gotten worse. Have we made any difference at all in the last forty years? We had such dreams."

My voice tapered off. Actually I hadn't been talking a whole heap, and it was the most I'd spoken all night, and I think my friends wanted to encourage me. They waited for me to continue. But, instead, there was a long pause. I'd run out of things to say. I saw Mos shoot Al a look.

So I said, "It's just that all I'm seeing is the futility of it all. You know?"

Al cleared his throat, "It's not that bad. Surely."

Mos blinked at him, "Are you kidding!"

"I mean, we were going to change the world, weren't we."

Al shrugged, "We did change the world…"

"…Yeah, for the worse!" said Mos. "Look at that clown in the White House. He's dragged the country – and the world – back a hundred years."

I looked at my two friends, "Do you think, in the end, that it's actually possible to effect real change?"

For once Mos couldn't think of anything to say. But Al finished swallowing his food, laid down his fork, took a sip of his drank and nodded his head gently.

"Yeah, I think we can make a positive difference. A few things come to mind. For example, in this country, we got rid of slavery. We improved infant mortality. We made working hours and work conditions more humane. There are many diseases which have been eradicated, like smallpox. Women now have the right to vote. Er, overseas, we've battled with many diseases, and some we've beaten, and some like AIDS we're still fighting, but we're nearly there. And I think we'll win in the end. We've fought tyrants all around the world, and many of those countries now have workable civilized leaderships. And, sure there's still way too much poverty in the world, but I believe the situation's better than it was. So, yeah. I think it's possible to effect real change."

And he picked up his fork and carried on eating.

Mos and I stared at him. It was the longest speech either of us had heard him make in a long while. Shit, it might have been the most we'd *ever* heard him say about anything.

"Well then, I guess maybe it is," said Mos, good-naturedly.

"Yeah." I said.

But my mind was on something else. I hadn't meant could the *world* bring about change. What I'd really meant was could I make any difference. Because right now I didn't think I could. Right now I felt as though it was irrelevant what I did. Almost as though I was formless and invisible. My arms always felt heavy these days. And my head felt as though it was filled with cotton wool.

Mos had given me a packet of Prozac. Good old Mos! Always ready with the meds. But I felt like the last thing I needed was to be more out of it. As it was, I found it profoundly difficult to marshal my thoughts. To focus on anything.

Except for one permanent impression. One grindingly repetitive impression: "Something is missing."

And something was missing. Even though we'd only been married for six months I missed Marie so much. A part of myself wasn't there. How could that be?

\*\*\*

I eased the car into my parking spot in the Network parking lot, pulled on the handbrake and switched off the motor. I sat there for a moment, then climbed out and headed for the building where my office was. As I was walking through the lot George Colorossi saw me and waved. George was a dour character, not given to joviality. A wave was a large gesture from George. As we drew abreast I 'hi'd him, "Hi."

"Hi."

"Shitty traffic." said George, not really looking at me, but focusing on not spilling his Styrofoam cup of coffee.

"Yeah," I said, even though my own traffic had actually been pretty good this morning. But I wasn't looking for a discussion this early. Especially about traffic conditions.

We walked together in silence, each lost in our own thoughts. At the entrance we swiped our security cards and pushed open the door. Down the hall I could see a small crowd gathering. This was quite unusual. Normally people would go straight to their desks and hunker there for a while as they absorbed the previous days viewing figures and the latest gossip. And prepared themselves for whatever lay ahead in their day.

But today it was different. Today there was a buzz in the air. And something was definitely Up!

As we arrived at the group I could see that many people were holding copies of the *Los Angeles Times* and either reading a certain page avidly or pointing to a particular article. Voices were being raised. And the level of excitement obviously wasn't one of joy.

Barbara Graden greeted us.

"Did you see?"

I stared at her blankly, but George responded, "No, what?"

"The deal with MRG went through. We're now working for them.'

"Great!" said George, and shook his head. "I'd better go and start working on my resumé."

And he schlumped off to his office.

"So, what d'you think?" asked Barbara, as she walked with me towards our respective offices.

"Maybe it can work out."

"You think?"

"Not really, no."

"It's alright for you Max. You'll go on forever. You know on-screen women have a use-by date. If I get squeezed out of here I'll never work again."

"You're fine Barbara. You're still young and beautiful…"

"…You're so sweet Max…"

"…And they're bound to want to keep you. If you want to stay, that is."

"What do you mean?"

"Well, MRG has a pretty tawdry rep. Many people think they're worse than Fox."

"Mmm." She thought for a moment. "Still, it's a job. And I only have a few good years."

In the general office we both dipped into our correspondence trays to collect the latest. I examined my collection carefully. There didn't seem to be anything too ominous. Barbara was doing the same. She pulled out one envelope addressed to her in spidery writing, tore the side off and slipped out the single sheet of notepaper. I saw her smile.

"Something interesting," I asked.

She answered me as she continued to read.

"A fan letter," she intoned. "Oh, how sweet. I bet this guy's over eighty…. Never mind." She looked up at me, "a fan letter's a fan letter, right?"

"Definitely better than anthrax." I said. "Have you seen this?"

I waved a piece of paper in front of her.

"There's going to be an internal videocast from head office at…"

I checked my watch, "any minute now. Think this is it?"

She shrugged, "Yeah, probably."

All around the general office monitors were being switched to the internal channel. Eyes flicked towards the screens and, apart from the odd hushed telephone conversation, the office quietened in anticipation. The network ident dissolved to a picture of the network CEO sitting between two strangers sitting erect in their chairs.

Someone in the office called out, "Who are those guys?"

I stared, fascinated, at one of the screens

The CEO's face was drained of color, as he looked down at his notes.

"He looks like they've taken him hostage…."

"…Looks to me like one of those terrorist videos…"

"…Perhaps they're going to behead him…"

"Shhh."

The CEO cleared his throat and looked into the camera.

\*\*\*

Afterwards I ambled into Mike Kenny's office. Mike was seated behind his huge, very messy desk. He was passing a piece of paper to a young man who was leaning across the desk on the other side of the desk. He wore his hair in the fashion of the day, which basically looked like he'd just gotten out of bed.

"Caroline said you wanted to see me."

"Oh, Max, good. You saw it, I suppose?"

"Uh huh."

"Yes, well….Max this is Brad."

Indicating the young man.

"Hi." I said, barely looking at Brad.

"Very soon Brad's going to be your executive producer."

It was one of those strange moments in time. I knew I had heard something, but felt sure I hadn't heard it correctly.

"I'm sorry?"

"Yeah. Brad's going to EP the show."

I looked at Brad properly now. He looked like he should still be in school. I wasn't sure whether I was meant to laugh or not. One of Mike's little jokes perhaps. I waited for the punchline.

"No, really! You heard the speech. We're going to be integrated into the MRG Network."

"So…?"

Brad smiled at me. Actually it was a pleasant smile. Like an innocent young boy. But there was something about it that made me wary.

"So there are bound to be a few changes. A few rationalizations in human resources."

I had a feeling of déjà vu. But, for the life of me, I couldn't remember from where.

Brad held out his hand, "I heard about your wife. I'm sorry. I am sorry."

"Yeah, well…"

I looked closer at Brad. He really did look as though he was about Tommy's age. Christ! Is this the way it's going to be? I knew there were going to have to be changes. But this was ridiculous. I turned back to Mike.

"And what about you?"

Mike laughed, "Oh, they've offered me a job in New York. Not sure yet whether I want to decamp there at my age. Besides there's Beverly to consider"

Mike was an old school journalist who'd started with newspapers and magazines and then moved on to television. At one time, like me, he had also been a foreign correspondent, but his wife had become sick and needed him on hand. And the network, in recognizing his skill as a producer, had stuck him in an office.

"Actually I'm considering going freelance. And, you know, there are a couple of books I've always wanted to write. But Brad here is the rising star. He's been EP-ing the music channel"

He said it with a completely straight face. But when he looked at me there was mirth and cynicism in his eyes.

"Yes," I thought, "that about sums it up."

Mike and I had spent many, many hours over quiet beers across the years chewing our way through the political landscape of world affairs. We held pretty much similar beliefs and opinions, but it had always been fun to play the devil's advocate or take a different view. What on earth was I going to talk to this boy about? Dance music?

So, of course, I said, "Well, welcome aboard. I'm sure you'll like it here."

"I'm sure I will Max. In fact I like it already." He stood up. "I'm going to leave you two to it. I'm sure you've got lots to talk about. Lots."

He started toying with his Blackberry.

"Max can you come here tomorrow at, say, nine-thirty. I've got a few ideas I want to toss around with you."

I raised an eyebrow as I caught Mike's expression.

"Sure. Nine-thirty. See you then."

"Good. Thanks. Mike, later? We can talk later?"

"Sure," said Mike.

And Brad turned on his heel and strode out purposefully.

I shook my head slowly. "Really?" I exploded in mirth, "Really?!"

"Yep! That's the way it's going. They're going to change the network completely. Frankly, I'm glad to be leaving."

"When?"

"Today…"

"…You're kidding!"

"Nope."

"After all these years…"

"…Oh, I'll get paid. I've actually negotiated a pretty good settlement." He smiled broadly. "Big silver lining."

***

I was sitting in my living room. The television was on, but muted. I had my feet up on the coffee table, and a glass of whisky sat snugly in my hand. In front of me, on the table was the urn containing Marie's ashes. I took a sip of the whisky as I reflected on how surreal everything felt. Somehow I couldn't quite get a grip on things.

One of the things that I like best is to walk. Not in the countryside. I like to walk around strange cities. Over the years I've reported from hundreds of cities. And always, as soon as I had any time to myself, I would take off and just wander around. And, most of the time, I couldn't speak the local language. I was curious, and would seek out all the plazas and all the little back streets. The feeling then was one of interested detachment. And it had a surreal air to it.

But now, in my own home, I'd again begun to feel like I was in some foreign country where I didn't speak the language and didn't know the customs.

So naturally I addressed the urn, "And how did it come to this?" I asked, half to myself and half to Marie. "Life was so great. And now everything just got completely turned on its head."

Don't get me wrong. It wasn't that I felt sorry for myself. There was just this feeling of enormous loss.

\*\*\*

The next morning, at nine-thirty precisely, I walked through the general office towards Mike's office. Except, of course, that now it was Brad's office. I paused for a moment before walking in. Brad was wearing a wireless telephone headset, and he was talking as he paced around the office. I wasn't sure whether to walk right in, but Brad turned suddenly and saw me.

"Hey Max, come in. Come in, come in.....Yeah, come back to me with some ideas…"

This latter was obviously addressed to whomever was on the other end of the phone, but he carried on looking at me while he spoke on the phone.

"No, something new. Something good. Right! Yeah, well gotta go….So how are you this morning?"

It was a moment before I realized that Brad was now actually talking to me.

"Oh, er, okay."

"Caroline!" Brad suddenly yelled out, "Two coffees."

"Nothing for me thanks," I said, "I'm good."

"Caroline!" Even louder, "Scrub that. Now…" And Brad ushered me to a chair even though he himself continued to pace.

"…Sit down, sit down. Good, good."

I was beginning to realize that Brad seemed to have a habit of repeating things. He was dressed in black pants with a black T-shirt with the inscription 'Make it Real'. Perhaps that had something to do with it. Maybe repeating yourself made things real. Then I realized that the T actually read 'Make it Reel'. "Right then!"

Brad launched straight into it, "Max I've looked at some of the stuff you've done over the years, and I gotta tell you I think it's terrific. Terrific…"

"…Thank you…"

"...Yeah, some pretty mind-blowing stuff. Mind-blowing. Anyway, I've got a special mission for you. We need to do a piece on the rising price of gas and what effect it's had. So I want you to grab a camera crew and head out to the burbs and shoot some vox pops. And some vox moms…Vox pops and vox moms…"

He chortled at his 'little joke'.

"No, actually," he continued, still chortling, "make sure you get young people. Preferably sexy chicks."

I looked at him aghast.

"Um, Brad, you know, don't you that I'm a *foreign* correspondent…"

"…Yeah. Let me stop you right there. We need to get something clear. With the new team we're going to be taking a kinda different tack. We're going to be skewing much younger generally with this network because that's where the real disposable income is. And maybe we might lose some old farts…"

I winced.

"…Old farts who want to see starving kids in India and who want to analyze the news to pieces generally. But we're going to focus on what's important to Americans. We're going to bring the news back home. We're going to be looking more at what happens here in…."

"…Don't other…"

But Brad was in full flood.

"…Because *this* where it's at. Where it's *at*. We're not looking to give civics lessons. So we'll be cutting right back on foreign stories. We'll still be taking some of the Iraq stuff, of course. But we're gonna put a more positive spin on it. Not focus so much on all the death and destruction…"

"…Just the good stuff…" I offered, mockingly.

"…Right! The good stuff. You got it. You've got it. Gee, I can see we're going to work well together."

I stood up. "Brad, what you're asking me to do is cadet stuff. You don't need me for that. I'm a foreign correspondent. That's what I do. I go to foreign places and I report from them…"

"…"I'm sorry Max, but we're going to be cutting our budgets right back. Especially overseas travel. That's another reason to focus more on the States. And then there's the other thing," he added ominously.

"The other thing?"

"Yeah. The other thing."

And now he had a look on his face that was a strange mixture of apologetic and gleeful.

"As I said, we're going to be skewing much younger. So what that means is that we're really going to be looking for younger faces on screen. If you know what I mean?"

Oh sure. I knew what he meant alright. And, if I hadn't known before, the knowing look Brad now gave me was enough to make it plainly obvious.

"But, if you stay…"

"*If* I stay?," I thought.

"…I can promise you that the next major hurricane story is yours. Okay?"

"Well, gee!" I just couldn't help myself, "that's really very gracious of you Brad."

But Brad had clearly had an irony bypass. He just powered right through the facetiousness, completely ignoring it.

"Not a problem, Max. Not a problem."

# Chapter Six

The restaurant on North Maple was Stanley's idea. He always liked to meet in high quality restaurants. Especially if I was paying. And not just paying for the meal, but paying Stanley's fees as well. I always thought that this was pretty iniquitous, that my lawyer would always insist on his meetings taking place in a restaurant. I mean, it wasn't as though he didn't have an office. Or as if he took the price of the meal off his bill.

On the other hand he was a good lawyer. So, over the years, I had put up with it.

We were already into the main course before Stanley got around to the matter in hand.

"So, I had a look at your employment contract...."

He took a bite of his steak, chewed it, and followed it with a swallow of wine.

"...And?" I asked, finally.

"...And..."

And he took another maddening sip.

"...And I don't think they have a leg to stand on. It states clearly in your contract how you're employed. For what purposes. And, as you know, what your entitlements are viz a vis travel expenses, etcetera, etcetera..."

And he carried on eating.

"So?"

"So," through a mouthful of food, "it's watertight."

He swallowed. Sipped. And continued.

"You can't force them to send you anywhere, of course. But you certainly don't have to do the other shit if you don't want to. Basically you can just stay at home until they send you overseas if you want. But I got to ask you, is that what you want? To stay at home, I mean."

I shrugged, "Not really."

"No, I didn't think so."

Once again he forked up a slice of steak and vegetables. And then he made that pinched face. You know, the one where you're not sure whether someone is going to throw up or orgasm.

"You know, this is amazing. You really should have tried it."

But I was only toying with my food anyway. My appetite hadn't followed me into the restaurant. I could've eaten at a burger joint for all the pleasure I was getting from this meal.

A waiter came by to nail his tip, "Everything alright here?"

"Oh yeah," said Stanley. "This is great."

The waiter smiled, visualizing a large tip. And he backed away.

"So I have to ask you," Stanley said finally. "Would you like me to negotiate a settlement for you?"

I thought about this for a moment.

"Yes. Yes I would."

Stanley dabbed at his mouth with his napkin.

"So what will you do? You know you're going to find it difficult to get another job at…"

"…At my age?"

"Mm. Have you given any consideration to that?"

I finally abandoned my food and leaned back in my chair.

"Not really. Maybe I'll write a book like Mike."

"About?"

"Dunno" I laughed. "Any ideas?"

\*\*\*

The surreal feeling only enhanced the floating feeling that I'd been experiencing. For nearly four weeks now my life had been so different. For one thing, when I got up in the morning time seemed endless. I had recently gotten into the habit of going jogging first thing. Although I had kept myself fit in life, even paying infrequent visits to the gym, this was actually a novel experience. At first my body had objected strongly. But, after a while, my legs began to appreciate being able to stretch; my throbbing head cleared; and my lungs welcomed the opportunity to expand to their full capacity.

Of course thoughts would pass through my mind. But I let them do just that. Pass through. And so the jogging became a form of meditation. I focused on my breathing, and took pleasure in measuring my step. I'd bought a new, expensive pair of trainers that supported my feet and ankles well. So I often felt, even with my slightly rickety knees, as though I was actually floating along.

And, all this time, Stanley was still talking with the network. It hadn't been quite the watertight case that he'd said it would be. Natch! So they were still negotiating.

In the meantime I jogged in the mornings. Then I came home, took a long shower, slipped on an old T-shirt and a pair of shorts, and ate a hearty breakfast.

After that I would sit and read the paper for a while. Well, I didn't actually read it – as in 'absorb any information'. My eye would travel down the text. Up and down and across. And then I'd turn the page, and do the same all over again. Mostly I had no idea what I'd just 'read'. Occasionally there would be an article about a subject with which I was familiar. Then I'd pay a little more attention. But, generally, if you'd asked me what was in the paper that day I wouldn't have a clue.

And I studiously avoided anything to do with Iraq. It still reminded me too much of Marie.

I read the newspaper for the same reason I spent hours on the internet every day: because I told myself that I was going to write a book, and I was conducting research. Some thought would prick me, either first thing when I woke up or when I was out jogging. And I would follow that thought to the net, where I would look something up. And then something else would catch my eye, and I'd follow that. I made copious notes and saved hundreds of files. But, in the end, all I had were notes, and no clear idea what to do with them.

My body might have become fitter, but inside all I felt was emptiness. Like I was hollow. It wasn't because I was alone. After all I had spent a good part of my life alone, and had no trouble keeping company with myself. Of course it was the double whammy of losing both Marie and my occupation. Sometimes I'd sit for long periods with my jaw resting on my hand, my eyes closed. I was trying to... Trying to what? To think of something? To remember something, or someone? To make contact with a part of myself that just didn't seem to be there.

And now I was talking to myself as well. Especially when I watched television. I would make observations out loud, "As if anyone would believe that!" or "God! That woman's ugly." or "Yeah, sure. Like that would happen!" Other times it would be something like, "Now, what shall I have to eat? No, don't feel like that. Oh, I know..." Simple things Nothing that I worried about exactly. But I did notice what I was doing, and sometimes I wondered whether this might be the onset of Alzheimer's.

I'd started watching television a lot actually. In a way it had become company for me. And a salve. At first it was CNN and the news shows. Then it was the documentary channels. But, eventually, I graduated to shows like 'Oprah'. More and more I found myself involved in what was being said.

And it was on one such show that they started talking about grief, and how important that was as a process. Nothing new, of course. But I did wonder whether this was something I needed to do. Something to *do*. To really grieve for Marie. And, maybe, to grieve for more than her. Because, in reflecting on my life, I had also started thinking about myself as a younger man. And I missed that man, and who he was and the life he had.

"Perhaps I need to grieve for that too," I said to myself. "Perhaps I need to acknowledge that I'll never be that age again….and let go of it."

This was hard. Where do you start with all this stuff?

***

"I've got great news for you…"

This time Stanley hadn't even waited for the food. He'd come rushing into the little restaurant off Melrose, right up to the table where I was sitting waiting for him. Stanley jerked his chair back and threw himself into it. He exhaled deeply and smiled as he looked at me, pausing for effect.

"…They've capitulated! Not only will you get what's due to you, the balance of your contract, bonuses etcetera, but I've also wangled a small golden handshake."

He paused again, to let it sink in for me.

"Plus…plus, listen to this. A small output deal…"

"…A what?..."

"…An output deal. They've got first refusal on two documentary specials if you want to produce them. On any subject you choose. Within reason, of course."

And he sat there beaming at me, waiting for the plaudits to rain down all around him.

"Isn't that great? What a package!"

I was stunned. My mind tried to process what Stanley had just said, and the implications. Stanley continued to beam. Eventually I connected his brain to his mouth.

"So that's it?"

The smile left Stanley's face.

"Whad'ya mean 'that's it?' That's a terrific package. I mean. It looked like, for a while there…"

"…No I didn't mean 'is that all'. I wasn't being unappreciative. No, Stanley, you did a fine job. Thank you. It *is* terrific."

And the smile returned. Stanley poured a glass of water and put it to his lips.

"What I meant was," I continued, "that's . That's the end of my career."

"You're not happy?"

"Oh, sure I'm happy. With the package. Thank you, I mean it. It's just that I was kind of hoping…," I ended somewhat wistfully.

"What? That they'd keep you on?"

A pause.

Then a very quiet "Yeah. Kinda." from me.

"Oh, I see. Well, it doesn't have to be the end of your career per se. You can get another job. I mean, there'll be a few minor restrictions, but you can…"

"…I think we both know that's not going to happen Stanley. Nobody wants to hire a sixty year old man…"

"…What about the docs…?"

"…That was good. I'm glad you were able to pull that one off. I just don't see myself as Ken Burns right now though. Maybe in the future. You know. In the meantime…"

Then silence. And neither of us spoke for a moment. Then Stanley grabbed up the menu and looked around.

"Do they have waiters here? 'Cause I'm starved."


After lunch I left the restaurant and started walking. At first I thought I was going back to my car. But my mind was preoccupied and I actually walked right past it without realizing. It was only when I arrived back at the Melrose intersection that I started taking note of where I was. The heat of the summer had gone now, and the day was warm and pleasant. I did, after all, have plenty of time on my hands, and it seemed like a nice idea to just enjoy the day and stroll around. I began to notice the traffic going past, the people in the street, and the buildings I was passing.

There was something about the Bodhi Tree Bookstore that captured my attention. I couldn't be sure why. A rack of free newspapers caught my eye, and I started thumbing through them, "looking for what?"

Some beautiful music was wafting out of the shop and it called to me like a siren's song. The short stairway drew me like a magnet and, somewhat cautiously, I made my way up the steps. Then I stopped at the top and peered inside. The interior of the shop was evocative. It reminded me of shops in the sixties. And it reminded me of myself in the sixties. There was a headiness and a richness that made me feel instantly at home. I looked at the array of objects, jewelry and books and was drawn deeper into the shop.

Wandering to the book stacks at the back of the shop I noted that the stacks were arranged by subject matter. And then I realized what I was doing here, and I started looking around for a book about grieving.

I began pulling out the occasional book, briefly reading the back cover, then sliding the book back. More than anything it was a pleasant way to pass the time. Sometimes my body would sway gently to the music. And, in this way, I lost myself for a while.

There were a few other people in the shop, mostly doing the same as me, quietly looking through what the Bodhi Tree had to offer. Occasionally one of them would take their prize to the counter. And then, in a little while, they might be replaced by someone else. But mostly I was unaware of who else was there. So I was surprised when I heard a voice behind me.

"Are you looking for something in particular?"

I turned around slowly to see a young woman with long blonde hair and a pleasant smile on her exquisite face. I assumed that she must work here.

"Er, yes. Kinda."

"It's just that I noticed you've been looking at a lot of books, but you don't seem to be able to find the right one."

"No, well…"

How do you tell someone that you're looking for a book that might explain why your wife died and how you might live the rest of your life without her? And how do you tell someone that you're wondering what happened to your life anyway?

"…I guess I was looking for a book about grieving, but I keep getting side-tracked. There are so many amazing books here on so many different subjects. In a way they're all interesting. But also none of them seems to quite do it for me.

"Oh, I see. Hmm. Well, I think I saw a couple of books over here…"

And she moved to the end of the stack where her eyes wandered over a row of books. I couldn't help notice how beautiful she was. And, from somewhere deep inside me a tiny, tiny spark ignited. It was so subtle that I didn't actually realize that it had happened.

"…Let me see," she mused. "Ah, yes, I thought so."

And triumphantly she extracted two books from the shelf.

"I think either of these might be of interest."

With a smile she handed over the books. I checked them out and smiled back at her.

"Yeah, great. Thanks. What terrific service. You sure know your stock…"

"…Oh, I don't work here," she smiled. "But I do spend a lot of time here. I guess I just like the feeling."

"Yes, me too."

I looked at her empty hands.

"So, d'you ever buy anything?"

She laughed, and I was taken aback at not only how white her teeth were, but that she seemed to have not one filling. Oh, the fluoride generation! But, most of all, I couldn't help smiling back at her.

"Sure, I buy stuff sometimes. Otherwise I don't think they'd let me keep coming back."

"Right."

And we laughed together this time. And it felt good.

"Well," I said, "thanks again."

And I turned to go. But as I turned I heard her say a strange thing.

"Say, you wouldn't like to go for a coffee would you? There's a really nice place, the Urth Caffé, just up the street."

"Well, er…"

I was struck dumb. The idea of going for coffee with this beautiful young woman would have obviously been highly appealing before. But now…now it was the furthest thing from my mind. Also I wasn't sure whether I was ready to try and communicate.

But she just waited patiently and smiled into my eyes, and I couldn't help myself.

"That would be nice," I said.

We walked up Melrose together.

"My name is Max."

"And mine's Angelina."

"Ah, my guardian angel," I said, trying for some humor, not really knowing what to say.

"Actually Angelina means Messenger. Did you know that?"

"So have you come to bring me a message?"

"Maybe," she said, mysteriously.

But the intrigue had to last a little while longer, because we'd arrived at the Urth. We found a table outside, and a waitress came immediately to take our order.

When the waitress had gone Angelina sat looking at me quizzically, her head tilted to one side. With the sun shining directly on her hair, I noticed that it was actually several subtle shades of blonde, some of which resembled spun gold. I was thinking of something to say, but she broke the silence first.

"I know you, don't I?"

I suppose that she meant that she recognized me. That I was a 'personality'. Well, this was Los Angeles, and there was always half a chance that, if you asked someone that question, they'd answer, "Sure, I'm in the movies." Or something like that. But I didn't expect that, so I started to disagree.

"Oh no. I don't….."

Then I realized.

"Oh! Maybe. I guess you *might*. I do….that is I used to do some foreign reporting…"

"…On the Viva Network?"

"Yes…"

"…See, I was sure that I knew you. Yes, I've seen some of your stories. Wow, you go to some amazing places."

"Yes, I've been very lucky. I have to say that in my life I have been to some really interesting places and met many remarkable people. I've been very fortunate. It's something that I'll always treasure. Sadly, however,…"

The waitress returned and placed our coffees on the table.

"…Sadly I'm not with Viva any more."

"Sadly?"

"Yes. New management. New ideas. Apparently they're not into 'civics lessons'.

I tipped some sugar into my coffee and began to stir.

"So…..is that what the grieving is about?"

"Er, no. Not really. My wife died recently, and I, er…"

"Oh, I'm sorry."

I thought to myself, "Why do people say 'I'm sorry' at times like this?" It sort of becomes automatic. In fact I do it myself. What are we sorry for? That the person's dead? When we didn't even know them? Sorry because we brought the subject up, committing a faux pas? Or because maybe we hurt someone? "Yes" I thought, "That's really the reason. Because we might have hurt someone's feelings. So, maybe there is some compassion left in the world."

"Was she ill?"

"What?"

"Your wife. Was it an illness?"

"No…Yes…Actually it was an aneurism. She hadn't been ill before that. Not that I knew."

I sipped my coffee.

"She wasn't very old. Thirty-eight."

"That's awful!"

"Yes."

"Have you talked to anyone about it?"

"My friends. They've been very supportive."

"And you talk to them about your feelings?"

"Well…in a way."

"Do you talk about how much you miss your wife?"

Then I could see that she'd obviously realized that maybe she was being too personal, and she tried to pull it back.

"I'm sorry, I don't have the right to ask you that. It's way out of line."

"No, it's okay."

I thought for a moment.

"We talk about some things. But, you know…guys being guys, we don't get into that kind of stuff too much."

"Gosh, no wonder you feel the need to grieve."

"Yes."

I acknowledged her observation quietly.

Each of us was lost in our own thoughts for a while. She sipped her coffee, weighing up whether to say something or not.

Finally she said, "Look, I know someone I think you might be interested in meeting."

I looked into her eyes. They were a startling shade of blue. And for a moment I was mesmerized by them.

"I live with a group of people in the valley," she began. "There's a guy there who's pretty wise. He's really helped me a lot. I think you'd get a lot from him. If you like, you're welcome to come and meet him."

"When?"

"Right now if you like."

"Oh, I don't…" I started to protest.

She saw the doubt on my face.

"…His name's Manson."

It took a second.

"Just kidding!"

And we both laughed. It felt good.


On the trip up into the Hollywood Hills I realized that it had been the first time I'd laughed properly since….since Marie. I was following behind her small Dodge sedan in my BMW up Laurel Canyon Boulevard, the tail of her car snaking around the bends. She was a pretty good driver, going just fast enough but keeping the drive easy.

We were into the hills now, heading for Mulholland. The traffic had been relatively light and the sun was shining, and I was feeling okay.

And now she was indicating that we were going to turn off. She gave plenty of warning, and then swung off. I focused on following her as we twisted and turned along the various roads.

Angelina slowed down and indicated that we were going to make a right, and her car pulled up to two large gates. She pushed the buzzer and spoke into the two-way. The gates slowly rolled open, and I followed her car up a long, sweeping driveway.

I was greeted by a fantastical architectural vision. I was used to some of the extraordinary properties that had been created in California, but this was definitely something special. In a way it reminded me of a huge, square wedding cake. There were square porticos, a multitude of towering, square columns, and huge oblong windows. The whole edifice gleamed an incandescent white, like cake-icing in the sun

There was a large square plaza in front of the building, and Angelina pulled to a halt some distance from the enormous double doors at the top of a set of steps. I parked beside her and we both climbed out of our cars. Angelina smiled at me, "Welcome."

"What's this place?"

"This is where I live."

I looked the place over and whistled softly.

"Rich daddy?" I asked.

She laughed and, instead of answering me, took my hand and led me towards the steps. As we approached one of the doors opened and a young man wearing a loose white tunic stood in the doorway. He smiled at Angelina.

"David, this is Max."

"Welcome Max," said David, holding out his hand and smiling..

I shook the young man's hand. It was firm and strong, but there was also a gentleness.

"Thanks."

To tell you the truth, I wasn't a hundred percent sure about this place. There was just something…. Something what? But Angelina encouraged me inside.

The interior was just as grand, but simpler. The large lobby was twenty feet high with a white marble floor. A sweeping white marble staircase rose majestically upwards. There were also a great many closed doors, but the only objects were some arrangements of flowers and a few modern sculptures.

A man and a woman were passing through the lobby, both dressed in identical tunics to David. The hairs on the back of my neck started to prickle. What was this place! Maybe now might actually be a good time to leave. I was just about to make my excuses when Angelina looped her arm through mine genially, and led me onwards.

"Come on I'll introduce you to some of my friends."

"Angelina, this place…?"

"…Yes?"

How do you say, 'This is a pretty weird, fucking place and your 'friends' are creeping me out a bit'? Especially to a beautiful woman like this with a sunny disposition who seems to bear you no harm.

I shrugged, and let her lead me to the rear of the lobby, where she pushed open a door that led to a large inner courtyard, in the center of which was a square, white swimming pool. Around the outside of the courtyard were more porticos and more columns.

Lazing beside the pool lay a half dozen young men and women, reading books, chatting and enjoying the sun. None of them wore the white tunics. In fact they all wore very little. All the women were topless, and everybody sported a tiny thong. The feeling was relaxed and warm, and I started to feel more relaxed as well. After all, this was really no more bizarre than the homes of several eccentric producers I'd had the privilege of visiting.

Angelina led me over to where two of the women were quietly chatting.

"Hannah, Mary, this is Max."

They both looked up and slid their sunglasses down their noses so they could getter better looks. Mary (or maybe it was Hannah) raised her eyebrows and smirked at Angelina. Hannah (or, perhaps Mary) smiled coquettishly at me, "Welcome," she said. But in a very different way to David.

Angelina pointed, "Over there is Jonathon. That's Samuel," she said, as the young man completed a perfect dive into the pool. "And that's Rebecca and Simon…Come on I'll show you more."

She led me back the way we'd come, and through the lobby. Slowly she opened one of the doors widely and touched a finger to her lips.

She whispered, "This is the library."

The library was vast, with thousands of books covering all the walls. Inside two young men were sitting at a long wooden table studying.

"We encourage study."

"We?" I wondered. "Who is 'we'?"

She gently closed the door and led me across the lobby to another door. Inside was a large dining hall, also with long tables. But the hall was empty.

I was impressed by the place, but I was beginning to feel like really I'd seen enough when she approached another door. However, this time she knocked tentatively on the door.

After a short pause the door cracked open a little, and David's face appeared. When he saw Angelina he nodded.

"Could you wait here just a moment," she said to me sweetly. "I won't be long."

David opened the door just wide enough for her to slip through and then closed it. Left alone in the lobby, I looked around. Curiously, I could feel a certain of peacefulness begin to came over me. I shut my eyes for a moment and breathed in deeply.

"Are you alright?"

Angelina had reappeared beside me.

"Yes. Sure. What's happening?"

"Remember I said that there's someone special I'd like you to meet? That he's really helped me a lot?"

"Uh huh."

"Well, he's inside this room, Max. But there's something I want to say. I think Gabriel is very wise. But you must make up your own mind. If he has something to offer you all well and good, If not, well…"

"Thank you Angelina.

She pushed open the door again and, taking me by the hand, she led me into the large room. The entire rear wall was ceiling to floor glass, and sunlight flooded into the room, making the other walls appear even whiter than they were painted. Otherwise this room was like the rest of the house: white marble floor; some floral arrangements; very few furnishings; and a lofty ceiling.

At the far end of the room was a small group of people. An elderly man with white hair sat upright in a high-backed armchair. A beautiful young woman with long, sleek black hair sat on the floor at his feet. And, to her side sat two men, one in his thirties, the other looked to be in his fifties. Each member of the group was dressed in the same loose-fitting, white tunics.

The elderly man was addressing the others in a quiet voice. So much so that I could see that they had to almost lean forward to hear properly what he was saying. No-one in the group turned to look at us. They just kept their attention on the man. I noticed that there was a general feeling of peace and tranquility in that room.

Angelina ushered me towards an empty chair in front of the man. It was only as we approached the group that the man stopped talking and looked up at me. The others too looked up. Each had a look of serenity on his or her face.

Without speaking Angelina indicated to me that I should sit in the chair, and she took up a position on the floor next to the other woman. The elderly man looked at me for a long time, studying me, unspeaking. He had a kind face, and it was clear that he was appraising me. But, eventually, I began to feel uncomfortable. Just as I felt my eyes wanting to wander away from the man's, he turned to Angelina. It was her cue to speak.

"Gabriel this is the man I spoke of:, Max."

She twisted to look at me. As did the others.

"Max, this is Gabriel. I hope you don't mind, but I've told him about your loss."

Gabriel smiled kindly at me, but didn't speak for a moment. When he did finally speak his voice was soft and mellow.

"Angelina has told me that your wife died recently."

"Yes."

My voice cracked when it came out.

Gently, almost lovingly, Gabriel asked, "Is there some way we can help?"

"I, er, I've found it difficult. Of course…"

Gabriel just nodded his head, encouraging me to continue.

"…And I…I've been thinking about grief. And Angelina…"

I looked down at her.

"…thought you might have something…..that I might be interested to meet you," I said sheepishly. 'How strange!' I thought. I'd met so many people in so many walks of life. And many of them were really high powered. But I'd never felt like this before.

"Ah," said Gabriel.

Again he looked deep into my eyes without speaking. A part of me wanted to scream 'Get the hell on with it'. But, strangely, the rest of me was content to just sit there, waiting for the old man.

"Was your wife's death expected?"

"No, actually, it came right out of the blue. A real shock."

"Yes, I see."

A long pause, then:

"You're right, of course. Grieving is necessary for those left behind….But grieving is a process, and it has many stages….Often, as in your case, the first stage is shock. This can be very difficult and dangerous. It sometimes feels like a part of *you* has died…"

"…Yes," I breathed the word out almost under my breath.

"…And frequently you will want to die too. This is a good opportunity for you, because a kind of awakening can happen. If you can develop an awareness, this is an opportunity for your own growth."

I had no idea what Gabriel meant, but I let it ride for a while.

"This shock will, eventually, be replaced by the next stage. Often this can be anger….This is good. It is the first indication that the healing can begin…But here too awareness is needed. If you feel anger now it is important that you *be* angry. But be aware at *what* you are angry. For example the person on the other end of the telephone who makes you angry is only a trigger for the anger that already exists inside of you…."

Gabriel gazed into my eyes to see if he was getting through to me.

"Yes?" he asked.

"Yes," I said.

"Mmm. Good….Sadness too will be there. And many tears. Has that happened for you?"

"I never…" I started to say. But instead: "No, not really."

"I see…."

And he rested his chin in his hand for a moment.

"…Tears too are natural. They are a way to express the sadness. 'Express' is an interesting word, don't you think. It has many meanings. One of them, of course, means to convey or articulate….However, another meaning is to extract or squeeze out. By extracting the tears you are helping to flush your system of its sadness....And this is very important. Because other stages can be depression, loneliness, and helplessness....The more you 'express' your feelings, the less you will sink into the black pits that await you....And, here too, talking about your feelings is good."

The old man gave a little laugh. This surprised the hell out of me, because Gabriel had seemed so serious up until now.

"We men aren't meant to be good at talking about our feelings. However, that isn't always true. Also we often deal with stuff in other ways....But, at this time of sorrow, it can be really good to talk about what's going on inside of you."

Gabriel tapped his own chest gently. And, again, he stopped talking and gazed into my eyes.

"I'm sure you actually know all of this. So forgive me if I seem to be preaching..."

"...Oh, no. It's fine," I protested, "It's actually good to hear this stuff."

"Thank you Max for indulging an old man."

Gabriel smiled warmly at me.

"So, yes. Grieving is indeed a process. That is important to remember. That is, because it is a process it means that things will, eventually change for you. So, may I make a suggestion: If you start to experience these feelings of helplessness and loneliness, go deeply into it. This may surprise you. You could, for example, put on some really sad music and crawl into bed with a photograph of your beloved. And, if you allow yourself to go deeply into the emotions and perhaps even feel sorry for yourself, then you will be surprised. Because these feelings will not last and they will disappear much sooner."

I wasn't exactly sure about this. Somehow I couldn't imagine myself wallowing in self-pity in this way. But I just nodded. Angelina reached up a hand to touch my leg, and she left it there for a moment, gazing into my eyes. I reached down and covered her hand with my own. It seemed the most natural thing in the world. Gabriel waited for us, and then started speaking again.

"May I ask you Max whether, in some way, you feel guilty for your wife's death?"

I thought for a moment.

"Not exactly," I responded, "But I guess I do feel guilty that I didn't know she was sick. And…" I thought this through for a moment, "It's possible that I….feel guilty that I couldn't save her. Couldn't stop her from dying."

"Yes….And may I also ask you whether you blame her in some way?"

'What a question!' I thought. 'Why would I blame her for dying?' It seemed a most extraordinary question and, at first, I was confused and…a little insulted. But, in the silence that followed the question, I realized that there was truth in the supposition. A part of me did blame Marie for dying. Wow! And, not only that. I also realized that a part of me was actually angry at Marie. For dying? Wow! When I answered, my voice was raspy.

"Yes…I guess I do blame her a little."

"Mmm. It's good for you to see that. Because in the seeing you can do something about it. Forgiveness can happen. Both of yourself…and your wife.

"Yes, I see."

"There is one more thing that you must do: You must acknowledge the loss to yourself. Because there is always a tendency to hang on. I'm not saying you must *do* something. There is no doing. But there is acceptance and surrender. And, with that acceptance, you will be able to let go. Remember, you are not being disloyal to your wife or your wife's memory. You are simply setting her free, and you are setting yourself free. And you can still love her. But now that love will be peaceful and joyous."

Gabriel opened his eyes wide, and peered deeply into my own eyes, as though he was looking into my soul. But the feeling didn't make me feel uneasy. On the contrary, I felt more relaxed and peaceful than I'd felt for some time.

# Chapter Seven

There have been many times in my adult life that I've wanted the advise of an older, wiser man. Over the years, when times have been difficult, or when I'd had decisions to make and didn't know what to do. Relationships have sometimes been a mystery. And I've often felt that, in dealing with women, a few words from someone who'd been in the same position might've proved invaluable. I had even fantasized about being in a tribe and going to talk with the tribal elders, men of such supreme wisdom that you just knew they could be relied on.

The trouble was that previous generations had not lived through what I and my peers are now living through. Life often seems more complicated. Many times I had actively sought out older men and tried to talk with them about life. But they were as mystified as I was. Perhaps more so. This was virgin territory for everyone.

So the time that I'd just spent with Gabriel had not only moved me, it had been an eye-opener.

Behind the house was a beautiful garden. Not large, but obviously tended with care. There were a great many plants bearing flowers of different hues. And the neatly-trimmed lawn in the middle was green and lush. I sat in an armchair mulling over what Gabriel had said. I'd been sitting here for over an hour now. Alone. Angelina had asked me to stay and have dinner with them. And now she was in the kitchen with some of the others preparing the dinner.

And the journalist in me also wondered what this place was. And who was Gabriel? Obviously a special man, but was this some kind of cult? The fact that they all dressed alike certainly pointed in that direction. But, right now, I didn't really care.

Hannah, one of the women that I'd met earlier, came towards me from the house. She carried a small tray that bore a tall glass of something.

"Angelina asked me to come and see if you're alright. And to bring you this."

She held the tray out for me to take the drink.

"Thank you."

I took a sip, and was surprised to discover that it was a piña colada. Well, whatever this group was, they certainly weren't *too* ascetic.

"Mm. I'm fine. In fact I feel very good….This is a beautiful place you have here."

"Yes it is."

"What do you all…..I mean is this some kind of, er, group?"

Hannah laughed. It was a very pleasant laugh.

"Oh, I think I'll let Gabriel explain. He's much better than me at that kind of thing.

Later, Angelina showed me into the dining room where everyone was now seated. Altogether there were about a dozen people, with Gabriel seated at the head of the table.

Angelina had now put on a white tunic. And I couldn't help but notice that she looked stunning. Her eyes shone, and there was an aliveness to her that I found invigorating.

"I'm glad you decided to stay."

"Thank you. So am I."

Angelina joined David in serving the food out and then she sat down next to me. I watched them all lower their heads as David said grace.

"Lord, we thank you for the blessings of this day, and we offer our gratitude for the bounty of this food and wine."

Jonathon was sitting on the other side of me. He smiled at me and poured wine into my glass. I noticed that there were several bottles on the table of both white and red wine.

The food that had been served was arranged in the middle of each plate, in the manner of good restaurants. But I couldn't make out the ingredients. Certainly several colorful vegetables, thinly sliced. And certainly some south-east Asian odors like coriander and ginger. And perhaps some kind of fish. Everybody else was tucking in, so I did too. Whatever it was, its taste was delicious.

"Okay?" asked Angelina.

"Mm. It's terrific. Did you cook this?"

She laughed.

"I helped. We all pitched in. Glad you like it."

Jonathon turned to me.

"Angelina tells me you're in television. Actually," he chuckled, "she says you're quite famous. Is that right?"

"No," I protested, "I'm basically a journalist. But for longer than I can remember, I've been a foreign correspondent."

"So you travel for a living?"

"Yes, but it's more than that. I get to see so many things that you wouldn't ordinarily see."

"Sounds great."

"Yeah. I think I've been very fortunate in my life. I've met some of the most extraordinary people, many of them famous, but many of them not. And I've been to some astonishing places…It's been a very rich life."

"You talk as though it's over."

"It is. Kinda. The job, that is, not my life."

I turned to Angelina, who was standing and starting to remove dishes.

"A new chapter in my life, I guess."

I finished my food to let Angelina take away the plate. As she and David disappeared to collect the main course I turned back to Jonathon.

"This is a beautiful house you have here."

"Yes, it's modeled on the principles of the Temple of Herod the Great in Jerusalem."

Hesitantly I asked, "And tell me….is this some kind of commune?"

Jonathon smiled politely, "Yes, you could call it that. Although that's a rather old-fashioned word."

"Yeah," I laughed, "I am rather old-fashioned…And is the comm… the group built around any particular principle?"

Jonathon hesitated for a moment.

"Er, yes. We're Judasians."

"Jew what," I blurted out..

"Judasians. We look to Our Lord Judas Iscariot to guide us…"

"…Really?" I couldn't believe that I'd actually heard right. "Wasn't Judas, er, you know….?"

The others at the table fell silent and turned to listen to the exchange. Jonathon chuckled. This was obviously familiar territory to him. I was feeling embarrassed, and Jonathon could see it on my face.

"That's alright. We generally get that reaction. But then, that's part of the point you see."

I waited for him to go on. But, instead, it was Gabriel who spoke. When he did, it was again gently and with great love.

"Most people are aware of how close Judas was to Jesus. And most people believe that Judas betrayed Jesus. In fact, nothing could be further from the truth. What Judas did, he did not only with the complicity of Jesus, but specifically at his request."

My mouth fell open.

Gabriel continued, "It was Jesus's destiny to be put on the cross. If he had simply disappeared and left the country his teachings may well have died out and everything that he had worked for been lost. And so Jesus approached Judas not only as a close disciple, but his closest friend. And he asked him to do the most difficult thing he could imagine. He said to Judas: 'You will exceed all of them. For you will sacrifice the man that clothes me.'

"At first Judas protested, of course, and refused to do it. He told Jesus that he was afraid. And that, while he understood that this was Jesus's destiny, he didn't want to be the cause of it. But Jesus exhorted him and told him not to be afraid. He said, 'Step away from the others and I shall tell you the mysteries of the kingdom. And, although you will be cursed by generations, this is your destiny as much as it is mine, and you must fulfill your destiny'"

My mind started to spin. I couldn't believe I was hearing this. I finally gathered my wits.

"And the thirty pieces of silver?" I asked.

"Ah yes," smiled Gabriel, "The thirty pieces of silver. That seems like such a damning piece of 'evidence', doesn't it. Well, actually, it was important that no-one be suspicious and think that Jesus had put Judas up to it. However, when Judas went to the Garden of Gethsemane to meet Jesus and kissed him, it was not to identify him, as many people believe. After all Jesus was well known. It was to kiss him good-bye, a kiss of love. Because Judas loved him so much, and he knew what was about to happen. And, although Jesus obviously made a great sacrifice, it was

Judas who made the greatest sacrifice, living forever in opprobrium while Jesus will live forever in the highest esteem.

"But Judas does not live in opprobrium with us. Because we understand what he did…and why. And we remember the 'mysteries of the kingdom' that Jesus spoke of. And he also said to Judas, 'It is possible for you to reach it, but you will grieve a great deal.' These things are what we study. And, you see, Judas knew all too well about grief."

When he said this he smiled at me, because this was obviously a message especially for me.

I hadn't realized that the main course had been served and that my wine glass had been re-filled. Neither had I realized that Angelina had slipped in beside me once again. Now she took my hand and smiled beatifically at me. She pointed to my plate – another beautifully arranged plate.

"Your food will go cold."

"Thank you." I said to her and loaded up my fork with some of the delicious food and tasted it. "Mmm." I said approvingly to her. "This is great. Thank you."

"You're very welcome." She said warmly.

But I was still gripped. I finished chewing my mouthful, swallowed and turned back to Gabriel.

"So you *are* Christians?"

Gabriel paused only slightly.

"To say that we are Christians is like saying that we are human beings. What we are doing here goes so much further than mere Christianity. Our practice goes deep within our souls, inasmuch as it is about awareness, even to the point of enlightenment."

Now I finally looked around me. All eyes at the table were focused on this conversation. But I had the strangest sensation, because this did not feel like some bizarre cult. The smiles on the people at the table were not plastic smiles – these were not Stepford people. I could see the sincerity written on their faces.

"I see." I said. A ridiculous thing to say really, because I didn't see at all. Nevertheless I had no more questions to ask right now. So I thanked Gabriel and concentrated on my food and wine.

At the end of the meal Hannah and Mary started clearing away the dishes, and I began to help. But Angelina rested a hand on mine and shook her head.

"It is their turn tonight. Guests are not expected to help. It's enough for you to simply enjoy and to engage with us."

She began to top up my wineglass, but I put my hand over it.

"I think I've had enough. I'll never be able to drive if I have any more."

She laughed.

"Well, as far as that's concerned you've probably already had too much. But I respect your decision not to have any more."

And she put the bottle back down.

I tried to figure out how many glasses I'd had. The trouble was that my glass must have been re-filled without me noticing. I always enjoy drinking wine with a meal. But I must have quaffed rather more of the admittedly pleasant wine than I'd imagined.

"Perhaps I'll go outside and clear my head."

How old was I? Nearly sixty? Did I still believe that, if you could just get some fresh air you'd be alert enough to drive home?

I stood up, perhaps a little unsteadily. But that was because it was difficult to get out of these chairs, wasn't it? And I'd been sitting a long time.

"I'll come with you," said Angelina.

She looped her arm through mine in a friendly gesture that also helped me to walk fairly steadily. She showed me how the French windows led directly from the dining room to the garden.

Outside it was delightful. The heat of the day had given way to a beautiful, balmy evening.

"Let me show you something," she said with delight.

We strolled together to a part of the garden where there were a number of rose bushes of different colors and different delicate scents.

"Check this out. Isn't it heavenly?"

And she inhaled deeply. I inhaled deeply too and nearly fell over.

"Whoa, steady on boy!" she laughed, and put her hands on my shoulders to steady me.

"I'm fine," I said, "Just shouldn't have breathed in so much so quickly….Mmm, you're right though, it is heavenly."

Her arms were still around me and our faces were close. With the moon gleaming in her golden hair and lighting her face she looked luminous and exquisite. Her clear blue eyes examined me with amusement. And then, still looking into my eyes, she leaned in towards me and very gently brushed her lips against mine and kissed me tenderly.

The feeling was electric. Electric and thrilling. But also surprising. I certainly hadn't expected this. And it was a moment before my brain connected with my mouth.

"Are you trying to seduce me?" I asked.

"Would that be such a bad thing?" she said.

I looked at the lovely young woman in my arms. And only one thought filled my head. The words that came out of my mouth were pure reaction. I spoke them without thinking. In spite of what I'd recently been through, and in spite of how I was feeling only a few hours before. Where does this reaction in men come from? Is it so deeply rooted, such a primal urge, that it overrides any other emotion?

"Actually that would be rather nice," I said.

"I was hoping you'd say that," she said, with a sweet smile. "Come on."

She led me across the garden to an annex of the house which was equally striking. There were several rooms there, presumably all for sleeping. Her room was spacious, but not huge. When I looked around I noticed that there were two single beds, one on either side of the room.

"My room-mate is away. So we won't be disturbed," she said.

Now that I was actually here I was beginning to feel slightly uncomfortable. A moment of reality kicked in. Was I really going to do this? My mind flicked to thoughts of Marie. It felt like a betrayal of her. But was I going to remain celibate for the rest of my life? If not, how long was a decent time to wait? A few months? A year? Five years? When Angelina reached up and touched my chest I decided to simply let the energy carry me along. I could feel the life in her, and I wanted to give myself to that.

I responded to her kisses, and there was no doubt that something was very much stirring inside me. And not just inside either. I was becoming highly aroused. She drew me over to one of the beds and lay back, gently pulling me on top of her.

I responded to my own urges. I kissed her fleshy lips, and was met with a corresponding passion from Angelina. Then she arched her neck and I kissed her there, unbuttoning her tunic top and following my fingers down with my lips.

Her full, rounded breasts protruded from the top of her simple white brassiere and, when I kissed them, she started to moan with pleasure. I placed a hand on one of her breasts and gently rubbed the nipple through the brassiere. The moaning increased. Her eyes were closed, and she started to squirm with pleasure. I was about to slide the strap down when a very strange thing happened. I looked down at this exquisite creature under me. Her beautiful face shining in rapture. Her beautiful *young* face shining in rapture. She was young, much younger even than Marie. And I thought how lucky I was to be right there with her. And simultaneously I also remembered how much older than her I was.

My lips were close to her ear now, and I whispered into her ear.

"I'm not sure this is right."

"Why?" she gasped.

"Because…." Really difficult to say, this, "I could be your father."

"You haven't seen my father," she whispered back, and turned her head to face me and kiss my lips.

And with that, and the alcohol coursing through my veins, it was the last thought I gave to that subject because she rolled out from under me and sat astride me. Then she slipped out of her top and reached behind her back, unhooked her bra, and let it fall to the bed. The sight of her full, beautifully curved breasts with the small pink nipples sent an extra shot of adrenalin racing around my body, and I could feel my penis beginning to stiffen.

Angelina leaned down and rested one breast close to my lips, and I responded to her invitation, taking the pert nipple into my mouth and sucking at it. At this she started moaning again. I cupped her other breast in my hand and squeezed it gently. The moaning became more throaty and now she pushed both breasts into my face.

After a while she broke away from me and began to unbutton my shirt. I started to help her and then, as I yanked my shirt off, she stood up and let her tunic pants slip to the floor. For a moment she posed for me, wearing only her thong, enjoying me enjoying her. Then her hands were at my zipper, sliding it down to expose the bulge beneath. She kissed the bulge briefly and giggled, then she tugged at my pants and pulled them down.

When we were both naked she lay down beside me and we wrapped our legs around one another and I became lost in her.

I wasn't sure what happened next. I remember her reaching down to touch my penis. And I remember the slight frown on her face. I had thought that there was no problem, but I followed her gaze down, and realized that I wasn't as stiff as I'd thought I'd been.

Angelina blinked and bent down to kiss me and to take me into her mouth. But somehow, although I enjoyed the sensation, and I admired her technique, instead of getting harder I started to get softer.

Now Angelina had a slight air of unease. Not to say panic. She began to rub at my penis with her hand. Without success. So, instead, she rolled on top of me again and sat astride me. She wet her fingertips and, reaching down, moistened herself. Then she took my now limp penis and tried to put inside her.

I, of course, was dismayed. This was turning into a disaster. However much I pushed, and however hard she wriggled, my damn cock just wouldn't go in.

Eventually we both realized that it was no good. I tried to push her back down on the bed. I thought that if maybe I went down on her it would be some consolation. But now Angelina was dejected. She lay down beside me and held me. Like a friend.

"It's okay," she said.

"No it's not," I said. "This doesn't happen to me."

I felt wretched.

We lay like that for some time. Eventually I spoke.

"It must just be too soon," I managed to say.

"Yes," was all she said.

After a while she got up to go to the bathroom. When she returned she climbed into the other bed, curled up and went to sleep. I was pissed off. Pissed off with her some. But mostly with myself. And it was in that state that I drifted off to sleep.

I dreamt that I was in Israel, reporting on the latest round of non-talks between the Israelis and the Palestinians. There was hope, however, if both sides would just accept that Judas was able to walk on water. But nobody wanted to be the first to acknowledge it. And although Judas had a rocket propelled grenade launcher, he couldn't get it to fire. So he took it along a public access path right into the heart of the Garden of Geffen. In the garden I was just smelling the roses when my cell phone rang. It was Mike, telling me to go directly to Iraq because Jesus was being held captive and they needed the story.

When I got to Baghdad I was met by a messenger who told me that I had to go immediately to a particular hotel room. The messenger whispered the room number in my ear.

Inside the hotel room Marie was stretched out naked on the bed. She smiled at me and indicated with a finger for me to come closer to the bed. I was very happy to see her, but there was a nagging worry at the back of my brain that I couldn't remember. "Silly boy," said Marie. "Everything is okay." And she stroked my face, then my chest.

I leaned down and kissed her lips. Then I began to gently kiss all parts of her body, moving slowly downwards. Marie was in ecstasy and small guttural sounds escaped her lips. I, too, became highly aroused, and I was about to climb on top of her. But first....

I turned over and partly woke up. I was aware that I was in a strange bed. This, of course, was not unusual in itself. But I knew there was something different about this bed.

I was aware too that I had a massive erection that was so stiff that my penis was flat against my stomach and it felt as though the tip reached to my navel.

And then I remembered where I was. I looked over to the other bed, where Angelina was fast asleep. I badly wanted to make up to her for my deficiency a few hours earlier. I also very much wanted to feel better about my sexual prowess.

I lay there for a moment, thinking. I took my cock in my hand, just to make sure. I didn't want any mistakes this time. And then I made the decision. I pulled the covers back, climbed out of bed, and moved over to where Angelina lay sleeping. She looked as beautiful asleep as she did awake. Perhaps I could wake her quietly and we could pick up where we'd left off.

I slid her bedcovers back and eased myself into the small space beside her. She stirred slightly and turned her face towards me. Her face truly was exquisite.

I could feel her sweet breath, and brought my lips slowly closer to hers. When our faces were millimeters apart Angelina opened her eyes……..and screamed in terror.

"Aaghhhhhh!"

Now, of course, I can see it from her point of view. She'd woken from a deep sleep to find a strange man on top of her, and it seemed worse than any nightmare.

I backed away. But Angelina, still partly asleep, was terrified. And she screamed again. If anything, even louder. She sat up and backed away from me, still screaming, her breathing fast and ragged.

The bedroom door flew open and David and Jonathon rushed in.

"It's okay…." I started to say.

"….Angelina?" said David, ignoring me. "What's happening?"

"I….I….I don't know."

She was still confused, and wasn't even sure herself what was happening. I was still standing there naked. So I decided to retreat to the other bed and cover myself up.

"It was all a misunderstanding…." I started to say. Then realized how stupid that sounded. "She…Angelina…was asleep, and I woke her by mistake….must have startled her."

Both men eyed me suspiciously. But Angelina was calming down now, and her breathing was returning to normal. She frowned.

"Maybe I had a nightmare." She said, unsure now whether that actually *had* been the case.

"Are you sure," asked David, "because…."

"….No, I'm fine. But thanks for coming in."

She wrapped a sheet around her and looked at her clock.

"Maybe I'll get up and make a drink."

Both Jonathon and David were obviously reluctant to leave her alone with me. But Angelina swung her legs off the bed and stood up, wrapping the bed sheet tighter around her. The first light of dawn was just beginning to show itself through the bedroom window. And now Angelina managed a wan smile.

"I'll be okay. Really."

# Chapter Eight

"One club"

Mos closed his fanned out playing cards and nodded to himself.

"One no trump."

Al mulled over his hand for a moment, "Pass."

I spoke up quickly, "Two diamonds."

Mos and Al and Harry and I were playing bridge. It was something we did once in a while. This time around it was at my place. While poker was all the rage those days, the four of us actually enjoyed bridge more. There was something about this card game that was more satisfying. Sometimes things could still get tense, especially between partners. And we still played for money, even though it was only for a few dollars. But this way nobody felt gypped, and it generally kept everybody feeling friendly. Many years ago we'd established the partnerships. Mos and I played together because I could handle Mos' occasional tantrums better. Not only that, but Harry and Al had devised a system where it seemed they could almost read each others minds sometimes.

"Pass." said Harry, and shrugged.

"Two hearts." from Mos.

"Pass," from big Al.

"Three hearts," from me.

"Pass," from Harry.

Mos looked at me quizzically, in an attempt at telepathy.

"Three spades," he said slowly.

"Pass," again from Al.

"Four hearts."

I said it as though it was the only possible bid.

Harry closed his hand and smiled at his partner.

"Pass," was all he said.

Harry Bonaventura didn't hang out as much as the rest of us. He was a television scriptwriter, mostly working on police procedurals. He'd got his break on *Hill Street Blues* many years ago, and now found steady work on each new police series that came along. The producers like his dialog work especially. They think he has a special voice. Maybe it's because he was originally from New York. But, whatever it is, Harry has kept pretty busy steadily churning out scripts.

The other thing that kept Harry busy was dating. Although he was nearly sixty and a veteran of three marriages, Harry always seemed to be going out with some young model, actress....or whatever. He was still good looking, tall and slim with a thick, silvery mane of hair. But probably the real secret to his great success with women was that he was a genuinely happy man. And with that came a warm friendliness and strong confidence. Nothing ever seemed to rile him.

"Pass," said Mos.

"Pass," said Al.

"Uh huh," Mos said. "Okay.....Then four hearts"

Al placed the two of clubs on the table, and Mos took my cards and laid them on the table face upwards. He studied them thoughtfully, then looked hard at his own cards. I stood up.

"Who needs a fresh drink," I asked, gathering glasses.

Mos held his out without looking up.

"I'm good." said Al.

So, that was it? You just left her there?" asked Harry, handing me his glass.

"Yeah. What else was I going to do?"

Mos selected a card and Harry followed with one of his own.

"You gonna see her again?"

"I doubt it. I mean, it wasn't as though I was looking for a relationship anyway. Especially so soon...."

I let it trail away as I collected clean glasses from the kitchen and poured the drinks. I hadn't meant to share this experience with everyone, and had only told Mos quietly. But, Mos being Mos, it didn't stay quiet for long. "It's good that you're getting out and about," he'd said. And then turned around and told the others a shortened version of the story. I was embarrassed by the episode, but the guys had gone easy on me, not ragging me too much. In the end I was glad to have talked about it.

"'Cause if you're not," called out Harry, "can you give me her number. If she's half as stunning as you said, I'd love to meet her."

"I'm sure you would." Al said to Harry. Then, when I returned, he said. "Was she trying to make you for a convert, d'you think."

"I'd convert," said Harry. "If she's a real babe I'd convert to fucking Islam if necessary."

"Can we play these fucking cards please," said Mos, trying to concentrate.

The others complied for a few minutes in silence as I handed out the fresh drinks and sat back down.

Harry took a trick. Then Mos made one from my hand. And it was Al's turn. He took that trick and started playing club cards again triumphantly.

"Shit!" said Mos, "I could have sworn we had it."

"Never mind." I said, "We're doing okay."

Mos took a swig from his new drink.

"I don't get these girls anyway. I mean, all my life I've been trying to understand women. And, just when I thought I might have them figured out, along comes this new generation. I swear they're nothing like women from previous generations.

"More confident," said Harry.

"Their mothers and grandmothers worked hard to get all their rights…" said Al.

"….And their fathers worked hard to give them a car….and a cell phone….and all the clothes that they can nearly wear. I mean, what's that about? They walk around with their tits hanging out and their asses sticking out of their pants. And then, if a man dares to look, they scream blue murder. 'Sexism', 'male chauvanist pig', you name it…"

"….I like it." Said Harry.

"Yeah, I like it," said Mos, "except when I get caught by my wife looking."

And we all laughed.

"Plus you can never get them to leave home, the girls or the boys,"

And we all laughed again because this was the bane of Al's life. He and Rita had two kids, both in their late twenties. After college each of them had come back home to live. Their daughter Emily, fortunately took after Rita. Fortunately because it would have been most unfortunate if she'd looked like Al. But Emily's long blonde hair, good looks, and vivacious personality meant that there were always both young men and young women coming to call on her. And, since Al worked at home, the distraction was often difficult for him.

His son Stevie, who *did* take after him, also worked from home, trying to establish his own small internet design company. The result was often mayhem. Which was not the way Al liked things.

"I'm trying to bribe them now." laughed Al, "With real money. Even offered to help finance an apartment each. But no go. We made them just too comfortable I guess.

***

"Dad, I'm coming round at eight to collect you. We'll go together."

It was Katie.

"Are you sure this is a good idea?"

"Of course! This is an important gig for Tommy."

"So why didn't he mention it himself?"

"You know what Tommy's like. Anyway, it'll be good for you to get out….."

"….I get out."

"Where?"

"Here and there. What are you, my social secretary?"

"Sure. Why not!"

Well, she was actually ten minutes late. Although that wasn't bad for Katie. But she insisted on driving, which I wasn't too keen on. In the end I gave in, and she whisked me off in her little coupe.

"Where is this thing?"

"Santa Monica. But we've got plenty of time."

"So why are you driving so fast?"

"Dad." She actually turned and looked at me, throwing me a dirty look, "Are you going to be a pain all evening? Just relax."

I jabbed a finger at the stopped traffic that she was approaching very fast. "Hey!"

She threw on the brakes and managed to pull up in time. Turning to me she gave a little shrug and a cheeky grin.

"Sorry. I'll drive a little slower. Alright?"

"Thanks….So, is this Tommy's new band?"

88

"It could be. At the moment they're still trying some things out together. But if things go well tonight he says they're considering playing together on a regular basis."

She found a parking spot not too far from the venue, although her parking left something to be desired. Katie didn't so much park the car as abandon it, and I looked over my shoulder ruefully at the car as we strode off together down the street.

At first I thought we were going to a steak joint but, although it was part of the same building, the venue turned out to be next door. There was a big sign on the door, reading 'Tonite: Open Mic Night'. As we pushed into the crowded bar I pondered that double spelling of 'night'. "I guess English is what you want it to be these days," I thought.

The hubbub of the crowd mixed with the music in the background. There was a pool room beside the bar, with players at all the tables. And on the other side of the pool room I could see a small stage, where I could just make out a young girl with an acoustic guitar who sat on a bar stool.

Katie checked her watch.

"Good. Plenty of time. How about a drink?"

"I'll get 'em," I said, "What would you like?"

"Tequila?" said Katie.

"I don't think so. You're the designated driver, remember. I'll get you a soft drink."

She pulled a face at me.

As I approached the bar I realized that the various television sets in the lounge were actually showing the girl playing on the stage. And now I could hear her singing. She was good in that sad-but-defiant-sounding manner of many young female singers today.

At the corner of the bar I saw a face I thought I recognized, but couldn't be sure. Then I remembered who it was, the raven-haired girl dressed all in black that Tommy had brought to the funeral. She was standing with a small group of people, but Tommy wasn't amongst them. She caught my eye, then looked away.

But she must have remembered who I was, because then she looked back and smiled at me. She gave a little wave and then carried on talking with her friends.

I carried my beer and the diet Coke back to where I'd left Katie. She was talking with a guy about her own age.

"Thanks dad. This is Alan. Alan this is my dad."

I didn't really feel like making small talk. But, fortunately, neither did Alan.

"Yeah, I've got a pool table waiting for me, so excuse me."

I looked around.

"Nice place."

Katie raised an eyebrow. I guess she couldn't tell whether I meant it or not.

"No, really!" I said.

"It's alright"

"So, when does Tommy play?"

"After this girl, I think."

Then I saw Tommy arrive at the small group where, 'what-was-her-name? Oh yeah, Anastasia' was standing. I love seeing my kids in other company, completely oblivious of my presence. They always seem like different people. More free somehow. Tommy was laughing and highly animated. He put his arm around Anastasia. She leaned into him and whispered into his ear. Then he turned around and saw me and Katie. He registered a look of surprise when he saw me, and immediately came over.

"Hey dad! Thanks for coming."

Tommy kissed Katie on the cheek and, as always, I had the urge to hug my son but, for some reason, felt inhibited from doing so. Was it a message I was picking up from Tommy that he was uncomfortable with being hugged in public, or was I just imagining it?

"Thought I'd come and support you."

"That's great dad. Hope you like it."

He looked over at the stage.

"I'd better get going."

"Sure. Good luck."

"Luck, dad?" then laughed.

I shrugged, "Well whatever you wish someone these days."

Why do my children always make me feel so old?

"It's okay. Thanks again for coming."

And, with a smile to his sister, Tommy went over and grabbed Anastasia and they went through the pool room together.

I looked around the room. Most of the people there were much younger than me. How long had it been since I'd been to a place like this? I tried to think. Not this century. Wow! 'Not this century'! That definitely made me feel old.

Where had all those years gone? I was reminded of a cartoon I'd seen once that said, "How did I get over the hill without ever getting to the top?". But I wasn't over the hill yet. Was I?

"You want to sit down?"

That's Katie, looking after me as always.

"Is there somewhere?"

"Yes, follow me."

She led me to a nook in the corner of the lounge where we could still see through to the stage and also see a television screen. And where she knew I'd be comfortable.

"I know you don't like to stand up for too long. Oh, there's someone over there I've been meaning to catch up with for the longest."

She turned to me and made a sweet face.

"Do you mind?"

"Not at all."

And I really didn't. I was happy to sit there and wait for Tommy and his band to come on.

"I won't be long."

"Take your time."

As she rose to go to see her friends I saw a face I thought I recognized as well. It was just the flash of a profile of a young man. Then I laughed to myself, because the guy I thought this was would be sixty today. And I laughed again.

What was the guy's name? Garry? Larry?....No Barry,. That's right. He had lived in the same house when I was at Berkeley. That house just off Telegraph in, what? Sixty-seven, sixty-eight? What an incredible time that was. The whole fucking hippy thing. I smiled as I remembered myself in those days. The long hair and scrawny beard. The beads. Oh Christ! Those clothes. And the fucking beads. How could I! At least I never wore flowers in my hair. Not that I could remember! But there were flowers everywhere else. And candles and incense. There seemed to be color everywhere. And psychedelic posters on the walls – especially that one I always loved of the naked girl lying down covered with different colors of body paint. And everyone wore buttons and T-shirts with slogans on them. One of my favorites was always 'If you love someone let them go. And if they don't come back hunt them down and kill them.'

There was a lightness then. An innocence. And a passion. Even though there was a war *then* – the Vietnam one – everything seemed to be treated differently. There seemed to be more creativity and originality in everything. Music and clothes and art and literature. A freshness. An air of experimentation.

Free choice. Free expression. Free love. Especially free love. What was her name? I remembered how we'd spent the evening together, talking and listening to the new Dylan record. Smoking a little weed and drinking a little wine. Alice, that was it. Oh, Alice, sweet Alice. Fresh-faced and lithe of limb. With long, brown hair that almost reached her ass. I took her to bed and we made love very slowly. There was real joy in each other, discovering and playing. And tormenting and satisfying each other. On and on all through the night.

And then, without any sleep whatsoever, we'd gone for a pre-dawn stroll. The dark, bluey-grayness was just beginning to lighten and an occasional bird tested its song. We'd walked hand-in-hand in a blissed-out state. And suddenly the silence was pierced by the sound of a fire engine that tore round a corner, streaked past us and stopped in the next street. We'd hurried to see what was happening, and there we were confronted by the surreal sight of a church on fire. But there was no-one else there, not a soul, only the firemen. We stood and watched for a while as the sky got lighter and lighter. And then we turned around and walked back to the house off Telegraph and went to sleep.

I thought about those days. We were going to change the world, weren't we? Tear down the walls. All the barriers. In politics, in religion, in all the arts. Tear 'em down and make sure that our children never had to go through the restrictions that we'd had to go through. And we *did*. We successfully ripped down so many of the walls. "But," I thought, "as it turns out, all those walls that we so diligently and passionately tore down, those walls that we thought were keeping us in, were actually keeping some bad things out. Who knew!"

I thought about how things were today, with so many boundaries gone, and wondered whether we'd gone too far. Ah, well.

I was brought out of my reverie by a roll of drums, punctuated by the crash of cymbals, followed by strangulated guitar chords and microphone testing, "One, two. One two." I didn't need the television to hear the band tuning up. And there was Tommy, standing in the front, playing a few chords on his guitar and then adjusting it.

Katie slid into the seat beside me.

"Okay dad?"

"Sure honey. So, here they are."

Yeah. Tommy looks good, don't you think."

Then, with a quick count, they were off at breakneck speed into a boisterous number. It was Tommy's voice, but it wasn't his voice somehow. I had heard my son sing before of course, but I'd never seen him perform in public quite like this. And, not only did he look and sound the part, Tommy projected something special, some singular charisma. And he certainly put his mettle into the performance.

Apart from the drummer there were two other guys on guitar and Anastasia on keyboards. All of them had microphones and gave Tommy great musical and vocal support. As a band they were pretty tight, and the sound was great.

I looked up at the television monitor, and saw Tommy singing his heart out. A strange lump came into my throat. I had often thought how overworked the word 'proud' was. People were 'proud to be Americans'. Or this sponsor is 'proud to bring you' this television program. I was 'so proud of her'. But here I was, seeing my youngest child standing up there on stage, and an overwhelming feeling flooded through me. And, yes, I would say it was pride. Not because of anything I might have done, not my own ego. Something more ephemeral than that. Somehow I was proud *for* him and proud *of* him.

The number came to an end and, barely waiting for the enthusiastic response from the audience, the musicians went straight into a slower, freewheeling number. Tommy's voice had a faint rasp to it now that emphasized the emotion of the words, and I forgot that this was my son and found myself caught up in the performance.

After the set I wanted to go right up to Tommy, but it was difficult because he seemed to be surrounded by his friends and he was obviously enjoying that. So I waited patiently close by, on the perimeter, for Tommy to turn around. And, when he did, I gave him a big thumbs up and a smile.

"That was great Tommy. I really loved it."

"Thanks dad," and he smiled back at me, "I'm glad you were here."

"Me too. Buy you a drink?"

Tommy held up the longneck, "I'm covered. But thanks."

Then Tommy was kidnapped by two girls, who dragged him off to the other side of the lounge. And I lost him.

# Chapter Nine

The phone rang just as I was walking out the door. I stood there for a moment, deliberating whether to pick it up or just leave. In the end the answering machine got it. But curiosity got the better of me, and I stopped to listen who it was.

"Max? This is Brad. From the network....?"

I groaned.

"....Okay, I want you to know there are no hard feelings. From this end. We did what we had to do, and you did what you had to do. So, no hard feelings. Anyway, to *show* you there are no hard feelings from this end....I was talking with a producer friend of mine, and she's looking for someone like you for a pilot they're putting together. Thought you might be interested. It's not for us of course, but it could stand a good chance. Anyway buddy..."

"*Buddy?*"

"....I gave her your number. I hope that's okay. Not this number of course. I wouldn't do that. Your cell number. So, I hope that's okay. Alright....well, good luck.....Oh! Her name's Stephanie....Yeah, well good luck."

I stood in the doorway, listening to the message. "Oh Christ, now what? Well, it could be a gig. Maybe something I'd enjoy. Who knows."

I locked the door and walked to my car thoughtfully. I threw my gym bag in the back and drove off.

The gym was only a short drive from my house. I could have run there, but I didn't want to get too exhausted. Ha-ha. I parked in the underground garage, and took the elevator to the gym on the third floor.

"Hi Max."

Julie signed me in. Julie was one of the most athletic girls I had ever seen. She oozed sheer athleticism. I imagined that she even looked sporty in her sleep. Her body was taut and lean, and the muscles on her bronzed arms and legs rippled softly as she moved. Her gleaming white teeth twinkled at me as she spoke.

"Haven't seen you for a while. Been overseas again?"

"No. I, er.....you know, personal stuff to attend to."

Why couldn't I just say 'my wife died'? I found that really curious. Maybe because there something very final about saying that out loud.

"Uh huh. Any classes today?"

"No, just the usual."

"Okay. Well, if you need anything…"

"Thanks Julie."

I strode to the Mens' locker room to change. The rhythmic music from the aerobics class pulsed throughout the gym, and I couldn't help but pick up my pace as I walked.

Harry was already there, and just tying his laces as I walked in.

"Hi."

"Oh hey."

Harry stood up, "How're you doing?"

"Pretty good."

He waited as I stripped off and changed into my shorts and tee.

"I'm glad to be back here though. I've been feeling a bit rusty."

He smiled mischievously, "I saw some new girls?"

Up until Marie's death Harry and I had met at the gym each Wednesday, unless I was away. First we'd warm up a little. Then go to the machine circuit and follow it round. Then the main event as we joined the row of exercise bikes right next to where the aerobics class – mostly women – were doing their thing. Both of us loved to watch and compare notes. A little harmless fun. But today I wasn't really in the mood. Nevertheless I went along with Harry.

"One very hot chick started last week. Great bod."

"Blonde?"

I knew Harry's preference was for blondes.

"No, brunette. I think she's here. Wait til you see her."

Inside the cavernous room we strolled past the large group of weight-lifters studying themselves narcissus-like in the huge mirrors as they heaved the metal around. There was a sprinkling of women with strange distorted physiques, who looked as though they'd been digitally altered, their womens' faces put on mens' bodies. But most of the weight-lifters were muscle-bound men with thick necks, broad chests and huge, bulging leg and arm muscles.

We began our warm-ups, stretching the muscles gently until we felt we were ready for the machines. Then, one by one, we followed the circuit around.

I was out of breath by the time we finished.

"You okay pal?" asked Harry.

"Yeah, I'm fine. I'm just out of practice."

I climbed onto a bike and Harry took the one next to me. He nodded his head towards a tall, willowy brunette in the middle of the class.

"That's her. Hasn't she got a great body?"

"Definitely."

"Gets you all out of breath, huh?"

Because I still *was*. Out of breath, that is. So I stopped pedaling for a while, and examined the woman thoughtfully.

"How old would you say she is?"

"I dunno. Thirty, maybe thirty-five."

"Yeah, probably. You really can't tell these days, can you."

"Nope. Nobody looks like what they used to. I mean, I remember when my dad was my age, fifty-five...."

"....fifty-eight...."

"....Yeah, fifty-eight," laughed Harry. "When he was my age he was an old man. And I don't just mean from my perspective as a young man. He really was old. He'd pretty much given up on life and was looking forward to retirement, and then to maybe a few years after that. Nowadays we're just getting started. This is just like the beginning of a new phase in life for us."

"Sixty's the new forty...."

"...That's right. For men anyway. Of course when I was forty I was going through all that angsty mid-life crisis shit. But now we're free and clear, with a new confidence."

I started pedaling again, and we pedaled quietly together for a while in rhythm, our eyes roaming over the women who were moving energetically on the floor in front of us. At one point I turned to look at Harry. But his eyes were fixed on the vision in front of him. I wouldn't say he was practically salivating, but he certainly was eager. Was I like that too normally? Wow!

I guess he realized that I was looking at him, because he turned to me then.

"The thing is, I guess, that we look after ourselves a lot better than our parents' generation. We try and eat well. Most of us have stopped smoking. We exercise and try and stay fit and keep our weight down. We stay out of the sun so we don't get melanomas. We go for regular check-ups for prostate cancer, colon cancer, heart...."

"...We have Botox injections and plastic surgery And hair transplants, and we take pills for everything ...."

"...That's right," laughed Harry, "And we get massages and frequent sex. And we enjoy life. Well, I do."

The music in the aerobics class sped up, and our pedaling sped up with it.

I took a long time showering and getting dressed. When I left the locker room it was just in time to see the willowy brunette writing something on a piece of paper and handing it to Harry. She smiled at him as she left, and Harry followed her out with his eyes.

"Phone number?" I asked.

"Uh, huh," replied Harry, without taking his eyes off her.

I shook my head in incredulity. "Juice?"

"Yeah, there's another babe in there that I thought you should see."

"You're like a kid in a candy store, aren't you?"

Harry thought for a moment.

"I guess I am. Come on."

***

When I got home I threw my sweaty gym gear into the washer. I still wasn't emotionally used to being by myself, but I was coping better with the practicalities. I'd established a routine, and I'd also organized Louisa, a chubby, middle-aged Mexican woman to come and clean for me. She always had a smile for me. And she often shopped and cooked for me as well.

But she wasn't coming today, and there was nothing prepared. I'm not a great cook. I'd always had someone else to cook for me, first my mother. Then later Lisa prepared all my meals when I was at home. And when I was away I ate out.

I put the coffee on, then looked in the refrigerator thoughtfully, and pulled out a loaf of bread, some butter, a hunk of cheese and a tomato. I sliced the cheese and the tomato, and laid the pieces carefully between two very thick pieces of buttered bread, creating a huge doorstep of a sandwich.

I examined my handiwork approvingly, then poured some coffee and carried it all into the living room to the coffee table where Marie's ashes still sat in the middle of the table.

I put the plate down on the table, sipped my coffee, and gazed at the urn. I could feel that Marie's spirit was still there in that urn. Not that I thought she was still here, of course. But I couldn't help talking to the urn as though it was actually Marie. Sometimes I had long conversations, and other times I tried to work things out by talking to the urn. Naturally I knew that I was really talking to myself, but there was something comforting about this man-urn relationship.

"So here we are again," I said out loud.

I picked up my plate and took a bite of the sandwich. I chewed for a moment, then spoke out again.

"Harry was in good form today. I don't know how he does it. You never really got to know Harry, did you? Well he's something else. A real babe-magnet. Amazing at his age."

I took another bite of the sandwich and started to chew. But it was a substantial mouthful, and I had difficulty swallowing it. I chewed harder, and I was just bringing the coffee mug to my lips, hoping that I could wash it down, when I felt a sharp pain in my chest. I winced, and froze for a moment.

"This is silly," I thought, and spat the rest of my mouthful out onto the plate, breathing deeply. I looked at the mess in disgust. Mostly disgust with myself.

"Yuck!"

I stood up and carried the plate into the kitchen and let the mess slide into the pedal bin. As I put the plate into the sink my cell phone rang. I answered it automatically.

"Hello."

"Hi. Is this Max Wheeler?"

It was a woman's voice.

"Who wants him?"

I was always cautious with strange voices these days. And sometimes even with familiar voices.

"My name is Stephanie Roth. I'm a television producer. Brad Anderson gave me this number."

Brad Brad. My ex-executive producer. Or ex ex, if you like.

"Oh yeah, Brad called me."

"Oh great!"

Very enthusiastic.

"I'm so glad. Anyway, we're producing a pilot for a new show and wondered whether you're interested in coming in to talk about it…"

"…Talk about it…?"

"…Yes. Since you're not….Since you might be available now we thought you might be interested."

"What kind of show is it?"

"It's a lifestyle show for cable. Brand new concept. It's called *You Show Me Yours*…."

"…Sort of a porno thing is it…?"

"Ha ha."

Big laugh, perhaps just a little too loud. And perhaps just a little too brittle.

"Oh no. Ha ha. It's about different skills that we all have. The first half of the program you show me what you do and how you do it and I try and do it. Then, in the second part, I show you how I do my thing, and you try and do it. See?"

I did see. Sort of.

"The thing is everybody who comes on the show is a celebrity. You know, magician, actor, sports person. That sort of thing."

"And you want me to describe how to be a foreign correspondent?"

"Oh no." More laughter. "We were interested in you hosting it."

That really stopped me in my tracks.

"Really?"

"Yes. Look, we've got a whole treatment that I can email to you. It describes it in more detail."

I looked at the urn on the coffee table and shrugged. When I spoke, it was more to myself. And Marie.

"Why not."

"Oh great! Brad gave me your email address…."

Good old Brad.

"…so I'll send it right now and, if you like it, maybe we can make a time for you to come to our office."

"Whereabouts are you?"

"Burbank."

"Sure, why don't you do that."

"Great. So, nice talking with you Max."

"Nice talking with you. Stephanie."

"Why not?" I said to the urn, as I put the phone down. "Maybe it's time for a change of direction."

I'd been working on a book in the last month. Well, that's actually putting it a bit strongly. I'd been jotting down some notes in an old exercise book. Mostly my own experiences, things that had happened to me overseas. Little stories that I found interesting or amusing. The thing was I hadn't been able to come up with a structure. And, besides, it truly wasn't something that I was burning to do. It was more a time filler. What *was* I burning to do? That was the problem! I didn't know. So why not do something like this. It was still journalism in a way, wasn't it?

"Um, not really," I said out loud. "But it might occupy me for a while. That wouldn't be so bad."

Without really realizing what I was doing, I began to rub my chest thoughtfully.

\*\*\*

The fabulous Libby had outdone herself. All the chairs and tables were specially decorated with miles of ribbon, matching the decorations to the house and gardens, matching Libby's fabulous dress. She had found the most sublime caterers who'd presented varied and interesting delicacies and appetizers followed by a wide selection of mouth-watering buffet items. The Veuve Cliquot champagne was chilled to the perfect temperature and it was all served with polite aplomb. A music group, who matched the chairs and the tables, etc, played at just the right volume and with just the right amount of intensity.

Rose petals had formed a path from the valet-parked cars up to the deck. And Mos and Libby had greeted every guest with delight and pleasure. Even the weather was playing its part, with the late summer sun in the clear blue sky just the right temperature. Well, as Libby had said, "You don't celebrate your J wedding anniversary every day."

Indeed you don't.

I had arrived fairly early, and had watched the other arrivals with interest.

"You know Lisa's coming, don't you?" Mos had asked.

"Yeah, I figured."

"She and Lib have always been close."

"Yes. It's fine Mos. It really is."

"And you know she's bringing a man, don't you?"

"Yep, that's fine too. Good luck to her. I hope she's happy. I really do"

Pause. Then me again: "Do you know anything about this guy?"

"Yeah, I met him once. A tennis party thing…"

"…You go to tennis parties? Since when…?"

"….It's Lib's new thing. All the women wanted to do something to keep fit. So they decided to play tennis together. And that kinda developed into tennis parties with husbands and families."

"So what's he like?"

"Who? Oh, Ron…?"

"…She going out with a Ron….?"

"…Yeah, what's wrong with that. It was my father's name…He's, er, he's a good-looking guy, I guess. About our age. In the business."

There is only one *business* in LA. Actually, of course, there are lots and lots of businesses, but only one *business*: The Movie Business. Or at a pinch the Television Business.

"Some kind of producer I think."

"Uh, huh…Family?"

"I don't know. That's all I heard.

Now from where I stood on the deck I could see Lisa arrive. The car she came in was a very large Mercedes. Was I paying for that or was it Ron's car? A tall man with distinguished, wavy gray hair handed the keys to a valet, and I could see him palming the guy a banknote. "That must be Ron," I said to himself.

"Hello Maxy."

The sexy voice that breathed into my ear was familiar. I knew who it was without turning round.

"Hello Kitty."

Kitty Reynolds, or as she now was, Kitty Reynolds-la Paz-Ljubicic-Goldernberg had been well named by her parents. She was so feline it was almost as though she purred when she talked. And her lissome body sashayed when she walked.

When I turned around and looked into her eyes I felt as though I was staring into the eyes of a cat. She held me lightly by the shoulders and kissed me on both cheeks, European style. She didn't do air kisses, she actually brushed her lips against my skin. The scent of her perfume, although light, was intoxicating…and very expensive.

"So how have you been Maxy?"

She was the only person in the world that called me that. The only person in fifty years who could get away with it. Even though she was over fifty now, her face was exquisite. I assumed she'd had a little help there, but she was still a looker. And I still found her body incredibly sexy.

Somewhat unnecessarily, she brushed an invisible strand of golden hair away from her face. It was only a faint gesture, but it enabled her to push out her breasts as if to say 'Hey, look at these. Wouldn't you like to hold them in your hands or nuzzle up against them?'.

"I've been okay Kitty. And you?"

"Oh, I've been okay too. Like you I'm still recovering from a bereavement, of course."

The thrice-married Kitty's last husband, the late Gerry Goldernberg had been older than her. A great deal older in fact. And he'd left her with a bundle.

"Oh look, there's Lisa and, er, do you know that man?"

"I'm reliably informed his name's Ron. But I couldn't say for sure."

"Are you and Lisa…You know?"

"What, friends? No, I wouldn't say 'friends'. And I think she still hasn't forgiven me. But we can talk to each other civilly."

"And you? What are you doing with yourself since you left the network?"

"Oh, this and that."

I was watching my ex-wife and her friend as they arrived at the house and were greeted by some of the guests. But Kitty wasn't done with me yet.

"So, Maxy, now that your marriage is over and, with your recent…sad loss from your *short* marriage," In other words a relationship that was easily gotten over, "I guess you're a free agent again. Does that mean you're…. available?"

I hadn't really considered myself like that.

"It's a little too early for that just yet Kitty. I'm still grieving."

"Of course." And she gave me a sweet smile, "So when you think you're ready, why don't you give me a call."

She reached out a finger and stroked my cheek softly.

I wasn't paying attention. I was watching a certain couple who were now surrounded by a small cluster of friends. I guessed that it would have been a point of honor for Lisa to have brought someone to the party. To show Libby and Mos. And all their friends. And me. That she was still desirable. Could still get a man.

Ron put his big arm around my wife's….strike that….my ex-wife's shoulder. The act was not so much protective as possessive. Big Ron was making a statement to all assembled here: This woman is Mine and she is With Me. I thought that generally it was the sort of thing that men might do at the beginning of a relationship when they're still not quite sure of Their Woman.

"So," I thought, "this is a new relationship."

And I thought back to my own first years with Lisa. A memory came to me of that year when we'd moved to London, England so I could take up the job at TVAM. That summer when she'd been pregnant with Jack. When, as I had said, we'd turned from being a two-Wheeler family to being a three-Wheeler family. What a magical year that had been. A young couple just starting out with everything to look forward to. A brand new job in a new country that was exciting.

I had majored in English at Berkeley. And, in particular, literature from twentieth century England. Lisa, too, had been an English major, and had originally been excited to go to England with me until she found out she was pregnant. She wasn't keen on giving birth in a strange country away from her family and friends. Even if it *was* England. Her indecision had paralyzed us both for two terrible weeks. Then her mother had persuaded her that it was an extraordinary opportunity. And she had offered to fly to London to be with her daughter for the birth.

We'd found a beautiful apartment in Belsize Park quite close to the studios where I worked. And it was also close to the Olde Worlde charm of Hampstead, with its cozy pubs and twee shops and restaurants. And its literary, artistic and intellectual connections. And we had made friends with a small group of expatriate Americans who had given us both support.

As Lisa's belly continued to expand we both fell in love with London. We would walk for hours, exploring London's streets. In the evenings we'd seek out Italian restaurants and French bistros. Here we fell in love all over again.

Lisa took a course, learning massage, so that she could massage the baby. And, in turn, she taught me what she'd learnt. Often we'd spend hours in our candle-lit incense-filled living room swapping massages. And afterwards we would make love.

She woke me one morning about three a.m. At first I thought there was something wrong, until she whispered in my ear, "I *need* some Chinese food."

"What d'you mean," I mumbled.

"I have the strongest craving for some Chinese food...."

I looked at the bedside clock.

"...Honey, it's..."

"...I know. But if I don't get Chinese I think I'm going to die."

"You're kidding me."

She just smiled at me and nodded.

"Okay."

I struggled out of bed and into some clothes. And together we drove around London's streets until we actually found a Chinese restaurant that was open. The manager gave us a strange look, but willingly brought us the menu.

Actually we weren't the only customers. There was also a Chinese family silently enjoying their own meal.

Afterwards, when we got home, I managed to steal a couple of hours sleep before I went off to work.

My employment at TVAM was fun too. I could almost feel the creativity crackling in the air. Everything seemed to be new, and people would arrive in the morning raring to go with innovative ideas, and ready to cross frontiers.

After Jack was born we'd take him in the pram for long walks on Hampstead Heath or Primrose Hill with their glorious views over London.

The contract had only been for one year, and both of us had been sad to leave London, where we'd been young and in love. We swore we would go back some day. Well, I went back. Several times. Alone. But we never got back there together.

I spent a good hour at the party trying to avoid Lisa. Whenever I saw her and Ron moving in my direction I'd slip away to another part of the house or garden. So it caught me by surprise when I turned a corner and found myself face to face with my ex-wife. Not only that, but she was alone.

"Have you been avoiding me?"

"No…yes….kinda."

"Why?"

"You know."

She got huffy, "No, actually Max, I don't know."

"I just thought it would be easier…"

"…Don't you think that's a little childish?"

I just shrugged.

"Actually I was looking for you"

"Why?"

"To tell you Maggie's pregnant again."

"Who…?"

"Your daughter-in-law Maggie. Remember her? She's married to your eldest son. You always were a selfish bastard…."

"…Always…?"

"…Everything had to be about you. You and your job…"

"…Look," I said defensively, "I just wasn't sure who you meant. Anyway, thanks for letting me know."

She had a way of getting under my skin like no-one else. I could be perfectly calm one minute. And then she'd say something, and I'd become defensive and start to get mad. I decided that maybe it would be better if this was the end of the conversation. But Lisa hadn't finished.

"Max, how long since you've seen your grandson. Or even spoken with him on the phone?"

"I don't know Lisa. It's been a difficult few months for me you know. I just lost my wife…."

Lisa didn't like to hear me call Marie that, and she froze up even more.

"Well I think you should at least make the effort Max," she said in a brittle voice.

"Thanks for the advice. By the way, who's your boyfriend?"

"Ron is not...Ron and I are just..."

"...Just good friends?" I interjected, laughing.

"No. Actually, if you must know, we're more than that."

I was still smiling.

"Where did you meet him?"

"Jenny introduced us. Ron works at the same studio as her."

And after she said it she looked me square in the eyes, daring me. Just daring me to say something offensive. I was stunned for a moment.

"Your daughter introduced you to your lover?"

Acid now: "Yes. Is there something wrong with that?"

"Er...I guess not. It just sounds a little weird, that's all."

"Oh, and marrying someone the same age as your daughter isn't weird?"

"I won't feel guilty Lisa. Don't try and make me guilty."

"You abandoned me Max. Just turned round one day and said 'Hey I want a new life'. Never a thought about me. You *should* feel guilty."

I shrugged and there was silence between us for a moment.

"I'll call Jack," I said quietly, and began to turn away.

"Don't do it for me," she called after me.

I looked back and was about to say something but thought better of it. Instead I turned and walked away.

# Chapter Ten

I drove through Burbank searching for the street. I found the intersection and cruised along until I found the right number. Pulling up outside the production offices I looked around. This building was like all the other soulless structures around here, featuring large slabs of gray concrete. A sign outside read 'Roth Marker Productions'. The parking spaces for the offices were filled by other vehicles, so I left the car in the street and walked into the building.

The reception area was deserted and I wasn't sure what to do. I looked around, but could see no sign of life. But, just when I thought maybe I could call them on my cell phone, a young woman flung herself through a door. She seemed taken aback to see me standing there.

"Hello? Can I help you?"

She started flipping through some files, looking for something. Clearly, helping me was the last thing on her mind.

"Max Wheeler to see Stephanie Roth."

My name obviously meant nothing to her. Perhaps she'd never seen any of my work. Perhaps she was too young, or just didn't give a shit.

"She's in a meeting right now."

What was it with meetings. Whenever you call someone these days they're always 'in a meeting'. Around the world, at any one moment, there must be billions of meetings happening. Maybe, eventually, the whole world will just end up being one big meeting.

I checked my watch. Yep, this was the right time.

"I have an appointment. She asked me to come in at this time."

"Really? Because she's kind of busy."

She found whatever it was she'd been looking for and was about to leave.

"Yes, *really*. Perhaps you should check."

She was just about to protest, but thought better of it.

"Hold on," was all she said. And disappeared.

Moments later another woman appeared. This one was older, maybe late thirties. Attractive in a busy, all-business sort of way. She wore dark pants with a cream blouse, and her brown hair had blonde highlights in it. She marched towards me with her arm held out stiffly towards me. I couldn't tell whether the smile was real or not.

"Hello Max, I'm Stephanie Roth. Sorry to keep you. Come on through."

She ushered me back through the doorway. As we walked past the young woman I noted that she didn't look in the least embarrassed. Merely disinterested.

Stephanie hustled me along a corridor. At the end she pushed open a door that opened into an office which was massive, but seemed to be filled with two huge desks, several large flow charts, stacks of files, and various pieces of production paraphernalia. Behind one of the desks sat a man with a dour gray face that matched his hair and his suit perfectly. He was leaning over a desk, busily searching for something. He didn't look up when we walked in.

"Did she find....?" He started to say. Then he saw me.

"Oh."

"Max, this is my partner Adam Marker. Adam this is Max Wheeler."

"Yes, of course. I've seen you many times." He leaned over his desk and stuck out his hand to shake.

"Would you like something? Some coffee?" asked Stephanie.

"No thanks, I'm fine."

"Well, sit down. Sit down."

She really was a friend of Brad's.

"What have you been doing since you left the network?"

"Oh, considering my options."

Isn't that what you were supposed to say?

"And working on a book."

"Really? What about?"

"My experiences in the field."

"Yes, I'm sure there are many things you could write about. It would make a very interesting book. I'd love to see it when it's done. Now how much do you know about the pilot?" asked Adam.

So much for small talk. Obviously these people were *very* busy.

"Well, Stephanie did tell me a little on the phone, but maybe you'd just like to start from the top."

At this point Adam Marker actually sneaked a look at his watch.

"Okay...*You Show Me Yours* is an original concept that builds on a highly successful formula that we've established with several of our shows which draw on reality in terms of peoples' actual real lives and their various talents and blends that with an entertainment aspect so that the audience becomes enmeshed in the lives of others and while the subjects retain their mystique they also become the 'friends' of the folks sitting in their living rooms or wherever."

This mud-like explanation he delivered in one single tone, actually without drawing a breath, so that I found my thoughts drifting. I studied Adam and began to speculate on how old the guy was. I mused to myself, "He could be anything from thirty-five to sixty. But he's probably only about forty. Hmm"

Stephanie Roth, sensing my torpor, decided to take over from her partner.

"As I mentioned, the show is divided into two parts. In the first part one of the celebrities will take the other celebrity, and of course the audience, into their world. For example, let's say we have a racecar driver and, oh, a famous chef. The racer shows the chef how his team sets up the car, how he prepares for a race, what's involved, how he trains, etcetera – because it's more physically demanding than many people think. Then he introduces us to other people in that world, blah blah blah, and they round out the picture. Then the racer takes him around a circuit in car. And talks us through it. And *then*, dah dah! It's the *Moment of Truth*! The chef has to drive the car. And we see how well he does. D'you see?"

I thought that maybe I did see. But I couldn't be sure.

"And then," continued Adam, "In the second half the chef takes the racer to his restaurant and they go through the same procedure. And, of course, the racing driver then has to prepare a meal and so on and so forth."

There was a pause while they both drew breath. At this time I felt that maybe I was meant to say something. But the best that I could manage was, "And you've sold this to a network?"

"We've sold the *concept*," said Stephanie hurriedly, "to cable."

"Now we have to show them a pilot," continued Adam. "And that's where you come in. We're interested in you auditioning to host the show. To be our catalyst as it were."

They both looked at me expectantly. The word 'auditioning' didn't escape my notice.

Eventually I managed, "You know I've never done anything like this? I'm...."

She jumped in, "Yes, of course. We're familiar with your work. But we thought that maybe you might like the challenge of something different. And, as far as we're concerned, we believe that you have the personality to carry it off and make it exciting. And, I should say, bring just enough gravitas to the show."

"Thank you," I said.

"Tell me," asked Adam, "Do you have an agent?"

"Er, no. I've never really needed one."

"I see. And would you feel comfortable discussing money?"

"Oh sure. But first I need to think about the project. You say you want me to audition?"

"Yes," said Stephanie, "It's something we always do."

I was starting to get a strange, tiny feeling at the back of my neck. Somehow I was beginning to have difficulty imagining myself hosting any show, let alone this one.

"Tell you what," I said, "Let me think about it."

I stood up.

"Of course," said Stephanie. But she could already sense that I was about to turn them down.

"I'll give you a call at the end of the week." She said. "See what thoughts you might have had."

Adam shook my hand fleetingly and apparently had already moved on to something else as he began to study something on his desk. Stephanie showed me out.

In the reception area the young woman again ignored me completely as I walked through. I was going to say good bye, but then thought 'fuck it'. And left.

Driving back home I ruminated on the experience I'd just had. 'What a waste of my time', I thought. I was angry with these idiots for dragging me all the way over there to talk about something that I shouldn't have considered for a nanosecond. And I was mad at myself for making the trip. Why? Why had I come? It wasn't as though I was desperate for work. Or someone to talk to, for that matter! In fact Stephanie had given me the outline on the phone. I should have politely – or otherwise – simply said, "That's not what I do. I'm a serious journalist who reports from overseas on world events and also conducts interviews with world leaders."

That's not to say, of course, that I hadn't sometimes done lighter pieces. But, essentially, I'm a foreign correspondent. I'm definitely not some kind of game-show host, glorified or otherwise. Well, stuff Stephie! So, why on earth had I gone? Because Brad had recommended it? Surely not. And auditioning? Would I ever do that? Well, maybe, if it was for the right kind of job. But…I rubbed my chest gently.

The traffic ahead was backing up. I looked to see if it was one particular lane or all of them. Even though I wasn't in a hurry to get anywhere I still didn't relish the thought of yet another California traffic crawl. But all the lanes were grinding to a halt. I let the car decelerate and sighed deeply as I pulled up behind a huge trailer that had slipped into my lane. Great! Now I couldn't even see ahead and what was happening there.

To my right was a big black Hummer and to my left was a large SUV with the whole family hanging out its windows trying to look ahead. I began to feel a little hemmed in, in fact strangely claustrophobic. I paused in my thoughts when I had to brake suddenly as the guy in the Hummer pulled out of his lane and forced his way in front of me. 'What a prick!'

Our lane slowed, and the Hummer driver decided to push his way back into the lane he'd come from.

Now the next lane was starting to slow again, and I could sense the Hummer about to try and shove its way back in front of me again. Now I was starting to get pissed. What did this clown think he was doing! And why did he think he had the right to just shove in wherever he thought fit! I sped up and closed the gap, so that he couldn't squeeze in. However, in spite of that, he just kept coming. I was determined not to give way. And he was obviously determined to shove in. I guess he thought that, because he was bigger, he could just go where he wanted. But my blood was up, and I started to get angry.

He lowered his window and started waving at me.

"Hey asshole," he screamed. "Learn to fucking drive!"

What? *He* was the one who needed to learn to drive. I turned to look at him. He was a mean-looking fucker, with large tattoos on his arm and neck, and even extending to his head. My heart was beating fast, and I wasn't sure what to do. I could feel pure rage inside me, and I was also aware that not all the anger had to do with the current situation. It was like I had a backlog of anger that I needed to vent.

I wanted to scream back at him to go get fucked, but my sense of self-preservation suggested that I should keep my mouth shut. But I didn't want to give into him. So, instead, I just looked ahead and kept on driving, hugging the tail of the truck in front of me.

We drove like that for maybe a minute, although it seemed longer. My heart was still racing. And then suddenly the Hummer's lane shot forward and my lane slowed slightly. And he was gone. I kept watching out for him. But he must have kept slipping through the lanes ahead of me. It took a long time for my blood pressure to come back down and for my head to stop pounding.

Eventually I calmed down and relaxed. After all I had nowhere special to go. No urgent meeting. Nothing to do at all actually.

And that was another thing. What *was* I going to do with my life now? Since the book wasn't really coming along, perhaps I should consider writing press pieces. But what about? Maybe I could call that editor guy at the *LA Times*, what was his name? George something. He'd said if ever I wanted to write something he wanted to be first in line to see it. Okay then, I'd call George – if I could find his business card.

Then, of course, there was the other thing. I've always been a bit too lazy for 'real' journalism. I was happy to make notes for my camera pieces. But that's all they were, notes. Generally I did as much research as I could, then winged it. And, actually, the network had always liked my spontaneity. It had become my style. One that other correspondents had tried to emulate over the years. "And not always successfully", I thought ruefully.

I was also getting itchy feet. One thing that I liked about being a foreign correspondent was the foreign bit. I simply loved to travel. I thought about when I'd got my first overseas gig after England. Lisa and I were living in New York then. It was the mid seventies and Lisa was pregnant with Jenny. Times were tough, and we were finding it difficult to make ends meet. Having Jack at home meant Lisa couldn't get full-time work. And she'd had to leave her part-time job at the restaurant because the size of her belly was making it hard for her to get around. I was still trying to make a reputation as a journalist, writing for various magazines and newspapers.

I'd written some freelance pieces for the *New York Times*, and one day I got called into the foreign editor's office. Saigon had fallen to the North Vietnamese a few months before, and now other countries 'in that neck of the woods' were in danger of following suit.

Something was happening in Indonesia, he'd said. There'd been a military coup in Portugal, and the Portuguese, who'd controlled this island, East Timor near Indonesia, for five hundred years had simply packed up and left. Now Washington was saying that the communists were about to step in and take over. And the Indonesian government was claiming that it was going to be worse than the Cuban situation. Gerald Ford and Henry Kissinger were going to be in Jakarta for a summit meeting. Anyway, the usual journalist who would have covered this story was sick, so would I like to hop over there for a couple of weeks and find out what the hell was going on?

Would I!

Lisa didn't want me to go, but this was the chance of a lifetime. Besides the money was way too good to turn down. And I'd be back long before there was any chance of the baby being born. She was worried about me being in danger. And also worried that she'd end up a widowed mother of two.

Apart from England the only country I had visited was Mexico. And that was only to slip down to Tijuana for a couple of days when I was a student. So the idea of winging it across the world was thrilling. But the first reality that I came across took me aback: the eternity it seemed to take to get there. By the time I reached Sydney, Australia I felt like I'd been in the air for days. I'd wished that I'd had more time to spend in this strange downunder country. But it was a quick overnight stop, then a hop to Darwin, and I climbed aboard a small plane headed for the East Timorese capital Dili.

On board the plane was another journalist, an Australian called Roger, who was also going there to cover a story. He was delightful company and, naturally, we got talking. The focus of Roger's story intrigued me. Apparently five young journalists working for Australian television had also traveled there two months before. There was talk of Indonesian forces invading East Timor, and they wanted to cover the invasion. Risky at the best of times. They shacked up in a house in a village called Balibo, where the local guys – the Fretilin – were based. The journalists began to prepare for the thousands of members of the Indonesian military. But the invasion hadn't come.

"We're not sure exactly what happened next," said Roger. "But we do know that all five journos were killed."

I couldn't help my sharp intake of breath.

"Yeah, a real pisser," said Roger bitterly. I knew two of those guys, and they were good blokes.

"How'd they get killed?"

"That's the mystery. And that's why I'm going there to find out. The Indo government says they got shot in the crossfire between two rival East Timorese groups. I'm not so sure. 'Cause these guys had painted their house with signs to make sure everyone knew who they were and what they were doing there."

It took me a while to get used to the clingy, humid climate, but I was enchanted by the East Timorese. They were mostly very gentle people with their own special charm. Their Portuguese heritage had lent them dignity. But everyone I spoke to was nervous about the possibility of a coming war. No-one wanted that. But neither did they want to be controlled by Indonesia. I spent two weeks talking to as many people as I could and making notes. I even took some photographs on my borrowed camera.

There was talk of Indonesian troops infiltrating and massing on the border with Indonesian West Timor. Many of the people I spoke to were getting really worried. One day I awoke to a buzz in the air. The elected government of East Timor, fearing they were about to be invaded, had proclaimed the Democratic Republic of East Timor.

Occasionally I'd bump into Roger, who wasn't making much progress.

"I keep getting different stories," he said one night in a Dili bar. "Some blokes I talked to reckon that about a hundred Indo commandos came ashore and met up with a bunch of pro-Indonesian East Timorese. And these were the ones who killed them. One bloke even swore to me that there was some fighting, but Fretilin survivors ran away and the fighting had finished. But then the Indo forces just executed the journos. I'm still talking. How about you?"

"I had a couple of good interviews today with two members of the East Timor government. Both highly articulate men." I took a swig of my beer. "And I'm going to Jakarta in a few days to cover the summit meeting."

But the summit was a dull affair. I flashed my *New York Times* accreditation, but still couldn't get close to anyone. I was stuck with the press conferences and one brief meeting with a lowly American diplomat. Then President Ford smiled and waved good-bye as he and Henry Kissinger departed. And I flew out the same night.

The next morning the Indonesian navy bombed Dili, and thousands of Indonesian paratroopers and marines landed on the beaches of East Timor.

Later I found out that the next day Roger had been captured by the Indonesian forces and shot dead. His body had been thrown off a wharf and was never seen again.

When I got back to New York I pulled my notes together and filed my story. Sadly it was spiked and never used. In fact there had been only one mention of the invasion: a forty-second item by Walter Cronkite on the CBS Evening News. That was the last mention of East Timor on the ABC, NBC, or CBS evening news for the next decade and a half.

But I never forgot.

The traffic in my lane began to slow again, and I started fiddling with the radio. I found a channel that was okay. I looked over at the car next to me and saw a young woman talking animatedly on her cell phone.

The traffic had completely stopped now, and absent-mindedly I studied her face, which was really all I could see. It was a pretty face with a vibrant youthfulness that was quite captivating. I thought about how men like to look at women. Even when I'd been married to Lisa I'd looked at other women. And the more attractive they were the more I looked. I never thought there was anything wrong with it. It wasn't as though I was being unfaithful to my wife, not even in my mind.

The young woman laughed out loud at something. As she did, she half turned towards me, and must have seen me out of the corner of her eye looking at her. She turned fully towards me, still laughing. Something about this woman smiling as she looked at me made me want to smile too. When I smiled back at her she acknowledged me with her eyes but turned away again and carried on with her conversation.

My lane started to move then and I was glad. We made it a full thirty yards before we had to stop again. And, when we did, the next lane started to move, and I ended up right next to the woman's car again. I couldn't help myself. I turned to watch her again. She seemed to have finished her conversation now and was more aware of the road and the other vehicles around her. She saw me and flashed a small smile. I lowered my window.

"Can you see what it is?" I asked.

She rolled down her window, "Sorry?"

I pointed at the big truck in front of me and shouted, "I can't see the road ahead. Can you see what the holdup is?"

"Probably an accident," she called.

I was looking at her, trying to think of something else to say, when she pointed in front of me. I turned and saw that my lane had taken off again.

"See ya," I shouted, and drove off.

I looked out for her car next time I stopped, but didn't see her again.

When I eventually came to the accident it was a bad one. Cops were directing the traffic around a four-vehicle pileup which was surrounded by ambulances and recovery vehicles. I looked to see if the Hummer was there. Half hoping...? Hmm. But it wasn't there. I could see that a sedan was upside down, and what must have been the driver or a passenger was lying prone on the road. Paramedics were attending to the man and also to someone still stuck in the car. Police were talking to a truck driver leaning against his truck, which was blocking the lane. And yet more paramedics were attending to the occupants of the other two automobiles.

I could see all this because the traffic was crawling slowly past. In truth the traffic could probably have gone faster, but everyone wanted to look and see what had happened. Including me. Why do we do this? Why do we gawk when something horrible happens? What's the fascination? Perhaps we somehow want to see the worst that can befall us. We want to see the gore and the misery of our fellow human beings. Maybe their misery will be our salvation. Maybe their suffering will mean we won't have to go through this. Or perhaps we're just preparing in case the worst happens to us. And so we can practice the hurt and the pain and the total fucking disaster that it will wreak on our lives.

# Chapter Eleven

Mike Kenny was already standing at the bar when I arrived. I spotted the tall, imposing figure with the ruddy Boston Irish countenance right away. Mike waved anyway.

"What'll you have?"

"What are you drinking?"

The question was superfluous really. Mike was a beer man. And he drank a lot of it. He pointed to his glass.

"Yeah, I'll have one of those."

Mike found the barman's eye and made a signal for two more of the same. The sound of karaoke drifted in from the other room. It was still early, and the bar hadn't filled up yet. Someone in a half-decent voice was singing an old Paul Simon song, and I found myself almost humming along. A man I'd never seen before waved at me. I acknowledged him anyway, and peering into the other room I saw that it was a young guy in his twenties singing. "And so it goes," I thought, "Everything old is new again."

The beers came, Mike paid, and we carried them over to a table.

"Good to see you Max. How've you been?"

"Oh, okay, you know. It's been a few months now, and I guess I'm getting used to it all. Not so much *accepting* it. Yet. But sort of realizing that something's happened and I have to try and move on. Tough though."

"Yeah," said Mike nodding. He sipped his drink thoughtfully. "Plus, I guess, in a way you've had two losses."

I looked at him questioningly.

"First your marriage to Lisa, then Marie. Kind of a double whammy."

"I guess. Although I never thought of it that way. I suppose I was so busy feeling guilty about Lisa that I never really considered the marriage a loss to myself. Besides, I had Marie."

The words still tore me up, and Mike caught the rasp in my voice. We both pulled on our beers, neither quite knowing what to say. Then Mike thought of something.

"Well, a triple whammy really, if you count the job."

"Yeah."

"How'd that all turn out?"

"Okay in the end. I got paid out on my contract you know. Which was good, although I'd rather be still doing the job."

"Uh huh."

"And what about you? You left the network I hear."

"Yep...."

"....And...?"

"...And I'm working for a brand new company called InterVod."

I shook my head, "I haven't heard of them. What is it, cable?"

"Nope. It's an advanced form of podcasting."

I looked at him blankly, the term was vaguely familiar, but I didn't know the details.

"What casting?"

"Don't tell me you don't know about podcasting. M'boy it's *the* delivery platform of the twenty-first century."

I was still baffled.

Mike cleared his throat, all the better to declaim: "Podcasting is a method of distributing audio and video multimedia over the internet. You can download a bunch of files or they can be streamed directly to your computer, your BlackBerry, or even you cellphone. The kids started it all, of course, with music videos. But now just about anything and everything is being podcast."

"...And you...?"

"...We're doing it with news segments. We create bite-sized news segments for video broadcast. We call it vodcasting. And soon we're going to offer an add-on service doing more of the kind of stuff that you do...."

"...You're kidding me! Is there much demand for this kind of stuff...?"

"....Is there! Yahoo have been paying a journalist since last year to do it, and now he's getting a couple of million hits. It's fucking huge Max. Nobody has any time these days. People are stopping buying newspapers. And the newspapers don't really care. They all have their own websites, and with the new media they don't have to worry about printers. They can give more immediate news, which can be updated in seconds. And they can sell more advertising on the web. Plus it can be directly targeted. For example, you read an article about automobiles and there's an ad for new cars. And now they're building vodcasts directly into their sites. But we've got our own site. It's the way of the future kiddo."

And he drained his glass. I watched him with mock wonder. Well, the look I wanted to put on my face was *mock* wonder. But actually I was pretty impressed.

"Well, look who looks smug."

Mike gave me a Cheshire-cat smile.

"So how does it work?"

For an answer Mike held up his glass. I finished my own beer, stood up and walked to the bar. The song from the other room was one I hadn't heard before, but the girl who was singing it had a sweet voice. I gave the barman his order and while I waited I looked over at my old friend. Mike sat back in chair, looking relaxed. Actually he was looking more relaxed than I'd seen him look in years.

"So," I said, when I placed the drinks down on the table and sat down. "Give."

"It's essentially the same as you and I have been doing for years, but with fewer constraints. I still have a team of people like you doing stories. And they still tape them themselves and beam them back the way we've started to do the last few years. The only difference is they also do the full edit and send it back as a package. And I have a few young geeks in the office who upload the stories to the web, etcetera. I don't have the network pricks to worry about. And I don't have to worry about selling the stories either. We have a wide charter.

"And I don't have to concern myself with selling advertising. I can just sit on my tush and relax. Matter of fact I don't even need to be in the office. I can go fishing if I want and take my wireless laptop, and do business from there."

He took a pull on his new drink.

"Oh….," he said, wiping a little froth from his upper lip, "…and the other thing. We're doing fewer breaking news stories and more color stuff. So I have less stress all round."

"Does it pay?"

"Who? Me, the company I work for, or the people in the field?"

"The latter. Well, all really."

"Not the kind of money you've been earning. But it's not bad. And, yeah, we're about to break even in a couple of months, and after that I expect we'll be making big bucks.....Why," he said after a moment, "are you interested in joining us?" And he gave me a sly smile.

"Maybe. Depends."

"On what?"

"Could I choose my own stories?"

"Within reason, yeah. Got any ideas?"

"Some. Most of them overseas stuff of course."

"Of course. As it happens," he smiled again, "I'm looking for a good overseas guy right now. What d'you think?"

"Can I come and see your operation before I decide?"

"Sure. Drop by tomorrow. There's not much to see, but I'll show you all we've got."

***

"Choo want somesing else Mister Wheeler?"

Louisa had just laid on the coffee table in front of me a mug of coffee and a toasted muffin.

"No thanks Louisa. That's great. Thanks."

"Okay den, I finissed all the cleaning. I see you Friday. Good bye Mister Wheeler."

"Bye Louisa, thanks again."

"Choo welcome," she called out, as she picked up her bag and slipped out the door..

I sipped the coffee. I put down the mug and was reaching for the muffin when my eye fell on the urn in front of me.

"I gotta do something about this," I said out loud. "It's time to let you rest in peace. Over-time really."

I broke off some of the muffin and was just about to put it into my mouth. But, instead, I paused.

"What should I do Marie?" I asked. "Where would you like to be? This isn't your home. And I should do the best thing by you."

I bit down on the food thoughtfully. "Let's see, you were born in Morocco, but taking your ashes back there doesn't seem right. France has often been your home, but I'm not sure about that. Where in France? Paris? Maybe. I know you lived in Marseille for a few years, but I'm not certain whether that was home to you at all." For a moment I flashed on Baghdad, where we'd met, then I shuddered at the thought.

Hm, nowhere seemed obvious. I sipped some more coffee slowly as I thought about our brief time together. I had no doubt that she had given me a new lease on life. Or that being with her had wrought changes in me that I wouldn't have experienced if I'd carried on living my life in the same way. Changes that I liked. Changes that I was eager to continue.

What divine accident had brought her into my life? Or was it an accident? I'm not a huge fan of the concept of predetermination, but it was certainly possible that this was just my fate. My destiny. And, if so, what next? Was there some kind of lesson to be learned? Should I be doing something special with my life?

I sighed deeply and began to eat the rest of my lunch just as the phone rang. It was Jack.

"Hey dad."

"Jack!" I was genuinely pleased to hear from my oldest son. We didn't talk half as much as I'd like. But then that definitely wasn't Jack's fault.

"Just thought I'd call to see how you're doing."

"Thanks Jack. I'm doing okay."

I suddenly remembered what Lisa had told me about Maggie.

"Actually I was meaning to call you."

"Yeah?"

"Yeah, I ran into your mom at Mos and Libby's anniversary party. She told me Maggie's pregnant. Congratulations. When's the baby due?"

"Thanks dad. She's due in just over four months."

She? They already knew the baby's gender.

"Everything's okay, is it?"

"Sure dad...."

"....It's just you already know it's a girl..."

"....Well they did a routine ultrasound, and they asked Maggie if she wanted to know what sex the baby is and she said 'sure'. You know what she's like...very practical. Besides, this way we can make proper preparations. And, of course, Toby's thrilled. A little sister!"

I remembered when, each time Lisa had got pregnant, we'd held off from telling people for as long as possible. But that was just superstition. We didn't want to jinx the baby.

"Well, congratulations anyway. Any plans to come West?"

"No, not at the moment. Actually the doctor's asked Maggie not to fly right now. Nothing serious," he said hurriedly. Perhaps a little too hurriedly, "It's just a delicate time. You know."

Maybe everything wasn't as okay as Jack said. "Or maybe," I thought "they just don't want to fly out here.

"Well, as long as she's alright. So, what else has been happening?"

"Oh not much. As you know I got a huge bonus from the bank…"

Did I know? I couldn't remember knowing. But then, although I was proud of Jack for doing so well, I wasn't too sure about the field he was in. I could never shake the feeling that merchant bankers made their squillions off the backs of the Poor and the Downtrodden. Perhaps that was why my level of interest in my son's profession was somewhat limited.

"….So we're plowing the bonus into our primary asset: the house…."

"Christ, he actually talks to me like a banker," I thought.

"And we're doing major renovations. Besides we're going to need extra space with another child on the way. And what about you dad? What have you been up to?"

"Not too much. I finished all the legal stuff with the network, so now I'm a free agent."

"Any idea what you're going to do?"

"Not really. There are a few things in the air," I said loftily. Why didn't I share with my son what I was considering? Was I afraid of Jack's reaction?

"Oh, and I went to see Tommy play not so long ago," I said, changing the subject. "He was pretty good."

"Yeah, I downloaded his song. He's definitely got talent."

Silence. Both thinking what to say.

"You heard about Jenny, I guess?" Jack asked finally.

"No, what?"

"Her promotion. She's doing really well at the studio now I think she's going to be head of business affairs next year."

"Wow! No, I didn't hear. That's terrific. Thanks for letting me know. I'll call her."

"Yeah, she'd like that"

I wondered whether Jenny's promotion might have had something to do with Ron. Or was I being unfair to my daughter. After all she was definitely a talented girl. Strike that, a talented woman."

I checked my watch. Time to move. I had said I'd be at Mike's new office in an hour's time.

"Actually Jack, I have a meeting I have to go to…"

"….I'd better let you go then…"

"….Yeah. But thanks for calling, Jack. It was very considerate. I appreciate it."

"Not a problem dad. Good luck with your meeting."

"Thanks Jack. And give my love to Maggie. Tell her how happy I am to hear the news."

"Will do dad. Bye."

"Bye."


InterVod's offices were in Century City. I followed Mike's directions up to the swish new suite. Very spacious and modern, with lots of groovy design elements. The elevator opened into what felt more like an expensive nightclub, but better lit. A receptionist sitting behind a black marble desk looked up as the elevator doors opened. I walked towards her and was just about to ask for Mike when she smiled at me and said, "Welcome Mister Wheeler." *There* was a surprise.

"Hi. I'm here to see…."

"….Mike Kenny, yes." She looked down at her futuristic mini switchboard. "He'll be with you momentarily. He's just finishing up on a conference call. Can I get you something?"

"No, I'm good, thank you."

"Is it still windy out there?" she asked with a pleasant smile.

"Er, no, the wind's dropped," I said.

"Excuse me," she said, as the light blinked on her switch and took the call.

I sat down in one of the ultramodern armchairs and flicked through a trendy magazine

"Oh, I think Mister Kenny's finished his call."

She pushed a couple of buttons, "Mister Wheeler's here....Thank you."

To me: "He'll be right out."

"What a great receptionist," I thought. "A bit different to the last one."

"Thank you, er...?

"...Myra," she said, and beamed at him.

"Thank you Myra."

Mike appeared then, his voice booming out in front of him.

"Hey Max. How's the head?"

He shook my hand and led me away from reception.

"I'll live. But I can't take it like I used to."

"Yeah. Know what you mean. Come on, let me show you around. Such as it is."

We walked back the way Mike had come, through double glass doors. The area inside was lit by discreet lighting. As we walked past a long row of reasonable size cubicles I could see that none of the individuals seemed to over twenty-five. More like college kids. Most were male, although, here and there was the occasional girl. All were casually dressed, and all sat relaxed in their ergonomically designed chairs. And each sat in front of a computer with a large plasma screen. Most wore headphones or earbuds which seemed to be connected to MP3 players.

"These are the guys taking the individual items and uploading them to the various websites and other platforms," said Mike.

"They look pretty relaxed."

"Yeah well, in the main, there's no pressure. Just a steady flow of product. They do it at their own speed. But they're all extremely efficient, and I rarely have any complaints. They can take time out whenever they want, and actually take as long as they like – I'll show you the facilities in a minute – but, mostly, no-one ever abuses the privilege."

Sensing our presence, a young man wearing a back-to-front baseball cap swung around and waved at us, then returned to his computer.

"This is how it all works. You send your package down the line to us. It arrives on their screens. They have a list from me where it's going to and they send it. Simple, huh?"

He moved on and I followed him. Mike pushed open another glass door, and we found ourselves in a huge recreation space divided into different areas. There was a place with a few modern armchairs and a huge widescreen television and also various games like air hockey; a hang-out place to sit for coffee and other drinks, and I could see a small buffet with various plates of food.

By the large floor-to-ceiling windows, screened off by a bunch of plants, were a bunch of cushions. A young woman sat cross-legged on one of the cushions with her eyes shut, possibly meditating. And, behind a partition, was a small gymnasium, with some of the very same machines that I used. Two guys working the machines ignored us and focused on their stretches.

"Impressive huh?" asked Mike.

"Sure is."

"The company likes to look after the staff. They especially want them to stay healthy. If you look at the food and drinks over there which, by the way, is all free, you'll see that they encourage healthy eating too. Come on."

And we exited through another set of doors, along a corridor. This was flanked by another long row of cubicles. But these had sound baffles because, inside each cubicle, I could see that someone wore a telephone headset and all of them were talking animatedly into their sets.

"This is where the hard sell happens. All these people are selling advertising and making deals. We could use agencies or call centers. But the company prefers to keep it in-house. Better control. And this," he said, arriving at the door to a large office, "is where I spend most of my time. When I'm here, that is."

He walked towards a huge desk, pausing at a small recessed bar where there was tea, coffee and chilled soft drinks.

"You want some coffee? Or maybe something else?"

"Just some water would be good."

Mike opened the door to the chiller.

"Sure, sparkling or still?"

"Sparkling,"

He handed me the chilled bottle and motioned to a guest chair. He, in turn, was just about to dump his frame into a large chair behind his desk when a woman walked into the office.

"What a stunner" I thought. Obviously one of the perks of Mike's job was to have this gorgeous woman as his secretary. Or possibly his assistant. Maybe mid-thirties, she was tall and slim, with shoulder-length sleek black hair. Her face with its slightly oriental-shaped eyes was exquisite. And she carried herself with great dignity.

"Oh, hi Amy. This is Max Wheeler…."

"….Yes, of course….," she said.

"Max, this is Amy Apple….My boss."

She stepped right up close into my personal space and stuck out her hand. I took it and almost had to hang on to prevent myself from falling over backwards from surprise as much as anything. Surprise that this striking young woman was my wily old friend's boss. Mike smiled broadly at my astonishment.

"Amy is the CEO of InterVod"

She smiled at me sweetly. "Mike has told me all about you. Are you going to join us?"

Right in. No messing. Quite a girl.

"I'm…I'm not sure…."

"….Mike tells me you're writing a book."

"Yeah…."

"….About your experiences?"

"Yes, kind of…."

"I'd love to read it when it's published. I'm sure it'll be fascinating. How's it going?"

"Well…I've made quite a few notes, but…" I spread my hands.

She laughed, "Can't get into it, huh?"

"I thought it would be fun. Truth is it's harder than I expected it to be. It's not the writing. I never have problems with that. It's just…Some memories…."

"So, *are* you going to join us?"

I paused a moment, then grinned at her, "I guess so."

"Good." She said with twinkling eyes. "Welcome aboard. Mike will brief you. Then let's you and me have a talk."

And she turned and left me standing there with my mouth looking like a fish. Mike finally fell into his chair.

"Something else, isn't she?" he said.

# Chapter Twelve

"That was great."

Mos, Harry and I were at Al's place. Rita was working, and he'd wanted to try out some new recipes on us. Dishes from Chile: Empanada de Pino, a kind of turnover with meat and olives and egg, that had come out a little dry; and Cazuela de Vacuno, a soupy kind of dish also with meat and corn and rice and lots of vegetables, that had been more successful. Mos put down the cutlery on his food-free plate and wiped his mouth.

"So, are you breaking out the old bullet-proof vest?"

"Looks like I may be"

"You know," Mos said, "Kevlar? I always figured that was invented by a couple of guys called Kevin and Larry. I have this picture of them, standing in the back room, mixing all kinds of stuff."

He laughed, "You know, all kinds of strange smells. Their wives are always complaining. But these guys are amateur inventors, and they're always trying to come up with shit. Mostly it's just junk. But, this one day, they try something different and then they go outside for a drink and a smoke. And when they come back there's this hard, thin layer of stuff sitting in the bottom of their container. They pick it out and then they get a surprise, because it doesn't weigh as much as they think it should. Huh? What's this? 'There must be something we can do with this', they think. But no, nothing!

"So they give up and leave it in the back room. Middle of the night one of them has a nightmare: he's being chased by bad guys who are shooting at him. So, what does he do? Holds up this crap that he and his pal had made that day. And, guess what? The bullets bounce off it. That's terrific he thinks and wakes up. 'Wow!' he thinks to himself, 'I know what we can do with the stuff: We can build walls out of it!!'"

We'd all been following him on this long yarn, laughing as Mos added more and more color. At the end there was an explosion of mirth.

Then Harry joined in, "So Kevin calls up Larry the next day and tells him about his dream and what he thinks they can do with the stuff. But Larry, who's the smart one, says 'why don't we build suits out of it, like medieval suits of armor'."

More hilarity.

And Al finished it off, "But Kevin says 'no they'd be too bulky. But we could just make vests to protect the chest and the heart, because that's where most people get hit. So they both agree that they have a hit on their hands. And Larry says "What shall we call it. I know...Larkev!"

"But Kevin says, 'Nah, that doesn't sound right. We have to call in Kevlar. Has a better ring to it. And that's that."

And we all burst out laughing.

Then Harry says, "Actually it was Kwolek."

"What?"

"A woman called Stephanie Kwolek invented Kevlar."

"What?"

"You're kidding!"

"A woman invented Kevlar?"

"No way!"

"Yep, I'm afraid so. It just so happened that I recently had to find out...."

"....For a script...?"

"....Actually, no, for some research I was doing for a guy I know who's doing a documentary film. Turns out that apparently Stephanie was working with DuPont way back in the sixties...sixty-six I think..."

"....And she was dreaming that she was being shot at..."

"...Yeah, maybe. Anyway, she came up with Kevlar..."

"...Well..."

"...And you know they use it for all kinds of stuff, for brake linings...."

"...You're kidding..."

"...Sure. And boats, space vehicles..."

"...That makes sense..."

"...Building materials, er, parachutes..."

"...Parachutes?..."

"...Well she should go down in history..."

"…Yeah, well, she did. She invented dozens of things. She's even in the National Inventors Hall of Fame…."

"…Inventors have a Hall of Fame…?

"…Doesn't everybody! Don't pharmacists have a Hall of Fame…?"

"…If they did, Mos would be in it for sure."

Later, while Al was showing Harry something on his computer, Mos and I were sitting in front of a ball game that neither of us was really watching.

"So, how've you been? Really." asked Mos

"Not bad….Maybe getting ready to move on with my life. You know?"

"Uh, huh."

It had just come out without me thinking too much. Was it true? Was I ready to move on? One way and another this had been a hell of a year. Now, maybe, it was time to try living in the present. To see what life held for me. Could I do that? Could I put the last few months behind me and move on? Unconsciously I rubbed my chest gently. Mos noticed what I was doing.

"You okay there?"

"What?"

"Your chest." He pointed to where I was rubbing.

I looked down. "Oh, sure. Sometimes I just get a little sore here that's all. It's nothing."

"How long since you had your last checkup?"

"What checkup?"

"You know, for your heart."

I laughed it off, "It's nothing. I don't need a checkup. My heart's fine." I tried to change the subject. "And you? What've you been up to?"

Mos let out a deep sigh, "Yesterday I went to the funeral of an old school friend. He was my age and now he's dead. Wow! I mean, you start to think it could happen any day. And it's something I'm starting to think about a lot. Tell you the truth, I think I'm becoming terrified of dying. Every week now I hear someone I know has cancer or some other terrible thing. We used to go to weddings all the time. Then it was bar mitzvahs These days it's funerals. And now every time I get a headache it's a tumor. Every little thing in my chest is a heart attack. And every pain in my stomach is stomach cancer."

He leaned forward towards me. "But the thing is it feels real….My grandfather, God bless him, was like that. He was always worrying about every little ache and pain. They used to call him a hypochondriac, he always had some kraink or other."

"And how old was he when he died?" I asked, seeking to console him.

"Two years younger than I am now."

It was one of those 'boom-tish' moments. I wasn't sure whether to laugh or not. Mos saved me.

"So you see," he continued, "it runs in my family. What if I have my grandfather's genes as well as his mishugas?"

"Mos….you can't go on worrying like that. You'll….you'll…"

"…What? Kill myself? I know." And now he laughed, and I joined in. "And that's the craziest part of it. We were told a few years ago that fear and worry bring about cancer. I don't know if that's true. But I realized that I was afraid and worried about getting cancer." He shrugged. "So, what to do?"

"Have you talked to anyone about this? I mean a professional."

"Nah. I talk to Lib, but she just laughs at me. I tried talking to a physician acquaintance of mine once, but he just told me not to worry."

"What you need is a strategy."

"Ah hah! You're absolutely right. That's exactly what I need." He placed his forefinger beside his nose. "And it so happens that the last few days I've been developing one. Listen to this: I call it the Pseu-nami Theory. Like Tsunami, but it starts with pseu, you know like pseudo. It works like this. I think of all my feelings like waves, okay? And sometimes a big wave comes along, okay? But here's the thing: just because it's a big wave, it doesn't mean it's a tsunami. It could just be a big wave, a Pseu-nami – a pseudo tsunami. So I could look at aches and pains and lumps and bumps in the same way. See?"

I didn't see. But I encouraged him nevertheless. "It seems like a plan to me. Besides, you'll probably live forever."

"Well, not forever. But at least long enough to see my kids do well and my grandchildren grow up a little."

We both mused on this for a moment. Then Mos carried on. "How about you? Would you like to live forever?"

I pursed my lips for a moment, thinking about the question.

"No, of course not, not forever…But, like you, I'd like to be around for my family. Besides…"

Besides what? Besides what? What *did* I want to do with my life?

"…Besides, I just have the germ of a feeling that there're things out there….places for me to go. I don't mean geographical locations, but places within myself…experiences to be had…a kind of…oh, I don't know…. a kind of expansion….. I think…like you…that, yeah, life is short. That, who knows how much time I've got left. And that maybe there is something else I should be doing before I die."

I knew what I meant, but realized that I was babbling. Fortunately just then Al and Harry walked in.

"That sounds pretty deep," said Harry.

"Yeah," I said. "That's life for you."

A moment's silence, then Al spoke, "So, a few rubbers?"

"Sure, why not."

\*\*\*

"I'm glad you called me. This is nice."

I was sitting with Jenny in a restaurant garden in the Canyon. I'd almost had to beg her to come. "To celebrate her promotion" I'd said. "Not such a big thing," she'd replied. Then a big discussion whether it should be lunch or dinner, because she never had time for lunch, and worked late as well, usually grabbing something to take home and warm up. In the end I'd persuaded her to have Sunday lunch with me.

I'd picked her up and we'd driven together. It was a lovely day, and there hadn't been much traffic. She sat quietly beside me as I drove. Answering my questions, but not initiating any conversation.

Jenny had always been this way with me. A little shy, a little reticent. I stole a quick look at her, but she was looking straight ahead through the windscreen. A grown woman now, she still had a look of vulnerability about her, something that she's always had. I remembered her as a young girl, a happy-go-lucky little thing living in Jack's shadow. She'd adored Jack and would have done anything for him and always loved to be around him.

But there was one particularly horrendous day when Jenny was six and Jack would have been nine. Always an independent child, Jack had gone off doing his Huck Finn thing and Jenny had tagged along behind. Jack loved to climb trees and was as nimble as a cat. Jenny, on the other hand, was scared of heights, and had stood at the bottom of a tree watching her brother disappear into the heavens. He'd encouraged her to climb up as well, bur Jenny was too scared. For some reason Jack had egged her on and, reluctantly, she'd begun to climb upwards. She'd done pretty well, finding good footholds and pulling herself up to the branches until she'd reached about nine feet. Then she made the mistake of looking down. That was when she became really scared and started to panic. Jack had tried to calm her down and reached down a hand for her. She tried to grasp his out-stretched hand, but lost her footing, then slipped and completely fell out of the tree.

The first that Lisa and I knew about it was when Jack appeared, running towards us, white-faced and panicked. He was finally able to tell us what had happened and Lisa and I charged off to where Jenny lay unconscious on the ground.

Lisa hadn't wanted me to move Jenny, but I ignored her and scooped my daughter up in my arms and rushed with her to the car as quickly as I could manage without shaking her about. We drove to the local hospital with Jenny lying prone on Lisa's lap in the back. When we eventually made it to casualty we endured hours of painful uncertainty while we waited for the results of the tests. Eventually the doctor told us that Jenny had a hairline skull fracture and that she was severely concussed. She also had a minor fracture in her right arm and grazing on her face.

They kept her in hospital for ten days while they waited to see if there were more serious consequences, but thank God there didn't seem to be any. Although I visited the hospital every day and Lisa stayed with her as long as she could, Jenny was a changed child after that. She still trailed Jack around, but she spent more time alone, reading and playing with her dolls and toys.

Inside the restaurant as we waited to be seated I tried to engage my daughter in conversation.

"How've you been?"

"Pretty good." It wasn't sullen or resentful. She just seemed to have little to say.

"And this promotion? What will you be doing?"

"You know," she shrugged, "Same old, same old." Then she smiled at me. "I got a new car space. Closer to the door. So now I don't have to walk so far." And, magically, she smiled.

"Jack says you're going to be Head of Business Affairs before long."

"Oh, I don't know about that."

Our name was called, and we were led to a table. The next few minutes were spent studying the menu. But I knew that it didn't matter how long Jenny stared at the huge piece of cardboard she was going to order what she always ordered.

"I'll have a Caesar salad," she said.

"Are you sure? There're some nice things here."

"I'm sure."

"Well maybe I'll have the same. I'm trying to lose a few pounds." I picked up the wine list. "How about some wine? A little light white?"

She shook her head. "Just some sparkling water please."

Seeing us lower our menus the waitress came to take our order. "What can I get you folks today?"

"Two Caesar salads and a large bottle of Perrier please."

"Okay. I'll be right back."

"How about you daddy? What have you been up to since, er....?"

"Not very much. You heard about the network?"

"Yeah, that was rotten for you....So are you, like, looking for something else?"

"Well I wasn't, but then I got offered two things..."

"...Great!"

I laughed, "One of them wasn't. I think they wanted me to be a game show host or something."

"Really?"

"Yeah. But with the other I'd be working with Mike Kenny again."

"At another network?"

"Mm, no, not really. Have you heard of podcasting?"

"Sure, hasn't everybody? Why d'you ask?"

"Because that's what this new company does. Apparently I'll be doing pretty much what I've always done. But, instead of writing about it or sending it to a network to put on air, it's going to be sent to people's computers, cell phones, whatever."

"That's cool. Welcome to the twenty-first century. I wouldn't have thought you'd get into that."

I looked at her quizzically. "Why not? Are suggesting that I'm some old fuddy-duddy?" And I made a pretend screwed-up face.

"No, of course not…Well,.." And now she actually laughed. "You are a bit old-fashioned…."

"…Really…!"

"…Yes. But it's okay. Everyone expects someone of your age to be old-fashioned. It would be too weird otherwise."

I pretended to be hurt. "What d'ya mean 'someone of my age'? I'm not that old!"

The waitress appeared with the Perrier and poured it into our glasses. She set a basket of sliced French bread on the table and disappeared. I absent-mindedly took a piece of bread and broke it up, popping a small piece into my mouth and chewing it slowly, then I swallowed it.

"Tell me about Ron," I said.

Jenny just placed her palms on the table in front of her and stared at me.

"What?" I asked

"Is that why you asked me to lunch? So you could talk about Ron?"

Had I? Was that in the back of my mind? No, of course not. But I was curious about one thing.

"No it wasn't. I wanted to see you. We haven't seen each other, just the two of us, for a long time. I was just making conversation, and I thought he worked with you, maybe helped with your promotion…"

"…He did no such thing!" She shook her head and breathed out her nose in disgust. Then she spoke very slowly, "Ron had nothing to do with my promotion. I earned that all by myself. Shit!.."

I wasn't used to hearing Jenny say words like 'shit', and it jarred on me a little.

"The hours I put in on that job," she continued, "I totally deserve that promotion. That and more! I'm there sometimes eighteen hours a day. And often seven days a week…."

"…I'm sorry…," I started to say. But she cut me off.

"…Ron is actually a producer. He works in a totally different department and there's no way, even though he is a pretty important producer, there's no way he could…"

The waitress arrived with our salads. She set them down and looked at each of us.

"Would you like something else?"

"No, that'll be fine thanks," I said.

After the waitress left we both started nibbling at our salads in silence. Eventually I put down my fork and reached out a hand to her.

"I'm sorry baby. I really didn't mean to imply that you couldn't do it by yourself. I believe in you." I looked her in the eyes. "I totally believe in you."

She pulled her hand away from me and picked at a bit of salad.

"Let's just let it drop," she mumbled, into her food.

"Fine by me," I said to the top of her head.

It broke my heart to hurt her. I really hadn't meant to do that. I toyed with my own salad, wanting to change the subject and restore some feeling of goodwill between us. I tested several subjects in my mind and rejected them all as being too provocative, especially the question of Jenny's love life. In the end it was Jenny who found the right thing to say.

"So, did you hear about Tommy?"

"No, what?"

"He's been offered a record deal by a major record company."

"Really? That's great! I went to hear him play not so long ago. I thought he was terrific. I was very proud of him."

It was barely noticeable, the little wince that she gave. But I picked it up. Her left hand was resting on the table and I tried reaching for it again. This time she didn't remove her hand. And she also held my gaze when I looked into her eyes.

"You know honey. I really am proud of *you*…"

"…I know daddy…"

"…Actually I don't think you do know how proud I am. I've watched you flower into this amazing woman…"

"…Dad…!"

"…who has gone out into the world and really made something of herself. And I've seen you do this all by yourself without any help…."

"…Dad, please! You'll make me blush."

But I could see that she was pleased. And in the silence that followed, when I covered her hand with my own, she smiled at me. Somewhat wanly, it has to be said, but a smile nevertheless. But what she said next knocked me completely off center.

"So daddy, tell me what happened with mom. How come you stopped loving her? I mean you two always seemed so close. And you were together for more than half your lives. How could you do that to her?"

"Maybe that was just it. We *were* together a very long time. I think…I think we just kind of outgrew each other."

"Whatever happened to 'til death do us part'?"

"Honey…"

I could feel the frustration building up in me. The frustration of not being able to explain it to myself properly, let alone my daughter.

"…Sometimes I'm surprised that two people can actually live together at all….You know I didn't *do* anything to your mother. We were in it together…"

She started to protest, but I held up my hand.

"…It was a partnership between two adults, equal in every way….And, you know, you're wrong. I didn't stop loving your mom. I still love her, but in a different way…."

This was coming out all wrong.

"…Look, people change. Especially over a period as long as thirty-some years. And circumstances change too….I think one of the things that happened was that I was away so much and your mom just got used to doing without me. She created a life for herself where she didn't need me…Oh, of course, she needed me in some ways, but not really. Look how she's managed this last year…."

"…Dad, she was *devastated*."

I paused and exhaled deeply.

"Yeah, I know," I said finally.

"And Marie?" she asked tentatively.

I was about to shout at her or something to stop her in her tracks. The last thing I wanted right now was an attack on Marie and my relationship with her. But then I realized that Jenny wasn't attacking me. She genuinely wanted to know.

"Marie was just there. She…she might have been the trigger for the end of our marriage, but she wasn't the cause. We found each other when I was…ripe, I guess. Ripe for that moment and that person. It certainly wasn't her fault…"

"…I didn't mean…"

"…No, I know you didn't baby."

I looked deep into her eyes. I saw now how green her eyes were. Funny, I hadn't actually known that before. When did that happen? When we brought her home from the hospital her eyes had been clear blue. She'd been such a placid baby. It was part of the reason that Lisa and I had gone on to have two more children. Jenny just sat there and smiled at everyone. I thought about those many, many nights when I had gotten up to feed her, leaving Lisa to sleep as much as possible. I would carry Jenny downstairs carefully and rock her gently as the bottle warmed up. And then I'd take her into the living room and cradle her as I sat holding the bottle for her to suck on and she gazed at me with those wondrous blue eyes. Sometimes I would lean forwards with my nose pressed against her scalp, inhaling that heavenly aroma unlike any other. And, when she'd finished with the bottle, she would gurgle happily.

"I know our divorce was hard for you," I said. "And I know how tough it was for your mom. I'm not stupid. But I fell in love with someone else. With the way things had been at home for such a long time, didn't I deserve a chance at some real happiness?"

But the thought of that now-missed happiness saddened me. Marie and I had our brief golden moment, flying to the sun. But, Icarus-like, our moment had been all too brief. And now I was never going to be with her. I was alone.

Jenny must have seen the sadness in my eyes. And, this time it was she who covered my still-outstretched hand.

# Chapter Thirteen

The next day started simply enough. Mike gave me a full in-depth briefing on how to do the job. Truth be told it didn't take long, because most of it was already so familiar. Mike showed me how the production and planning were organized. I saw a breakdown of the various types of reports and mini-productions that the company undertook. My specialty, of course, was going to be overseas reports. Mike introduced me to Amelia, who was going to be my production manager and main point of contact. She was pleasant enough, but seemed to be overwhelmed with her task. She barely had time to sit down and talk before she was whisked away to solve yet another production problem.

In Mike's office we talked about the types of stories I was going to cover. Mike said that at first they just wanted color pieces. But he understood that they were going to sign a new client soon who would be wanting more hard-edged news stories. Possibly front line stuff. Was that okay?

"Sure", I said. That was exactly what I was looking for. What surprised me was how much product they wanted. It was definitely going to be a stretch, especially until I got up to speed.

Amy Apple arrived to take us to lunch to celebrate my joining the company. The three of us caught a cab to a new Italian place in Beverly Hills that I'd never heard of. Of course it was full, but Amy's assistant had made reservations, so we didn't have to wait too long. It was just the sort of place that I had grown to hate. There were shiny white tiles on the floor and all the walls reflected and accentuated the crashing of cutlery by the scurrying waitpersons and the scraping of chairs. Because it was so noisy the customers all had to shout at each other in order to be heard. And the more they shouted, the louder everyone else shouted. This was punctuated by occasional screams of laughter. And, scoring the whole production, was blaring Italian opera like some mad cacophony.

The result was that, however hard I tried, I could barely hear a word anyone spoke. I tried concentrating very hard. And even reading lips. But it was no good. So I just tried to let the whole thing wash over me and nodded my head occasionally to try and look as though I was participating.

There was San Pelegrino and Lambrusco to drink; grissini to nibble on; and fish, chicken and salad to eat. But afterwards I couldn't remember what I'd eaten. As soon as I'd put down my fork the memory of the food disappeared forever.

At one point Mike scraped his chair back and got up. I assumed he was going to the toilet until Mike shook my hand and disappeared out the front door. I tried asking Amy where Mike was going, but I couldn't hear her answer. She carried on talking over the coffee, and I carried on nodding my head. When the bill came she confidently took it and, without even looking, dropped her Platinum card on it. As we got up to leave she asked me a question. Again I smiled and nodded at her.

Her chauffer-driven car appeared and we climbed in the back. My ears were still ringing, but at least it was relatively quiet in the back of the car. I was mildly aware, as we passed the Farmers' Market, that instead of it heading back to the office, it was driving along Fairfax. Amy turned to me and gave me a warm smile just as the car pulled into a gated community, and pulled up at security.

"Where's this," I asked.

"My place, of course," said Amy as though it was really obvious. She noticed the look of puzzlement on my face.

"You're down with this?" she asked, somewhat bewilderingly.

"Er, yes."

What else could I say!

So......What? My boss had brought me here to screw me? Wow, that was a switcheroo. Was I 'down' with it? I wasn't at all sure. On the one hand Amy was a beautiful woman. An angelic, unlined face that could belong on a model. The body of a model too. But not one of those scrawny catwalk chicks. Amy was slim and lithe, but when she pressed against me I could feel her ample swollen breasts, and I became excited.

I reflected on how two beautiful young women had wanted to make love to me. Well, maybe 'make love' was a bit strong. But have sex with me. And I also reflected on how much older I was. I couldn't understand it. It wasn't as though I had a reputation as a great lover. To be honest, I always considered my skills to be fairly average on that score.

So, as I say, I was getting *very* excited. On the other hand I really wasn't looking for sexual adventure. I actually wanted to be faithful to Marie...well the memory of Marie anyway. I could still feel her spirit, and I was reluctant to let go of that. Then there was the other thing. My encounter with Angelina hadn't exactly covered me in glory. I thought about that night ruefully. Even though I'd been responding to her game…her attempt to maybe draw me into the tribe…I'd wished that it had turned out differently.

The décor inside her apartment was interesting and definitely not what I had expected. There was a slightly old-fashioned air to the place, with its heavily wooded window frames and doors. But the furnishings were the big surprise. The whole place was decorated in full-on Chinese style, with what looked like authentic antique Chinese lanterns, drapes, knick-knacks and a luscious Chinese carpet. I let out a low whistle.

"You like it?" she asked,

"Yeah, it's great."

I looked again at her smiling oriental eyes.

"You're Chinese?"

"My mother's Chinese. My father's Jewish. Hence my name."

"Apple?"

"It used to be Appel, but I changed it."

"It's in interesting combination."

"Actually the two cultures have a lot in common. More than you might imagine. Anyway, it's never been a problem for me."

She moved in close. I became aware of her light, but heady perfume. "But enough about me. Let me show you the rest of the place."

She took my hand and led me straight into the bedroom which was, if anything, even more exotic than the living room, with red satin and black lacquer, candles and small statues. She gently pulled off my jacket, then, placing her small purse on the night stand, she sat down on the bed and reached out for my belt, drawing me towards her. She gave me a mischievous look then started very slowly to unbuckle my belt. Immediately my body began to respond.

"Amy," I wanted to say, "Why me?" But instinctively I knew the answer. She was 'collecting' me. I was a trophy that she was adding to her collection. A new employee that she was going to 'have'. I was used to this predatory behavior in men, but I'd never come across it with women. Very slowly she unzipped my pants as she gazed up at me, a whimsical smile on her face. But I wasn't about to cede complete control to her. Instead I lay down beside her, drew her towards me and kissed her deeply. Her lips were sweet and succulent, and I became even more aroused.

I reached down and took hold of the edge of her top. She lay unmoving as I drew it upwards and over her head, exposing the soft, milky skin where her small, but beautifully shaped breasts heaved above her black, lacy brassiere. I could see her nipples harden and reached out for her. Instead she rolled over and deftly unzipped her tailored pants and pulled them off in one motion, revealing her brief black panties.

I barely had time to enjoy looking at her before she climbed on top of me and began to skillfully unbutton my shirt. I reached behind her with both hands and grasped a firm buttock in each, kneading them gently. Amy leant forwards and kissed my chest, allowing her kisses to go lower and lower until she reached my navel. Then she hopped off the bed, grasped the cuffs of my pants, and jerked them clean off. Her eyes widened slightly when she took in the expanding bulge in my shorts. Excitedly she ripped them off as well. I started to sit up but she softly pushed me back down. I was feeling vaguely uncomfortable, as though the roles were being reversed. Mostly in my life it had been me taking the lead.

I expected her to come to me then but, instead, she moved away towards where her MP3 player was docked beside the bed. She expertly selected some tracks and waited briefly until the music began to play, then she began to dance sensually to the rhythm. As she slowly writhed to the music her hips swayed and she raised her arms above her head so that her breasts jutted forwards. And, as she sashayed towards me, she held my gaze, the corners of her sensuous mouth turned upwards.

She'd reached the edge of the bed now and her arms went behind her back, unhooking her brassiere and allowing it to fall to the floor. Then, still holding my gaze, she put the tips of both forefingers into the sides of her panties and very slowly drew them downwards over her hips until they fell in a little pile on the floor. She kicked them away with a little flick.

Now she was swaying backwards and forwards and, as she did so, she began to lean over me until her breasts were hanging right in front of my face, almost brushing my lips.

I was beginning to enjoy the performance, and I smiled at her as she looked down at me, first at my face, then along my body until she came to my now fully-erect penis. She knelt down beside the bed and put her hand on it, then kissed it gently. From somewhere she produced a condom, which she rolled onto me. It was all that I could do not to explode then and there.

Amy stood up again and cocked her head to one side, as if to say "what shall we do now?". Then, as though she was mounting a horse, she swung a leg over until she was kneeling astride me. She reached down and found my stiff cock, and it seemed as though a look of pure pleasure filled her face.

I stretched out a hand to cup a breast with one hand and squeeze it gently, rubbing the nipple a little with the edge of my thumb. Still holding my penis she closed her eyes and began to thrust her chest forwards, until her breasts were pushing into my face. I took the other nipple between my lips and ran my tongue around it, then drew it in and flicked it with my tongue. She sank down and placed me inside her, and began very slowly to rise and fall, gently riding me.

I became aware of what seemed at first like a slight change in the music. Then I realized that it was a cell phone chirruping. Without losing her rhythm, Amy leaned over and picked up her purse, pulling out her cell.

"Hello," she said softly. She still had her eyes closed.

I couldn't hear whoever was on the other end of the phone, and I didn't really want to. I was surprised that Amy had taken the call. But I was even more surprised that she could carry on talking calmly as she was fucking me, with barely a change in her voice as she sped up the pace, sliding up and down me as smoothly as a machine.

For a moment I wondered who was on the other end of the phone and what they thought. But I didn't linger on this thought for very long because I was focusing as hard as could on not exploding into her. My chest was tight, and I could now feel a throbbing there.

Amy paused for a moment and I opened my eyes to see why. Her eyes were shut, but she was obviously thinking about something. Then she returned to riding me. Faster and faster now until I couldn't hold on any longer. And, at that moment, she arched her back and held both arms high in the air. Which also meant that the phone was as far from her mouth as possible when she let out a long low moan.

Not knowing who was on the other end of the phone, I restrained his own vocal stylings, and simply allowed myself the pleasure of releasing the pent up energy and blasted off, releasing the pressure in my chest at the same time.

Amy still had her eyes shut. But she slowly brought her arms back down, putting the phone back to her ear, listening to what the caller was saying.

I tried to imagine whether the caller had any idea what had been happening while they were talking. Probably not. But I had certainly found the experience stimulating.

Amy slid off me and rolled over, lying on her stomach beside me. I slipped off the condom and tied a knot in the end.

"Tell him that it's impossible….Well, get him to call me….okay....?" she said.

I noticed for the first time that Amy had an exotic tattoo at the base of her spine that stretched right across the small of her back. I reached out and idly traced the pattern.

"Alright, I'll talk to you later…Yeah, okay….Bye." And she flipped the cell shut, then turned to me.

"Hey lover. Okay?"

I decided to play it casual, "Sure," I said. But then I couldn't resist: "How are you able to do that?"

"What?....Oh, that," she laughed. "I'm a woman. Women are good at multi-tasking. Didn't you know? Besides," she smirked, "I'm also a Gemini. Which basically means I can multi-multi-task."

She picked up her watch from the night stand and checked the time. Then she gave me a lecherous look.

"How about another go-around?" she asked.

I wasn't sure I was ready for it, and I paused just long enough to let her know that I had some doubt.

"Wait a minute," she said with a twinkle in her eye. And she hopped off the bed and I watched her pert rump disappear into the en suite, and return moments later with a damp wash-cloth. She very carefully washed my penis and my balls. It was almost a loving action. Then she flung the wash-cloth on the floor and replaced it with her mouth. I was amazed that I could feel myself begin to stiffen again. Any other time I would have had to wait for an hour or so for this to happen.

"You….must…be….able….to perform……magic." I managed to say.

She stopped for a moment. "Oh, I can," she smiled up at me and opened her hand to reveal a new condom.

***

The next day I had already parked my car and was walking towards Mike's office when I became slowly aware that I was no longer feeling Marie's energy as strongly. It had been with me all this time. And now it was as if she was gradually fading away. I stopped and closed my eyes. No, she wasn't gone completely. But her being there was definitely fainter than before. And this really saddened me.

"Well, it looks like you passed the final examination," Mike had said, smirking to himself.

"You know? Did she *tell* you?"

"She didn't have to. It's what happens. Consider it a form of hazing."

"Best damn hazing I ever had!" I laughed. I thought for a moment. Then, "Did you...?"

"If you think I'm going to answer that question you're insane. I've got a wife and family."

But Mike was smiling all the same. And I was pretty sure I knew the answer.

"Anyway," said Mike, "to other matters. I've got your first gig. Wanna know where you're going?"

"Sure."

Mike held up an airline ticket wallet and gave a cheesy grin like a game-show host, "You're going to South-East Asia!" he announced like a game show host.

"Really? Great."

"Yeah, we have a bunch of stories we want you to do in Malaysia, Thailand and Cambodia. First port of call is a color story on the Iban people. You know, headhunters! They're at a real tipping point in their culture where they're losing all the old stuff..."

"...That's a relief..."

"...Not just the headhunting, but everything else as well."

He handed me a manila folder,

"Here are the basic facts. However, I'm sure you can dig up plenty more. And while you're there I want you to do a couple more stories. One of them is another color piece."

He handed me another folder.

"And this one's about the deforestation of the jungle. That's a more serious piece and I'm sure you'll do it justice. Then it's on to Thailand for a piece on female kick-boxers."

Another folder.

"And another on a rapping monk. Nice guy, by all accounts. Then to Cambodia. This is a story we can use widely. It's about glue-sniffing…."

"…They do that in Cambodia…?"

"…You'd be surprised! Especially the kids. It's getting to be a big problem. And two more stories. One on Angkor Wat, and another on Cambodian American criminals that have been deported back there."

As he spoke he handed over more folders.

"The details are all here as well."

"That's a bunch of stories."

"Sure is, but that's the way we work here. Is that going to be okay?"

I just shrugged 'okay'.

"Course we might think of something while you're over there. Or something might break."

Then Mike bent down, picked up a case and placed it on his desk.

"And this is your gear."

He flipped the lid on the case and opened it up. Inside were a number of items: A video camera no bigger than seven inches long; a laptop computer; a satellite phone; various microphones and a few other bits and pieces.

"This is it?" I exclaimed. "The camera looks like a toy!"

"I know, your dick is bigger! Well that, my friend, is the very latest in HD digital three-chip broadcast quality videography. You'll find the picture is extraordinary."

Mike plucked the camera out of the case, switched it on, flipped open the LCD monitor and handed it to me. Then he sat down at his desk.

"Do you remember when you not only traveled with a crew, but sometimes we had to pay excess baggage on your flights for even the simplest gigs…?"

He waved a hand over the case.

"Well, this is all you need now. That one small case. You can shoot it all on that camera. And that laptop has a sophisticated edit suite loaded onto it, and it connects to the sat-phone so you can immediately send it back to me...."

Mike held up a hand, "I know what you're going to say: You're no editor. Well, we'll give you a crash course over the next couple of days. By the time you leave in three days time you'll be totally on top of it."

I looked through the camera's monitor.

"So?" said Mike, "you gonna be okay with this?"

"Absolutely. Wow! Just when I thought it was all over for me too. I think I'm looking forward to it."

Mike scribbled an address on a piece of paper and handed it to me.

"Here. If you go and see this guy Prakash Veraswami tomorrow, he'll show you how the edit suite works and how to get the best out of it. Come and see me again before you go and we'll have drink and I can answer any questions that might come up."

"Okay."

***

Over the next couple of days Prakash taught me the finer points of editing, from the technicalities of the computer software to the creative aspects of overlay or B roll material to transitioning and the use of music and various effects. It was an intense course in the dark art of edit suite. Then Prakash watched as I cut together two five-minute stories from raw footage. Finally he deemed me ready to go out on my own.

I actually enjoyed the experience. I love learning new skills. And this one was going to turn me into a version of the consummate mini-documentary filmmaker.

There were many subtle aspects which I'd never considered. And, best of all, it also taught me indirectly what to film and what to not waste my time on.

After two days I was raring to go. At the end of the second day I met up with Mike in a bar,

"How'd it go?"

"Pretty good. Your pal Prakash is a decent guy."

"Isn't he though. So, are you all set?"

"Yep....You know Mike I'm looking forward to doing this. I want to thank you for it. It's the first thing I've looked forward to in quite a while."

"Hey, don't thank me. We needed someone and I thought you'd do a swell job...."

"....Bullshit...!"

"....Actually not. I could have got some kid out of film school who would have eaten it up. But I know I can trust you to do a totally professional job. And that's important to me."

He sipped his beer.

"You will have noticed however," he continued, "that this is very much a no-frills employment. You'll be traveling coach and staying in two star joints."

I sighed. "Yeah, I did notice that. It's not really what I need at my age. But I'll put up with it. For a while."

# Chapter Fourteen

The steady hum from the aircraft's motors was at once soporific and, at the same time, vaguely disturbing, not really allowing me to sleep properly. But that wasn't the only thing which prevented me from falling into the arms of Morpheus. Squeezing my six-foot frame into the seat had been just about okay, even though my knees pressed in hard into the seat in front. But I never have been able to sleep sitting up, and the airplane seat only tipped back so far. Since sleeping pills don't really work for me, I'd tried drinking alcohol. This had allowed me to nod off for what was probably a little over an hour. But then someone walked by my aisle seat and nudged me into semi-consciousness. And the light from the guy playing solitaire on his laptop in the seat next to me kept me awake. I tried the mask provided by the airline, but found that too irritating. Then I began to wriggle. And the more I wriggled the less sleepy I became. In the end I gave up. I started fiddling with the remote for the movies, but couldn't find any movies that I wanted to watch.

So I just sat there in a state that was halfway between sleeping and wakefulness. Which, in a way, was similar to feeling halfway between living and dying. And, in this state, for some reason I began to believe that I was on my way to see Marie. And I could see her in the distance holding her arms out wide, welcoming me.

I ran towards her, a broad smile on my face. She tilted her head to one side, somewhat coyly....somewhat shy. But she held out her arms to me nevertheless. And I felt as grateful as I'd ever been for anything in my whole life. I didn't so much take her in my arms as engulf her. I wrapped my arms around her, and she was me and I was her. I closed my eyes and, for quite some time, I held her and just breathed gently in and out, my cheek pressed into her hair. It almost felt as though our hearts were pressed together.

"What a relief! I thought I'd never see you again." I said.

"My love, my love. I've missed you so much." She replied.

I pulled away from her a little. Just enough to see the tears begin to trickle down her face. I raised up a hand and with a finger wiped away a tear. When I put the finger to my own lips I could taste the saltiness there. She smiled a brave smile.

"It's too late, you know." She said valiantly.

I had no idea what she was talking about.

"What d'you mean?"

Marie caressed the side of my face with her fingers. And this time, when she smiled at me, it was with a mixture of tenderness and regret and joy and sadness and....love.

"Too late for us." She said finally. "I'll always be there. But you have to travel your own road now. And I have to...."

A light shone into my eyes. A bright light. And something about the light stopped me from hearing what she was saying, and stopped me from seeing her. A flood of redness replaced the light and I became aware of other sounds around me. Sounds of voices and movement.

When I opened my eyes I took in the rising bustle of passengers straightening themselves, pointlessly trying to calm their hair and standing up, stretching and reaching for the overhead lockers.

The seat-belt sign chimed on and flight attendants arrived to fold up trays and seat backs. And I knew that was the last time I would ever see Marie. And the last time I would feel her presence around me. And a shroud of sadness fell around me, which caused me to sit unmoving and dazed amongst the flurry of activity.

As the plane touched down at Kuala Lumpur airport many of the passengers craned their necks to peer out of the windows. But I just sat there, gazing straight ahead of me. And even when the plane came to a stop, and all the passengers rushed to win the race of who could be first to get their baggage and pass through customs, I continued to sit in my seat, frustrating and annoying the people beside me. I was reluctant to lose the final fragment of my connection with Marie

But, in the end, I was forced to capitulate, and I too rose and, zombie-like, reached for my carry-on from the locker and shuffled down the aisle.

Somehow or other I found my way to the Airside Transit Hotel inside the airport, where I could crash until it was time to catch the plane for the next leg of his journey.

When I awoke I was surprised that I'd actually fallen asleep at all. I guessed that it had been a combination of emotional fatigue and physical exhaustion. I was used to waking up in strange beds, but this small room was no more strange than many where I'd spent a night. I checked my watch and pulled and prodded myself out of bed and into the shower. Mechanically I checked out of the hotel and grabbed some coffee before heading for the departure gate for my flight to Kuching in Sarawak.

During the short hop there I began to realize that I was back in the saddle, and I started looking forward to the job in hand. I pulled out the notes that Mike had given me. "Holiday Inn." Well, that wasn't too bad. At least in this part of the world I could stay in a semi-decent place without breaking the bank.

A name and a phone number were written underneath the hotel's address. Abdul Hashim was going to be my minder. I hoped that he knew his stuff. Over the years I've worked with the full range of minders from the almost criminally useless to those without whom life would literally be impossible. Once in Iraq I even had a man who was prepared to risk his own life in order to save mine.

But I needn't have worried. Because Abdul was actually waiting for me when the plane arrived, and he smoothly steered me out through the clammy air to a waiting car, where the driver Tariq was dusting an already immaculate Mercedes.

"I have arranged a boat to take us up the river." said the portly, mustachioed Abdul. "We can go in the morning, if that is alright with you,"

"That's fine. It'll give me a chance to get my bearings and do a little research before we go. Any chance of talking with any timber people?"

There was a long pause before Abdul answered.

"I don't think that will be possible." Was all he said.

I was going to protest, but one look at Abdul's face and I knew that the subject was closed. "Hmm. So it's going to be like that," I thought. Had Abdul been bought off? Or was he too lazy? Or, more likely, he was just afraid of the power that was wielded by those tearing down the rainforests and selling them for woodchips.

And so my research consisted mostly of seeing the tourist sights and checking out the history of the area in the museum of the White Rajah, learning about how the British used to control Borneo, the third largest island in the world. I'd also brought with me some literature about the Iban people, the local inhabitants. People who live in the jungle on the river, cultivating rice and pepper. These were people who only sixty years before used to be headhunters, taking the heads of their enemies in battle. I'd read that, apparently, a taken head was believed to bring strength, good luck and prosperity to the community. So much so that it was common for brides' fathers to demand human heads as dowry from the bride-grooms. "And tomorrow," I thought, "I'm going to sleep in one of their longhous-es. "Old habits die hard, but that better be one they've gotten over."

When it came time to leave early next morning Abdul insisted on carrying my camera case and my overnight bag out to the waiting car.

It was a gray day with a heavy, overcast sky. But the highway was straight and smooth, and Tariq was the consummate driver, making the drive a pleasant one. On either side of the highway the fields stretched away into the distance.

At first Abdul tried to engage me in conversation, but I wasn't really interested in chatting. After a while he gave up, leaving me to enter a state of suspended rumination. In fact I was surprised when just over two hours had gone by and we stopped for an early lunch at a little roadside café.

I asked Abdul to order for me and went looking for a john. It was only when I was in the middle of relieving myself that I thought about the fact that all my gear was in the car. "Trust is a wonderful thing." I thought. When I returned every eye in the café was on me. I wondered what Abdul had told them about me.

The food was simple but tasty, although the portions were small. But I wasn't really hungry anyway, so that was fine by me.


About a half hour after we left the café we turned off the highway onto a road that became progressively narrower and more winding. The Merc slowed so as not to bump its underside on the now rutted and potholed road.

Eventually, after we turned yet another bend, splashed through a small ford, turned another corner, there was the river. Tariq pulled over and turned off the motor, and we all climbed out.

I looked around. There was a small landing stage poking out into the river alongside a slipway. Beside it sat a small wooden general store that was stuffed with all kinds of goods. As I walked about, stretching my body Abdul disappeared inside the store, returning a moment later with three plastic quart bottles of water. He handed one each to Tariq and me, then looked at his watch.

"He should be here soon."

"Our guide?"

"Yes, our guide. You want to wait in the car?"

"No, I need to move my body. It gets a bit stiff these days."

"Yes, mine too." Abdul looked up to the sky. "It might rain."

"That's all right. How long will it take to get up the river?"

Abdul shrugged, "Perhaps one hour. I have never been to this longhouse."

We heard gentle splashing and a craft appeared like I'd never seen before. It was long, maybe thirty feet long, but only about three feet wide, and pointed at both ends. And it sat very low in the water. A young man stood at the front of the longboat holding a substantial pole which he used to push any flotsam out of the way as another, older, man at the rear guided the boat to the landing stage and cut off the outboard motor. The young man hopped off and tied the boat up.

The man with the pole had a big grin on his face.

"I think this is him," said Abdul, and went over to talk with the man. They shook hands and spoke a few words that I couldn't understand. Then Abdul returned.

"Yes it is him. He wants to buy some things at the store. Five minutes, he says. Okay?"

"Sure," I said.

Abdul spoke a few words to Tariq in Malay, and Tariq opened the Merc's trunk and hoisted out my bags, smiled at me and stuck out his hand.

"He is going now. He will come back tomorrow to collect us," said Abdul.

I shook Tariq's hand, feeling the roughness of it. Then Tariq shut the trunk and climbed back into the car. Abdul picked up my bags, called out something to Tariq who was slowly driving off, and started walking towards the landing stage.

"We can wait in the boat if you like."

The boat rocked gently as I gingerly climbed aboard. There were no seats in the boat, just occasional struts to perch on. The old man indicated to me to sit in the middle of the longboat and Abdul handed me my bags, which I set down in front of me, and immediately opened my camera case and took out the video camera. Time to start work.

The journey up the river was peaceful. The only sound was the purr of the outboard as it propelled us along. Nobody spoke. The young man at the front pushed away any logs that appeared, and the old man maintained a constant speed. Occasionally we would pass another boat and everyone would wave lazily. And, sometimes, we would pass people on the bank or children playing in the water. Now and then a longhouse sitting beside a landing stage might appear. I filmed it all, but otherwise I sat quietly, for the first time in a long time at peace with myself.

After about an hour and a half we encountered more forks in the river and it began to narrow. At the same time the sky darkened and a few spots of rain began to fall. I looked up, wondering whether I needed to put the camera away. The others looked up too, but still nobody spoke.

Now the trees that lined the river banks seemed to close in on us, and sometimes we even had to duck our heads to avoid the branches that stuck out and threatened to take out an eye or assault our bodies.

The boat was going slower and slower now as navigation became more difficult. I was just putting away the camera to protect it from what had now become heavy rain, when I realized that we were pulling up at a slipway. The old man spoke a few words to Abdul, who shrugged but said nothing in return as the young man jumped onto the bank and began to haul on a rope to pull the boat part way up the slipway. Then he tied the rope to a tree. The old man threw him another rope and he made that fast as well.

"He says the river is too shallow from here. The water has gone" Abdul said to me. "We will have to walk the rest of the way."

He climbed out carefully and I handed him my bags before stepping out myself.

"I'll carry these." I said.

"I have nothing to carry. I can take one." said Abdul.

"Okay. Thanks." I handed him my overnight bag.

The mud on the slipway nearly brought me unstuck, but I just managed to keep my balance. Both the Iban men laughed when they saw me struggling to stay upright. And, when I recovered, I saw their faces and I couldn't help grinning back at them.

We all set off up the grassy hill away from the river, and I expected that the longhouse might be at the top of the slope. But, when we got there, I could see no sign of habitation, and we just carried on walking. The old man seemed remarkably spry for his age.

After a while the trees thinned out a little and the four of us fell into a pattern, the two Iban striding out ahead, followed by me, and Abdul lagging along behind, obviously not used to any form of exercise. As we walked, the pattern became more exaggerated. Then I lost sight of the two men in front, and had to guess which path they had taken.

When the path unexpectedly split, one way going upwards and to the left, the other upwards and to the right, I wasn't sure which path to take. I stopped still in my tracks. Both of the men in front of me had completely disappeared. I looked behind me. There was no sign of Abdul either. I listened, but could hear nothing. Perhaps I'd already taken the wrong path.

Then it hit me. I was in the middle of the jungle in Borneo and I was lost. I had no idea what I should do. I'd never felt more alone in my life. Then I started to panic slightly, my heart beating rapidly. I looked around wildly and was thinking about the viability of retracing my steps, when Abdul appeared. I could have kissed him. Almost.

Simultaneously the younger Iban man called to us from above.

"Is all okay?" wheezed Abdul.

"Yeah," I grinned. "You?"

"I think."

And we carried on walking upwards, following the trail. The rain was coming down harder now, and I wasn't sure how waterproof the camera case was. "I guess I'll find out." I thought.

Then we were near the top of the incline, and either the rain was easing off or the jungle canopy was protecting us better. At the very top we all paused to catch our breath.

"You're sure you don't want me to carry my bag?" I asked Abdul.

"No, I will be okay."

A few words from the older man and Abdul grunted at him. Then we were off again.

We walked for an hour. There was very little light now, and I had no idea where we were going. Sometimes we were walking upwards, sometimes down. And, as far as I knew, we could have been walking around in circles. The rain started pelting down again and water plastered my hair to my face and soaked my clothes. My breathing was becoming labored but, when I opened my mouth to breathe properly it filled with rainwater. I thought I was going to completely dissolve.

Eventually we came to a stream. "What now?" I thought. But the young man simply waded into it, and we all followed. I was glad that at least I was wearing boots, because God knew what I was stepping on. I also wondered what else was in the stream. Leeches? I'd experienced leeches before, and it wasn't nice.

I missed my step a couple of times, and almost fell into the water. I'd brought a lightweight jacket, which I'd put on in the boat. But that was soaked through now, as were all my clothes underneath. And now water was sloshing around inside my boots. I'd been in torrential rain before, but I'd never gone cross-country trekking in it. I began to feel as though I was actually becoming water as it poured down on my head, streamed down my face and saturated my body.

Then we were clear of the stream and wending our way down a narrow path. As we brushed against bushes and branches that jutted outwards, even more water would be deposited on us. If that was possible.

And, just as I was beginning to believe that I'd died and gone to some watery hell, at long last I saw some lights ahead sparkling through the trees. Was this our destination? I prayed that it was. Literally prayed. I even muttered the words out loud to myself. And, yes, after walking for another few minutes I looked upwards and saw that we were at the foot of a huge wooden structure. The two Iban began to climb up long flights of wooden steps and Abdul and I followed them. Me feeling more than bedraggled.

Eventually we reached the top and quite suddenly we appeared at the end of a long wooden balcony. And, blessed joy of joys, there was a roof over our heads.

There were several people on the balcony, sitting on mats and, as one, they all turned to see the new arrivals. But I stood, frozen to the spot. Eventually I put down the case and began slowly to try and peel off my sodden jacket. All the while water continued to drip off my head.

The younger Iban man had immediately disappeared when we'd arrived, but now he reappeared. He had taken off his wet clothes and put on a sarong. Now he held out a thin towel each to Abdul and me. He spoke some words to the disconsolate Abdul, who nodded then turned to me.

"He has some dry clothes." He said it like 'clothies'. "He says we can change over there." And he pointed to a small room off the balcony. "You can go."

I saw Abdul's unhappy face. "Why don't you go first." I said.

"Oh no…"

"…Sure. I'll be fine. Go."

So Abdul did. And when he returned, drier now, I could see that his spirits were better, even though his dry clothes were too small and ill-fitting. I picked up my overnight bag and went to the change room. Inside I found that it was actually a bedroom with two small single beds. I unzipped the bag and looked inside. The few things I'd brought had not in fact gotten rained on, but they were damp. So I stripped off my soaked clothes and toweled myself thoroughly. Then I put on the clothes that I had been lent. Iban men were obviously a lot smaller than my six-foot frame and the bottoms of my legs stuck out like those of a circus clown. But I didn't mind, it was such a relief to be dry.

As I walked back I could see why they called them longhouses. Because that was precisely what it was: a long house, like a wooden cabin, maybe a hundred feet long. The balcony, which was perhaps twenty feet wide, ran the whole length of the house. And off it were a series of doors, presumably leading to rooms just like the one I'd come out of. There were many more people on the balcony now. All staring at me. And there were some curious children peeking out through some of the doorways as well.

Abdul beckoned me over to where he was sitting amidst a small group. He briefly introduced me, and there were smiles all round. I had no idea what was being said, but I smiled back. Then I excused myself to check the camera case. I was relieved that I'd decided to leave the laptop and other gear back in the hotel. And, fortunately, the seal on the camera case had held, and no rain seemed to have got inside the case. I was concerned about condensation inside the camera though, and wondered whether it was going to be a problem.

Curious eyes watched me as I held up the camera, switched it on and flipped open the LCD screen. I held the camera low and pressed record and very slowly panned across the whole balcony. Then I tried a couple of slow zooms and got some delightful inconspicuous close-ups.

A couple of adventurous teenagers came and stood behind me to see what I was doing. And there were a few giggles. More kids came to see what was happening. But these were not ignorant natives. The people in this longhouse had seen a camera before. What was delightful though was that nobody posed for the camera. Those people in shot simply continued what they had been doing.

I hit stop and rewound. Then I played back what I had just shot. There didn't seem to be anything wrong with the camera or the picture, although the low light made the picture a little grainy. The kids behind me loved to see playback and more than one reached out to try and take the camera from me.

"Mister Wheeler" called out Abdul, and beckoned me over.

I went over and Abdul introduced me to the now much larger group of people. I wasn't sure of the procedure but, although nobody shook my hand, they all seemed relatively pleased to see me. As I sat down a couple of men even tried talking directly to me and Abdul haltingly interpreted. But, because the rain was still noisy outside the exposed balcony, I couldn't quite make out what Abdul was saying, so I fudged it. Several women sat with large baskets in front of them sorting something, and I asked him what they were doing.

"It's pepper."

I thought I misheard, and asked again.

"They grow pepper here. They sort it to sell," he laughed. "I think the pepper you put on your food in America comes from here."

The women nodded at me and smiled as though they understood. From somewhere out the back a small group of younger women appeared carrying trays with food in bowls. They set them down and, almost instantaneously, more Iban appeared to come and eat. I counted to a little over forty men, women and children.

A woman shyly handed me a bowl that contained some rice and a little fish and some yams. Gratefully I ate the food slowly and looked around me at this large family group, all sitting on mats eating quietly.

When I was done a woman came over with a large bowl, ready to ladle out some more. I made that face: putting my head on one side and kind of smiling apologetically. Although it was good, I didn't want to take food from their mouths. Besides, in spite of the long day and my cross-country hiking ordeal, I wasn't that hungry.

A teenage boy that I hadn't noticed before came over and sat beside me. I nodded at him and smiled.

"You have enough?" the boy asked in English.

Somewhat taken aback, it was a moment before I replied.

"Yes. Thanks....You speak English?"

"Yes, I speak....little....I learn television. You want...see?"

Then I remembered why I had come there.

"Sure. Why not."

I ran the camera as the teenager and a couple of his friends took me through one of the doors, and the boy pointed proudly at a television that sat perched high up on a shelf. He climbed up and switched it on. It was an older model, but it was color. And, although the picture was a little fuzzy, the boy proudly changed channels a couple of times to demonstrate the set's versatility.

"We see many things. You American?"

"Yes, I'm American."

"We see you country. I will go you country."

"I know Gudge Bush. He is you country, yes?"

"Yep, I'm afraid so."

"Gudge Bush funny man."

I laughed, "He sure is."

"You want to see house?"

"Yes, I'd like that."

The boys joyfully took me on a tour of the longhouse. There was a long row of rooms that each led off the main balcony. It seemed that each family had its privacy if it wanted it, but that most activities were communal. In a way it seemed like the perfect existence. But Mike had told me that their lives were becoming less communal and more isolated from the group. Partly due to Iban families having televisions and other modern devices in their rooms.

Abdul was still sitting talking quietly with a small group. On the way back to talk with him I couldn't help noticing what, at first sight, appeared to be an ornament suspended from the rafters high above. And then I realized that what I was looking at was actually three heads. Were they real? They seemed smaller than they should be. Had they been shrunken, or were these actually replica heads? When the boys saw me looking at the heads they laughed. I still wasn't sure whether they were real or not.

I had brought a lightweight sleeping bag with me in my overnight bag, and I was delighted to discover that the plastic bag that it was stored in had prevented too much moisture from seeping in. It was a warm night, and I didn't really need to get inside the sleeping bag. But there was only that and a mat to sleep on. And when I woke up the next morning my body was stiff and sore all over. I got unsteadily to my feet. Abdul was still asleep. It was just getting light and, although it had stopped raining, the air was filled with moisture. It rose up from the ground as mist, illuminating everything with a mysterious glow. I went to the edge of the balcony and looked out and down into the jungle. Birds were beginning to test their songs, and I could hear other creatures foraging around. Down below a few scrawny chickens scratched around in the dirt.

There is an expression in documentary filmmaking which they describe as 'shooting the shit' out of something, which basically means filming every single possible thing that there is to film. That morning I shot the shit out of the longhouse, its inhabitants and its environs. The Iban were very polite and very cooperative, and I was grateful to them.

Eventually, when it was time to leave, Abdul told me with a smile on his face that there was now enough water in the river for us to take a smaller boat from there. And that we wouldn't have to walk back to the longboat. I was as relieved as he was.

The smaller boat took us to where we'd moored the longboat and we transferred to that and continued along the river, stopping occasionally so that Abdul could show me where great tracts of land had been exposed by deforestation.

"The trees here were virgin trees. You know what that means? The same trees as thousands, millions, of years ago, that nobody had touched. And now men come from Malaysia and China and make this.

I would have liked to have hired a helicopter from which to film, so that I could show how bad it really was, but I didn't have the budget for it. Nevertheless, I found a couple of people in Kuching who were prepared to talk on camera and, when I finally got back to the hotel, I was able to edit both stories into two very credible pieces. I had to spend several very intensive days doing it, but I was pleased with the results. And, when I uploaded the pieces to Mike, the response from him was more than favorable.

"Keep up the good work," he said.

# Chapter Fifteen

The two stories in Thailand were more entertaining: the female kick-boxers and the rapping monk, and I was able to have fun with them. The girl kick-boxers were feminine but very tough. However, they seemed to make it more like a dance than a brutal fight.

The monk was great. He rapped in Thai, but tried a few words of English. His rhythm was impeccable, and I felt he could even have a career in the States if he wanted. And if he learnt more English.

I was getting to know the edit suite too, and it was starting to come easier. I even had a little time to myself in Bangkok before I moved on again. It had been a while since I'd been there, but nothing much had changed. Maybe the traffic was a little crazier, if that's possible. And cell phones and internet shops seemed to be everywhere. Apart from that, it was pretty much the same. I started to relax a little, and even got myself a massage. But I'd forgotten that Thai massages tend to be what you might call 'deep tissue', and it was very painful. When it was over I felt like I needed a nice relaxing massage.

I flew directly from Bangkok to Siem Reap in Cambodia. Siem Reap had left behind the horrors of the Vietnam war times, and the little town had grown into a major tourist destination because of the Angkor Wat temples. I had seen them before several times. But now they hid a dirty little secret. Hundreds of kids begged around the exquisite structures. And many of them were begging not for food, but for glue to sniff. They moved around in gangs, and the game was to hire babies from their mothers for the day. Then they'd sling the infants on their hips and try and find someone to beg from.

With as little as fifty cents the kids could go to a bicycle repair shop and buy some Mustang tire repair glue. And that was all it took to turn their poor undeveloped brains to mush.

I filmed some kids begging. Of course when they saw me they swarmed around me like seagulls with a half-eaten sandwich. Knowing what the money would be used for, I was in a quandary. If I just filmed them without giving them anything I felt that I'd be exploiting them. If I gave them money then I was pretty sure what it would be used for. It was the old journalist's dilemma. Do you film a man bleeding to death, or do you take him to a hospital?

And, besides, I actually wanted to see for myself if it was true about the glue. And, of course, to film them sniffing it. So I handed out a few dollars, and watched as a few of them left. I started to follow them, and the rest of the kids followed me. I hoped I wouldn't get taken for a pedophile, something that was far too common in Cambodia.

But it was hopeless. I stood out far too obviously. All that happened was that none of the kids would let me alone. The problem was that Siem Reap was too small. I decided that I'd have to move onto the capital, Phnom Penh sooner than I'd planned. Sometimes a story went down like this.

I gave up trying to film the kids and started walking away. But they continued to follow me, holding out their hands and pleading in Khmer. They were incredibly persistent, and I couldn't shake them off. Obviously they believed I was good for a few more dollars. Finally I half-ran across a busy road, taking my life in my hands. Even then two of the older boys tried to follow me. So I hurried on and zigzagged through a couple of streets. There I stopped and laughed. "What am I doing?" I said out loud, "Running away from a bunch of kids." It wasn't as though I felt threatened. Neither was it the handing out of money. I was happy to give the kids some dollars. Lord knew they needed it more than I did. It was more the nuisance aspect of having a braying bunch of kids hassling me, that's all.

There was an international press club overlooking the river that I had been to before, and I made for that. It was in a modern building, and I found it again quite easily. I walked upstairs and found a free table on the balcony with a nice view of the river. A waiter came and I ordered a beer. Then I looked around to see if there were any familiar faces. Not recognizing anyone I decided to have a look at the footage I'd just shot to see if any of it was useable. I bent down to pull the camera from its case.

"Max? Is that you?"

I looked upwards. Yep, I'd recognize that ass anywhere: Linda Farrell. I straightened up and gave her a lopsided grin.

"Hello Linda, how are you? Why don't you sit down."

She looked at her wrist. Her watch had twisted around. She swiveled it so that she could see the time. When she was younger Linda Farrell had been a Great

Beauty. A real heart-breaker, with an exquisite face that radiated allure. She also had the body of an angel. In her late forties now, time had been good to her. Well, time and several million bucks in the bank back home in DC. Some of it she'd inherited and some she'd married. But the result was that she really never needed to work another day in her life. So traveling the world taking photographs was something she did for love, not money. And it showed. Her work, while not quite in the same class as Marie's, was pretty good. And she frequently sold it to some of the world's top magazines. She perched on a chair and gave me a warm smile.

"Actually I'm on my way to meet someone, but....I haven't seen you since.... "

"....Must be four years. How've you been? You look terrific."

She always took a compliment well.

"Thank you. I've been pretty good. Certainly nothing to complain about. And you? I hear you've had a tough year. I was sorry to hear about..."

"...Yeah, I've had better...."

"...So what are you doing in Cambodia? Are you on vacation?"

"Nope. Got a new job. This is an assignment."

"Oh, terrific!"

She looked at her watch again. "Look, this is insane. I really have to go." She stood up. "But, what are you doing later?"

"Nothing much. You wanna catch up?"

"How about dinner. Here. Say eight o'clock?"

I shrugged. "Sounds good to me."

She bent and kissed my cheek. Then flashed her eyes at me.

"I'll look forward to it. Ciao."

And she swept out.

"Well," I thought, "How about that!"

I spent the rest of the afternoon taking B-roll shots. Anything that I could think of that might be useful coverage for the story. The camera had a useful zoom lens on it, which allowed me to get some good discreet shots.

Back at the hotel I showered, shaved and changed my clothes. It was a warm night and I had no need of a jacket. I looked in the mirror to check my appearance and an old, familiar feeling came over me. It was as if I was going out on a date.

Well, I was going to have dinner with a beautiful woman. Dinner and… I paused for a moment and shut my eyes.

Eventually I opened them and spoke to myself in the mirror, "Life goes on." Then again more softly, "Life goes on."

Though a little humid, the warm night was pleasant enough as I crossed a bridge and then walked beside the strangely green river that snaked through Siem Reap. The half moon had a halo around it, giving off a slightly eerie light.

The press club was filling up, and I was wondering whether I should have reserved a table. But when I arrived they promised me a table would be available about eight fifteen. I ordered a whisky at the bar and felt at home. The energy in places like this was as familiar as my own home. More so in a way. I'd hung out in these kind of places all my working life. There were a couple of faces here that I vaguely recognized, but nobody that I could put a name to.

I'd known Linda Farrell for more than ten years. Well, 'known' wasn't exactly right. We'd hung out in the same circles, known the same people. I'd always found her to be pleasant company, and we shared interests in many of the same subjects and seemed to have similar senses of humor.

I saw her before she noticed me. She stood in the entrance, poised and elegant, looking around. When she saw me she smiled and sashayed over.

"Hello," she said, bending to kiss my cheek.

"You look pretty stunning." Because she did.

"Yes, I thought so tonight."

"And modest."

"Oh," she chuckled, "I never was modest Max. You know that!"

A barman came over.

"Gin tonic please."

"And I'll have the same again." I said, holding up my glass.

"So what…?" I began to ask, just as she said, "Tell me all…" And we laughed together.

And that was how the evening continued. With the rapport between us flowing like a dance. Together we remembered many of the places that we'd both been to, although not always at the same time. And we shared news and gossip about people we knew. Later I told her all about marrying and then losing Marie. She'd heard some of it of course, but she was interested to hear it from me.

She wasn't traveling so much these days, she said. "Getting old." I looked her up and down and flattered her and told her how young she still looked. And how beautiful. She said, without a beat, that it wasn't a question of beauty, but thank you. And, in any case, it was simply that she had less urge to travel.

The food wasn't great and the bottle of wine was extremely average. But the view was terrific and the atmosphere lively. And the company was great.

I told her about the work I was doing. She'd heard of podcasting, and had even downloaded a few things herself. We talked about how media was changing and fragmenting and how it would affect our work. We seemed to have similar views on most things and I felt very relaxed in Linda's company, and she in mine.

Eventually it came time to leave. I settled the account and, quite naturally we rose as one and left the restaurant. She took my arm as we walked back along the river towards her hotel, talking all the while. And when we arrived at the front entrance she stopped and turned to me.

"Thank you. It's been lovely seeing you again. I've enjoyed myself this evening."

"Me too," I said, and then seized the moment, "But it doesn't have to end now."

"Oh, it does, I'm afraid," she said looking at her wristwatch. "I'm flying to Bangkok tomorrow,"

She saw the look of disappointment in my face.

"Oh, Max," she laughed, "Did you think I was going to sleep with you? Silly boy! No, not tonight…But thank you for the offer. Very sweet of you."

She leaned into me and kissed me lightly on the lips. I could feel the warmth of her skin and smell the scent of her perfume, and all I could do was to stand there helplessly.

"Goodnight Max. Happy trails."

And she turned and walked into the hotel. I watched her go in and, as the doors closed behind her, I shook my head and left. I felt incredibly foolish. How could I have misjudged the situation so much? What was happening with me? Five years ago I would never have had that kind of expectation. It would simply have been a dinner of old friends and colleagues. Now….what? Maybe it was my experiences with Amy and…What was her name? The girl from the Judasians? Oh yes, Angelina, my angel. Or was I now trying to use sex to dispel the pain

As I walked back across the bridge to my hotel I felt like kicking myself. And I also felt horny. Well, too bad about that. "Damn fool," I said to myself out loud. An old man wearing a straw hat, pushing a bicycle towards me looked at me when I spoke, thinking that I might be talking to him, but I just shook my head and walked on.

***

At the airport next morning I was hoping I wouldn't run into Linda. I was still feeling embarrassed about my assumption. But she had said that hers was an early flight, and thankfully there was no sign of her by the time my flight to Phnom Penh was called. I was still a little hung-over from the duty-free whisky that I'd drunk to try and douse the throbbing in my groin.

The flight was short and, before I knew it, I was on the ground and in a taxi headed for my hotel. They checked me in as soon as I arrived and I asked if there were any messages. The receptionist looked.

"No sir, nothing."

A bellhop carried my bag to the small elevator. Beside the door was a large sign on the door showing a picture of a handgun with a diagonal red line through it. I wasn't sure whether to feel more secure or less.

Inside the room I unpacked, set up the laptop and began to dump the Siem Reap footage onto it. I was about halfway through when the telephone rang.

"Mister Wheeler you have a visitor. A mister Samnang."

Samnang had come highly recommended. He was going to take me on a tour of the city that most people would never see. He had worked with several of the numerous NGOs that were based in Cambodia, and his English was fairly good. He'd also arranged for Prang, a cab driver, to drive us around. The cab looked like it was a model that was thirty years old. But, in spite of the driver's name, the bodywork, paint job and the chrome on the car were immaculate.

The traffic goes quite slowly in Phnom Penh which is a good thing because there seem to be few rules about which side of the road to drive on, when to turn, or anything else. It also meant that Samnang was able point out interesting subject matter for me to film. And Prang was often able to pull over.

"There are so many children in Phnom Penh. I think maybe sixty, sixty-five percent of population is children."

"Really! I wasn't sure whether to believe that figure or not. But there certainly seemed to be a lot of kids on the streets. "Why so many?"

"I think because parents have HIV/AIDS. So cannot look after children. And maybe die also. So children must look after selves. They come from other parts of Cambodia too. Run away from home. Come to Phnom Penh. Look there. See. There is gang."

I asked Prang to stop as soon as he could.

"Can we talk with them?" I asked.

"We can try."

The driver stopped the car and waited with it as I walked back with Samnang, stopping occasionally to film the gang from a safe distance. Eventually we were spotted, and I put the camera down. A couple of older kids were shouting at us.

"What'd they say?" I asked.

"This one very angry. But the other ask for money for filming him."

"Please tell him I can give them a little money. After. If they will talk for a few minutes."

Samnang translated and, at first, they were all reluctant. But the boy who had asked for money agreed. Then the others also nodded their heads. They walked off down a side street and Samnang and I followed. I felt like the Pied Piper in reverse, with some of the kids skipping and laughing as they walked. A little way down the street they came to a humpy, a sort of home-constructed tent built right on the earth of the sidewalk. I asked if it was alright to film as the boy burrowed around in the back of the humpy and pulled out a bundle wrapped in an old, dirty cloth. He unwrapped it to show what was inside. I asked if I could film them sniffing the glue, and several of the kids obliged. Then one of the boys said something to Samnang, who translated it for me.

"He said they only have glue. But many of their friends have heroin and...." He couldn't find the right English word. "Meth...?"

"...Methamphetamines...?

"...I guess, yes."

I looked at the kids. There were about ten of them now. They ranged, as far as I could tell, from sixteen down to five years of age. I carried on filming as they handed the bag with glue to the youngest, who eagerly took it. Again I was in two minds as to whether or not to interfere and try and stop it or to carry on filming. But the young boy only had the bag for a short time, then handed it to me. I held it to my nose for a second. It was strong-smelling and made me dizzy, and I wondered how the children could tolerate it, let alone be attracted to it. I passed it back to the older boy who also held out his other hand for money. When I handed over a few bills the boy asked Samnang whether he'd told me about the monkeys.

"What monkeys?" I asked, when Samnang translated.

"There is a district of Phnom Penh called Daun Penh. Here there are many, many monkeys. Maybe hundreds of them. They live in trees, and sometimes they jump down and sometimes bite and steal also. Now they steal glue bags from people as well. They have become bad. Now they attack people. Very bad."

"Can we go there?"

"Of course."

It was starting to rain now. I thanked the kids and Samnang and I walked back to the car.

For the rest of the day we drove and walked around the city. Samnang took me to places where there were pickpockets and teenage prostitutes, and gangs of kids with babies on their hips and kids stealing from shops. And by the time we'd finished I had more than enough for my story.

That evening I sat in the tub with a glass of well-deserved whisky and let the steam from the hot water soothe my body. I was tired, but it felt good. When I finally climbed out of the tub I thought maybe I'd get room service instead of going out to eat. I wrapped a towel around my waist and picked up the folder that sat beside the telephone and flipped through it. The room service menu seemed to be fairly limited, and there was nothing that really appealed to me. So I gave in. I knew that there was a restaurant in the lobby and that I wouldn't have to go outside.

"So that's what I'll do."

But, as I sat, I turned over some more pages and read details about other hotel services. Apparently there was a gym on the top floor, and they also offered an in-house massage.

"Might be just what I need," I said out loud. Then I remembered the massage I'd had in Thailand and laughed. If I was going to get a massage I'd better check that it wasn't a deep-tissue one.

I slipped on some clothes and went downstairs. There were no other customers in the hotel bar so I took my drink through to the restaurant. When I walked in there was a blast of laughter. It seemed like a family party was happening in the rear of the place and I thought maybe I wouldn't be able to eat there tonight. But a couple of people waved me in and a stunning girl wearing a traditional costume came towards me smiling.

"One person?" she asked.

I returned her smile, "Yes, just one person."

She turned and led me to a table. The sarong-like skirt was wrapped tightly around her and, as she walked, her ass danced in front of me hypnotically. As I sat down she handed me a menu and cleared away the redundant cutlery on the other side of the table.

I looked around the brightly decorated restaurant. For some reason I thought about the Bow Thai Restaurant off Fairfax and wondered what the guys were doing tonight. Maybe I could get a good Cambodian recipe to take back to Al.

Maybe not! The food wasn't really that great and, although I'd enjoyed watching the waitresses glide by as they served other customers, I was happy to leave.

As I rode up in the gun-free elevator I noticed a sign with a photograph of the gym. It was still quite early so I thought "What the hell!" and decided to go and have a look.

I was met on the top floor by a smiling woman wearing traditional costume.

"Yes sir? You want massaase?"

She asked the question so sweetly. I could see two or three exercise machines sitting in darkness. So this was the gym! Well, maybe tomorrow I might jump on the exercise bike.

"Massaase in your room, yes?"

Idly I asked, "How much?"

"Eight dollar sir."

Eight bucks for a massage?

"Soft and gentle, yes." I asked, not looking for a repeat of my Thai experience.

"Oh yes sir. Very soft. Very gentle. You want choose?"

And before I could answer she beckoned me to follow her to the next room. The room itself was divided in two by a glass wall. On the other side of the glass sat maybe eight or nine young masseuses all wearing white leotards.

"You choose, yes."

I looked at the girls. Okay, I definitely didn't want anyone too beefy. But there wasn't much danger of that. On the other hand a couple of the girls looked like they could barely massage a child. Some just sat there, waiting for my decision. But one girl smiled at me and rubbed her forearms. Why not. I handed over the money and the woman wrote me a very neat receipt. At least I assume it was a receipt. It was all in Khmer, which I couldn't read. I looked around, but couldn't see a massage table.

"Where?" I asked.

"In room." And she said something to the girl who went trough the same forearm-rubbing and smiling routine and started walking towards the elevator.

The ride down to my floor was like any elevator ride, with neither of us talking or even really looking at each other. I led her along the hallway and ushered her into the room. The first thing she did was walk straight to the television and turn it on, adjusting the sound to make it louder.

"No, I don't think so," I said, turning it off again.

She didn't protest, but instead mimed to me that I should take off my clothes. I went into the bathroom, took off my clothes and had a quick shower. While I was there I heard the television come back on. And when I returned to the bedroom with a big towel tied around my waist she was sitting on the edge of the bed, glued to a variety show. Again I turned it off and mimed "too loud".

"Not relaxing," I said. "I want nice relaxing massage, okay?"

"Okay." She said, almost cheerfully, and patted the bed for me to lie down.

I lay on my stomach with my face resting on a pillow, and she worked my back. She was pretty good, firm but gentle, and her small hands found my knotted muscles and I began to relax.

Almost too soon she patted my back gently and flipped her hand, obviously indicating for me to do the same with my body. So I obliged, and she got stuck into my legs, again kneading them gently but firmly. She obviously enjoyed massaging my legs because she seemed to put a lot of energy into it, pushing my legs wider and wider as she worked my thighs.

I was enjoying the massage and feeling quite relaxed now. But I could also feel something else. As she rubbed my thighs I could feel my cock starting to swell. In fact I was grateful that the towel was still covering me. However, she seemed to think the towel was more nuisance than anything else, because she lifted it higher so that she could get into the top of my thighs. My eyes were shut so I couldn't see whether she'd noticed my erection.

Then she sat up quite suddenly.

"You want....?" She asked, nodding her head.

Over the years I had received massages in many countries. And sometimes the girls had asked me if I'd like "a little more". Or "a happy ending". And a couple of times I had gotten a hand job. Once it had been pathetic, like my mother doing it. But the other time was an experience I was happy to repeat.

"Okay," I said, "why not."

She smiled at me and disappeared to the bathroom. When she returned she had a towel wrapped around her and was holding the white leotard in her hand. She sat on the side of the bed, reaching for the small wallet she'd brought in with her. From the wallet she took out a condom packet. That was when I realized it was going to be more than a hand job. My first instinct was to say 'no'. But then I became curious.

"How much?" I asked.

"Thirty dollar." she said, turning back to me and handing me the condom packet.

Then I thought, "Every man's fantasy, isn't it? Have a beautiful girl give you a great massage, then fuck you."

I realized she was waiting, and reached for my own wallet, pulled out a couple of notes, and handed them to her. As she neatly folded the money and tucked them away a thought occurred to me.

"How old are you?' I asked. Although she certainly looked like a grown woman I needed to know she was at least over the age of consent.

She didn't get it at first. Then she showed me with her fingers: twenty-three. And she switched off the light.

But, although the room was in semi-darkness, there was just enough light coming in through the thin curtains for me to see her untying the towel and letting it slip down. She came and lay beside me on the bed and I looked down at her body. She had a beautiful body, with small but shapely breasts. And, although she wasn't tall, her legs and buttocks were well-formed, and her light brown skin was soft and taut. She seemed almost shy with me as I very gently stroked her shoulder, then moving downwards cupped a breast and brought it to my lips. She shut her eyes and trembled slightly as I ran my tongue over a nipple.

With my other hand I felt the curve of a buttock. She pushed towards me and I could feel my erection stiffen even more, beginning now to press against the lower part of my belly. My breathing became heavier and more intense.

She rolled over slightly and lay on her back, spreading her legs. I thought about waiting to let the energy build. But I was ready now. Ready to explode. And I didn't have to wait until she was also ready. I reached out and grabbed the condom packet and tore it open with my teeth, then rolled it on.

She had her head tilted upwards expectantly. For a moment I let myself enjoy looking at her exquisite little body. Then I lay on top of her and slowly pushed into her. I went carefully to make sure she was big enough. But I needn't have worried. She even managed to wear an ecstatic look on her pretty, heart-shaped face as I began to pump faster and faster. I held her tightly, feeling her breasts against my chest.

Then I exploded. And it was over.

She waited for a minute, then eased herself out from under me. I watched her as she slipped back into her leotard, picked up her wallet from the night stand and headed for the door.

"Thank you." I said.

She said nothing, but gave me a flicker of a grin and opened the door. Then she was gone.

I gazed at the closed door for a while as I drifted off to sleep with a contented smile on my face.

# Chapter Sixteen

The telephone was insistent. I reached out and plucked it from its cradle. I wasn't sure what time it was, but it felt like the middle of the night.

"Mmm" was all I could say.

"Daddy?"

"Katie? Is everything…?"

"I'm fine daddy…But Granny Phyllis is not looking so good."

Granny Phyllis was my mother. Over the last few years her health had been deteriorating generally. She'd already retired to Florida, But then I'd had to find a nursing home for her in to stay in so that she could be looked after and given proper care. And, recently, Alzheimer's had reared its unpleasant head. I tried to go and visit her whenever I could. But, in the last six months, she just didn't recognize me at all. It was always distressing for me. And, worst of all, I could see that she knew that she *should* recognize me. And that was very distressing for her. I knew that she probably didn't have too much longer to live, and I'd often wondered what would happen if I was out of the country. Now I knew.

"The home called mom. They said they didn't know how much longer…."

Long silence.

"….and mom called me. I said I thought you were out of the country. I called Mike. I hope that's okay…."

"…Of course…"

"…Anyway, he gave me the number for this hotel."

"I'm glad you called. I'll try and get on a flight today. How long…?"

"Maybe just a few days."

"And you?"

"I'm okay in myself. But…"

I could hear the catch in her voice

"I know sweetie, I know. I'll be back as soon as I can."

"Daddy I'm so sorry….I wanted to fly down to Florida. I mean it's Granny Phyllis….But I have to stay in town…I have a thing…"

"…It's alright sweetie, you don't have to…"

"...But you'll be all alone. I've called the others, and they're all... tied up too...."

"It really is okay. I'll be fine. And I won't be alone. I'll give her your love, okay?"

"Yes daddy....Have a safe trip."

"Thanks sweetie."

So it had come. This call. This summons. Now it was *that* time.

I called downstairs and asked whether they could help me change my flight: "Emergency." And "my mother." And "first available."

They'd "try and do something" they said, and would I like "breakfast in my room?". I demurred. Not a time to be alone. Plenty of time for that.

And so, dreamlike, trying not to think too much, I shaved and showered and slowly dressed and went downstairs for breakfast.

But all I really managed was some coffee. And afterwards I went to reception, and they'd managed to book me a business class seat on a plane leaving in the afternoon. And could they organize a taxi to the airport? "Yes, of course, sir."

"Thank you."

And I turned. And then I didn't know where to go. Back to my room? I didn't feel like it, but I had to pack anyway."

I had just walked in through the door when the telephone rang. I picked it up absent-mindedly. It was Mike.

"Your daughter. Katie..."

"Yes, she called me. She told me she'd spoken to you."

"Sorry to hear about your mother."

"Thanks.....I'm on a flight this afternoon. I'll catch a connection to Miami."

"Okay....Max?"

"Yeah?"

"How d'you get on with the story there?"

"I've got enough to cut this one together. But I haven't started that."

"Okay. Don't worry about that. Call me from Florida...when you have time."

"Will do."


Time. When I "had time". Time wasn't going to be the problem.

I packed the few things that I'd bothered to unpack. Then stood in the middle of the room.

174

"Now what?"

Well, I could carry on shooting. I might get something that I didn't already have. I picked up the camera case and headed out. The sky was darkly overcast and threatening when I left the hotel. I paused outside, deliberating whether to turn left or right. I wondered whether it would matter. There must have been many times in my life when, if I'd just turned left instead of right or right instead of left, my whole life would have been different. The thing was I wouldn't know.

And before I knew it I'd turned anyway and was walking along and thinking and wondering how life might have been different. I was so preoccupied that I didn't notice the spots of rain.

"All in all" I thought, "I wouldn't have wanted to do it differently. I've had a terrific life. Correction, I *have* a terrific life. As I'd said to Gabriel: the people I've met, the places I've been, the things I've seen. I wouldn't give that up for anything." I'd never been rich, but I'd always had enough money. A decent house. I'd been lucky. And here I was, almost sixty with a healthy body, and with most of my hair. Why would I swap this life for anything else?

And then the heavens opened and torrents of rain crashed down on me. It was like someone had taken an ocean and tipped it upside down. All around me people scattered and ran for cover. I looked about for somewhere to run to. Nothing was obvious. A closed nightclub, a huge building site with no cover, a temple with a locked gate, I just stood there, trying to shield the camera case. My clothes were now completely soaked through. The rain was lashing at my face and driving into the top of my head. I'd never felt so wet in my life, even when I'd been with the Iban. Water was starting to form a small lake on the primitive sidewalk, meaning that I had to trudge through it. And now there was water inside my shoes, which squelched as I half ran, splashing, along the street, looking for somewhere to go. I began to feel as though I was going to melt. Or get washed away.

The traffic, which was normally chaotic, was now sheer madness, with bicycles, scooters, motorbikes, small cars, vans, buses and trucks all trying to avoid the deepening lagoons of water that were spreading across the road, and all trying simultaneously to avoid each other. And, one after another, they would spray even more water over me, drenching me and now almost making me feel as though I was about to drown. Meanwhile incredibly, it seemed as though – if anything – it was raining even harder. I started to run wildly along the street. But the wind was pitching the rain into my eyes and, with my head down, I couldn't see where I was going. I hadn't run as fast as this in years and I started to get a stitch in my side. My breath was becoming more labored and suddenly I winced as a sharp pain attacked my chest, forcing me to pause for a moment before I could move on.

I looked to the side, and saw a group of men huddled in the doorway of a shop and wondered whether there was room inside for me. As I headed for the entrance the men moved aside and let me through. And, finally, I was out of the rain.

I stood inside the shop, the water dripping off me and forming a pool on the floor. I could see that I was in an internet café and that most heads were looking in my direction. A young woman behind the counter reached down and pulled out a piece of fabric. She held it out to me tentatively.

"You want?"

I took the material gratefully and wiped my face and hair.

"Internet?" she asked.

I wasn't sure that I wouldn't drip all over a computer and short it out and all the other machines in the place. But I could still hear the rain pelting down outside, and then I realized that I hadn't checked my email for a couple of days, and maybe this was a good thing to do anyway.

The woman pointed to a vacant computer and I headed for the chair. As I did, I realized that the chair was further away than I'd thought. And I was obviously more tired than I'd imagined, because my legs became kind of jelly-like. I lifted the left one and examined it. The rain was still coming off it. Except that the rain wasn't coming from the outside of my leg, but…from inside his leg. Wow! This rain had really soaked through. The other leg too had water leaking from it.

As I put one foot in front of the other I could hear a squelching sound. I looked down and could see that water was sloshing over the sides of my shoes. This wasn't right somehow. I thought that maybe I'd better sit down and take off my shoes to let out the rest of the rainwater. Just in case there were any fish in there.

Sitting on the floor was better, and I felt more comfortable. But, actually, lying down would be *more* comfortable. So I did that. And, as I looked up, I could feel more water pouring down onto me. The water was coming in the form of a jet pointed right at my chest. And I wasn't sure that the water jet wouldn't drive a hole straight through. I lifted a hand to try and stop the jet, but more water was coming from inside my arm. I waved the hand in front of my face and spread my fingers, only to see water seeping out from between them.

There was so much rain that the whole of the place was filling up with it. And the level was so high that it was enveloping me and coddling me. Then it was over my face and the level was rising towards the ceiling. And I was underwater. I shut my eyes and let the water swirl me about and the eddy took my body and I floated around. I began to feel at one with the water. There was no division between the water around me and my body. I was the water. The feeling was pleasant enough, but there was something that wasn't quite right.

A voice whispered in my ear, but I couldn't understand what the voice was saying. A part of me wanted the voice to leave me alone, but I was also afraid of *being* alone. I strained to understand what the voice was saying, but it was still no good.

"I'd better open my eyes and look." I thought to myself. But I didn't open my eyes immediately. The effort was too much. "A little harder." I thought. And so I managed first one eye, then the other.

I was looking into the concerned face of the young woman in the internet café, who was kneeling beside me. She looked very worried, but I had no idea why. She spoke to me in Khmer, which I couldn't understand. I noticed that there was an older woman behind her. The young woman turned to the older woman and, although I still couldn't understand, I knew that it had been a question.

Now I realized that there were several other people gathered around me. And then it struck me that I was actually lying on the floor.

"Probably not…the best thing to do." I muttered to myself.

Although they probably couldn't understand what I'd muttered, the fact that I was talking brought an audible sigh of relief to the two women. The older one said something sharply to the other people gathered around, and they began to move away.

I tried to sit up and the young woman reached behind me to help. And, even though she was a lot smaller than me, her support helped me and, by holding my arms behind me, I was able to prop myself up. At long last she smiled at me, then turned and spoke again to the older woman, who disappeared behind a curtain.

The other customers were back at their computers now, the drama old news. I became aware that the men were still sheltering in the doorway. Now, with the exception of one, they'd also turned around to peer back out into the storm, waiting for their moment.

The older woman came back with a small tray bearing a cup of tea which she held out to me. I was recovered enough now to be able to sit without supporting my weight, and I took the cup.

"Thank you."

The older woman smiled as I tentatively sipped the hot green tea.

What had just happened? Obviously I'd fainted or something, but why? I could feel some kind of pain in my chest. Had I had a heart attack? But wasn't it meant to go down one arm or something. My mind was fuzzy, and it was difficult to think. I began to feel foolish sitting there, and grabbed hold of a chair to take my weight so that I could stand up. I discovered that standing up was not a great idea just yet. So, instead, I sat in the chair and sipped the tea again.

"Okay? You Okay?" asked the younger woman.

"Okay. Yes, I think so, thank you. I'll be fine."

"Okay."

The older woman motioned to me to drink more tea. So I did. And I began to feel stronger. I smiled at them encouragingly, then waved at the computer. The two women nodded at me.

I turned to face the computer and set the cup down on the computer table. I could see the women still studying me from the other side of the café, obviously still concerned. So, partly to allay their fears, I started tapping at the keyboard, logging onto my email. Then I shut my eyes and exhaled deeply as the computer whirred away.

When I looked at the screen there were a couple of dozen messages, but most of it was spam about penis enlargement or cheap Viagra. "Hmm." But I was pleased to see a message from Katie, which I opened. She'd sent it just in case she hadn't been able to get me on the phone. In it she talked about my mother and how much she meant to her. Absent-mindedly I rubbed at my chest to ease the residual pain there as I read.

I knew that all my kids were fond of my mother, but I hadn't realized the full extent of how much she meant to them. I never had much contact with *my* grandparents. My mother's parents had lived in Canada and they rarely made any form of contact. And, after the accident when my father died, I hadn't heard much from my father's parents either. Once in a while I'd visit at a friend's house at Thanksgiving or Christmas and there I would see the three generations together. At those times I felt a little envious. Otherwise it really didn't bother me. In fact, if anything, in a strange way it had given me a sense of freedom. Not so many people to worry about. So my own childrens' attachment to their grandparents bemused me a little.

There was an old message from Mike, obviously sent before Katie had phoned me, giving me the lowdown on some new stories to cover.

Tentatively I looked around. Nobody was staring at me now. Even the two women were engrossed in their own conversation. I turned back to the computer, and rested my jaw in the palm of my hand as I gazed at the screen. But I wasn't seeing what was written there. Instead it suddenly hit me that my mother was dying. And that I was going back to the States to see her for the last time.

*** 

I thought about her all the way home. Well, not *thought about* exactly. A fragment of a memory would pop into my mind and I would see it and hear my mother's voice and I would remember something about the event, then it would all drift away. Maybe I had cut my knee falling off my bike or something. And there would be mom dabbing gently at it – kindness itself. Or when I graduated and I'd looked out into the ocean of faces. And there she was looking as proud as could be.

These reveries sustained me all the way home. I must have sat through five movies, but I couldn't have told you what they were. Or who was in them. At some point I fell asleep. But, again, I had very little memory of when that was.

And then I stepped out into the humidity of Miami airport. In South-East Asia there's a softness to the humidity. Here it was different. It was simply oppressive. I was sweating before I even reached the taxi stand.

Even though I'd been traveling for the best part of a day, I asked the cabbie to take me directly to the hospital. I had no idea exactly how long my mother still had left. I could find a motel later.

For so many years of my life I had seen my mother through the eyes of a child. Oh, I'd watched her getting older, and noticed the lacework of wrinkles decorate her face. And I'd seen her lose her once-beautiful figure and become somewhat

179

stooped. But it was only in the last few years that I'd really seen her through different eyes. As I watched she'd changed from middle-aged to old to elderly. But, as I sat beside her bed, I felt that the woman lying there was someone that I was only half familiar with. And that, to some extent, part of her had already left.

She'd had her eyes closed as I walked in the room. But she opened her eyes when I approached her, and her eyes hadn't registered even a glimmer of recognition. I could have been a doctor or a television repair man or someone come to murder her, she couldn't have peered at me with more indifferent eyes.

Now I sat in a chair beside her, holding her hand. And, although she allowed me to hold it, she in no way held my hand back.

"She's getting pretty strong dosages of morphine," said the nurse, adjusting a drip. "She's been in quite a lot of pain."

"D'you think she has any idea what's happening?" I asked.

"Yeah, we get asked that a lot. I have no idea. But, personally, I always try and treat a patient with respect as though they *do* know. Just in case, y'know…"

She stretched up to make an adjustment to the drip. Then, as she began to smooth the bedding, she said "Your brother was here."

"My br.….? Oh, yes."

"I think he went to get some coffee. He's been here since yesterday."

Did I notice a hint of recrimination in her voice?

"I was overseas," I felt obliged to explain. "Working in South-East Asia, My daughter called me."

"Well you're here now."

"Yes, I'm here now."

As she headed for the door I wondered why I felt that I owed this woman an explanation. That I needed to tell her that I'd been in South-East Asia, reporting on international events. That it had taken me nearly twenty-four hours to get here.

As the nurse left I turned back to my mother. She looked frail, as though the life was being slowly drained from her. Her eyes were shut tightly now, "trying to ward off some particularly bad pain," I thought. "What must it be like? Did she feel utterly alone? Or was there someone…some thing – maybe some spirit – there to guide her?" Now her eyes were open again. She looked down at the hand that I was holding, and then up at my face with complete bewilderment. Her lips moved but I couldn't understand what she said.

"What mom?"

She looked at me and spoke louder. But "On the table," was all she said. I patted her hand.

"Yes mom."

She closed her eyes again, and I studied her face. She'd been a beautiful woman when she was younger, with fine cheekbones, a delicate, straight nose and exquisite, sparkling eyes. As I studied her, I could still see that woman. I didn't see the lined forehead, and the aged face kris-crossed with a spider's web of lines. With my free hand I stroked her brow lovingly. My mother. My one connection to a time past. My time past. My childhood, my school years. The rock of my life, who was always there. Not that I'd spent much time with her in recent years. After Billy-Bob swept her off to Montana and I had begun my world travels, I'd visited with her less and less. At first Lisa and I had made the long trek with the kids, but we stopped doing that because it got to be too difficult. So I'd just go by myself. And then somehow even that just got to be less and less.

After she lost Billy-Bob, about fifteen years ago, my mother had come west a few times. But then she'd moved to Florida and in recent years it had just been phone calls. Up until lately. When the Alzheimer's started I tried to visit. But, more and more, she just stared at me.

"I should have come to see you more often," I whispered to her now. "I should have made the effort." I sighed deeply. "Too late now."

I leaned over her and kissed her forehead.

"Hi."

I looked up. A short middle-aged man stood in the doorway. With a start I realized that it was Elliott. Even though we were half-brothers. Elliott and I were completely unalike, in build and stature and in demeanor. And maybe it was because he was so bald that, even though he was twelve years younger, people always thought that it was Elliott who looked like he was the elder brother.

"Hi. Have you been here long?"

"Yeah. Came yesterday."

A man of few words, Elliott.

"I was overseas…"

"…Yeah, I heard…"

"…I just got here."

I pointed to my bags in the corner of the room. Briefly I again wondered why I did that. Did I need to justify myself somehow? My relationship with Elliott had never been comfortable. Maybe it was the age difference. Maybe it was that we had different fathers, different lifestyles, different lives. Hell, we were just too different. Elliott had lived in Montana most of his life. Now he was an animal doctor specializing in cattle. He spent half his life with his entire arm up the backside of a cow. And, even after 9/11 and Afghanistan and, shit yes, Iraq, he still had no concept of world affairs. It wasn't that he was unintelligent. He just had a kind of tunnel vision about life's priorities. Consequently he seemed to have no interest in my life whatsoever.

Elliott came and stood on the other side of our mother. And that was the other thing. After all these years I still couldn't comprehend that she was somebody else's mother as well.

Her eyes were still shut and her breathing was becoming less even now. And it had a slight rasp to it as well.

"Morphine." said Elliott.

"What?"

"She's pretty dosed up on diamorphine. For the pain. On top of the Alzheimer's, it means she's really out of it."

Elliott dragged over another chair and sat down. And he too shut his eyes and exhaled deeply, the emotion now beginning to show on his face. And an understanding passed through me. That this man too was about to lose his mother. And that she was precious to him. And I looked at my half-brother's face and felt more compassion for him than I'd felt in years. Somehow it touched my heart, and in that moment it began to really sink in that my mother was dying. And I began to miss her already. I sighed deeply, and rubbed my eyes.

"You okay?' asked Elliott.

"Yeah…Well, you know. Sure….How long…?"

"I spoke with a doctor. He didn't know. Said it could be weeks or just hours. Best guess was a couple of days."

In the end it was four days and three nights. I spent most of that time at my mother's bedside. Occasionally she'd open her eyes and look at me and open her mouth to speak. And I thought, "This time, this time." Maybe she would recognize me. But of course she didn't. And sometimes she seemed to be in pain, and that was the hardest thing for me. I wanted so much to soothe her brow and take it all away, just as she'd done for me when I was a small child.

Elliott was also there. Often the two of us sat in complete silence, gazing at her or staring at the television which was high up on a bracket with the volume turned right down. If you watched it for long enough it meant that either you developed a crick in your neck or you slid down in your chair so that you ended up with a painful, twisted back. So then one or other of us would go for a walk. But both of us felt guilty if we were away for too long, and we'd hurry back just to sit in the chair again. Funnily enough, at that time, we never had a real conversation. There seemed to be a peacefulness in that room, and each of us seemed content to sit quietly and reflect on our lives.

Finally, in spite of our vigil, she slipped away in the middle of the night when we were both asleep. We arrived one morning to be met with the news. There were a few formalities to be gone through and that was that. Then nothing. But we'd become so used by now to our little routine that we weren't sure what to do. And leaving the hospital now meant a total acknowledgement that she'd died, and neither of us was ready for that. Just yet.

So we went for coffee.

"Did she talk to you about what she wanted?" I asked.

"You mean…?"

"Yeah. I know she wanted to be buried not burned. But did she ever tell you where?"

"Not really. I always thought next to my dad…"

"…In Montana…?"

"…Of course…."

"…Because, I mean, there's a choice. She grew up in Pennsylvania, which is where her family is, And *my* dad. But she lived here in Florida for a few years. She might have picked something out here. Then there's California…"

"….Why would she want to be buried in California?"

"Because that's where I live. I'm only saying. Did she say anything to you? Or maybe leave a will?"

"Yeah, there's a will somewhere. But I don't know if she put *that* in. I'm pretty sure she would have wanted it to be in Montana."

I looked at my half-brother. I didn't really want to have to traipse out to Montana if I wanted to visit her grave. But I also really didn't feel like arguing about it.

"We'll look in the will." Was all I said.

# Chapter Seventeen

It was a relief when my plane touched down at LAX. The trip to South-East Asia had taken its toll on me. But the emotional experience of the last week in Florida had completely knocked the stuffing out of me. Wearily I disembarked from the plane and trudged through arrivals, paying little attention to anything around me.

As I waited for the car park shuttle bus my mind was blank, so focused was I on just getting home.

Mercifully the freeway was unclogged and gave me a fairly swift ride back home. I parked the car and turned off the motor. And relished the absence of sound and the thrumming of the motor. I lay back in the seat and stretched my neck. It had been a long time since I'd felt as dog-tired as this.

Finally I climbed out and dragged my bag out of the back, pausing at the front door because I suddenly couldn't remember locking the car doors. Then I heard in my head the echo of the beep as I'd pushed the button on the key ring. Okay.

I pushed the door key into the lock and almost staggered in, dropping the bags as I kicked the door shut. When I turned and tottered into the living room the first thing I noticed was the urn containing Marie's ashes.

"Oh no. I have to do *something* with you my darling. Enough is enough. Especially after this week. But not now. *Definitely* not now. Tomorrow."

And I flopped down on the settee and fell instantly asleep.

Some time in the middle of the night I half woke, but at first I couldn't figure out where I was. When I realized I breathed out deeply and started pulling off my clothes, leaving a trail all the way to the bathroom where I stood wavering over a torrential and never-ending piss, before staggering off to find my bed.

Dawn was just beginning to glow through the bedroom window when I next woke. I could make out familiar silhouettes as I lay enjoying the feeling of being in my own bed in my own room.

"Nice to go traveling," I thought, "but so nice to come home." And then my fifty-nine year old bladder forced me out of bed.

I stood in the shower until it ran cold, letting the water wash away the knots from my body. And by the time I'd shaved and brushed my teeth thoroughly I was beginning to feel human again. I brewed a pot of coffee while I rummaged for something to eat, finding only a single pop-tart which I dropped into the toaster. "Shoulda called Louisa," I thought.

Although it was a beautiful early Fall day, Santa Monica was uncrowded. I found somewhere to park easily. Then I went around the car, leaned in through the passenger door and unhooked the seatbelt that had been safely holding the urn in place. Hugging it to me, I gently kicked the door shut and locked the car.

I felt very self-conscious during the long walk along the pier. Even though I tried to act as nonchalantly as I could, the urn seemed to attract some attention. Or was I just imagining that? There were a few families on the pier, and it was the children who stared at me. Did they know what I was holding?

I tried just looking ahead and trying to ignore anyone I met. But I was distracted about half way along by a woman coming towards me who seemed to be having some kind of manic attack. She was gesticulating wildly and shouting out. I thought she was coming straight at me, and my first response was to feel protective of Marie. Partly, of course, in case the woman knocked the urn from my hands. But also, strangely, for the peace of mind of Marie's spirit. I found that to be most odd. Because, never in my life, could I remember imagining the spirits of the dead. Even as a child.

I crossed to the other side as I saw the woman coming closer and closer, hoping that she would not come swinging over to my side. And then, when she was only yards away from me, I noticed the wire dangling from her ear and the tiny microphone attached to it near her mouth. And I realized that she was talking to someone on the cell phone which I could now see her clutching tightly. Obviously she was having some kind of argument and, in fact, passed right by me without seeming to see me at all. I laughed to myself about how stupid I'd been.

As I advanced along the pier the wind picked up and wisps of my hair started to whip against my face. The tide was in. and I decided that I didn't need to go right to the end. I stopped and looked around at the beach and the headland behind. Marie and I had come down here many times. It was a place that she was fond of. And that was one reason why I had chosen it. But also because, as I looked out across the rolling waves, out towards the deeper ocean, I knew that this was a way I could set her free. And she had always been a child of the world. A free spirit in the best, most meaningful, aspect of the phrase.

The wind was watering up my eyes now. In my heart I would like them to have been real tears. But I knew that the hurting in my heart was real. And I knew that I had loved Marie and would always love her.

I pulled the top off the urn and set it on the ground at my feet. Then I shut my eyes as I felt, rather than thought, a silent prayer. At first I gently tipped out just a little. Fragments of her dust floated in the air. Then I upended the urn and followed the clouds of ashes as they swirled around, gusting this way and that, and then sank below me into the ocean. I didn't take any notice now of the few people around me watching what I was doing.

"Good bye my love," I said.

I closed my eyes again and, for the briefest possible moment, wondered about following the ashes down into the water. I imagined my body falling through the air, almost flying, until it hit the water and passed through the surface. And I imagined going down and down, with the water enfolding me, absorbing me. Until, at last, I finally merged with the ocean. And my whole being turned liquid – became water. I had deliquesced, and was no longer solid

An enormous sadness overcame me. It felt like I had lost a part of myself. Something that I would never see again. I was overwhelmed by a sense of separation. And there was a yearning in my heart. A longing that I knew would now never be fulfilled. Part of myself had been ripped away.

Mark Abrahams had been my doctor for more than twenty years. He'd steered me through minor ailments and encouraged me to have all the checks. But it had been some time since I'd had the full cardio. Now Mark sat at his computer, composing a letter to a cardiologist. He tapped a few more keys and read what he'd typed. Then he added a few more words, saved the page and hit the print button.

"This guy's good. If there's something to find, he'll find it," he said

"I'm not really looking for anything," I drawled.

"I know, I know. But if there's something there you need to know. And, besides," he chuckled grimly, "I don't want you suing me for malpractice."

"So this is all about you?"

"Of course. Isn't it always?"

Mark plucked the letter from the printer, folded it and slid it into an envelope. He scribbled an address and phone number on the envelope and handed it to me.

"Look, you've been through quite a bit lately. At your age…"

"At *my* age…?

"…Yes, at *your* age. There are men fifteen years younger than you – men who seem to be perfectly healthy – dropping dead. So at *your* age it certainly doesn't hurt to err on the side of caution. Okay? Now, is there anything else I can help you with today?"

"Nope."

"Good."

I stood up to leave.

"By the way, I was sorry to hear about your mother. When's the funeral?"

"Couple of days. In Montana. My…brother's organizing it all."

"Okay. Take it easy."

"I will doc, I will."


I felt strange visiting a cardiologist. Was this going to be the pattern now? Specialists for this, that and the other? I'd never really been sick in my life, and I certainly didn't relish it now. But the cardiologist's offices reflected the proximity of Rodeo Drive. It was more like a boutique hotel, with its concealed lighting and swish furniture. The receptionist was swish too. With her model looks and couture dress she looked anything but a receptionist. Nevertheless she handed me a clipboard with several pieces of paper, and a long list of questions.

"If you could kindly fill this in."

A real Jessica Rabbit.

I looked at the questions. Details of my health for my whole life practically. I hated with a passion filling in forms. But I gritted my teeth and dug in. And, after wracking my brain for over fifteen minutes, I managed to complete every page. I handed it back to the receptionist when she got off the phone. I was hoping for straight 'A's.

"If you could kindly step on here."

She meant the weighing machine. I hadn't weighed myself fully clothed for a very long time and was staggered to see what it was. I was about to make excuses, but realized that was probably unnecessary. She didn't seem to be bothered by my weight. She made a note, lifted the phone and spoke quietly into it, then turned to me.

"Doctor Li will see you now. If you just go along that corridor. It's the first door on the left."

Doctor Norman Li was an extremely jovial man with twinkling eyes and broad, Chinese features.

"Ah yes, Mister Max Wheeler. How are you?"

"Well, I was rather hoping you might tell me that."

"Yes, of course." The cardiologist roared with laughter. Finally he said, "You have come for a heart check. I hope my receptionist looked after you."

"Er, yes."

"Good, good. She gave you my bill for five thousand dollars...?"

"...What!...."

And the good doctor again roared with laughter, "Okay, that's the heart check. Well, you seem to have survived, you must be alright! No, no, just kidding! Could you take your shirt off please."

At first I wasn't a hundred percent sure *that* wasn't another gag, but I decided to play along. As I stripped of my shirt, a beautiful oriental girl in a white lab coat came in with my notes, which she handed to Doctor and then smiled sweetly at me.

"Thank you Katie."

"Oh 'Katie'. I have a daughter called 'Katie'", I said, then immediately felt foolish. She smiled at me again. But all she said was, "Really."

"Okay," said Doctor Li, "Could you please lie up here on the bed."

I hopped up on to the day bed and lay down. The doctor wrapped a blood pressure band around my arm, pumped it up, and started applying his stethoscope to my chest and back.

"Uh huh.....Muh huh." he said.

"Do they teach you that at medical school?" I asked. "Are there special classes in 'doctor-speak'?"

This set the doctor off laughing again. "Oh yes, right after the classes where they taught us to write unintelligibly."

Katie began to examine my chest intensely, almost sensually rubbing a finger over it. Memories of Cambodia flooded back to me. But Katie looked at Doctor Li quizzically. He, in turn, saw the uncertainty on my face.

"Don't worry," he chuckled, "She just wants to know whether she should shave you or not. We need the contacts to make a good connection....What do you think? Is he is too hairy?" he asked her.

"No, I think he will be okay," she said, and began to smooth a cold gel on my chest. When she'd finished she picked up a handful of leads, like carburetor leads, and started sticking them to my chest.

Then she held the other end of the leads as we all moved over to a walking machine, similar to the one in my gym. I felt like a dog being led on some strange kind of leash.

"Do you do much exercise?" asked Doctor Li.

"Try to," I said, as Katie plugged in the other ends of the leads to another machine connected to a computer.

"Good."

He switched on the walker and I began to amble along.

"This isn't much of a test." I thought to myself.

But after three minutes Katie and the good doctor read and noted the readout from the computer, checked my vital signs, then turned up the speed of the walker. Now it was genuine walking speed, but still no strain.

Eventually they got the speed to a point where I really was having to push. And now I was sweating.

"Ah, I think we have found your point," exclaimed the doctor. "Can you carry on for another couple of minutes?"

"I...think...so," I puffed.

For some reason Doctor Li seemed to find it all amusing. I could feel the blood throbbing through me but, I realized, there was no pain in my heart. I pushed on harder, silently counting out the seconds to myself. At last Doctor Li hit the button and the machine slowed and then came to a stop. I was still breathing heavily, but I managed a sigh of relief.

"I thought you said you worked out," laughed Doctor Li.

"I...guess...not as...much...as I....should," I managed.

The doctor checked my blood pressure again and nodded to himself.

"Okay. Please come over here and lie down again and Katie will remove all the spaghetti. When she's done please put your shirt back on and come and see me in my office." And he disappeared next door.

I did as I was asked and, after Katie had removed all the leads, she wiped the gel from my chest and smiled sweetly at me as she handed me the towel to finish wiping myself,

I was still buttoning my shirt as I walked into Doctor Li's office. The cardiologist was typing some notes on his computer and waved to me to sit down. Eventually he saved the file, turned to me and looked at me inscrutably. Then he picked up a plastic model of a heart which had lurid colors and removable parts.

"This is your heart. Well, not *your* heart of course. If it was *your* heart," he laughed, "you'd be dead and I wouldn't be sitting here talking with you."

What a joker!

"I'm sure that you know that your body is able to function because blood is being driven around it, yes…?"

"…Yes…"

"…Good. So, about five liters of blood circulates around your body every minute. And what drives it?" He held up the model, "This beautiful pump: the heart."

He demonstrated the chambers of the heart as though they were rooms in a house, and then described in detail the pathway of the blood as it received oxygen from the lungs and delivered it throughout the body. Even though he'd obviously given this talk possibly thousands of times, I could see that he was relishing it. I knew some of the details already, but actually found it interesting. On the other hand, enough was enough.

"So…?" I asked.

"So? Well, you will be pleased to know that I can't see anything seriously wrong with your heart. There are some minor matters, but nothing that shouts at me. Okay?"

"Yes," I said, highly relieved. Actually, it was only when I breathed out and realized just *how* relieved I was, that I also realized how worried I'd been by it all.

"It's possible that you have some interference in these small arteries here," he said pointing at the model. "And I'd like to study your readouts in more detail. I'd also like you to have some blood tests. But…" and he paused.

191

"…But?" I wondered.

"…Tell me. How has life been for you in the last few months? Have you had much stress?"

"Well, my mother's just died. And a while back I got fired from my job. And that came right on the heel of my wife dying."

"Mmm, I see," was all the doctor said for a moment. Then, "So would it be fair to say that you've been experiencing some stress?"

"I would say that's fair to say, yes."

"Yes, so most probably that is your answer.…But we'll finish the tests just in case, okay?"

"Okay."

"Good. Katie will take your blood and I will send all your results to doctor…" he checked the letter, "Doctor Abrahams."

***

The first sign that I read after I got off the plane read 'Welcome to Billings Logan International Airport, gateway to the big sky and beyond'.

Billings, Montana. "Definitely 'beyond'. Possibly even further than that." I thought, and wondered about it being an international airport, and how many tourists came here from, say, Paris or Tokyo. "Probably not too many,"

Elliott's wife was called Elizabeth-Anne. She'd been very attractive once. But that was a few years ago. Now her body had filled out so much that her waistline had disappeared, and her once-pretty face had become flabby and jowly. I almost walked right past her. And I would have if she hadn't called out my name.

"Elizabeth-Anne?"

"Yep. I guess it's been a while."

"Too long. How've you been."

"Oh, fine. Just fine."

We walked together in semi-silence, broken up with patches of polite questions. She was an unassuming woman, as far as I knew a good wife and mother. But I'd never managed to get close to her. Figured out how she ticked. It was as though we existed on parallel but separate universes.

"I was sorry to hear about your…wife." she said.

There it was. That nanosecond of hesitation between 'your' and 'wife', as though she wasn't quite sure what to call Marie. Because, I guessed, in Elizabeth-Anne's mind, Lisa would always be my wife. And Marie would be something else. But I understood that this was *her* world, a world of simplicity where everything had its place. And second wives didn't really figure in that world for her. What a shock she'd get if Elliott left her and married someone else. But, what were the chances of that happening?

"Thank you," I said politely.

"You came here alone? None of your children are coming?"

"Nah, they've all got their lives. And they're all pretty busy. You know."

"But she was their grandmother!"

"Yeah…,"

I just let it hang. What was I going to say? In fact I would have liked them all to be there. Lisa too. But the truth was they were all too busy. No-one had time for anything these days. Not even family funerals. And they sure as hell weren't going to fly out to Montana for a funeral. Not even Katie.

We climbed aboard the family's ginormous SUV, and Elizabeth-Anne spent an agonizing five minutes trying to reverse out of the parking place.

I had offered to stay in a motel, but Elliott and Elizabeth-Anne wouldn't hear of it. The couple lived in a large house just outside Billings. Their daughter Brandy was in her third year of college, but had returned for the funeral. She was sitting on a stool in the kitchen talking quietly with her brother Gary when Elizabeth-Anne brought me in.

"You remember your uncle Max?" asked Elizabeth-Anne somewhat unnecessarily.

"Yes, of course," said Gary, "It's not been that long. How're ya doin'?"

Both Brandy and Gary were what you might call 'large'. "Welcome to the twenty-first century," I thought.

Brandy came over and kissed me on the cheek, and Gary reached out a paw for me to shake.

"You've got my room," said Gary. "If you want to wash up I'll show you where it is."

He hopped off the stool and grabbed my bag. I shrugged and followed him.

"Where are you sleeping?" I asked.

"With my bud next door. It's okay." He pushed open his bedroom door. "I cleaned up as much as I could." he said without any hint of an apology.

"It's fine. Thanks very much for this…"

"…No biggy…" said Gary, and left.

I looked around me at this teenage boy's room, and was instantly taken back to my own teenage years.


The first surprise was to discover that Elliott was a vegetarian.

"You would be too if you saw some of the things I've seen," he said. "Boy, I could tell you some stories."

"Not right now, honey," jumped in Elizabeth-Anne.

"Don't worry, I wasn't going to…."

"…Max, whyn't you have some more pot roast. You know this recipe comes from Judy H. Martz, who used to be our Governor. It's her own special recipe."

"No thanks, Elizabeth-Anne. It is nice though…"

"How 'bout some more potato pie. It's Gary's favorite, isn't it Gary?"

"I'm doing just fine thanks."

"But you've hardly eaten anything…"

"…Honey, leave the man alone. He's a grown man. If he wants some more he'll take some more. He knows if he wants more food. Right Max…?"

"…Honey. I know he's a grown man. I'm just being sociable is all."

"Well, I'll have some more," said Gary reaching out an arm for the potato pie.

"How's Katie?" asked Brandy, "She was very sweet to me when I visited Los Angeles last year."

"She's fine. She's just sorry she can't be here."

Family! Not the area where I'm at my best. I know men who love to be surrounded by their families, by uncles aunts and cousins. Men who revel in familial activities. But I had always been different. Not that it bothered me a lot. I figured I was just a different breed. Was I antisocial? The truth was I didn't actually like people very much…..Although I wouldn't have broadcast that to the world…..Sure, I had a few friends that I felt very good about. And my kids, of course. I loved them. But, people generally? I was *interested* in them, but I didn't really *like* them very much. Actually I often preferred animals.

Elizabeth-Anne brought a platter in from the kitchen.

"Now I just know you're going to have some my strawberry crispies. I made them specially for you.

Elliott had arranged everything with the funeral home. And, to be fair, he'd done a good job. The casket was modest but, I thought, strangely suited my mother's taste. If it had been up to me, of course, I would have had a closed casket. But Elliott had wanted it this way. Just so we could all have one last good-bye.

There were about three dozen people in the chapel. Close family, old friends. Some people I had never met and had no idea who they were. They could have just wandered in for all I knew. Maybe that was their hobby, going to funerals. I knew people with stranger hobbies.

Elliott walked up to the casket and stood silently beside it. He gazed down for a long time, then bent and kissed our mother's face. Then he turned and faced the mourners,

"There is a quality in people that seems to me to become rarer and rarer every year that I'm alive. The quality I'm talking about is 'goodness'. A guileless willingness to be there for other people and to do good in the world….My mother had that goodness. In this dog-eat-dog world that we seem to find ourselves living in, she was a rarity. She was, in every sense, a *good* woman. Just like it says in the bible. In her life she had many friends and an abundance of acquaintances. And she would willingly go out of her way for any one of them. Go that extra mile. And, in return she inspired loyalty and respect. She was loved too. Not just by her family, but by the whole community…."

At this point, for some reason, he looked directly at me. I had been thinking about Elliott's words. "Would anybody ever describe *me* in that way?" I wondered.

"….She was the best mother a child could have. And the best wife a man could have. She loved my father and always took care of him, and I know that he loved her too. And I speak for my own children when I say that she was also a loving and beloved grandmother. She will be sorely missed by everybody…And now I call on my brother Max to say a few words."

This caught me completely off-guard. *Of course* I was expected to speak. Why hadn't I realized that? There I'd been, drifting along to Elliott's words, and not even giving it a thought. Plus, I wondered whether as a 'television person', they'd all be expecting something special from me. Maybe I should have asked Harry to write something for me. I was okay at speeches. But this was ridiculous! This was my mother for Christ's sake! Almost reluctantly I moved to the front, where Elliott reached up and hugged me. That was a first! I couldn't recollect any time when the two of us had hugged.

I turned to look at my mother. She lay in waxy repose, dressed in her best clothes. Amazingly, many of the cross-hatching of lines that had congregated on her face now seemed to have softened and, in some cases, disappeared. She looked not so much peaceful as untroubled. Nothing could touch her now. Not the good things nor the bad stuff. I leant over her and kissed her forehead. It was as cold as ice. And I thought to myself, "This is not my mother. This is a wax effigy of who she was. My mother is someone else. And, now, some*where* else."

I turned to face the expectant group. And slowly began to speak.

"My bro…" a frog caught in my throat, and I cleared it, "My brother Elliott has already spoken to you about how special my mother was. I'm sure each one of you…." and I paused briefly to look at them all, "…could tell a number of stories about how she touched your lives."

What the hell was I going to say? A small, white-haired elderly woman wearing a black dress was sniffling. I wondered who she was. Then my mind went numb and I shut my eyes and tried to collect my thoughts. But nothing would come. I decided to risk it, to just start talking and see what came out of my mouth. I began hesitantly.

"My mother was there for me every day of my life. I have so….so many memories of her from when I was a child. She also gave me many gifts," (What! Where was I going with that?) From a GI Joe that I might desperately have wanted, to a smile on a cloudy day. But…but I think the greatest gift she gave me was that she believed in me."

And then it just came tumbling out.

"Even as a small boy, if I said I wanted to *be* something or *do* something, she immediately supported me. In her eyes I could *do anything. Be anything.* She gave me that great gift and, if I am anything at all today, it is entirely because of her. She gave me not only her unconditional love, but her unconditional support. I may not have spent as much time with her in recent times as I would have liked. But, whenever we talked on the phone, she would tell me that she knew that we were close. And that was true. She was the best mother a boy could have …and the best mother a man could have."

I twisted around to gaze down at her for a long time, then whispered, "Thank you."

I cleared my throat again and turned back to the assembly. I wanted to say something else, but the words just wouldn't come. I wanted to tell them all about how, after my father died, my mother had been everything to me. And that, even after she re-married, she always gave me her attention. That, even though my own children hadn't gotten to spend much time with her, whenever she and I spoke she unfailingly asked about each of them by name. And always sent a card and a little something to each of them on their birthdays and at Christmas. But nothing else would come out of my mouth. So I just dropped my head and walked back to my seat.

A couple of other people spoke briefly, then everybody headed out to the cemetery. The ground was all prepared, with green edging around the gaping hole. It was when I arrived at the edge of this deep opening in the earth that I began to fully realize the permanence of the situation. That they were going to put my mother, my mom, in this hole in the ground and I would never see her again. I desperately wished I could cry. I wanted something to wash away the feelings that I was experiencing. To extinguish the pain. But, although my eyes burned and I could barely swallow, not a single tear fell from my eye.

As the service continued I became more dazed. I barely heard the words spoken. I watched as the casket was lowered into the cavity and the first few spadefuls of soil were shoveled onto it. But there was a roaring in my ears and a feeling of cotton inside my head. My body became zombie-like, with a deep, deep enervation. Somebody passed me a shovel, but I couldn't have told you what I did with it.

More words were spoken and then it was over. People turned to one another to hug and to support. A few of the men shook my hand and muttered a few words. I had no idea what. Elliott again gave me a tentative half hug, as did Elizabeth-Anne, but I found it hard to get my body to respond.

And that was that.

# Chapter Eighteen

Back in Los Angeles I called in to see Mike.

"You didn't have to come in just yet, you know that."

"I know. But I can't just sit around at home Mike. You know me better than that."

"Yeah....Sorry to hear about your mother. Was it...expected?"

"Yes, pretty much. She'd had Alzheimer's for some time. And there were other things. You know, in some ways it was a relief. Especially for her. She really didn't know which side was up anymore."

"But still tough on you."

A pause. This part of it was still sinking in with me.

"Yes," I said eventually, "it is."

Neither of us spoke for a while. I was lost in my thoughts and I guess Mike didn't want to impose anything on me.

Eventually I let out a deep sigh and looked up.

"Well, life goes on. How are things here?"

"Okay. We're still growing steadily."

Before he spoke again he looked towards the door.

"But........There are rumors that Amy will sell out. One guy even mentioned Murdoch. But I think they're just rumors...at this point."

"But the company's just getting started!"

He shrugged. I wasn't quite sure where that left me.

"So you've got more work for me?"

"If you want. Are you sure you're ready for it?"

"'The show must go on.' Besides it'll occupy my mind. Which will be a good thing. So, what've you got?"

"Tell you what. Let me look through some stuff and talk it over with Amy. Speaking of whom, have you seen her at all?"

"No. Although she actually sent me a note about my mother. Which I thought was nice."

"Yeah, she can be like that."

"Tell me, does she really own all this?"

"Sure. Why not. I think her old man and some of his friends originally put up the money. But she's a smart cookie. She developed the whole thing and she got the details and the dynamic right. And she's got incredible radar, very plugged in. It's because of her that it's successful."

Mike's phone buzzed and he picked it up.

"Yep…Oh, hi." Mike smiled at me and mouthed, "It's Amy." Then, into the phone, "Yes….No, we didn't….Naturally….Uh huh…Sure. By the way, Max is here…Yes, will do…okay."

He put the phone down

"What was I saying about her radar? She's amazing." And he shook his head, unbelieving. "By the way, she wants to see you. "'If you're up to it', she said."

Amy stood up as soon as I walked in. She came around her desk and kissed me lightly on the cheek.

"Max. How *are* you?"

Her tone was warm and sincere, but there was not a hint of the passion that we'd shared last time that I'd seen her.

"I'm okay. I came looking for an assignment."

"Are you sure? Don't you need time to…?"

"To grieve? Yes. But I can't just grieve to order. I think…I mean I was just starting to get over the loss of my wife. Now…"

I was silent for a moment, gathering my thoughts.

"I know it'll come Amy. But, I guess right now I just need something to occupy me. And you know this is something I've always loved. So…"

She looked deeply into my eyes. "Okay then, if you're sure. And if there's anything we…I can do just let me know. Okay?"

"That's very kind. Thank you."

She studied me in silence for a moment. I had thought that our previous encounter was a one-off. Now I wondered whether perhaps there might be a return bout. It wasn't something I felt like right now. But maybe sometime in the future.

"You're most welcome." Her smile was difficult to read.

I headed for the door.

"Max?"

"Yes," I said, turning around.

"Have you ever considered more of a management position?"

"You mean like Mike's job?"

"Yes, that sort of thing.

"Not really. I know what I'm good at. And…that isn't me."

I meant what I said. But I couldn't help wondering what she had in mind. She didn't tell me, of course. She simply smiled enigmatically. And I decided that it was time to leave.

\*\*\*

"So…what's been happening?"

Mos had invited me over to his house and we were seated on the porch. Mos had been most unlike his usual garrulous self. So quiet, in fact, that I knew there was something in the wind. Even now he held his silence a little bit too long.

"Mos?"

Eventually Mos let out a long sigh, "Libby found a lump." Was all he said.

"A lum…?" Then I realized the full significance. "What do you mean 'she found a lump'?"

"Just that."

"And…?"

"And….It's breast cancer."

"She had it checked?"

"Yes…She got the results two days ago…"

"…Two days! Why didn't you tell me before now?"

He'd been looking away from me this whole time, staring down at his shoes, as though he could find some answers there. Now Mos turned to me.

"With all your tsoris recently I didn't think you needed one more thing. I didn't want to burden you…"

"…It's not a burden. I'm your friend, aren't I?"

"Yes, of course you are. Which is why I'm telling you now."

"I should think so."

There was another long pause and Mos went back to studying his shoes. Neither of us knew what to say. But eventually, without looking up, Mos again broke the silence.

"And…you know…I always thought it would be me. All these years I've been worrying about getting this, getting that. And all the time it was Lib I should have worried about."

"You don't blame yourself, do you? I mean…"

"…No, I don't blame myself for the cancer. But maybe I should have sensed something…"

"…How could you have sensed something…?" I started to say. But when Mos looked up at me there tears in his eyes. And it shut me up immediately. So, instead I asked, "How bad is it?"

"Well, thank God it looks like it might be at a fairly early stage. The lump is quite small. They only caught it because she had a mammogram. You want to know a funny thing? Her sister thought *she'd* found a lump and was too nervous to go for a screening by herself. So she asked Lib to go with her. And, while she was there, she thought she might as well get screened herself….Thank God!"

"And how's the sister?"

"What?...Oh, the sister's fine. Turns out it was nothing. But God bless her. Because if it hadn't been…"

At this point his voice trailed off as his thoughts turned to what might have been.

Again we each began to ruminate, Mos on 'what might have been', while my thoughts of Marie mingled with my memories of my mother.

It was Mos who spoke again first.

"Crazy world, huh?"

"Sure is….So, is she getting treatment?"

"Yeah. Or, she will be. First they're going to take out the lump. And, while they do that, they'll do a biopsy. Apparently, if it's okay after that, she might have to have chemo or radiation. I'm not sure. If it's not okay then…. they might have to remove her breast."

The last few words struggled out of his mouth, and his eyes began to glisten. He blinked back the tears that were welling there. "Oh Christ! God knows I don't want to lose her. But, you know what? I also don't want her to have a breast removed." And now tears started to gently run down his cheeks.

"What are you worried about! Your sex life? You think you won't find her attractive any more? Surely at least she'd be alive."

Perhaps I was thinking about Marie at that time. Perhaps I was just making a point.

"Besides," I continued, "they can do good reconstruction work these days. *If* she has to have it they can fix her up."

Mos thought for a moment. Then the old irrepressible Mos smiled through his tears, "I guess....And she'd been complaining lately about having saggy tits. This would be a good excuse for a boob job. Wouldn't it?"

***

I had arranged to meet Mike in the same karaoke bar we'd met in before. Mostly social, but he'd had some ideas on some assignments for me and he wanted to run the ideas by me. I'd arrived on time and been waiting for twenty minutes with still no sign of Mike. My beer glass was empty and I decided to switch to scotch. The barman pushed the small glass towards me and placed a small pitcher of water beside it unasked. I handed over the money and fished out my cell phone. I dialed up Mike's number but it was engaged. But, just as I flipped the phone shut, it rang. It was Mike. Our calls had obviously crossed.

"Hey Buddy."

"Hey Mike, where are you?"

"I'm still here. In the office. Sorry, I got stuck. We had a new thing came in that I had to deal with right away. Are you there...?"

"...In the bar...?"

"...Yeah..."

"...Uh huh. I've been here about twenty minutes."

"Okay, can you give me, like, a half hour and then I'll know how it's going. Can you wait? Are you due somewhere?"

"No I'm not due somewhere. Where would I go?"

"I dunno. So that's okay?"

"I guess. Just call me and let me know, alright?"

"Will do. See yer."

I closed the phone and looked around. Someone in the next room was warbling a Beatles song and it sounded horrible. I sipped at my drink and checked out my fellow fun-seekers. A group of three guys were standing at the other end of the bar, deeply engrossed in a conversation. But I couldn't hear what it was. From time to time one or other of them would flick a look at a pair of attractive girls…Strike that!…Attractive young women, seated in the corner behind me. Both of them wore very low cut tops in the fashion of the day, their breasts spilling out like wenches or milkmaids. I tried not to stare, but I couldn't help myself. How could I *not* look. Any red-blooded man would be drawn to this spectacle as their luscious breasts threatened any second to free themselves and come tumbling undone. One of them had a top cut so low that I could see the tops of the pinkish brown areolas around her nipples. Sex hadn't been on my mind. It really wasn't what I wanted to think about at all right now, but I found it hard to tear my eyes away. I could hear that the two women were talking about a third woman. Presumably a mutual friend. I purposefully tried turning my head away from them, but couldn't help being drawn back.

The song, and the singer, changed. This time the guy had a more mellifluous voice, and I found myself caught up in the melody.

I took a sip of my drink, and was surprised to discover that the glass was empty. I ordered another one just as a party of two couples walked in and approached the bar. The place was starting to fill up now. The barman poured the drink and took my money. I waved away the change.

A television over the bar was silently playing out a game. The Dodgers, it looked like. I checked it out. Yeah, the Dodgers. I twisted my wrist to see the time on my watch. "Maybe I should get up there and sing something myself." I thought. "Nope. I don't *think* so!"

The two young women were both starting to look around the bar with edgy, nervous little looks. Were they too waiting for someone?

Now it was an Asian voice singing a Sinatra song in a quavering voice, totally lacking in understanding of where to give the right emphasis to the words. I thought of the many nights I'd spent in Tokyo and Seoul, in bars not too dissimilar to this. And my mind drifted vaguely to the hundreds of places that I'd visited over the years. In one way they all blended into one location. But then I reckoned that, if I applied my mind, I would probably be able to remember each and every place that I'd visited.

Now the women in front of me were stealing glances at me. Were they attracted to me? What was happening in my life that so many younger women were drawn to me? By focusing a little harder, I was able to hear what they were saying.

"What, that old guy?"

"Yes him. He keeps staring at us."

"Dirty old man! Don't you think that's so totally creepy. I reckon they should lock people like that up."

"Yes, it's disgusting."

It was a moment before I realized they were talking about me! "Jesus Christ!" They were talking about me. The 'old man'. "No, the 'dirty old man'. Holy shit! *Had* I been staring at them? Had I turned into that guy? When did he turn into *that guy*! I felt deeply embarrassed, and turned away from them. I could almost feel my face suffuse with shame. What was I thinking! I wanted to run from the bar and never return. And I felt so old!

My cell phone rang.

"Hey Max. Sorry buddy, I'm not going to make it. This is taking much longer than I anticipated."

"S'alright," I managed to say.

"You okay buddy?"

"Yeah, sure."

"I'll call you tomorrow, okay?"

"Sure. No problem."

So it was with a feeling of relief that I knocked back my drink and fled from the bar.

As I was climbing into my car I wondered whether I should drive. I tried to remember how many drinks I'd had. "Only three." I thought. "Three whiskys and a beer." That was okay wasn't it? I had a little buzz on, but I was okay to drive. I needed to concentrate, that was all. And probably get something to eat. That would be a good idea. I started the car and slowly pulled away. The traffic was light and I had no problems. I was careful to drive under the limit, but not too slowly. And to keep the car straight. "Straighten up and fly right."

I was about to drive through an intersection when the car in front pulled up unexpectedly. I slammed on the brakes. My car twisted and turned, narrowly avoiding parked cars to my right. I managed to pull up with burning rubber, inches from the car in front of me. I was about to yell at the idiot who'd stopped like that, then realized the driver had halted because of a red light. Oh, shit! I would have driven straight through. And then maybe *I too* would be toast right now.

"Better be even more careful," I said out loud to myself. Obviously I wasn't in as much control as I thought I'd been. Maybe I shouldn't be driving at all. So, what should I do? Pull over and park? And then what? Let's see, where was I? I probably could walk home from here. "Are you crazy!" I said, again out loud, "Walk home? In Los Angeles? "Not a good idea buddy."

So…what? Grab a cab? Good luck with that one as well. "No," I thought, "I'll find somewhere to eat ASAP." Then I realized that I was near The Bow Thai restaurant. I cruised along until I found somewhere to park, and gratefully eased the car to a stop. For a moment I just sat there and breathed out gently. Then I climbed out and walked to the restaurant.

The place only had a handful of customers, but nobody came to greet me. So I selected a table halfway back and sat down. I looked around. Even though it was a Thai restaurant it somehow reminded me of Cambodia, where I'd been only two weeks before. I picked up the menu. I'd eaten there so many times with the guys that I knew the menu pretty well. I quickly decided on fish cakes and my favorite chicken dish, and waited for a waitress to come.

While I waited my mind drifted to the experience I'd just had in the bar. And, again, my face suffused as I remembered how I'd misunderstood the girls' intentions. I exhaled deeply.

Eventually a waitress appeared almost silently at the table. She smiled at me a little shyly. I hadn't seen her before but she was very pretty. And, strangely, she reminded me of someone. I couldn't think who. I read out my order to her.

"You want something drink?"

"Yeah, I'll have…" I was about to order a beer, then realized I'd better have something else. "…How about a diet Coke."

"Okay."

As she walked away she swayed her hips in a slow, gracious fashion that excited and fascinated me. Then it came to me who she reminded me of. Of course! The girl in the hotel. The masseuse. *Masseuse?* That was classic. But I was loath to call her what she really was. I just wanted to remember her as 'the girl in the hotel'. I thought about that night. I'd enjoyed myself. It had been a nice experience. And the girl seemed okay about the whole thing. Or was she? She hadn't shown me any hint of displeasure. And…

A thought bubbled its way to my consciousness.

…And she'd certainly behaved as though she was doing what she was doing voluntarily. But was she? I felt like I'd taken a maturity pill. The journalist in me took over and I started thinking about sexual slavery. Is that what this girl was? Was she being held against her wishes, forced to do what she did against her will? Had she been kidnapped or, even worse, was her family being threatened? I searched my memory for any hint that it had been against her wishes. For the life of me it certainly hadn't seemed that way. I mean, she almost seemed to have enjoyed the experience, although I wasn't fool enough to believe that she regarded me as a great lover. Or was I? There was a moment, a brief moment, when I'd felt that. That I was actually giving her something. Giving her pleasure. And that she was responding because she was turned on. But I knew in my heart that she was just acting. But was it worse than that? Was she acting that she was okay with it when she really wasn't?

I went over the whole episode in my mind again. I had treated her gently, I knew that. I certainly hadn't hurt her. Ha! The Benign Rapist! No, that was too dramatic. I knew that she had probably had hundreds of men, and that I was just one of them. I couldn't take responsibility for her life. But that too wasn't right either. I *could* have said no. I could have refused to play the game.

But what if it all was her choice? What if this was her only chance to make a little money? That she could make more money this way than any other? And…what if she did enjoy it, just a little bit? Was it really such a bad thing? And, ultimately, can you actually take responsibility for someone else's life? I knew the answer to that one. I knew that, without men like me, her profession would not be able to flourish at all.

It was the return of the waitress that interrupted my self-torture. I exhaled deeply just as she placed the Coke and the fishcakes in front of me. She noticed the sigh.

"You okay?"

I looked up into her pretty, concerned face and forced myself to smile at her. "Yes, I'm fine thank you."

She smiled back, "Good. Have good meal. Okay?"

"Thank you."

This time I didn't watch her ass as she walked away.

*** 

I sat in Mark Abrahams' waiting room, flicking through a pile of magazines. Sitting there seemed to confirm that my doctor was paid too much money, because he always had the very latest issues of a whole range of magazines, none of which was ever dog-eared or had pages torn out.

Actually, if you had to wait somewhere, this wasn't a bad place. Apart from the classy magazines, Abrahams had installed expensively comfortable chairs. The lighting was restrained and classical music played in the background at just the right level. The receptionist would also supply you with a good coffee or tea if you wanted. Or even a chilled bottle of water. It was a place to relax. Which was just as well, because Abrahams was running late. As usual. This time it was a half hour so far.

After checking out the latest cars, clothing and furniture that I didn't need to buy I had just found an article that I was actually interested in reading when the receptionist called out my name.

"You can go in now."

Reluctantly I put down the magazine and headed for the doctor's inner sanctum.

"Ah Max."

"Hi Mark. How are you?"

"Never better. And how about you?"

"Well, I was rather hoping you might tell me that."

"Yes, of course. But I mean generally. How are you?"

"Not bad. A few minor aches when I wake up in the morning. But nothing to write home about. So….?"

"Yes, of course."

He flipped open my file.

"Okay, I've got the results of your blood work back…and also a letter from Doctor Li…Hmmm."

He read the results to himself for a few moments.

"Right. Well the good news is that Li doesn't see any major problems with your heart. He seems to think that the pain you've been experiencing…"

"…Oh, I wouldn't call it *pain*…"

"…What would you call it? *Pleasure*…?"

"…No, I mean it's not something that's been causing me…"

I wasn't quite sure how to end that sentence.

Abrahams put down the folder and peered at me over the top of his spectacles.

"Max, I know you're a brave-man-and-you-don't-want-to-cause-anyone-any-trouble, etcetera. But I deal with the real world here…"

I was about to protest that I too dealt with the real world, but Abrahams put up his hand to stop me.

"…Let's just get down to it, shall we. Basically your heart seems to be okay, and any pain you've been experiencing is probably stress-related. I say 'probably', because obviously we can't be certain. But, after all, the last few months have been very high stress for you.…Now, the other thing is that some of your levels are somewhat elevated. I'm going to prescribe some meds that should help that. I want you to take them for three months, and then come back and see me again. Okay?"

"Yep."

"Good. And, hopefully, there'll be less stress in your life in the next few months."

"I truly hope so."

***

It was a really hot day. I lay beside the swimming pool. Perspiration beaded down from my forehead and dripped into my eyes, and then formed tiny rivulets which ran down either side of my nose. I rubbed a hand roughly over my face and tried to wipe it away. But it just kept oozing out of my skin. At the same time I could feel pools of sweat growing under my arms. I rose languidly to my feet and, shielding my eyes from the burning sun, I peered into the blue sky. There was not a single cloud to be seen. I could see an airplane so high up that it was no bigger than a speck. I wondered where it was going. And who was on it.

The water was lapping gently at the edge of the pool, and I turned and looked down into it, enjoying the patterns that the water made as it formed, bumped up against the side, then dispersed again. I knelt down and scooped up a handful of water and wiped it over my face. It cooled me a little, but moments later I could feel that I was sweating again.

I stood up and placed my toes square with the edge of the pool. And, holding my arms out wide sideways, I shut my eyes and enjoyed the feeling of being in total balance. My breath was easy now. Slowly in and slowly out. And, for the first time in a long time, I began to feel at one with the universe.

Then, before even I knew that I was going to do it, I brought my arms forward, bent my knees slightly and sprang from the balls of my feet head first into the water.

It was cool and refreshing as I dove downwards, and I felt the silkiness of the water course against my skin as I glided through it.

The deeper I dove, the darker the water became. I could just make out patterns in the inkiness, patterns of swirls and tunnels. I swam towards one of the tunnels, peering to see what lay at the other end. But I couldn't make it out. As I swam, the tunnel itself began to twist and turn and form a kind of vortex. I was drawn deeper and deeper into the vortex, which began to change color from deep navy blue to a lighter blue flecked with patches of green and strands of white.

And I also realized that the consistency was changing too. Instead of clear water it was becoming viscous, like something from inside my own body. Like a mixture of fluids, in fact. Of mucous and sperm and perspiration. And, just in front of me, bright light illuminated shades of red and yellow which, when I got closer, I could see were blood and urine. My own blood and urine.

As I twisted and turned my body through the convolutions of the fluid vortex I began to feel that the various secretions and I were all part of the same entity, as though my whole body was becoming liquid and dissolving into itself.

But while I swam deeper and deeper I knew with certainty that something was missing. And, although I knew what that was, for the life of me, however hard I tried, I couldn't remember what it was.

I tried desperately to think. If I could just remember. If I could just bring that thought to the surface. I almost had it. But the threads of consciousness were intruding and that thing was retreating and drifting away from me. And the more awake I became the harder it was to remember.

And then finally, lying in my bed in a pool of sweat, I was sure that the thought was gone forever. And I'd lost it.

# Chapter Nineteen

I lay unmoving, staring up at the ceiling, engulfed by a deep feeling of sadness. A torpor and a deep enervation subsumed me completely.

I could perhaps have lain like that for the rest of my life if the telephone hadn't rung. I almost had to force my arm to reach out for the phone.

"Yeah."

"Max?"

"Uh, huh."

"You okay?"

'Not really' was what I wanted to say. 'It's all just a bit too much' might have followed. I could have said that to Mike too. But I actually didn't have the energy to go into explanations.

"Yeah, I'm fine. Just woke up, What's up?"

Mike seemed relieved.

"Amy wants you to come into the office for a meeting."

This was ominous. "Uh, oh! Am I about to get fired already?"

Mike laughed, "No, nothing like that. Actually it couldn't be further from the truth...."

"...Really? So what....?"

"...I'll let her explain. About eleven? Don't be late, she's a busy gal."

"Okay."

I held the dead phone for a while before I dropped it in its cradle.

"Now what?" I wondered.

I lay back on the pillows and shut my eyes. My mind was empty of all thoughts. I tried to remember what I'd been thinking about before the phone rang. But nothing came. It felt as though my whole body was hurting. And yet, when I tried to focus on a particular part of my anatomy, I couldn't identify any particular pain there. It was like a general ache.

Was I sick? Was it a virus of some kind? An illness? Some strange malady? I didn't think so. It was just a general malaise. I *felt* rotten, but it didn't have a thing to do with my body.

I knew I had to move. That I would probably feel better if I did. But it was hard to move. I had mummy-like bandages tying my whole frame to the bed.

I finally dragged myself up and staggered into the bathroom, where I forced myself to shower and painfully shave and run a comb through my hair. But when I looked in the mirror after I was dressed I thought that I looked just barely presentable.

"Oh well," I thought, "It'll have to do."

I loved meetings in Amy's office. Mike had told me that she'd had a feng shui expert do it out for her. But, whatever it was, it felt good in there. There was plenty of light, and a simple, uncluttered felling. And I usually felt like I could think clearly. Usually. But not this morning. This morning I couldn't seem to think at all.

"Are you alright Max? You seem a little preoccupied or something."

"Er....yeah....I'm fine. Just had a rough night, that's all."

We were sitting waiting for Mike. As usual. Amy didn't have a desk in her office, just several chairs, tastefully arranged around a low glass-topped coffee table. She rose from one of the chairs now. And, for a moment, I thought she was actually going to come and kiss me. Or something. But what she actually did was to pour a glass of water and set it beside me on the edge of the coffee table.

"Thank you."

Mike bustled in, "Sorry. Usual stuff." He fell into an armchair.

"That's alright."

I had been curious about this meeting. I couldn't imagine that they were going to fire me. But, if they were, did they both need to be there?

"So Max." Amy began. "We've been doing a bit of thinking....."

"Uh oh," I thought, "here it comes. Well it was okay while it lasted."

"...As you probably know, this is a highly competitive and very fast-developing scene. And we really have to stay on top of our game. Recently we've been noticing quite a lot of overlap with our competitors. So one of the things we've decided to focus on is more branding."

"Okay." I said, not really knowing where she was going with this. And why it mattered to me.

"That means developing some 'names'...."

She didn't make the quote marks in the air. Amy was too cool for that. But I got it. And....?

"...We're going to start building you up into one of those names. As part of our branding. If that's okay with you."

It wasn't really a question. But, nevertheless, I felt obliged to respond.

"Why, yes. Of course."

"I'm going to ask you to work with Mike to develop some themes."

"Themes?"

She looked to Mike to take over.

"Yes themes," said Mike, "maybe some kind of commentary. Probably political...."

"...But..."

"...I know, you've never done that kind of stuff. But I think it could work. And, with the mid-terms coming up, the whole country's going to be more interested. The thing is, everyone's attention span is getting shorter. So some snappy, pithy pieces, say five minutes, could really generate some interest."

"Snappy?" I thought to myself. "Pithy?" Was that me? Oh, well, might as well give it a try. Not exactly the new Dan Rather, but maybe I could do something interesting. Yes, it might work.

"Unfortunately we won't be able to do anything extra with your salary just yet...."

"Naturally." I almost said aloud.

"...But once you start attracting some decent sponsors and advertisers we could certainly take a look at that. So...anything?"

"Er, no."

"Good. I'll leave it to you and Mike to come up with some ideas."

"Okay."

And we were dismissed. Mike rose untidily to his feet. I wasn't sure whether I was meant to say anything else. Or, indeed, whether to shake her hand...or, perhaps kiss her. But I was saved from having to decide by the ringing of Amy's telephone.

As soon as we were outside the office Mike slapped me on the back.

"Great. Let's go and have a drink to celebrate. And to talk about some ideas."

\*\*\*

"So, I know you've never been really political…"

"…Oh, I wouldn't say that…"

"…No, hear me out. You've always been the consummate journalist, remaining impartial, never being partisan. But I know from our talks in private over the years that you definitely hold your own views…"

"…Of course…"

"…So what about sharing those views with others? Your opinion of how this administration is handling affairs. Iraq, for instance…"

"…Aren't there enough…?"

"…I think there's definitely room for your comments. As Amy said, in short snappy, pithy pieces. And stuff at home too. Habeus Corpus, for example. I know you were furious about that."

"Yes, I was. I am. I can't believe that while Bush pretends to espouse liberty and democracy he's happy to rip it away from us. And, the greatest hypocrisy of all, he does it in the *name* of freedom and democracy…"

"…Exactly…"

Mike handed the barman a twenty.

"…And I know there's other stuff that you have something to say about…"

"…Like 'Sneak & Peak'. Exactly what kind of police state are we now living in when the cops can just walk into your house and search it without a search warrant and without even telling you?"

Mike pushed over a tip to the barmen and picked up the rest of his change. The bar was quiet. It was a little too early for the after-work crowd and lunchtime was long gone. Here and there a few lost souls sat in the artificially lit interior. I picked up my glass thoughtfully.

"And then there's Darfur…..And Zimbabwe…."

"…That's my boy. I knew that, once you set your mind to it, that you'd come up with a whole string of ideas."

I smiled at my friend, "It just might work. Could be fun too. How frequently would you want the pieces?"

"I was thinking daily. Would that be too much?"

"Not if that's all I'm doing. And no travel involved?"

"No. These are purely thought pieces. I think we'd want you to be as balanced as possible but, of course, you'd have to be true to yourself."

"When would you want to start?"

"We're thinking in two weeks time."

I thought for a moment, then looked my friend in the eye.

"Well…it sounds like a great gig! What's the catch?" I asked, laughing.

"None that I can see…."

"…And you're not giving me this gig out of pity…?"

"…Pity…?"

"…You know, 'cause of what's been happening in my life…"

"…Shit, no. I don't feel *that* sorry for you."

And we both laughed.

An hour or so after Mike had left I still had my head down, making notes in the small journalist's notepad that I had carried with me, in one version or another my whole adult life.

So I never would have seen the woman come in. The woman who now sat at the other end of the bar studying me from time to time. A woman who, apparently was studying me with bemusement. The bar was filling up now. Some work-weary, others glad to be released and in a mood for celebration.

I ordered another drink and studied my notes. "Yes", I thought at last. It could definitely work. Kind of like having my own TV show, but in the new world. Well, that was okay too. I'd miss the travel. Or would I? Maybe it would be good to be working but not putting more strain on my body for a while. I breathed out and looked around.

At a nearby table a young woman sat by herself. She sat with her head resting in one hand, staring into space. Her face was enchanting, with high cheek-bones and wide eyes with long eyelashes. And her long, black hair was sleek and glossy. Her body, from what I could see of it, was stunning. I couldn't tell whether she'd just slipped in for an after-work drink or whether she was there to meet someone. She certainly wasn't looking around her. Perhaps, I thought, she was waiting to be picked up. A hooker? No, she was too pretty for that. And too well dressed for that. I considered that I might just be being a male chauvinist. Why shouldn't she just be doing what I was doing. Sitting there by herself having a quiet drink?

A voice behind me said, "Pretty isn't she?"

I turned around. I wasn't sure that the question was directed at me. I looked into her eyes: the woman who'd been sitting at the other end of the bar, and was now sitting on the next stool to mine.

"I'm sorry?"

"She's a pretty girl, isn't she?"

"Yes, I suppose so." Feigning indifference.

The woman laughed. Her face lit up and I could see that this older woman, although possibly old enough to be the other woman's mother, was herself something of a beauty. A still-pretty face, carefully brushed hair and a svelte figure. And the sparkle that remained in her eyes also held the promise of intelligence.

"You *suppose* so," She said, repeating his phrase. Teasing me. "Are you afraid to admit to me that you find her attractive?" And she laughed again.

"No, I supp…" And now I too was laughing. At myself. Finally: "Yes, I think she's attractive. Why? Is that a sin?"

"Not at all," she said, still smiling. "But I couldn't help noticing that you've been staring at her for the last five minutes…"

"…Well, I…"

"…So tell me. What's the attraction of younger women…?"

"…I'm sorry?"

"I mean, forgive me, you're…" and she appraised me for a moment. "Fifty-five…?"

"…Actually, I'm just about to turn sixty."

"Mmm. Not bad. You look after yourself…"

"…Thank you…"

"…You're welcome. But, here's the thing. That woman over there…That girl…is definitely young enough to be your daughter. And, quite possibly, your grand-daughter. Yet you were ogling her for more than five minutes. .."

I started to protest, but realized that was pointless. However, a little voice at the back of my mind did ask me why I was submitting myself to this interrogation. But the woman was already continuing.

"…And I'm sure that, given half a chance, you'd take her home to bed. Am I right?"

"Yes, I guess."

"You *guess*."

I gazed into the twinkling eyes in front of me. Twinkling eyes around which there was a fine web of deeply-etched lines. And then I studied her face more intensely. The woman had obviously been a great beauty in her time. Was *still* very beautiful. But I thought about the younger woman. And, as if to remind myself, I looked over at her. The tautness and smoothness of her skin, and what it would feel like under my fingers. That very elasticity that would seem to almost give me a feeling of life itself. And I knew that, to an older man, almost any younger woman was desirable. She didn't have to be beautiful. She just needed to have rounded buttocks, smooth skin, a flat belly and pert, non-saggy breasts.

She was still waiting for my answer, and she asked again, "So what's the attraction?"

I looked at the woman in front of me and I wanted to say to her: "Are you fucking kidding!" Instead I just mumbled, "Well, you know…"

"And do you do that much?"

"What's that?"

Sit, staring at women? Checking them over…!"

"…Certainly not…!" I started to protest. "Well, actually, I guess, sure. All men do. Apart from…you know. It's not like something you grow out of." Defensive now: "Anyway, why is it a problem? Don't women want to be looked at?"

"Of course. But most women don't want to be ogled. It's uncomfortable. And, frankly, a little creepy."

Is that what I'd been doing? Ogling? How long had I been doing that? It wasn't something I'd been aware of. Sure, I'd always found women attractive. Enjoyed looking at them. What man didn't? But I'd never been an 'ogler.' Had I? Did that make me misogynistic?…….No, I'd always told myself that I was a lover of women, an *admirer* of women. Was I objectifying them? No. And, these days, didn't women – well some of them anyway – look at men the same way.

But maybe this woman was right. Maybe I'd just been ogling. Holy shit! Well, if that was the case, it was time to change.

I became aware that she was studying me as I was thinking. Then, unexpectedly she asked, "Are you married?"

And a funny thing happened. Maybe it was being with a woman my own age – Was she my own age? – I said, " No, I'm divor…" But I stopped myself just in time. "My wife died."

The way she was studying me now I began to feel a little like a laboratory specimen.

"Ah….so you're not attached?"

"No."

"Hmm…"

She took a long sip of her drink. And, again, studied me, a quizzical look in her eye now. It was as though she was mulling something over in her mind.

Eventually she said, "Would you like to have dinner with me?"

The question caught me completely off guard. For a moment I sat there stunned. If I had tried to guess what might have come out of her mouth at that time I would never have guessed this.

She sat there patiently as I deliberated what to say. But, just as I opened my mouth to speak, my cell phone chirped in my pocket. I looked down in disbelief, as though I couldn't understand what it was. When I flipped it open I recognized Katie's number. I spoke into it automatically.

"Hello sweetheart, how are you?"

But there was silence at the other end.

"Hello?...Katie?"

Then I heard a small, unfamiliar voice.

"Mister Wheeler?"

"Yes. Who's this?"

"Mister Wheeler, my name's Janice. I'm a friend of Katie…."

There was something about the girl's voice that filled me with dread. What had happened to Katie? I knew it must be something terrible.

"I'm with her at her place. I think you…"

And then she choked a little and started to cry.

"…Could you come over here. Katie's not very well…"

I could feel that she was starting to lose it. I felt my voice, icily clear, trying to calm her down.

"…Janice? Is that your name?"

"Yes…"

"…Exactly what's the matter with Katie?"

The brief silence that followed was ominous. My mind went into a dizzying freefall. But, when Janice's spoke again, it came out in a whispered torrent.

"She-had-an-abortion-and-she's-really-bleeding-more-than-I-think-she-should.-and-she's-also-burning-up-and-her-mom's-gone-on-vacation-and-I-didn't-know-who-else-to-call…"

"…Did you call for an ambulance?"

"Yes, but it's been ages, and there's still no sign. And I'm really worried about her. What should I do?"

I was just about to speak when she cut me off.

"….Wait. There's someone at the door now. It might be them"

And I could hear the phone being dropped, and muffled voices in the background.

The sounds went on and on. I wanted to yell into the phone to ask what was happening. But I guessed that the paramedics had arrived, and they were dealing with Katie. And I'd just have to wait.

After an eternity Janice picked up the phone again.

"Hello? Mister Wheeler?"

"Yes, I'm still here."

"Oh good. Well, the paramedics came and they're looking after Katie. But soon they're going to take her to hospital."

"Okay. Ask them which hospital, and I'll meet you there."

"I will…And Mister Wheeler?"

"Yes."

"They say they think she'll be okay."


It was some time before I could find which part of the hospital she was in. But there she was: lying quite still, her eyes shut. Her face was pale. A nurse was adjusting an IV drip. A dark-haired young woman hovered in a corner, watching, her hand covering her mouth. I assumed this was Janice. She was obviously still very shaken. I caught her eye and nodded. As I moved to the side of the bed the nurse turned. I saw the question in her eye and quickly answered the unasked question.

"I'm her father. I came as soon as I could. How is she?"

The nurse, a squat Latina, finished her adjustment and made a note on clipboard.

"You have to talk with the doctor. He'll be back in a minute. He went to check on another patient."

And she left.

I looked down at my daughter. She seemed to be asleep. Perhaps they'd given her something. There was a chair nearby and I carried it over and sat down beside her, closing my hand over hers. Again I looked at the vulnerable face, and a small lump began to form in my throat. My heart hurt.

Sometimes, when my children were little, I used to creep into their bedrooms in the middle of the night just to watch them sleeping. This had always been a magical moment. Now I wished that Katie would wake up, just so that I would know she was alright.

A small voice behind me:

"I'm sorry Mister Wheeler."

I turned to Janice. She looked awful. She'd obviously been crying, and her face was streaked with eye make-up.

"What happened?" I asked gently.

"As…As I said…she had an abortion…"

"…In a clinic?"

"Yes, it was all quite legal and everything…I went with her. She wanted a friend there…"

"…And they just let her out?"

"Well, she seemed okay. It was only after she'd been at home for a few hours…."

She stopped suddenly when Doctor Prembhodi arrived.

"You are…?" he asked me gently.

"I'm Katie's father. Is she going to be okay?"

"Mister…?"

"…Wheeler…"

"….Mister Wheeler. Your daughter has experienced a postabortion triad…."

"…I'm sorry. A…?"

"…What we call a triad. Sometimes there are retained products of conception which can cause some pain, bleeding, and low-grade fevers. This is not uncommon.

Occasionally we get a certain amount of hemorrhage. We've given her an ultra-sound and, to be on the safe side, we've given her antibiotics in case she has an infection. And we are about to evacuate her uterus to ensure that there are no blood clots that may endanger her. She's lost a little blood, but she'll be okay. For the moment it would probably be best if you went for some coffee."

It was only when I returned with the two cups and set them carefully on the cafeteria table that I thought to ask.

"Where's the father?"

"Oh, Mister Wheeler. I don't think…"

"…Please. Call me Max…"

"…I think Katie should tell you all that…"

"…Janice," I tried to be firm, but not unkind, "Katie's not in a position to tell me anything right now, is she. All I want to know is why the father isn't here."

She looked down at her shoes and thought for a long time.

"He isn't here because he doesn't know."

"Why?"

"Because Katie dumped him…."

"…Really! Why?"

"She thought that the relationship was a mistake."

"Wow!"

I was silent for a moment while my brain computed this information. Then another thought struck me.

"Did he know?"

"What? That she was pregnant?"

She sipped at her coffee for a moment.

"I don't know….No, I don't think so. Katie didn't want him to know. She thought he might try and make her change her mind. And he was already pretty clingy. That's why…"

"I see."

"They work together."

"Pardon?"

"He works at the same graphic design place as Katie. That was part of the problem. It was all a bit claustrophobic."

221

"What's he like?"

She looked directly into my eyes and paused before she spoke. "Why? It's over. She'd already made her decision. He wasn't son-in-law material."

I didn't know what to make of this statement. But Janice, perhaps thinking that she'd spoken out of turn, broke the look and cast her eyes downwards.

We sat in silence for several minutes and I thought about my children and how they handled relationships. It felt very strange. When Lisa was twenty-eight she'd already had two children and was pregnant with a third. I wondered whether Katie ever thought about settling down. When she was forty? It wasn't that I was rushing to be a grandfather again. And it wasn't as though I wanted to impose any of my stuff on my kids. But, Jesus Christ! And then I thought again, as I so often did these days, how little I knew my children.

I looked at Janice. She was lost in her own thoughts, absent-mindedly tracing figures in some spilt water on the table.

"Are you and Katie close?' I asked.

"Yes," she said without looking up. "Well, you know."

"You work with her as well?"

"Me? No. I'm a yoga teacher. I hate computers."

She checked her watch and reflexively so did I.

"I wonder how it's going." I said.

"Yes," she said, thoughtfully. "I hope it won't be too much longer."

"You don't have to wait…"

"…No, I didn't mean that."

But my attention had been drawn to someone who'd just walked in. Mos looked drawn and pale, and he almost walked by our table without seeing us. I stood up to acknowledge my friend. Mos blinked, as his mind tried to compute the fact that I was sitting in the hospital cafeteria.

"Max? What are you…?"

"…they brought Katie here. She's having a small operation."

"Is…is she okay?"

"Yes, I'm sure she'll be fine."

I turned to Janice.

"This is her friend ."

Mos gave her a slight nod as he sat down.

"Lib's upstairs."

"Chemo?"

"Yes, she's on her second session."

"How's she handling it?"

"Not too well actually....I hate to see her this way."

He shook his head

"Yeah, I know.

I watched as my friend rubbed his tired eyes with his thumb and forefinger.

"Can I get you a coffee or something?"

"No, I'm fine. But d'you mind if I just sit here. I don't really have much to say."

"Sure. Of course."

At that moment I would have liked to put my arms around him. But something stopped me. Maybe it was because of Janice's presence. So the three of us sat in silence, each reflecting on our own thoughts.

# Chapter Twenty

I watched my daughter sleeping. Every so often she would frown as though she was trying to work out a problem. The IV tube that was stuck in her arm seemed to be irritating her, and sometimes she reached out her other hand to try and scratch herself, but somehow never quite made it.

Janice had left when the doctor told her that Katie was fine. She hadn't slept much the previous night and it had been a long day. Actually I had encouraged her to go home. I wanted to spend a little time with Katie alone. This might be my only chance. Jenny would be arriving soon and Lisa had cancelled her vacation and was flying back. I liked the idea of watching over my daughter. Especially now that I knew that she was going to be okay.

"Hey, daddy." She said slowly, slurring her words slightly. "What...?"

She had one eye open and was squinting at me. I could see that she was trying to figure out where she was,

"You're in hospital honey. Remember? The doctors took care of you."

"Mm, yeah....Am I alright?"

"You're fine. You did really well."

"I didn't do anything." She said shutting both eyes now.

I thought about asking her about the abortion, but immediately thought better of it. That could keep. Again she reached out to try and scratch her arm.

"You need me to get a nurse?"

"Mmwa?....No thanks."

I watched her lying there and wanted to....wanted to...what? To take her in my arms. Or something. She looked so vulnerable. I just wanted to protect her somehow. But, of course, I couldn't. Not really.

She spoke again without opening her eyes.

"How are you daddy?"

"I'm....I'm fine. Now that you're awake. I'm going to be good."

"Okay." She said and I thought she'd drifted off to sleep. But a couple of minutes later she surprised me.

"I have to leave her tomorrow."

"What?"

"I have to leave tomorrow because I have a very important job to do...."

"...Well, we'll see..."

"No, I have to."

"What could be so important?"

Now she opened her eyes and squinted at me.

"I gotta be better to organize your party..."

"...My what?"

"Your sixtieth..."

"....Oh, honey, I don't want...."

"...Sure you do..."

"...It makes me feel so old."

Katie shut her eyes again and the corners of her mouth turned up in an approximation of a smile. I said nothing. Just watched her. I was thinking about a day a long time ago, when she was six years old. Somehow or other she'd jumped into a swimming pool and banged her head pretty bad. We'd seen it happen and pulled her out quickly, but she'd got concussed. And I'd been worried. Had sat by her bed most of the night, keeping watch. Lisa said that she'd be fine, but I couldn't help myself. And, of course, Katie had been up the next day running around as though nothing had happened.

She spoke again without opening her eyes.

"Sly."

"What honey?"

"Sylvester Stallone. He's not old....And he just celebrated his sixtieth.....And Bill Clinton....Had a big sixtieth. He's not old either."

I laughed. "All right. You win. You can arrange whatever you like. But only when you're really better."

The smile curled on her lips again.

"Okay, that's a deal."

I didn't hear Jenny come in.

"Hello daddy."

She kissed me lightly on the cheek, then went around and kissed her sister, who was now attempting a smile of greeting.

"Hey you! How're you doing?"

"I'm fine. You didn't need to come down here."

"I know. I was just passing…."

"…Like hell!"

Jenny sat down.

"So, how are you really?"

Katie twisted slightly so she could see her, and winced from the effort.

"Really. I'm fine. A little sore, is all."

"I called mom…"

"…You didn't…"

"…She's flying back tomorrow…"

"…Jen, why'd you do that?"

"Because I knew she would have wanted to know."

"But it'll ruin her vacation."

"Well, these things happen."

"And did you call Jack too? And he is he flying over too…?"

"…Of course not! I mean, yes I called him…"

"…Jenny!..."

"…Look, he's your brother. He has a right to know. And, no, of course he's not coming…."

"…Good! Because it's nothing…"

I thought it was about time I jumped in. I'd always hated to hear the kids squabbling. But I was also afraid that Katie would get upset and have a setback.

"Okay, that's enough!

Actually I didn't know whether to laugh or cry. Because my memory flashed back to so many years ago, when the kids were little. And Lisa and I would take them for a road trip. Before we'd traveled half a mile down the road at least two of them would be squabbling. You could depend on it. It wasn't always the same ones. But somebody would be taking a dig at somebody else. And, before too long, somebody would be in tears. Did I miss those days? Yes and no. Hang on. Of course I did. Of course I'd like to be living those days now. But maybe with some of the knowledge I had now.

"You want to throw more water on."

"I dunno. It's plenty hot right now."

"Come on, don't be a wimp. This is nothing.

Mos and Al and Harry and I were sprawled out in the sauna. I was lying on a top tier.

"You know," said Mos somewhat defensively, "Different people have different metabolisms. Did you ever think about that?"

"It's not your metabolism," said Harry laughing. "It's that you're a wimp."

He climbed down from his bench, scooped up a ladleful of water, and hurled it on the coals.

"If you can't take the heat stay out of the sauna…!"

"…It's kitchen, you ass…"

"…I know. But it's sauna too."

"Well *I'm* melting," rumbled Al. "I don't think I can take too much more of this."

Yes, I thought, that's exactly what I feel like. But it has nothing to do with the sauna. Or rather it was like my whole life over the last few months had turned into one big sauna, where I was slowly melting and could do nothing about it.

"This is good for you Al. It'll help you lose some of that excess ballast you're carrying…."

"…I'll have you know this is not ballast. This is pure good living…"

"…What!" hooted Harry.

"I gotta get out of here." Said Mos.

He wrapped his towel around him and shoved the door open.

"I'll see you guys in the bar."

"Wait up," said Al. "I've had enough too."

He managed to wrap his towel around his rather large girth as he lumbered out of the sauna.

"What about you Max? You gonna desert me too?"

But I was still lost in my own thoughts. As the perspiration beaded on my forehead and dripped down, stinging my eyes, I began to feel as though my whole being was coming unglued. A crushing torpor overcame me, draining my vital energies.

"You okay buddy? You don't look so good." said Harry, "Maybe we *had* better wrap this.

He stood up.

"Come on, let's join the others."

Al was sitting on the change-room bench, his huge body still bright pink. We could hear the shower running with Mos under it.

"No, I'm fine." I said, "I just had a 'moment'"

"What, a Senior Moment?" asked Harry.

"No, just one of those....you know…times in your life when…"

I couldn't really explain to my friend what had just happened in the sauna. Could I even explain it to myself?

Mos appeared from the showers, toweling himself as he walked.

"What's up?" he asked

"Max just had a moment in the sauna, that's all."

"You should get a checkup. At our age you never know…"

"…I had a checkup. I'm fine!" I said, rubbing my eyes and trying to shake off whatever had descended on me.

"Well, if you're sure…"

I gave my best impression of a smile. But Al was looking at me as though he knew something was up.

"What?" I asked.

"Nothing." said Al, obviously not wanting to make me uncomfortable. And he began to slowly pull on his clothes.

Mos was looking at himself in the mirror trying, somewhat unsuccessfully, to arrange his hair into some sort of style.

"Do you think," he asked, "that as you get older that your hair loses its way? And, instead of coming out the top of your head it comes out your ears and your nose instead?"

Harry laughed. "In your case it definitely does."

"Here we go again," said Al. "Time for 'Getting Old' jokes."

"It's no joke." I said.

Mos slumped down onto the bench. "You're right, it isn't. It's too close to the truth. Jesus!"

He rubbed his eyes wearily as the three of us looked on. Finally Harry asked the question we'd all wanted to ask.

"How's Libby doing?" asked Harry.

"What?...Oh, you know...She's doing the chemo thing. And then there's radio. The doctors say she has a good chance. But Lib feels like shit. And who knows with this damn thing....You know what I've been thinking? What if she dies? What if I'm left by myself? One of those pathetic, lonely old men who talks to himself all the time. Who lives on cans of baked beans because he doesn't know how to take care of himself. Christ, I don't want to be that man!"

"No" I thought, "I don't want to be that man either."

"They found this guy the other day." continued Mos, "He lived in North Hollywood or somewhere like that. Apparently he lived alone. Had done for quite some time. I think his wife had died. Well the neighbors noticed this funny smell coming from his place, so they called the cops. When they eventually busted in they found him dead inside. And guess what? They reckon he'd been dead for at least six months. Christ! He'd been dead for six months and nobody noticed? Nobody missed him? How pathetic is that?"

He shook his head sadly.

"I sure as shit don't want to be that guy."

Mos stopped talking then. And we were quiet too. Almost as though we were holding a minute's silence for the dead man. Even though we didn't know who he was. Eventually it was Harry who broke the silence.

"Well, at least you have your children. That'll never happen to you."

"Yeah, you're right," he said quietly. "Thank God."

Mos mused on that for a moment then turned to me.

"By the way, how's your kid?"

I was taken off guard, unprepared for the question. I was still thinking about the man, dead for six months.

"What? Oh, Katie's doing well. Lisa broke her vacation to be with her and she's taken her back to the house for a while. But, actually, all she needs is some bed-rest and a little TLC, and she'll be fine. I just wish she'd told us. You know?"

"Sure."

But I still couldn't quite shake off the image of the old guy, alone in his apartment. In my head I could see the man, lying alone, his corpse slowly rotting away. And it had struck some kind of chord. And there was still a tiny voice in my head wondering whether I could ever actually become that man. I let out a deep sigh and Mos looked at me.

"You okay?"

I blinked at him, then realized what had just happened.

"Yeah. I'm good." I looked around at my three friends. "So, where're we going to eat?"

"I can't. I have a date," said Harry, buttoning his shirt.

"A *date*! It's, like, mid day!" said Mos.

"Yeah, it's a *lunch* date."

"Sorry," said Al. "I have some stuff I *have* to finish today."

Mos sighed. "Yeah, I'm sorry too, Max. I need to go and pick up Lib. I can do tomorrow though."

"Hey, er, not a problem," I said, "I was only thinking….you know…"

***

I was sipping my coffee thoughtfully. A previous customer had left behind a copy of *Daily Variety*. And I was flipping absent-mindedly through its pages when I saw the headline: "*You Show Me Yours* picked up". Sure enough the television network had liked the pilot, and had committed to a full series. Out of curiosity I read through to see who the host was going be. When I found the name I didn't recognize it. Hmm. I felt a small twinge. Maybe I should have done the show after all. Nah! It really wasn't me. And I knew it. At least I had…What? ...My integrity?...Yes, my journalistic integrity, godammit! Because now, of course, I had so much more journalistic integrity doing…What was I doing? Well, at least it was still journalism. Even though I didn't actually fully understand the whole vodcasting thing. I breathed out a deep sigh.

"Wow, that was a big sigh."

I looked up at the sound of the unfamiliar voice. And, at first, the face was unfamiliar too. When I was on air all the time I sometimes had strangers approaching me. Some, of course, just wanted autographs. But many felt at liberty to make very personal comments. Many didn't like my hair. They complained about my neckties. And some even felt obliged to criticize my expression, sometimes too severe, sometimes to jocular. I had grown used to it, and had learned to treat each person in a pleasant but slightly reserved way.

"Did you sort out your emergency?"

I frowned. Then it came back to me. The woman I'd been talking to when I got the phone call about Katie.

"Oh, hi."

She was standing beside me, and I had to twist my neck to look up at her.

"Laura." she said.

"I'm sorry?"

"My name is Laura. I don't think I ever got to tell you."

"Oh, of course…."

I wasn't sure whether to say anything else. But she remained, hovering above me.

"…Er, would you like to sit down?"

"I thought you'd never ask."

She sat down gracefully across the small table from me.

"So, did you sort it out?"

"Oh…yes….Thank you."

Sure as shit I wasn't about to go into details of Katie's hospitalization with a complete stranger.

"So, er…"

"…Laura…"

"…So, Laura…Is this a regular hang-out of yours?"

She laughed loudly and freely. And I noticed that when she laughed it brought a radiance to her face, and she looked quite beautiful.      "You make me sound like I'm in the James gang!" she said finally, and then laughed again. "No, it's not really my *hang-out*. But I do come here quite often. I live not too far away, and it's, you know…"

There was definitely something about her that was fascinating. And I was drawn to her playfulness. So much so, in fact, that it lightened my own mood.

"I didn't know there were any women in the James gang. By the way, my name's Max." I said, sticking out my hand.

She looked me squarely in the eyes.

"Yes, I know."

But she took my hand nevertheless.

"Don't worry," she said, "I'm not a celebrity stalker…"

"…Oh, I'd hardly describe myself as a celebrity…"

"…No I guess not." And she laughed again. Not at me, but at the sheer pleasure in the moment. And there was joy in her laugh.

She motioned to the copy of *Daily Variety* in front of me.

"Anything interesting there?"

"Not really. There's a TV series that they're going to make that they'd asked me to host…"

"…But you didn't want to do it?"

"Not really. It was just a bit too much…*tabloid television*, if you know what I mean."

And she laughed yet again. Gently. This woman sure laughed a lot. Well, I liked it. Maybe that was what I needed. People in my life who laughed more.

"You have a beautiful laugh."

"Why thank you." But this time she just smiled gently. "Actually I have been told that before. But, yes, I do know what you mean about tabloid TV. I'm not a big fan." Again she indicated the magazine. "So, you're not disappointed?"

"Well, actually, yeah. I was hoping the pilot would be a huge failure." And now it was my turn to laugh. "It would have given me a sense of righteousness. Now I just have to hope that the series is a failure. That would definitely make me feel better."

"An honest man. I like that."

"Well…I try at least to always be honest with myself. Y'know..if I feel like killing someone at least I acknowledge the truth to myself. Not that I'd ever act on it of course…"

"…Of course…"

"…Just that I don't pretend to myself that I *don't* have those feelings."

She tilted her head at me slightly quizzically. "That's nice."

"Nice?"

And again she laughed loudly. But this time it was at herself.

"Yes, kind of an overused word that, isn't it. I must try and improve my vocabulary."

I looked at my coffee cup, and realized that it was empty.

"I might get another drink. Would you like one?" I asked.

"Sure. Thanks. I'll have a cappuccino."

"With…?"

"Oh, you mean like soya milk or decaf or something? No, just a straight cappuccino please."

"How refreshing."

I signaled to the waitress.

"So, Laura, you know all about me…"

"….Oh, I wouldn't say all…"

"….Well, more than I know about you. What do you do?"

The waitress took my empty coffee cup and saucer and wiped the table.

"Two cappuccinos please"

"You gottit." said the waitress.

"It's a funny convention isn't it?" asked Laura, watching the waitress disappear behind the counter. "Defining someone by what they *do*?"

"Well, let's see…I could ask you what tribe you belong to. Or maybe where you grew up. Or perhaps your blood group. Yeah, I think it's a strange thing that we do. But what would you prefer?"

"Oh, I don't know. Maybe take someone on face value perhaps."

And we both laughed again.

"Yeah, that's going to work!" I said mockingly.

"So, what if I said I was a hooker?"

I studied her carefully for a couple of seconds, then smiled and shook my head. "No, I don't think so."

Why? Because I'm too old?"

"No. Just my senses tell me something else…"

"So, if you rely on your senses, and they already tell you something about me, why do I need to give you information so that you can pigeon-hole me?"

"Because…I don't know. Maybe my senses tell me what you you're *not* rather than what you are."

"Hmm. You've got an interesting set of senses there…."

I shrugged noncommittally and looked around at the few people who sat reading or talking quietly to one another. In the background I could hear the whoosh of the coffee machine. And I became aware of how relaxed I felt.

I turned back around to find Laura looking directly at me, a twinkle in her eyes. And I could feel how relaxed I felt with *her* as well. The thought crossed my mind that, when I'd been with much younger women at some level, that I'd always had to....what?...be on my mettle? To never quite relax? As though I had to prove something. But now there was none of that.

"So, er...?"

"...Laura..."

"...Yes, I'm sorry. *Laura*..." I said her name with respect. "What exactly *do* you do?"

"Exactly? Well, actually I'm a documentary filmmaker...."

"...You're kidding!"

"No, sorry. No kidding there. I make documentary films."

"What kind?"

"Mostly social commentaries. You know, righting the world's wrongs."

"Well I never."

"Surprised?"

"No...not really, I guess....So, do you get to travel much?"

"Oh yes. That's part of it for me. I love to travel. Which is great, because there's not much money to be made from docs. Unless you're Mike Moore, of course."

# Chapter Twenty-One

I never sleep well when I lie flat on my back. For some reason I can't seem to get my breathing working properly that way. And now it was labored and loud. So loud, in fact, that it even disturbed me. I rolled over onto my side and my breathing eased.

Automatically I pulled the covers over my shoulders as I returned to deep sleep. And to a new dream. The steam rose through the air in delicate strands. I peered through the steam, but couldn't see what he was looking for. I walked on and nodded to a woman I recognized. What was her name? I thought about trying to explain to her what I was looking for, but the words wouldn't come. She was behind me now and I was still trying to see it. But the mist was getting thicker. Why? This was meant to be easy. If only I could....Someone tapped me on the shoulder. I turned around and she held out her arms and kissed me on the cheek. Jenny? No, Katie. How nice!

I was about to ask Katie, but she drifted away. Something about it worried me. Was I going to lose Katie? And I needed to keep on looking. Feeling torn, I started to fret. I tried to see where Katie had gone. I twisted around, but she'd disappeared into the mist. I tried to call out her name, but there was a pain in my chest. I was beginning to panic.

I woke with a start. The panic was still there, but I couldn't remember why. Fragments of the dream remained, but the more I tried to recall it the more it disappeared. I was looking for something. What? And something about Katie. Yes. But what? Was she alright? Perhaps I should call her. I peered at the bedside clock. Twenty after three. Fitzgerald time. No time to phone anyone.

I lay in a state of semi-consciousness for almost an hour. I was wishing that I'd just drop off to sleep. But my brain kept trying to remember what it was I'd been searching for. I knew it was important, but it just wouldn't come to me. Finally I surrendered and switched on the light. Maybe a drop of Scotch would help me drop off. It often did. I pulled myself out of bed, threw on a robe, and blearily made my way to the living room where I poured a shot of whisky and carried it over to my favorite armchair. I felt the familiar burn as I sipped my drink.

I thought about turning on the television, but decided that it might actually fully wake me up and I felt that, if possible, I'd like to get some more sleep. I looked around the living room. It was nothing special. I was still paying money to Lisa, so I couldn't afford anything really flash. But I felt comfortable here. It was alright. I took in all the various artifacts that I'd collected over the years. Was this the sum total of my life? This place? And these things? I sipped again at the whisky and reflected on my life. If I was to die tomorrow what would my legacy be? Well, I had four great kids. But I couldn't really take credit for that, could I? Lisa gave birth to them all. And, truth be told, Lisa raised them all while I roamed the world.

So... what was I actually leaving the world? A bunch of interviews? A few miles of tape of...what? Maybe I shouldn't be so hard on myself, I thought. After all, what legacy did most men leave? If you worked in a factory or an office every day of your life what could you possibly leave behind? At best memories of a job well done. And wasn't that true of me also? Sure it was.

Ah, but then again, I was Max Wheeler. And, for some reason, I felt that I owed it to the world to ....To what? Do better? Bullshit! I thought again about the dream I'd just awoken from. Maybe this was its message. This searching. This rumination. Hmm.

Perhaps I should dedicate the rest of my days to Good Works. To Doing Something For Society. So that I could leave a legacy. But wasn't that just my ego speaking. The ego that needed to be immortal. To stand out from the crowd. And be remembered.

The rest of my days? That sounded like I was about to drop off my perch any moment. Idly I began to wonder how many more.....well not *days*, but years, I had left. How many more birthdays would I see? How many Christmases? Thanksgivings? Five? Ten? That didn't seem very many. They seemed like such small numbers.

"I guess I could live to be a hundred." I muttered to myself. But I didn't really believe it.

And then, for some reason I remembered the old Judasian. What was his name?...oh, yeah...Gabriel, who'd talked to me about the grieving process. How I needed to go through all the stages. I couldn't remember the order now. But, what were the stages? Of course there was sadness. And loneliness and helplessness.....And anger. Yes, I remembered anger. And, er,....vulnerability, yeah vulnerability. Well, I felt, I'd experienced all of those emotions since Marie had died. Was there something else? Because I felt as though I'd missed something. Hmm, something about forgiveness and letting go. Well, I wasn't sure what 'forgiveness' meant, but I certainly wasn't ready to 'let go' yet.

My mind flashed onto images of Marie: Laughing at some ridiculous thing I'd said or done. Holding my hand as we went for a walk. With her camera to her eye, capturing some amazing picture that, it seemed, nobody else could quite get. And, of course, in the wildest throes of passion as we made love. Abruptly I felt my heart almost torn from my body, and my breathing became heavy.

Shit! Where *was* I going with this life? I was about to turn sixty. This was.....well, not 'it' exactly. But possibly the last part of my active life. I had just so much juice left. And then, if I was 'lucky' – and not actually dead – I'd be on the scrapheap.

I took another sip of the whisky, and pondered on a man's worth. On *my* worth. Many people said that a man should leave the world in a better state than he found it. Could I claim that? Maybe. Depends which way you look at it.     Then, of course, there was the other worth. My monitory worth. I'd done alright over the years. Never been what you might call wealthy, but certainly comfortable. Even now, with this place and still paying money to Lisa, I was okay. All in all I could probably retire and, if I had no major crisis, I'd be alright......Yeah, I'd be alright.

Now, at last, I began to feel drowsy again. I drained the glass, set it down, and stood up. Yeah, I could sleep now. Good.

***

The exhibition was of photographs from various photographers. They'd come together to show the suffering in the world. Huge black-and-white pictures of gaunt or swollen-bellied, unsmiling children in Africa. Of bodies in the Middle East, torn apart by war and bloody violence. And of hospital wards stuffed with human beings. It was moving stuff alright. Some of it almost too painful to look at.

The problem for me was not that I'd seen so much of it in person. It was the exhibition itself. Even though it was being held by a major charity, instead of drawing attention to the plight of sections of the human race, this felt more like an art exhibition. That the people served only as objects to be artfully captured and rendered for artistic rather than humanitarian understanding.

I probably wouldn't have come at all if it hadn't been for Laura. In the coffee house, She'd slid her card over to me and smiled at me as she stood up. "Call me sometime," she'd said. After she left I stared at the card for a moment. Then I grinned as I tucked it into my pocket. 'I might just do that', I thought. And then, when I'd turned out my pants pocket, I'd found her card and on a whim decided to call her. She hadn't seemed surprised in the slightest to hear from me. And, right off, had mentioned the exhibition. Two of the photographers were her friends. Would I like to go? "Why not?" I thought at the time.

But now I wasn't sure. I looked deep into an extra-large black-and-white picture of a woman wearing what looked like sackcloth. She was squinting into the camera, and in her arms she held a crying baby.

"What d'you think?"

I hadn't seen Laura come up behind me

"Very impressive."

She looked at me for a moment quizzically, and then surprised me by bursting into laughter.

"I know. It's all a bit 'worthy', isn't it."

"It's not that," I protested, "'Worthy' I can take. It's just that....Well, in a way they're *too* good. You know what I mean? I feel like I'm looking at art..."

"...You are...."

"...Yes, but it feels like it's at the expense of the subjects. I mean, look at this woman." I gestured at the woman in sackcloth, "What will she get out of all this? Other than having her portrait taken?"

"Well, these pictures will end up being sold. And the proceeds will go to a charity that will help her. Or, at the very least, another woman just like her."

"Mmm, I suppose so. But I'm still not sure."

"So," she laughed again. "Do I understand that you've seen enough?"

I noticed again that she laughed a lot. I liked that. It made me feel like smiling as well. And that couldn't be bad. Could it?

"Yes, I think so. How about dinner?"

"Sure," she said. "I'm ready."

And she was. In the restaurant I had enjoyed myself immensely. She was easy to be with. And she seemed to enjoy herself as well. Again I realized how comfortable I felt in this woman's company. Conversation happened naturally between us, and we seemed to find the same things interesting or amusing. She continued to gently tease me sometimes. But I didn't mind, because she always did it warmly. And, sometimes, she could also be self-deprecating.

The food was pretty good, and the wine that we had chosen fitted it perfectly. She loved to travel, she said, and was interested in the places I'd been to. And she had some fascinating stories of her own. She'd started out as a researcher and had kind of fallen into documentary-making almost by default. She'd married one of the guys that she'd worked with, and helped him with his projects. And when the marriage ended eighteen years later Laura had been working on research for a film about selective abortion in India and China. She'd got so hooked into the story that she decided that *she* would make the film. She eventually got funding and made the film. And what d'you know? The film actually won a couple of awards at film festivals and even got picked up by a few cable TV channels here and there. Suddenly she was a film-maker. And, since that time, she had taken the opportunity to travel the world as widely as possible.

I couldn't remember exactly how it happened. But the next thing I knew I was in Laura's car and we were heading up Laurel Canon Boulevard. She surprised me by how fast she drove. Perhaps she was in a hurry to get there. Or maybe this was her natural exuberance. She certainly seemed carefree, her head thrown back, as she gently swayed to the music coming from the car's speakers.

I remembered the last time I'd driven up Laurel Canon. With…the little angel…Angelina. But we didn't drive as far as Mulholland this time. Instead she peeled off and 'arrived' in the driveway of a modest wooden ranch-style house surrounded by a wide variety of trees. I sat for a moment, slightly stunned to be suddenly not moving. She turned to me and smiled.

"Well, this is it. The terminus. This train don't go no further!"

She almost bounded out of the car, and I was surprised at how sprightly she seemed to be. At the front door she paused to fish her key out from her purse.

"What d'you think?" she asked squarely.

"Charming." I said. And it was. There was a definite warmth and allure to the place. She fumbled the key into the lock and threw open the front door.

"Yes, it is kinda charming, isn't it. Come on in."

And she led me directly into the surprisingly large living room, where she threw her purse onto a chair and turned towards me. And, before I knew it, she was in my arms.

I barely had time to take the dresser, the two bookcases stuffed with books and topped with knickknacks, the multitude of pictures hanging on the walls. And the queen size bed,

Laura slowly drew the blinds. She was half turned towards me, a winsome smile on her face. I grinned back at her and waited for her to come to me. But she stood her ground for a moment, toying with the energy, enjoying the moment. Then her hand slid to the buttons on her blouse and, as she looked into my eyes, very slowly began to unbutton them. I held her gaze, and mirror-image-wise, also began to unbutton my shirt.

She was playing it cool, but I could hear her breathing getting heavier. And throatier. We took a step towards each other at the same moment. And we both laughed. And when she was in my arms again I could feel her breasts thrust hard against my naked chest. I could only just smell the delicate perfume she wore. Gently I held the back of her head and pressed my lips against hers. She responded strongly, pushing back as her lips parted slightly, and I felt the restrained animal energy in her as she waited for me to make the first move.

There was no resistance from her as we gently toppled onto the bed and I started pulling at her clothes, all the while kissing her. I slipped off her blouse and paused for a moment before pressing my lips to the top of each breast, which bulged from her brassiere. As she moaned softly I slipped a finger under a strap and loosened it so that it hung down, exposing more of her. Then I loosened the other strap and, as I pulled downwards, both breasts were slowly exposed. She pulled back a little and looked at me curiously, to see what my reaction might be. But my smile seemed to reassure her, and she reached down, took both of my hands and gently lifted them so that they each cupped one of her breasts. I leaned forwards and, as I put my lips to each nipple in turn they began to harden.

She closed her eyes, and her breathing became more intense and more hoarse. Then she surprised me by leaning forwards and taking one of my nipples between her own lips and tenderly licking it. She looked up at me mischievously, and began to kiss my chest.

I ripped off my shirt and then started pulling at her clothing, freeing most of it until she lay there, wearing only her panties. I paused for a moment to study her body. She knew what I was doing and murmured, "Well?...Not bad for an old broad, huh?"

I didn't want to talk but managed to say, somewhat huskily, "Mmm, pretty damn good if you ask me."

She spread her legs and slipped the fingers of one hand inside her panties, slowly rubbing herself, her eyes fluttering closed. I unhooked my belt and pulled my pants downwards, exposing the stiffness which pushed out from my shorts. She opened her eyes and reached out one hand to place it on my erection. I moved closer towards her, covering her mouth with my own. She pressed hard against me and opened her mouth, allowing my tongue to penetrate her there.

I kissed her face, then slowly moved downwards to her neck and throat, and further down until I found her breasts again, which I began to lick. Simultaneously I reached both hands down to slip her panties right off. When I got them to her feet she kicked them away.

Before I could do anything else Laura turned onto her stomach and reached out an arm to the drawer of the bedside table. As I kissed each buttock she turned and smiled at me. Then she retrieved the condom packet from the drawer and handed it to me, inching her way back closer to me. Lying, looking up at me coquettishly.

"Here we go again", I thought.

And then: Bang! It flew into my head. That's when I remembered. That look. That look! It was the eyes. I remembered where I'd seen similar eyes before. Of course: Natalie.

Natalie Swanson had been my first true love. I was fourteen and she was still twelve, almost thirteen. We'd met at a party and, for me, it had felt almost as though I'd been hit by a baseball bat. I'd had occasional crushes on girls before, of course. And even fantasized about various actresses. Marilyn Monroe and Mamie van Doren were my favorites. But with Natalie it was something different. So much so, that I'd rashly gone home and told my mother all about her. I wasn't sure what response I'd expected when I told my mother that I thought that maybe I might be in love. But I certainly hadn't expected laughter.

It threw me for a moment. But then I shrugged it off. I just *knew* how I felt, and it didn't matter what anyone else thought. Including my mother.

And it seemed that Natalie was just as crazy about me. I started seeing her every Saturday night. We'd go to a movie or just hang around the drug store with our friends, talking and listening to the jukebox. And then I'd walk her home. When we first started going together she wasn't yet wearing a brassiere. I discovered this about the third Saturday when I slipped my fingers inside her dress. At first she tried to push my hand away. Then she shyly relaxed her grip. The next week I discovered that, even though there was really no need for it, she was now wearing a bra.

Sometimes, on sunny days, we'd pack a picnic and head out of town, spending the lazy days gazing up at the blue sky or kissing or just talking.

One time I even bought a dime store ring and presented it to Natalie on her birthday. She accepted it almost as if it was an engagement ring. For her she couldn't have treasured it more even if it had been a real diamond.

Our love affair lasted eighteen months. Then her family moved to Oregon. She was distraught, and promised to write every day. Which she actually did for three weeks. Then it became every other day, and finally settled into once a week. I wrote back. And one fine spring day, after I promised my mother that I would take extra special care, I set off to Portland to see Natalie. I spent a week with her, but it felt strange to both of us. We promised 'forever', and I flew home. We wrote once more each. And that was it. It was over. But I kept a photograph of her, pinned to the wall for several years. And what always returned my attention to the photograph was the eyes.

And here they were again. The same eyes. It was uncanny. Obviously the rest of Laura was very different. But I could see it now, and I smiled to myself.

"What?" she asked.

"Sorry?"

"What are you smiling at?"

"Well….you."

"Yes?"

"Actually….I just realized you remind me of someone."

"Sharon Stone? I get that a lot."

"No…Actually my first girlfriend."

"Oh, that's so sweet." She saw the look on my face, as though I thought she was being sarcastic. "No, really. I'm touched"

Then she reached out for my hand and put the condom packet into it.

# Chapter Twenty-Two

"So, how are things?"

"Mmnn, not so great. Libby was really hoping she wouldn't have to go all the way. Then they took her breast, and now they think they might have to take the other one as well."

Mos and I were sitting on the edge of Mos's swimming pool, dangling our feet in the water.

"I thought it was just…"

Mos turned and shrugged at me.

"…Yeah. So did I. So did Lib. Came as a pretty big shock to her. She still isn't coping with it very well. She's scared stiff of dying. So, all in all, she's not terrific…."

He kicked the water thoughtfully.

"Plus she's had a pretty bad reaction to the chemo. Each time it knocks her sideways. And she feels nauseous all the time. She's just about getting over the last dose, and starting to get her appetite back, and bam! It hits her again. Just the thought of food makes her ill. I try and cook her something to tempt her to eat, but she hates me being in *her* kitchen. And I can't cook anyway…"

He shook his head wordlessly, staring down into the water, and paused before speaking again.

"…And, of course, when she's upset then it affects me. Not just the eating, 'cause naturally I can't eat in front of her. But we're like this, you know," He crossed his fingers, "Something disturbs her it disturbs me too….."

He let out a big sigh.

"….But what ya gonna do? Life! Right? It's going to get you one way or another!"

We were both silent for a moment, watching the little ripples in the water catch the distorted light and reflect back a kaleidoscope of fractured blue sky. Each of us was lost in his own thoughts. Finally I just breathed it out: "Shit."

"Yeah," Mos shrugged and sighed again.

There was a long pause now. But then Mos turned to me. "And you? What's happening with you? Life still got you by the balls?"

I let out a wry little chuckle. "Kind of."

"You still grieving for Marie?"

I continued staring into the water. It was a while before I spoke. "Yeah...some...But...."

I wanted to tell him about Laura. But I didn't know what to say. That I'd had a nice connection with someone? Too soon. Too soon.

Mos knew me too well, and I could see that he was about to pump me for more information. But he obviously thought better of it and decided to change the subject.

"What about that new job of yours? How's that going?"

"Yeah, well that's another thing." I screwed up my face. "I'm kind of finding it difficult to work up any real enthusiasm for it. Funny, huh? Here's an opportunity to do something that I enjoy, and have control over what I'm doing. And, who knows, maybe make a difference in the process. And I feel..." I sighed. "I just feel 'what the hell!'."

"Maybe it's not the right thing."

"Maybe."

"What's not the right thing?" asked a familiar voice, as Harry plopped down beside me.

"This new job of his." offered Mos.

"Why, what's wrong with it? I thought you told me it was something you'd like to do."

"I did. I just can't seem to raise the enthusiasm."

"Well, all due respect. I mean I know it's less than a year since you lost your wife. But maybe you need someone in your life to give it a bit of sparkle."

"You think?"

I saw Mos throw me a look, but I decided not to go there.

"I sure do. As a matter of fact I might even know the right someone. Just your type, Great legs and beautiful red hair...

"...Oh no, not a redhead! That's the last thing he needs."

"Anyway," continued Harry, "This chick is insatiable..."

"...You mean she's *never* satisfied! said Mos "Sounds like my mother...!"

"…Exactly."

A shadow fell over Mos as Al lowered his large frame beside him.

"Hey." Was all he said.

"Hi Al."

The four of us sat on the edge of the pool, dangling our feet in the water."

"How's Libby?" asked Al.

"Holding her own."

"Rita said to say hi."

"Sure."

We all sat there in silence for a while.

"We gonna play bridge?"

"Sure."

And we all got to our feet in unison, and headed inside to where the card table was already set up.


"So is he going to do it?"

"One diamond….Who? Do what?"

"Bush…One heart…Now that the Democrats have control. Is he going to have to get out of Iraq?"

Harry studied his cards carefully, "Two clubs…Nah, the guy's too stubborn. You watch him, he'll probably try and send in more troops."

"You think…?"

"Three no trumps,"

Al stopped us all in our tracks.

"Pass."

"Pass."

"Pass…Nah, he'd never do that. Surely."

"He's going to be a lame duck president. There's nothing he'll be able to do now."

"Don't you believe it. There's still plenty of damage he can do."

"Well, if there's damage to be done, I guess he's the man for the job all right."

At the mid-terms the Democrats had just taken control of both the House and the Senate after twelve years of nearly unbroken Republican rule. And, although the Dems had declared that they would work closely with the President, everyone knew that he would now be more ineffectual than ever.

"So," Harry asked me, "Are you going to write about all this on your new blog…?"

"….His what…?'

"…This new thing that Max is going to do. His blog…"

"…It's not a blog. And writing doesn't come into it. Actually I'll be doing what I've always done. Well, in a way. The only difference is that the pieces I do may be shorter, and they'll be out on the internet instead of television."

"Well I think it'll be good for you," said Harry. "Something to get into. You've been pretty down-in-the-mouth recently. I think it's just what you need."

"Really!" I blinked. "Down-in-the-mouth? I mean, I knew I was a bit introverted, but…"

"…Don't listen to the mad old fart," said Mos, "You've had a tough time of it lately. One thing and another."

"Yeah," I mused.

And there was a charged silence amongst the four of us. Nobody really wanted to say anything more on the subject. I mean what was there to say?

It was Al who broke the tension. As he studied the dummy, almost to himself he muttered, "So where does that leave Rumsfeld?"

"What?"

"Rumsfeld? D'you think Bush will stand by him?"

"Oh, he's gone."

"You think?"

"Definitely!"

I led a card. And for a few minutes we focused on the game. Al took eight tricks in a row, but then lost the lead. Finally he made the contract, and breathed out a sigh of relief.

"For a while I didn't think you were going to make it there big man.", said Harry.

"Me too." whispered Al.

I was figuring out the numbers on a piece of paper. I drew a line under the last and laid the pen down.

"Well that's it. You win that one." I stood up and stretched. "I need a break."

"Good idea," said Mos. "Anyone need a top-up?"

"Yeah, I wouldn't mind," replied Harry.

I didn't recognize the apparition that appeared at that moment. The fabulous Libby. The indomitable Libby, who always lit up a room, almost crept in to where we were playing. She hadn't lost much weight, but her face was sallow and she wore a kind of turban on her head. Mostly it was the change in her energy that affected us as we all turned towards her.

"Hi guys." she said quietly.

I was immediately struck by the change in her, and I was moved by seeing her like this. I felt like I was seeing a different Libby, a new Libby. Almost seeing inside her to her vulnerable core.

Mos was on his feet. "Can I get you anything sweetheart?"

Her smile was wan. But it beamed directly at Mos, and I could see the connection between them. And, strangely, I was jealous of this connection. Of this loving bond. What I wouldn't give right now to have that feeling. And I knew instantly that what I meant was I wished I had Marie right now. That I could take her in my arms and care for her. If only…

***

Myra, the receptionist at InterVod's offices, greeted me with a smile.

"Hi Max. How are you?"

"Pretty good, thanks Myra. Is Amy available?"

Myra keyed in some strokes on her computer, and frowned at the screen, "Did she arrange a meeting this morning?"

"Actually no. I was just hoping she could squeeze me in."

I gave her one of my most beguiling smiles, "Any chance?"

"Well, it's a busy day," she picked up the telephone, "But let me see."

She punched in Amy's extension number and waited for the response. It came after a few seconds.

"Hi Amy. Max Wheeler's in reception….No….I don't know….Uh huh….Okay, thanks."

She carefully replaced the receiver and looked up at me and smiled sweetly at me.

"She said she's very busy. But, if you can give her five she'll find a few minutes for you, okay? Can I get you some coffee or something while you're waiting?"

"No, I'm fine thanks."

"Okay then."

As Myra went back to her computer I sat down and pulled out some notes I'd been working on. I read through what I'd written. I'd spent the last couple of days refining some ideas for my…. My what? What would I call them? Not broadcasts now. Narrowcasts? That didn't sound right. Podcasts? Vodcasts? Maybe. Anyway, I'd drawn up a list of about twenty ideas that I thought would work and I wanted to discuss them with someone, and Mike was away. The thought occurred to me that maybe I really ought to have waited for Mike to come back and talk with him first, and I was just about to suggest to Myra that I should postpone this impromptu meeting, when Amy appeared.

"Max, sorry to keep you waiting."

She came up close to me and touched my arm.

"Come in, won't you."

She swiveled her hips and shimmied back through into her office I followed her, admiring the way she managed to make a simple walk into a work of art. She sat on the two-seater sofa and patted the seat beside her.

"Come on Max. I won't bite," she laughed lightly.

I sat down beside her and straightened the pieces of paper in my hand.

"I've put a lot of thought into…" I started.

"…Never mind that for the moment." She interrupted me. "This is quite an opportune moment. There's been a development."

That stopped me. "What now?" I thought.

She smiled at me for a moment. Perhaps deciding where to begin.

"In the short time we've been operating we've already developed quite a reputation. So much so that, believe it or not, there've been several offers to buy me out…"

"…You're kidding…"

"…Absolutely not. We've got a terrific operation here." She almost looked affronted. "Anyway…." She paused again and looked me square in the eyes. "I've decided to accept one of the offers…"

"…What…!"

"…Somebody made me an offer I couldn't refuse…." She sighed deeply. "Oh, it was a lot of things really. We're doing well, yes. But development and start-up costs were higher than we anticipated. Plus, when we started, there was only a little competition. Now dozens of new sites are setting up every week, and it's going to get harder to define ourselves in the marketplace. And my backers are nervous. *Plus*…." She gave me another little smile. "I've been promised a seat on the board of the company that will take us over."

I was stunned. This was something I hadn't expected. I couldn't think of a thing to say.

"Well, I can see that I really have surprised you here."

"You sure have."

"The thing is," she continued. "The new owners want to run things their way, and they've asked me to cut staff. And it's last in first out, I'm afraid. And, unfortunately that includes you"

She reached out a gently put a hand on my arm.

"I'm sorry Max. Of course I'll be recommending that they take you on. But it'll be their decision, you understand?"

"Yes." I was still struck dumb.

She looked at me compassionately.

"I hope you're not too upset with me. I have to do what's best for the greatest good. I mean, they'll probably ask you to come in. But, even if they don't, a journalist of your reputation…."

She just let the sentence hang.

# Chapter Twenty-Three

"Hi Max. How's it going?"

"Paul! Where are you?"

I couldn't help smiling into the telephone when I heard the voice.

"Right here in LA. Actually, not too far away from you. I had to see someone."

"So why don't you come around."

Twenty minutes later I looked out of the window just as Paul's car pulled up outside my apartment building. I watched as Paul climbed out of the car and walked towards the building's front door. The intercom buzzed.

"Come on up".

I pressed the release.

Shortly afterwards I opened the door to see my old journalist friend standing there. Impulsively I threw an arm around his shoulders.

"Come in. Come on in. Good to see you."

"You too."

I ushered him into the living room.

"Drink?"

"Sure."

I poured us both a shot of whisky, and we clinked glasses and knocked it back. The two of us studied each other for a moment. I thought that Paul looked drawn and tired. He seemed to have aged since I last saw him.

"Sit down, sit down. Another drink?"

"Mm, maybe in a minute."

"How long have you been in the country?"

Paul shrugged.

"I arrived yesterday."

"And where were you? Where did you just come from?"

A slight beat before Paul answered, "Iraq."

"Oh."

"Yes."

"Shit!"

"Yeah."

"How long were you there?"

"Three months. I can't say it was fun."

"No? I thought you liked to get in the thick of it."

"Not this time."

In spite of Paul's demeanor, I could feel my own nostalgia for the place.

"Tell me. How bad is it? And do you still go to some of the little restaurants that we used to go to?"

Paul shook his head, "I have to tell you it's not a good scene there. You have *no* idea what it's like now. There's insanity in the air. Those who can afford it are desperately trying to get out. To go anywhere. People are terrified. Of course they try and lead normal lives. But they're scared shitless just to go outside. Even simple things like going to the market. Because those are exactly the places being targeted by the mad bombers. And it's hard for them to drive around. Gas is scarce, so some people line up for hours. But now they've started bombing those queues. Who knows when it's going to be their turn. And there're still huge numbers of families living without electricity, water, plumbing for God's sake!

He rubbed a hand over a weary face, "Maybe I will have another drink."

I got up to pour us both another.

"No, I never go to any of those restaurants. I never go outside the fucking Green Zone. The only safe way you can get from the airport into Baghdad is by chopper.

"And do you know what the worst of it is for me? For a journalist? I can't even get out to see it, to report on it. I can't even go and talk to people and ask them questions. It's just too dangerous. I have to rely on Iraqi cameramen. We pay them to go out and shoot stuff and bring it back to us....Thanks."

He took the glass from me.

"I've worked with six different guys since I've been there. Three have been killed. One was arrested by our forces for no reason. He's now in Abu Ghraib. So far as I can find out he did nothing wrong, just pissed someone off one day. One's working with someone else. And the last guy I worked with quit. He just couldn't handle it any more. He figured if he wasn't killed by the Sunnis or the Shiites, then the Americans probably shoot him at some checkpoint. His wife was begging him to stop.

"So it's like working with your hand behind your back. And we end up just telling half the story, because I know about as much as......as you about what's happening. There's no proper professional analysis or interpretation that I can give." He shrugged. "I figured there really was very little point in me being there. So I left."

He knocked back his drink.

"The place is a fucking mess!"

"Wow."

"'Wow' is right. 'Wow' indeed."

We both sat there speechless for a moment. Then Paul smiled wryly, realizing he'd been on a bit of a rant. "I'm sorry. So, how the hell are you?"

"*Me?* Oh…It's been….interesting."

Paul looked at me expectantly, but I was struggling to find the words.

"It's been quite a ride," I said finally. "I'm not sure what to say."

I shook my head. "These last few months…."

Paul was still watching me, patiently waiting. I exhaled deeply. "Yeah, quite a ride. Like…..Christ, it's such a cliché….like a roller coaster. I feel turned inside out and upside-down." I gave a little laugh. "I think, in some ways I would happily have swapped the last few months with you."

Paul opened his mouth to protest, but I held up a hand,

"But only in some ways. Mostly it's been a major learning experience."

I realized what I'd just said and laughed at my use of the phrase.

"'Learning experience'. I'm showing my age now, using psychobabble phrases like that." I knocked back my drink, and exhaled deeply again.

"So, how long are you in town for?"

"Just a couple of days. Then I head east for a week. And, after that I head off to Afghanistan."

He saw the look on my face and chuckled. "Crazy, huh!"

"Are you serious?"

"'Fraid so." said Paul, and chuckled again,

I was helpless to stop the mirth rising to the surface. And it felt like a weight was lifting off me. We infected each other, and before too long we were both roaring with laughter.

***

That night I had a terrible dream about being chased by three thugs in Venice. I had fallen into one of the canals, and was drowning. It was only a slow realization as I opened my eyes that it had been a dream. Relief flooded through me, although some anxiety and apprehension stayed with me and I was breathing heavily. My face and body were covered in sweat, and I could feel a cramping in my right calf. I tried to slow down my breathing, but it needed more effort. Thank Christ it had only been a dream. How good to be able to wake from it and return to some sanity. I turned my head towards the clock. It read 6:17. The dawn light was just beginning to illuminate the room. As I looked around my breathing finally began to slow down and the sense of foreboding began to lift.

I closed my eyes again and lay there for a long time, as all the muscles in my body relaxed. Finally I pulled back the bedcovers and slid out of bed.

In the kitchen I poured water into the coffee machine and reached into the refrigerator for the jar of coffee. I remembered as soon as I put my hand on the jar that it was empty. Damn! I'd meant to buy some more yesterday. For a moment I considered making some tea instead, but I really needed coffee. Only one thing for it. There was a convenience store not too far away. I could kill two birds with the proverbial and jog to the store.

I slipped on my shorts and long-sleeved sweatshirt, went through a few body stretches, then grabbed a bottle of water from the refrigerator and headed out the door. There was actually a slight spring in my step, and I decided I was looking forward to a morning jog. It had been a while. "Silver linings", I thought as I set off down the street.

There was still a pinkish color in the sky as I eased into my stride.

# Chapter Twenty-Four

With only light traffic around and practically no pedestrians. I enjoyed the freedom of stretching my legs. I soon fell into a loose, regular stride, and was almost sorry when I arrived at the store.

Inside was quiet too. One old man was wandering around with a couple of items in a basket. A young man, whose name-badge read 'Kevin', was squatting on the floor re-filling shelves, and a couple of young women – girls really – were thumbing through some magazines. I nodded to Ahmad, the Pakistani owner and went in search of the coffee. As I passed the two girls I wondered why they were talking so loudly Then I saw that one of them had the earbuds of an MP3 player shoved into her ears. Obviously she had to talk over the level of whatever was on her player. Were they just starting their day or just arriving home? One of them, with pink cotton-candy colored hair and a hunk of metal decorating her left eyebrow, was pointing at a photograph.

"That's where I'm going."

The other girl, who had a hoop suspended from a nostril and a slash of bright red lipstick and was wearing a short plaid skirt, leaned over and peered at the picture.

"Oh, it looks nice."

A dreamy look came into the first girl's eyes.

"Oh it is. I've had my tickets now for, like, nine months. And I just can't wait. I'm so looking forward to it."

I felt, rather than heard, the door open. For some reason I looked towards the door, and saw a man dressed in army camouflage and carrying a large sports bag. Instinctively I knew something wasn't quite right. Maybe it was the way the man carried himself, maybe it was a look in his eyes.

"I told you I don't want you in my store…" began Ahmad.

"…And I told you I don't take no orders from no stinking Arab," said the man in a steely voice. "I'm done with all that." He dropped the bag to the floor and quickly unzipped it.

"I'm not an Arab…" Ahmad started to say, but froze when he saw the man pull an M-16 rifle from the bag and cock it. He tried to edge sideways, possibly towards an emergency button under the counter.

"Don't even think about it!" barked the man.

Ahmad backed away from the counter and half raised his hands in the air. The atmosphere in the store was electric. Kevin was frozen into his squatting position, one hand poised in the air, still holding a can. I saw the old man with the basket was holding a hand to his chest as though he might have a heart attack. The two girls had dropped the magazine, and were staring at the rifle in horror. My own hand was still reaching towards the shelf for the coffee. I looked into the man's steely gray eyes, and the sight chilled me. There was that same thousand mile stare that I'd seen in some guys back from combat. That not-quite-here quality that was so disconcerting. There was something in the voice too. A coldness that had no human warmth in it whatsoever. Both the old man and the shelf stacker began to back away towards the rear of the store. I also felt myself drawn backwards, automatically trying to make myself as small as possible. I could feel a cold, clammy sweat breaking out on my face.

"Now." said the man, "You're going to apologize for what you said to me earlier. 'Cause I didn't have my life destroyed protecting stinking Arabs like you…"

"I told you, I'm not an Arab…."

But that was as far as he got. The man raised the rifle up and brought it within six inches of Ahmad's face. One of the girls let out a short, high-pitched scream. The man whirled around and, as he did, there was an eardrum-tearing explosion. And then another, louder and longer, scream. The girl with the pink hair collapsed to the floor. For a moment her friend just stood there, holding her hand to her face. Then she dove down to kneel beside her friend.

"Ashleigh! Oh my God!"

I could see the girl writhing on the floor, but I was frozen with fear.

The man with the rifle, completely unfazed, turned back to Ahmad. Perhaps he just regarded the girl as 'collateral damage'. He simply said to Ahmad, "Now, like I said, you're going to apologize for what you said to me earlier."

I saw a couple of faces, one black, one Latino, peer in through the glass door. Then they disappeared.

"I…I…I…" stuttered Ahmad. But he could bring himself to say nothing more.

"Ashleigh! Oh God! Someone please!"

The man twitched the rifle in Ahmad's face, which was now drained of all color. "That's right. Go on!"

"I…I'm….sorry."

The man's finger curled around the trigger. "Shit!" I thought, "He's actually going to shoot him."

"You're sorry for *what*?!"

"I'm sorry for what….I said." Ahmad managed to say.

I could hear the sound of police car sirens n the distance. At first it was faint, but then I could see that everyone in the store was becoming aware of them.

"Help her. You've got to help Ashleigh. She's dying!" yelled the girl with the nose-ring.

The man noticed Kevin slowly edging his way to the back of the store. He pointed his rifle directly at him. "You! Come here!"

Kevin reluctantly began to walk slowly back towards the front of the store.

Apart from the whimpering from the girl, there was now silence inside the store. But there were more police sirens and activity outside.

My heart was racing. I was wondering whether it might be possible to grab the rifle before anyone else got hurt. But one look in the guy's eyes was enough to know that I shouldn't take such a stupid chance. Here was someone who, although he'd actually shot someone accidentally, knew his weapon. And was presumably used to battle conditions. It would probably be suicide to try and interfere in any way.

The police sirens drew nearer. The man with the rifle cocked an ear, but otherwise didn't react. I looked into his eyes, and it seemed as though he may be considering his options. Or perhaps figuring his odds if there was going to be a shoot-out.

The girl who'd been shot was now making a very strange sound. Something between a moan and a gurgle. And there seemed to be a lot of blood around her. Some of it was bubbling out of her mouth.

I couldn't help myself: "She really needs help." I said.

The man swung the rifle and pointed it at my chest.

"What?" he said.

"The girl." I managed to reply. "She doesn't look good. She might die."

At this the other girl began to howl. She was leaning over her friend, rocking backwards and forwards. And saying something which was unintelligible.

The man considered the situation. But all he said was "Hmm."

Behind them the old man suddenly dropped his basket with a clatter, clutched at his chest again and fell to the floor. The noise startled everyone. Kevin went to his aid, and carefully helped the older man to sit up, resting his back against a drinks cabinet.

Two police cars screeched to a halt outside the store, their sirens still blaring and their lights flashing. For the first time the man showed some degree of concern. I decided to keep my mouth shut for the moment. This might not be the best time to speak again.

Four policemen cautiously appeared at the door, peering inside. The man reacted by shoving Ahmad and me back towards the two girls. A policeman held his hand to his eyebrows so he could see better into the store as he tried to sum up the picture. He called out: "Is anyone hurt?"

At first no-one replied. But, when he repeated the question, I risked an answer.

"Yes." I called. "One person's shot, and another is sick. We need an ambulance."

The man looked deep into my eyes, and at first it seemed as though he might react badly to my intervention. But, instead, he moved behind our small group and pointed his rifle at the girl with the nose-ring. She was now leaning over her friend keening, tears streaming down her face. The threat was obvious.

"Son," called out the same policeman. "You need to give yourself up. Everything will be okay if you do. We don't want anyone else to get hurt."

The response took a few seconds to come.

"Not going to happen." was all he said. And he chewed the side of his cheek thoughtfully, assessing the situation.

The brief silence was broken by the girl, "Please. You've got to help her. She's dying."

The man turned briefly and looked down at the girls. But he was lost in his own thoughts.

"And I think this man needs medical attention," called out Kevin tentatively.

There was activity outside the front door. A thin, balding man had joined the uniformed police officers. The flack jacket he was wearing distorted the lines of his suit jacket. He ostentatiously held up his cell phone as he pushed the buttons. After a short delay the store telephone rang. Ahmad looked at the man questioningly. The man shook his head "no".

All eyes were now on the man, waiting to see what he might do. I took another risk, "You have to let them take her out....She *could* die."

When she heard this it set off the friend wailing again. The man stared hard at me, but didn't speak.

"Really, man," I continued, pushing my luck. "Right now you've got trouble. But nowhere near as much trouble as if she dies....Let her go."

The man began chewing the inside of his cheek again thoughtfully.

The old man began wheezing. Maybe he'd heard my suggestion, maybe he really was ill. Without speaking Kevin implored the man with his eyes. But the man just stared back. The light was gone from his eyes. But it was obvious that he was still thinking through what his next move should be. When he eventually spoke it was to me.

"Let you all go? So they can come in here and start blasting me? You really think that's a good idea." And he gave a derisive little laugh. "I don't think so."

The phone rang again, but everyone ignored it as they waited for the man to make his next move. He, on the other hand, looked like he wasn't about to make *any* move whatsoever.

I have no idea where the next thing came from. Maybe it was everything that had been happening in my life lately. Maybe I genuinely didn't care what happened next. It sure wasn't from any sense of heroics.

"Tell you what." I said eventually. Let the girl and the old man go. I'll stay with you. You'll still have...three of us."

The man rubbed his nose with the side of his thumb while he considered my offer. Then he surprised me by picking up the telephone. As soon as he did I could hear the voice of the policeman.

"We can work this out son. It'll be okay."

"Sure it will." said the man. "I've got a few people in here. Some of them will be coming out in a minute..."

"...Good..."

"...Shut up!...You will *not* attempt to do anything stupid. Understand?"

"Sure. You're making the right decision."

"Yeah, right."

The man nodded to Kevin, "Take the old guy out." Then he turned to me, "Help her carry her friend out." He whirled around and pointed a finger at Ahmad. "*You* will stay here."

Kevin supported the old man as he rested an arm over his shoulder. The old man, still holding his hand to his chest, leaned on Kevin as they too moved towards the door.

"Don't shoot." Yelled Kevin, "We're coming out."

Together they shuffled out of the door and into the street. When he stepped outside two policemen wearing flak jackets grabbed Kevin. Another policeman took away the old man.

I recovered from my shock. Then I looked at the shop-owner. "What are you going to do?" I asked the man. "Shoot him."

"I might." said the man. And he almost smiled.

"Let Ahmad help carry her out. I'll stay with you."

The man narrowed his eyes as he looked at me. "You want to be a hero?"

"Not really." I said.

I figured that the guy would almost certainly shoot Ahmad and then turn the gun on himself. Whereas there was a reasonable chance he wouldn't actually shoot me. At least that was what I hoped. "I just think it'll be better for everyone this way."

"It may not be better for you."

I shrugged. Maybe the guy *would* shoot me. I closed my eyes. Shit, now what had I done!

"Okay." said the man eventually. "Take them outside. But you…" and he pointed the rifle directly at me, "You stay."

Ahmad and the girl very carefully lifted her friend and began to carry her towards the door. The police outside saw what was happening and backed away from the doorway to give them a clear exit.

Inside I could hear Kevin, still yelling at the police. Obviously they weren't taking any chances with him. Maybe they thought he might be some kind of accomplice.

The man was still pointing his rifle at me. I could feel my heart racing.

"D'you mind." I said. "You're really making me nervous pointing that thing at me."

But the guy didn't move it immediately. Instead he stared directly into my eyes for a long moment. Then he stepped slightly away from me, out of reach, and slowly re-directed the rifle towards the door.

As the silence became intense I wondered what was next. Finally I couldn't stand it any longer.

"Afghanistan? Iraq?"

The man turned on me. "Shut up!" was all he said.

I could see that he was obviously calculating what his next move should be as he thoughtfully rolled the thumb and index finger of his free hand. But then he surprised me. Quietly he said, "Iraq". It wasn't addressed to anyone, least of all me. It was as though the man was remembering being there.

"Bad, huh?" I asked softly.

The man sneered at me. "What d'you think?" But, after a moment's reflection, he added quietly, "Yeah. Pretty bad."

I was thinking to myself, if only I could keep this up. Establish some kind of rapport with the guy. Then maybe we might both come out alive.

"How long were you there?' I asked tentatively.

Again it looked as though the man wasn't going to answer. But finally he said, "Too long." He still didn't actually look directly at me. His focus was on the front doors of the store.

A long pause. Then, "Two tours."

The store phone rang again, and the guy at the door waved his cell in the air. But this time the phone went unanswered, and eventually stopped. Then the man surprised me again.

"When we were shipped out first. They told us it was for four months. Then it was extended. And finally it was twelve months. Then fifteen….."

There was a noise out the back and both of us wheeled around. Another noise, and there was a deafening explosion as the man fired off a round. I had a ringing in my ears, but I was pretty sure that the noise out back had stopped. I wondered if there had been someone there and, if so, whether they'd actually been shot.

The man stood listening. But there was silence. He showed no signs of fear, but I could see him trying to think through his next moves.

"Name's Max," I said. "Max Wheeler."

"Yeah…..Is that so." He turned to face me. "What do you do Max Wheeler?"

"I'm a journalist."

The man gave a little laugh. "Really! You going to write about this?"

I shrugged. "If I survive."

The man stared at me for a moment. "Yeah," was all he said.

The telephone started ringing again. We both watched it warily. The man exhaled heavily in frustration.

I said: "You could talk to them."

"What for?…..I've got nothing to say."

Eventually the phone stopped again and there was silence. I knew I should keep the man talking. That, while we did, there was some chance we might both come out of this alive. Otherwise the man might decide to do something impulsive. I searched my mind for something to say.

"What's your name?" was all I could think of.

It sounded pretty lame, even to my ears. But, to my surprise, the man replied.

"Kovaks ….Bob Kovaks." :

Then Kovaks squinted his eyes slightly as he looked me. "You been on TV?"

"Yeah."

"I thought I seen you."

Another pause as I tried to think of something else.

"Bad situation in Iraq."

"Uh, huh."

"What was it like there for you?"

A long silence. But, just as I was beginning to think that Kovaks wasn't going to answer, he said:

"First time we thought we knew what we were up for."

He said this without looking at me.

"We'd been jazzed before we left. Then we had our campaign. And, I mean, we'd won the "war" hadn't we. Saddam had been defeated. All we had to do was mop up, then we could go home. Ha!"

And that was all he said.

There were more cops now peeking in through the front door of the store. I could see two of them conversing. One was nodding in agreement. Were they going to try something. Something dumb. I worried that this might be the really stupid part where I could get badly hurt. Then the two cops disappeared from view. I wondered whether I could talk this guy into giving himself up. I flicked a look at Kovaks, and could see that he too had noticed the cops talking.

Kovaks started pacing around. I guessed that his pulse was racing. His eyes flicked again towards the front door, then the back of the store. "Oh shit!"

"Were the Iraqis pleased to see you?"

"Mm, what?...Yeah, at first. Most of 'em....."

But the soldier's attention wasn't really on what I was asking. Nevertheless I carried on.

"So what happened?"

Kovaks just stared at me. He stared at me hard, and for a brief instant I thought I might have pushed too hard. Maybe the guy might actually shoot me.

Instead he spat out: "Man, you really are a fucking journalist!" And I could see that he was actually starting to get angry. He moved towards me and brought his rifle up between us. His face was flushed.

"What is it you want to know, huh?"

I stammered, "I'm just trying to understand."

"Well, understand this....."

For the first time Kovaks raised his voice.

"...The whole place is a shit-heap! I have *no* idea what we are doing there. I thought it was to save the Iraqis and to bring them democracy! Well not a one of them is interested in fucking democracy. Not *our* kind of democracy anyhow! And some of them are trying as hard as they can to kill us.

"We never knew when we would go out on patrol whether we'd get hit. We never knew if we would come back alive. And that happened day after day after day. And, instead of a few months, it lasted for more than a year. And we just focused on staying alive."

He stopped talking and looked away from me. It seemed like he'd said all he was going to say. But he was just getting started. He turned back to me.

"Man I saw such terrible things. With the car bombings you'd get bits of bodies everywhere. You wouldn't know who belonged to what. And there'd be some guy or some woman with her leg blown off begging you to help. And, shit! There was nothing you could do. And the worst was the kids. I've seen babies completely charred black from fire. And kids screaming in agony. It got so I couldn't stomach the smell of steak in the chow hall. It reminded me of burning flesh and made me physically ill.

"And our guys too. I have one memory that never goes away. A soldier standing as close to me as you are now was shot in the head by an insurgent sniper. When he was hit by the bullet I saw his head just snap back and his brains splattered everywhere. All over me, everywhere. I still have nightmares about that."

I shuddered. But I kept my mouth shut. The anger had gone from Kovaks now. Instead there was something else. A sadness mixed with a kind of resignation. I looked at the man, wondering what was next. Could this sadness be the trigger for some awful event? Better keep the guy talking. I was about to ask another question when Kovaks spoke. And I realized then that the soldier actually wanted to share his story.

"Finally I got to go home. Of course there were no parades for me, no cheering crowds to welcome me. At first my wife was happy to see me again, relieved that I was still in one piece. But during the day I'd get depressed and at night the nightmares are bad. One night I woke up thinking we were being attacked and I slugged my wife. She got less and less happy to have me around. War changes you. It changes you forever.

"I think my wife was more relieved when I went back for my second tour. Anyways, she didn't stick around. One day I got an email to say that she'd had enough. A fucking email man. Shit!......

"....I was depressed enough as it was. Lots of the guys were. Tons of them survive on Zoloft and Ambien. But I just tried to get through one day at a time. And then it was tougher. When we arrived we were heroes. Now we were pretty much everyone's enemy."

He looked deep into my eyes.

"To be honest, when I got that email from my wife I totally lost it. I hated everyone, the Iraqis, the command, everyone. I'd go out in the morning hoping that I'd get taken out. It was only because of the guys in my squad that I survived. They looked after me. They became my family."

A distant look came into the man's eyes.

"Two of them in particular...."

A very long pause. And I watched as Kovaks' face became suffused and his eyes started to glisten.

"....There were two guys, Brody and Matthews. If it wasn't for them....and then, one day...."

And now I could see the tears in the man's eyes, and I felt real compassion for him. And I also felt envy for those tears.

"One day we were out on patrol...We'd been told to check out a particular house. There'd been reports of a shooter inside. We kicked the door in. There was a family there. No men, but two women and a bunch of kids. I don't know how many, maybe four, five. They all seemed to shrink back in the corner like they do sometimes. One of the women started screaming, and I think that set off one of the kids crying. We tried to calm them all down. Matthews knew some Arabic and he told them we were looking for the shooter, but they didn't seem to understand. Then we heard a noise in the next room. Brody pushed the door open carefully, but he couldn't see anything. But we all had a feeling that something was up. The hairs on my neck were standing up straight.

"Three of the guys edged into the room carefully. I was watching the family because something didn't seem right. The woman who was screaming was really starting to wail now. You know, the way that they do.

"I didn't see it. All I knew was that suddenly there was this almighty fucking explosion that knocked me off my feet. And when I *could* see through the dust and shit there was a hole in the fucking wall and Brody and Matthews and Alonzo were annihilated....I mean, one minute they were there, the next....."

Kovaks put his face in his hand. He was swallowing hard, trying to gulp back the tears.

# Chapter Twenty-Five

An unmarked police car pulled up outside the store, and the two senior offices who climbed out were greeted by a uniformed cop.

"Well?"

"We have one gun and one hostage." said the uniform.

"The other hostages?"

"He sent them out. One…a girl…was shot. Still alive. The paramedics took her to hospital. It looks like an old man had some kind of mild heart attack. They took him too."

"The guy inside?"

"He looks to be okay. He's got the gunman talking to him."

"Smart."

"Yeah."

"The rear entrance?"

"We tried that sir. There was a shot. One round."

"What weapons does this guy have."

"We're not sure. But we've only seen one, an M-16."

"Do we know what he wants?"

"Not at this time."

"You tried to call him?"

"Yes sir. He wasn't interested. Wouldn't talk."

"Hmm…..Is he shooting out here?"

"Not yet."

The senior officer, Inspector Garry Jackson, flattened himself against the wall, and slowly eased himself along so that he could see inside. He studied the scene for some time, then slid back to the others.

"You know who that is?"

"The shooter…?"

"….No, the hostage."

"No sir."

"That's Max Wheeler the television journalist. I used to watch him all the time."

He turned to the colleague that he arrived with.

"Look Wheeler up Eric. See if you can get a cell phone number for him."

"Sure."

Jackson turned back to the uniformed officer.

"You have any ID on the shooter? Or what he wants."

"No sir. Best we can understand, he'd had some kind of argument with the store owner. And he went back with a gun to sort it out We believe the gun might have gone off by mistake."

"He hasn't made any demands?"

"Nope."

"Oh great! The cavalry's here."

They both turned to watch as a vehicle with a SWAT team pulled up. Several heavily protected men bristling with weapons leapt out. Their senior officer marched over to Jackson.

"Hey Garry, what've you got?"

Jackson held up his hand to warn the other man to back off for a moment.

"Your boys can relax Brad. We've got everything under control here."

"I'm sure you do Bob. I'm sure you do. So we'll just take up our positions and be ready if you need us."

Jackson sighed resignedly. "Okay."

Eric returned with a piece of paper and handed it to Jackson.

"Took a bit of arm-twisting, but here's Wheeler's cell."

Jackson took the piece of paper and pulled out his own cell phone. He punched in the numbers, then turned to see what happened inside the store.

\*\*\*

Kovaks had been silent for some time, remembering his friends. Truth be told I wasn't sure what might happen next. It was quite feasible that Kovaks could put the gun to both or either of our heads and pull the trigger. Or the emotion that he was experiencing could just as easily steer him away from this path.

I had just decided that it would probably be a good idea to say something when my cell phone started ringing. At first it startled us both. I pulled it out but didn't answer it. Instead I looked at Kovaks to see what he might do. Kovaks, in turn, simply stared at the small device. It seemed to be ringing louder and louder. I looked at him questioningly. Eventually Kovaks gave a little nod and I flipped it open.

"Yes?" I said.

"Mister Wheeler, this is Bob Jackson from the LAPD. Are you all right?"

"I'm fine."

I realized what was happening. I looked towards the store window and saw Jackson wave. Kovaks noticed too, but didn't protest.

"Mister Wheeler can I talk with the man there with you."

"He wants to talk to you." I said, holding the phone out to Kovaks. But Kovaks shook his head. I put the phone back to my ear.

"He doesn't want to...."

"...Yeah, I saw." said Jackson. "Maybe I can talk through you. Is that okay?"

"Sure."

"Do you know the man's name?"

"Er, yes." I tried out the name: "Kovaks?" I looked at the soldier, questioningly, to make sure I'd got it right. "Bob Kovaks."

"Okay." said Jackson.

I could see that Kovaks was starting to become agitated. I watched as the policeman turned and repeated the name to a colleague, then back again to me.

"And, Mister Wheeler, do you know what Mister Kovaks wants?"

"Not really. I think we just have ourselves a little situation. And it's kind of gotten out of hand..."

At this Kovaks grabbed the cell phone and threw it hard down on the floor. Then he lifted the rifle and held it to my head. But he wasn't looking at me. He was staring pointedly out through the front window.

He yelled, "Fuck you!" And the blood rushed to his face

I couldn't help it. I started to perspire badly. I knew that any second could be my last, and I was finding it difficult to breathe. My eyes flicked between the gun and the front window where the cops were gathered. I saw them back away from the window. Kovaks saw it too, and he seemed to relax slightly, some of the redness going from his cheeks. It crossed my mind that the barrel of the rifle was so close that I could probably knock it to one side. Then what? Tackle the guy? A man who was fit and nearly a third of my age? Not a good idea. So what? Run like hell to the front door? Kovaks could bring me down before I'd made two strides.

I had been in tight spots before. I'd even feared for my life before. But I'd never encountered anything like this before. I could feel the sweat in my armpits, and trickling down from my forehead. I also felt a slight dizziness and my head was beginning to swim. I wondered whether I might faint, and I forced myself to keep breathing. As I did so, I couldn't help a small moan escaping my lips, and I felt ashamed.

When he heard the moan, Kovaks turned his face back to me. Obviously he could see the tension in my face.

"I'm not going to shoot you." he said.

"What are you going to do?" I managed to gasp

"I'm not sure" said Kovaks. He was silent for a moment. Then he said quietly, "Seems to me this is a lose-lose situation. I'm in deep shit. The only way I can get out of it is to shoot myself. And I didn't survive two fucking years of *that* to take myself out."

"You know," I said, "That girl's going to be okay. If you go outside now and let this thing go, it might not be so bad. Get yourself a good lawyer and you may not even have to do time…Post traumatic stress and all that…."

"…You know a good lawyer?"

"Yeah, I know a few. Not…you know, *criminal* lawyers. But I'd be happy to help you…."

"…Really?"

"Actually yes."

"Hmm."

Kovaks slowly lowered the rifle. I let out a little sigh of relief, but then watched in horror as the man pointed it towards himself.

"Please don't," I whispered.

Bob Kovaks stared at me silently, his breathing slow and even.

"Please."

The moment seemed to be endless. But, eventually, still staring at me, Kovaks allowed the rifle to slide to the floor.

I gave a little nod.

"Thank you," I said.

Kovaks response was a slight, mirthless snigger. Then he slowly turned and, raising his hands in the air, he headed for the door.

"He's coming out," yelled someone.

"Stand back!"

Even though Kovaks had dropped his own rifle, almost a dozen guns were trained on him as walked towards the door.

As soon as he stepped outside Jackson called out, "Okay stop right there. And kneel down."

For a moment it looked as though Kovaks might be having second thoughts. Maybe he might turn and head right back into the store. Or maybe he might just lunge for one of the cops and get himself taken out. But, a moment later, still with his hands in the air, he slowly knelt down.

"Good." said Jackson. "Now lie face down and spread your arms outwards. The soldier obliged and two cops immediately stepped forwards, one on either side. One of the cops cuffed his hands behind his back as the other frisked him. Then they both helped him up and walked him towards a waiting wagon.

Jackson called out to me," Okay Mister Wheeler. It's safe to come out now."

# Chapter Twenty-Six

I adjusted the temperature, tested it with my hand, then stepped into the shower. I allowed the water to pour down onto my head and splash over my shoulders. I stood there like that for several minutes, slowly breathing in and out. Then I held my face up to the torrent and felt the little needles of water sting my skin.

The steam began to build inside the shower cabinet, and soon I was transported to another world. For once my thoughts stopped, and I simply enjoyed the sensuous pleasure, losing all sense of time, feeling at one with the stream of water.

In the end it was the change in temperature which forced me out of the shower. I turned off the faucet and reached for a large towel to wrap myself in.

But my fingers never found the towel. Instead they inexplicably began to twitch. I tried to hold them still, but found that I couldn't. Now my arm too was shaking and I couldn't control that either. I tried to step out of the shower, but instead I started to tremble and convulse. Then, without warning, I collapsed on the floor, briefly losing consciousness.

When I came to I was hyperventilating, rapidly sucking in air and expelling it automatically. And my whole body was shaking. I tried to stop it, but found it impossible. Eventually I managed to draw up my legs towards my chest. As the seizure took hold of me I closed my eyes. I was scared stiff, not knowing what the hell was happening. The vibrations took over my body, and I had no choice but to just lie there and hope that the shaking would stop. And that I wouldn't die.

Finally the shaking slowed. But now I found myself unable to move, not because I was paralyzed, but because I was frozen to the spot, frozen almost by some exterior force. As I lay there in the fetal position my mind finally began to clear slightly.

"My God!" I thought "My God, whatever next!"

My body was feeling chilled from the tiled floor, and I knew that I had to try and move. In spite of almost overwhelming exhaustion I managed to drag myself up from the floor. Supporting my weight I reached out for my robe and struggled into it. Then, using the walls as support, I slowly staggered into the bedroom and fell onto the bed.

I thought that I should call someone. This didn't feel like a stroke, although at that moment I wasn't precisely sure what a stroke felt like. However, this could be something serious. Should I try and phone for an ambulance. Or perhaps a friend. If so, whom should I phone?

I managed to climb under the bedclothes and began to feel the warmth of the bed thaw my chilled body. Soon after that I drifted off to sleep.

I slept for almost twenty-four hours without stirring. As I gradually came to a small voice inside my head told me I shouldn't open my eyes. Not yet at least. Maybe in a few minutes. Maybe then. But my eyes deceived me and opened of their own accord. I had no say in the matter. And then I found my body easing itself out of bed. My mind also had no say in the matter.

I stood over the toilet bowl for a long time as I emptied my bladder, supporting myself with one hand resting on the wall in front of me. When I'd finished I breathed out a huge sigh.

"For this relief many thanks," I muttered to myself.

I took one look at the shower stall and turned away from it, recalling all that had occurred the day before. Instead I peered into the mirror over the sink. I felt fine now, but…..what the hell *was* that!

***

"I want to run some more tests…." Mark Abrahams held up his hand. "No, hear me out. How long have I been your doctor…?"

"….Too long….!"

"….Yeah, for me too."

This was familiar repartee for us. It covered the slight awkwardness of friends who also had a doctor/patient relationship.

"Frankly Max, my best guess is that you've been under a ton of stress recently, And this most recent experience …the hostage thing…"

"…Hardly a hostage…."

"…Whatever. This was the camel's straw. What I'm going to prescribe is rest and relaxation. Do nothing …."

"…But I've been doing nothing for a while now…"

"…Rest and relaxation. Stress-management. Re-charge the batteries. But…I want you to come in for a day to run the tests. Just in case."

"Well I guess I've got nothing better to do. When?"

"….Now.

I was about to protest. Then I just shrugged.


The day dragged badly, and I was bored stiff. They poked and prodded me and stuck tubes in me and wheeled me here and there to be sucked into dark mechanical tunnels. And, when that was over, they forced me to stay the night. I flipped channels on the television and thought of Bruce Springsteen. And, finally, I was left alone with my thoughts.

As I eventually drifted off to sleep, assisted by mild medication, I drowsily began to summarize my life. Again. The one thing I kept coming back to was the hole that I felt existed in my life. And, just before Morpheus swallowed me, my very last thoughts were of Laura. I realized that she was the one person that I wanted to hear from, and a smile began to spread on my face. And, just before my lights went out, I was wondering whether this was a woman with whom I could spend some time…..Maybe the rest of my life.

# Chapter Twenty-Seven

"You know, I wanted to thank you," she said. "I mean, it's quite an…."

"…An honor…?"

"…Well, I wouldn't go *that* far," she laughed. And the laugh filled her whole face. Her eyes twinkled and she wore a broad grin, and I thought I could imagine the girl in her, how she'd looked thirty or forty years ago.

"…No, well I mean you're the special guest. It's your sixtieth birthday party. And we hardly know each other…"

"…Except in the biblical sense …"

She didn't exactly blush, but her cheeks did take on a rosy hue.

"…Well, yes. But that's no…"

"…Laura." I rested my hands gently on her shoulders, "I want you here. And I want to introduce you to my family and friends. And I think this would be the perfect opportunity."

"Thank you," was all she said. And then leaned forward and kissed me softly on the lips.

We climbed out of the car and, as a valet took my place, we were immediately greeted by Katie, who was holding a kind of Hawaiian lei, which she slipped around my neck.

"That's for the birthday boy."

Then she wrapped her arms around me and kissed me. I was delighted to see my daughter looking so healthy.

"Happy birthday daddy."

"Thanks Katie."

I fingered the lei.

"Er, do I have to?"

Her face never lost its joyousness.

"Of *course* you do daddy…..At least for a while. Come on, don't be a spoilsport."

"Okay….Katie, this is Laura. Katie is my younger daughter."

"Hello," Katie said, and kissed Laura on the cheek. "Pleased to meet you. I'm glad you've come"

"Why, thank you."

Laura blinked, taken aback slightly. She hadn't expected to be welcomed so eagerly.

"Come on," said Katie, slipping an arm through each of ours, "There's a bunch of people here already. And they've all been waiting for you to arrive."

The venue for the party was Mos and Libby's house. When I had found out about this I'd been worried that it would be too much for Libby.

"Don't worry," Mos had told me. "She's finished the chemo, and she's feeling a bit better. She really wants to do this. And she's got plenty of support. Besides, it'll take her mind off everything else."

Obviously Libby – or somebody - had put a lot of thought into the party. Just as for Mos and Libby's thirtieth anniversary party, the garden looked beautiful. It was festooned with a great many elegant lights and groups of candles. And, in the cool early December air, the groups of bedecked tables and chairs were warmed by huge overhead heaters.

As we proceeded up towards the house giant speakers began to boom out the exuberant voice of Stevie Wonder: "*Hap*...py *birth*...day to you. *Hap*...py *birth*...day........"

I smiled. How many times had I heard this before? So corny, yet, in spite of myself I smiled. Maybe it was the sheer joyousness in Stevie's voice. Or perhaps it was that I actually felt really good to be here. And, in spite of everything, to be celebrating my sixtieth birthday. There certainly had been times when I thought I might not actually make it to this point. But here I was. And yesterday Mark Abrahams had called me to talk about the test results. Basically everything looked good. There was still a small question mark around a couple of minor heart arteries.

"But," said Mark, "If you promise not to sue me if it doesn't come true, I'd say that you could live to be a hundred."

And we'd both laughed.

"What a beautiful garden." said Laura, as we continued upwards. "Who did you say lives here?"

"My friend Mos and his wife Libby. There they are by the door. He's about my oldest friend."

The passage upwards was quite slow now, because people were stopping us to greet me. There were kisses for me and Katie, and interested looks at Laura, some of them direct, some of the more surreptitious.

We were greeted at the top by Mos, clutching a glass, and by Libby, wearing an extravagant hat over a colorful bandana. Libby promptly put her arms around me, nearly crushing the lei.

"Happy birthday Max."

"Thanks Lib. And thank you so much for all of this. I know it was…"

But she cut me off:

"….It was nothing Max. You know I can do these kind of things with my eyes shut. Now…this must be Laura."

She turned to Laura and embraced her. Which kind of took Laura by surprise, although she was clearly pleased.

"Welcome. And how nice to meet you. Although, unfortunately, Max has told us practically nothing about you. But I'm dying to find out."

As Katie slipped off, Mos beamed at me and tried a hug. But, with the glass in one hand, Mos was only able to give me a sort of awkward one-armed embrace. But he had a big, beaming grin on his face.

"Happy Birthday bud. The big six oh."

"Thanks Mos. Yeah, the big six oh. All downhill from here."

"Here, let me get you a drink. Champagne?"

"Sure. It *is* my birthday."

"Coming right up."

Mos brushed by Al's wife Rita as she came burbling out the door, talking a mile a minute. She had her arm around a slim, young woman whose blonde hair was drawn into a short pony-tail. I wondered who she was. Rita was propelling the silently acquiescing woman out towards the garden, but she stopped when she saw me, and came right over.

"Max, Cheri. A very, very happy birthday."

She gave me a little peck on the cheek.

"What a thrilling time and what a wonderful job Libby's done here. …Oh, hi Lib, I was just saying…"

"Thank you Rita. I heard. That's so sweet of you."

For the thousandth time I marveled at how two women who can't stand each other are able to appear to be so affable and friendly.

"Happy birthday Mister Wheeler," said the young woman. She actually shook my hand. And the handshake was firm like a man's, although not as strong. "I'm Sam, Jenny's friend."

"Thanks Sam." I looked around. Where is she?"

"Inside the house on the phone. Some business thing." Her eyes went heavenward, and I understood completely.

Mos returned with my drink and handed it to me. Al was only a few steps behind him..

"Happy birthday buddy."

"Thanks Al."

He raised his glass.

"Here's to you Max, a man I really respect." He drank from his glass.

I was taken completely by surprise.

"Why, thank you Al. That means a lot to me."

I indicated the house and garden.

"This is great, isn't it."

More people were arriving now, and I heard laughter as they made their way up towards the house. I turned back to find that Jenny had come out of the house, and was walking towards me with her arms outstretched.

"A very happy birthday daddy." She hugged me closely, and I saw that her face was slightly flushed.

"Thank you sweetheart. Lovely to see you."

Jenny was standing next to Sam now who linked Jenny's arm in what could only be described as a proprietorial way.

"You've met Sam?" she asked.

"Yes, I'm happy to say that I have."

The pair of them now beamed at me like a matched set. In my mind I was thinking, 'Is she…? Is this what I think….?'

From the look on Jenny's face it seemed that she was reading my mind. But she wasn't about to make anything easy for me. Well, this *was* a surprise.

And another surprise: I suddenly realized that the party of people approaching included not only my brother Elliott and sister-in-law Elizabeth-Anne, but behind them were also Brandy and Gary. Wow! This was a major gathering of the clans. Maybe I was dying, and nobody had wanted to tell me.

Elliott bellowed out: "Is that my big brother? Hey big brother, happy birthday."

I couldn't remember seeing my brother so jovial. Maybe it was the California air. And Elizabeth-Anne too was smiling. That really was something.

"Wow, I'm impressed. You flew across the country just to come to my birthday party?"

"Sure." said Elliott, pumping my hand. "After all, it's a very special one. And besides…" he added slyly. "..it gave us the excuse to take Gary and Brandy on what will probably be our last family vacation. We've got all kinds of stuff lined up."

Elizabeth-Anne kissed me somewhat primly, and so did Brandy. Then Gary shook my hand as well and muttered "Happy birthday". Then they all stood around, not sure what to do next. Fortunately the awkwardness was broken by Mike Kenny, who was standing right behind them.

"Hey Max! The best of Irish to yer. Well, this is certainly great!"

"Mike! I'm so glad you came. This is my brother Elliott and his family."

And then more people piled up behind them. And even more.

After a while I actually began to feel fatigued. Being the center of attention, and having to be 'on' and greet all the well-wishers was beginning to take its toll. Laura had been involved in her own conversations but nevertheless had obviously been keeping an eye on me. Now she could tell that I was beginning to wilt. She whispered in my ear, "Why don't you show me some more of this garden. Surely we can find a quiet spot to just sit quietly."

I was relieved, "Good idea. Come on, I think I know just the place."

To the side of the garden, away from all the lights, was a wooden gazebo which comfortably fitted two people in complete privacy. We sat down inside with relief. So much so that neither of us spoke for some time. Eventually it was me who broke the silence.

"I mean, this is great and everything. And, of course, it's nice for everyone to come. But……Well, it's all just a bit too much really."

I took her hand.

"But I'm glad you're here."

"Why, thank you kind sir. How very gallant."

"No, really. This feels good."

For a little while we looked into each others eyes as I toyed, absent-mindedly with her hand. Then she leaned over and kissed me gently on the mouth. It wasn't a long kiss, but we both felt the intensity of it.

"Yes it does." was all she said.

And we sat there enjoying the silence and each other's company.


After a little while I noticed her shiver slightly, and she pulled her coat tighter around herself.

"Come on," I said. "We should be getting back. 'Guest of Honor' and all that. Otherwise people might think I've been kidnapped by aliens. Or that we've eloped."

"Mmm," she said, not moving.

Then: "Max, I've been thinking a lot recently about what I want to do with the rest of my life."

"Yes?"

"And I think I'd like to spend at least part of it helping other people. In my travels I've seen a lot of privation of various kinds, especially some terrible poverty. So......it seems to me that....what I'd like most to do is to somehow help with world poverty."

"O...kay?" I couldn't see where on earth this was leading.

"And I've been checking out some of the micro-credit agencies.....I think that's what I'm going to do."

"I see."

"Yes.....And I was wondering....Is this something that appeals to you? Would you like to come on this journey with me?"

I looked at her for a long time before I answered. But I knew what I was going to say because it was all so obvious now.

"Yes," I said. "Yes, I *would* like to......"

Tommy suddenly appeared.

".....Hey dad, I was looking for you. Everyone's wondering where the Man of the Hour's got to. By the way, happy birthday man."

Tommy did that thing where he kind of bumped his shoulder against mine and touched the back of my hand with his fist.

"Thanks Tommy…This is Laura…This is Tommy, my youngest. He's a rock star."

"Yeah, right!"

He was self-deprecating, but I knew he was pleased at my description. He smiled at Laura.

"Anyway, are you coming inside? We can go the back way."

The kitchen was full of catering staff, busy preparing and carrying food. But the three of us squeezed our way through to the wall-to-wall guests.

"Hey, look who I found!" called out Tommy.

Many people ignored him, and carried on with their conversations, some having to shout because the hubbub was so loud. But several faces turned, and greeted me. Hands reached out to touch me as I walked through, and there were smiles on faces. I saw Lisa in the distance with, what's-his-name, Ron. She gave me a little wave and mouthed 'Happy Birthday'.

There was a heavy tap on my shoulder and I spun around to face Harry.

"Hey there old man."

"Not so much of the *old* please."

"Quite a celebration, huh?"

"Yeah. Pretty amazing."

But Harry's eyes were on Laura. I noticed and smiled

"Keep your hands off her Harry. She's spoken for."

"Really?....Really! Well done Max. She looks nice. Good luck to you."

Hey dad, there's someone upstairs who's been waiting to see you"

I shot Tommy a quizzical look. Then realized who Tommy was talking about. As I was about to climb the stairs I turned around to see whether Laura was still with me. She gave me a tentative smile as though she wasn't sure whether or not she should follow.

"Come on," I said, "I think I know who this is, and I'd like to introduce you."

"Okay."

She followed me up the stairs towards one of the bedrooms. Inside Maggie, the young, stressed-out mother, was dressing a four-year old boy. My beautiful grandson Toby. Jack stood patiently beside them holding his son's teddy bear.

Maggie looked up when we walked in.

"Here he is! See I told you granddad was coming. You'd better hurry up now."

The small boy beamed with delight at me, and tried to run towards me, even though he still didn't have his pants on properly.

"Danddad!!."

"Hey!" I said. "How's my little champion?"

I scooped him up and gave him a big kiss.

"Hello little man."

"Hello."

The little boy clung to me and bathed in my love. I cuddled him some more, and then turned and showed him to Laura.

"This…is Toby. Say hello to Laura, Toby."

She moved closer and tentatively held out a hand.

But Toby was too shy, and instead clung tighter to me.

"Oh well," I said. "This pretty lady is Maggie, Toby's mom. And this is Jack, my son and heir."

Maggie gave Laura a slightly strained smile as she struggled to pull up Toby's pants, but Jack came forward and took Laura's hand in greeting.

"Hello, welcome to the madness."

"You live in New York?"

"Long Island, yes."

"Jack doesn't like Los Angeles," I blurted out. "He says that in New York people say 'fuck you' when they mean 'have a nice day', and in Los Angeles it's the other way around."

Jack began to protest, but Laura laughed brightly. As usual, I could see Maggie's slight look of disapproval.

"Hi Maggie," I said, putting my spare arm around my daughter-in- law. She gave me a little peck on the cheek.

"Happy birthday Max." she said, and reached out to take Toby, who shrunk back into my arms.

"Baby", said Toby, shyly.

"Yes", said Maggie. "Of course."

She turned around and picked up a tiny bundle from the bed. Pulling back the blanket she revealed the exquisite face of a sleeping baby.

"And this," she said, "is Lucy."

My new granddaughter was beautiful, with delicate features and some blonde wispy hair. I was enchanted. Lucy gave a little moue with her lips in her sleep, and I leant over to lightly touch my lips to her forehead.

"She's exquisite," I said. 'What an angel!"

Toby reached out an arm to touch his sister, and I was afraid he might wake her, so I gently moved away. I could feel myself beaming with pleasure at being surrounded by my family in this way.

Jack reached behind him and pulled out a large, flat wrapped parcel. He held it out to me.

"Here dad. Happy birthday from us all."

"Thank you Jack."

"Toby, you want to hop off, so granddad can unwrap his present?"

The little boy shook his head, but reluctantly let his father take him. I took the parcel and studied it uncertainly.

"Wow, is this from you Toby? What could it be?"

Toby just shook his head again and nestled into Jack's legs.

I carefully unwrapped the present to discover that it was a large framed photograph of Jack, Maggie, Toby and Lucy.

"Oh, that's beautiful. What a great gift! Thank you."

"That's me." Toby pointed out to me proudly.

"Yes, I can see that. And what a great picture it is of you too. And your mommy and daddy. And Lucy. Thanks guys. I'll treasure this."

I hugged them all, and Toby had a wide smile of pleasure on his face.

"So, are you guys ready?" asked Tommy. "Dad's about to make a speech."

"I am? That's the first I've heard of it."

"Sure you are. Everyone's expecting it."

"But I haven't prepared anything."

"You'll be fine. You're the professional after all. Just a few impromptu words."

Katie joined me as Tommy led the little procession down the stairs. Everyone there seemed to be having a good time, mostly standing or sitting around talking. This didn't seem like the moment to interrupt the proceedings.

"Are you sure…?" I began.

"…Yes," chorused Tommy and Katie.

Jack stepped forward. He pulled a key out of his pocket and clinked it against his glass. The hubbub quietened a little, but several people carried on talking. So Jack spoke out loudly.

"Excuse me. May I have your attention. Hello!"

One or two guests outside obviously had no idea what was happening, and carried on talking. But most people became silent and turned towards Jack.

"Thank you. Ladies and gentlemen, we're all here today to celebrate with, and…." He turned to me. "…and honor a man who means a great deal to all of us…."

"…Stop, stop!" I interjected, "You'll make be blush…"

"…a man who means a *great* deal to all of us. A man who I am proud to call my father: Max Wheeler."

He raised his glass to me.

"Thank you Jack. I, er, hadn't realized I was supposed to make a speech. So I won't…."

There were some cheers from the back of the crowd which were 'shushed' down by others as I tried to formulate some thoughts.

"…I just think," I adlibbed, "that it's amazing that you've all come here to celebrate my birthday with me. And I thank you for that. Actually sixty isn't such a great age anymore. We keep hearing that it's the new fifty, and that fifty is the new forty. So, does that really make me forty…..?"

"…No chance." called out someone.

"Well, a good try, I guess. Anyway, time was that when men reached this age all they thought about was retiring and going fishing or something. But, today, I think this is when a new chapter starts in one's life…"

"…So what are you going to do…?"

"…Shush"

"Good question. Well, I guess I could go and write that book that I've been talking about for such a long time. Who knows, it might even generate that Pulitzer that seems to have consistently evaded me...."

Laughs all round.

"...On the other hand, I could take the advice of my friend Harry over there, and set up a shop in the Middle East. He tells me I could do a roaring trade in selling American and Israeli flags and other effigies for burning. There seems to be a permanent and strong market for that..."

A few titters, combined with a couple of 'shame's and one or two 'I-don't-gettit's.

"Yes, well never mind...."

I couldn't help turning then to briefly look at Laura.

"...But, somehow, I think existence might have other plans for me. Whatever it is, I would like to thank each and every one of you for coming here today to celebrate with me. As I look around me and see so many faces of my family and friends I really do feel blessed.....So thank you all very much...."

I paused then to take in and acknowledge everyone. And being surrounded by all these family and friends touched my heart. I felt moved in a way that I couldn't ever remember feeling.

Out of the corner of my eye I could see Toby whispering in Jack's ear. Jack told him 'no'. But, nevertheless, Toby pushed his way forward.

"My song. My song."

Jack tried to pull him back, but Toby was determined.

"He wants to sing this song that he's learned." said Jack. "I'm sorry."

"No, that's okay," I said. I indicated to Toby the large crowd of people, all paying attention. "Here you are Toby. This is your shot at fame. Let's hear your song."

Toby started out very quietly, almost a whisper, directly to me:

"I love you whether I show it or not. I love you whether you know it or not...."

There were calls from the back of the crowd: "Louder."

"....There are so many things I have to share inside my heart...Perhaps now is a good time to start..."

"Louder."

"They can't hear you very well Toby," I said. "Can you sing louder?"

Toby shook his head: No.

"Alright, I'll tell you what we'll do…."

Carefully I got down on my knees beside him and gently tried to turn my grandson towards the 'audience'. But Toby would only look directly at *me*.

"Let's sing it together, shall we."

He nodded his head.

Toby whispered the words to me, and I began to whisper them back one line at a time. Then, when we were ready, we started together…at roughly the same time:

"I….love you…whether I show it or not…. I …love you….whether… you….know it or not…. There are so many things I have to share inside my heart…"

As I spoke the words and looked into this child's eyes something very strange happened. A ball of energy began to form in my chest and force its way up into my throat.

"…Perhaps now…is a good time to start…"

My skin became warmer, and I could feel my eyes begin to prickle. And there was a slight roaring in my ears. I looked deeper into Toby's uncensoring, innocent eyes and tried to focus.

"I love you…."

Running in the back of my mind somewhere was all that had happened to me recently, especially in the last year.

"….whether I show it or not…"

Before I knew what was happening, the tears started to form in my eyes, tears I had never experienced. Tears of joy and of sorrow. Tears of regret and disappointment. Tears of relief and…yes…tears of love. They welled there for a moment and then began slowly to run down my cheeks, forming their own pathway. My vision was bleary and I felt like I was dissolving, but I didn't care.

Totally unaware of anyone else around me now, I took the little boy in my arms and unashamedly wept. Toby was a little scared at first, but then he brought his hand up to my face and tried to wipe away the wetness.

"It's alright danddad. Everything's alright!"

And it was.

# GREAT BOOKS

# E-BOOKS

# AUDIOBOOKS

# & MORE

Visit us today

www.speakingvolumes.us

www.ingramcontent.com/pod-product-compliance
Lightning Source LLC
Chambersburg PA
CBHW021509240626
47154CB00002B/565